ATLAS RISING

BECCA C. SMITH

Dedicated to the love of my life,
my husband Stephan Fleet.
I love you to the moon and back.

Chapter One
Friday June 3, 2321 9:06 p.m.

CHELSAN

Chelsan sat patiently in the back of the hover-limo waiting for Ryan to open the door for her. She didn't want to wait, she wanted to open the door herself, but he had insisted in his oh-so-cute-gentlemanly way and Chelsan figured she'd let him have his moment.

And it was the first 'normal' moment Chelsan had experienced in a long time.

It had been two months since Chelsan had taken down Elisha and her army of I.Q. kid clones, essentially saving the world, and she was finally going to do something that didn't involve her powers or protecting the planet from evil, a.k.a. her grandparents or some overgrown I.Q. kid.

Chelsan was going to prom.

It wasn't exactly her dream in life to go to a school dance, but in this case, it meant everything to her. It meant that she might be able to stop controlling dead things forever. That she could finally enjoy being a simple girl who just wanted to graduate high school in a few weeks and take a gap year with her amazing boyfriend.

A feeling of calm swept through Chelsan and an invisible weight lifted from her chest.

Yes.

Prom.

Ryan.

All was good.

The hover-limo door opened and Chelsan saw the love of her life standing in front of her. Ryan Vaughn. He held his hand out with a smile. A smile that said how much he loved her. A smile that made his eyes sparkle with adoration. The boy was crazy-stupid in love with Chelsan Derée and she felt the exact same way.

They looked like the happiest couple on the planet the instant Chelsan's hand clasped his own.

This was how it should be.

Two teenagers celebrating their last year in high school by going to the prom. Two teenagers who had lived through things that no one on this Earth should have to live through.

But it was all worth it to spend the rest of eternity with each other. Chelsan had already drank John Fortski's immortality serum, but Fortski was busy at work in his lab making more so Ryan and Chelsan's other friends could take it as well. Chelsan knew it would happen soon though and that felt pretty darned good.

Stepping out of the hover-limo, Ryan kissed Chelsan as if he couldn't help himself. Kissing Ryan always made Chelsan's brain explode.

"Okay, you two. You can at least wait until the end of the night to do all that." Nancy's voice carried over the noise from the parking lot.

Ryan gently pulled away as if what Nancy was asking them to do was utter torture, but he smiled at Chelsan. "We should probably do this dance thing."

Nancy and Jason walked over to them. Nancy had a huge smile on her face while Jason looked like he wanted to be anywhere but a high school prom. He was in his nineties and probably hadn't thought about proms in eighty years.

Of course, with Age-pro – another one of John Fortski's inventions – Jason, like everyone else who had money in the world, looked eighteen. Poor people couldn't start taking Age-pro until they were thirty. It was one way to separate the lower class from the upper class. Chelsan suspected her grandparents had something to do with that decision. It wouldn't surprise her at all.

Nancy looked radiant in a light blue, billowy dress that brought out the blue in her eyes. Jason wore a tuxedo, which suited him nicely. He was the most famous reporter on the planet – especially after the Elisha debacle two months ago – so there was always a crowd of looky-loos wherever he went. Tonight was no exception.

Jill and Max walked over to the group, another beaming couple. Even though Jill had once been Chelsan's mortal enemy, she ended up becoming a good friend. And now she could say, without cringing, that Jill looked amazing. Her long locks of black hair had the perfect amount of bounce as she and Max made their way to them. Jill's porcelain skin was in beautiful contrast to Max's ebony complexion. He was stunning in his tuxedo and perfectly shaved head.

Jill quickly warned Nancy, "Watch out. Joan is eyeing Jason like a hawk. I think she plans on making her move tonight."

Nancy responded to Jill's comment with an annoyed huff. "I swear if she tries anything…"

3

Jason kissed Nancy's cheek in response. "You want me to shove her and declare my love for you? Or maybe kick her in the shins on camera?"

"You kid, but I know you," Nancy said, her voice edging into the start of a rant. "*You're* the one who agreed to go to this dance with her to get in good with her dad. Did you think I forgot that?"

Jason paused, not sure what to say for fear of Nancy's impending wrath.

Chelsan interceded, "Nancy, deep breaths. Let's get inside and have fun."

"I'll play interference. You two won't have to deal with Joan at all," Jill said with determination. "Besides, it'll be entertaining torturing Joan."

"Torture?" Chelsan shook her head. "Jill, can we just have one relaxed, stress-free evening? I don't think I've ever had one of those. At least not in the last year."

Jill acknowledged that fact with a slight nod. "True," she sighed, "I'll keep damage control to a minimum."

"We can at least spike her punch with vinegar or something, right?" Eva said, walking up from behind with Bill in tow.

Chelsan immediately hugged Bill and for once Eva didn't seem to mind.

"Vinegar?" Jill nodded thoughtfully. "I like it. Annoying, but doesn't actually hurt anyone."

Nancy took a second, then slowly started to smile. "That I'd like to see."

Chelsan simply rolled her eyes with a smile and decided she'd stay out of it.

Bill's warm smile was one of Chelsan's favorite things in the world. They had never been a couple (to Bill's dismay), but they'd still managed to stay best friends. She called him her teddy bear with abs. He was tall, muscular, beautiful and endearing all wrapped up into one. Eva was his girlfriend and Chelsan still wasn't sure how she felt about that. Chelsan knew that Eva had seen the error of her ways, but it was still hard to forget that Eva and Elisha had tortured Chelsan, and it wasn't spiking her drink with vinegar. It was caustic acid being smeared on Chelsan's skin until she almost died.

Yeah.

Still on the fence when it came to Eva.

The eight of them walked inside the newly remodeled Geoffrey Turner High. A school named after Chelsan's grandfather. At least Chelsan could think of him without getting sick to her stomach anymore.

Baby steps.

The auditorium was stunning. The theme was 'Under the Sea' and the entire room was decorated in shades of blue or green with moving water holographically projected on the walls. Holographic fish swam all around them in beautiful schools and everything sparkled as if the sun was peeking through the ocean to the auditorium below.

Chelsan felt happy.

She felt safe.

She'd never forget that moment.

It was pure magic.

Present Time

Well, that didn't last long.

Prom had been amazing (except for the vinegar part). I ended up having some of the vinegar-spiked punch by accident. When I

5

spit it out, Joan figured out our trap and steered clear of the prank entirely. Total mission fail. Vinegar aside, the rest of the prom was way better than I ever could have expected, so I *thought* I would fall asleep and have amazing dreams about... I don't know... anything but an astral projection session.

And a dream with someone claiming to be *Atlas?* A freaking Greek god? That was just weird. I normally would have chalked it up to a bad dream, but I was familiar enough with leaving the astral plane to know when someone had jumped into my head.

It was always strange to me when people swooshed out of my noggin. Astral projection was bizarre in general. You'd think I'd be used to it, considering how much of my life seemed to be spent either sharing *my* headspace with someone else or me leaping into someone *else's* brain.

My grandmother, Roberta Turner (and astral projectionist extraordinaire), had taught me how to create a permanent 'Keep Out' barrier, but apparently this woman in my dream knew the secret code to breaking into my head. I still couldn't get over the whole calling herself a 'god' thing. Atlas. Seriously?! But she also called herself 'Kala,' so... which was it? Atlas or Kala? According to the woman, she had *become* Atlas, so I guess that made her both? If that was possible? Did that mean people could randomly become gods? And hello! Gods *existed?* And angels? And...demons?

Apparently, according to her, all of the above.

It still was a lot to take in though. You'd think accepting something supernatural would be old hat for me, considering I have the ability to control dead things. Not to mention my friends, Max and Eva, who have the same power. (Not as tricked out as mine, but they could handle themselves in a zombie fight). Even ex-evil Elisha had the same ability. I was beginning to feel unspecial, which was fine with me. I never liked being the center of attention, and being a 'World Hero' after saving the planet from an army of child clones (did I mention the clones were all of my father, Franklin Turner?!) with I.Q. Farm-evil-genius-kids' souls controlling their bodies…

Yeah, I know. I already sound nuts!

And grosser than that was the fact that the I.Q. 'kids' weren't kids at all. My grandfather had kept them in their seven-year-old bodies by using Age-pro, so some of them were over a hundred years old.

The clones/I.Q. kids all had distorted versions of my powers as well. Not surprising since my dad was the original source of the controlling-dead-things skill set. Combined with the sociopathic brains of the Collective I.Q. Farm's population making the decisions, each one of the clones flew to a major city in the world, rounded up armies of dead people and began their rampage of killing anyone that got in their way. And what made the whole thing more terrifying was the fact that as they killed more people, those dead bodies only added to their growing army.

It was a plague that couldn't be stopped.

But I did, with the help of Ryan, Max, Isabelle (who happened to be a three-hundred-year-old elite soldier with the power to stop hearts), and the last living Franklin clone who had an I.Q. kid soul stuck inside of him.

For a while, Ryan had the entire I.Q. Collective roiling around in his brain until Elisha finally purged their consciousnesses from Ryan's head and placed them into the Franklin clones' bodies. Ryan and the I.Q. kids were all still connected though, bonded in an astrophysical way. So, we had used Ryan's connection to all the I.Q. kids through the Franklin clone we had in our custody.

7

After that, I tapped into Isabelle's power and stopped all the clones' hearts, killing both the clones and the I.Q. kids all at once.

When the dust settled, the Franklin clone/I.Q. kid disappeared. We still didn't know where he was. We knew he was alive though because Elisha had given him Fortski's immortality serum. Unlike Age-pro, this serum was true immortality. You could be decapitated and your body would grow back. It did stop aging like Age-pro though, so the Franklin clone was stuck in his seven-year-old body *forever.*

Elisha and her clone/I.Q. kid army had almost taken over the world.

But we killed them all. Killed. The pain of it was still raw. It was the evil army or the world. We chose the world. Or, at least, I did. I didn't really give Ryan, Max, the clone or Isabelle a choice. Ryan told me daily that I made the right decision and that he would have done the same thing if it had been him. But it still hurt. *I* was to blame.

No one else.

Only me, Max, Eva, my grandfather, Fortski, Elisha and the Franklin clone had taken the serum. I just wished Fortski would hurry up so *all* my friends and family could take it.

I still couldn't believe Elisha was good now. I technically made her 'human' again by reattaching her soul to her brain (long story). Needless to say, after every horrendous thing Elisha had done, returning her soul had pretty much sent her to the looney bin. My grandparents, Geoffrey Turner (Vice President of Population Control) and Roberta Turner, kept Elisha at their Los Angeles Headquarters, where they gave her psychiatric help and could keep an eye on her. I visited her once and let's just say it didn't go over too well.

When was I going to wake up? I was still in dreamland. Usually after having 'visitors' I'd wake up by now. I wanted to tell everyone what I witnessed and hello? Gods! It was going to blow their minds!

Sitting in my imaginary oak forest was comforting, but I was starting to get bored. People always envied the fact that I could be conscious in my own dreams, but let me tell you, experiencing real time while you were asleep was a total time suck.

Suddenly my body felt like it was being tugged.

Maybe this Atlas/Kala girl was trying to pull me into her head? I wasn't sure if it was *safe* to look inside a *god's* brain. Still, seeing as I had nothing else to do (and I admit I was completely curious!) I decided to go with the flow and let my consciousness take me wherever it wanted.

The oak forest dissolved around me as if it were made of rain, the downpour quickly morphing into new scenery.

Then I saw him.

The Franklin clone.

Was it because I had been thinking about him? Maybe I *was* just dreaming?

The clone stood in a large room that appeared empty except for two of my grandfather's brain machines in its center. Long, sinewy tubes and wires draped from the ceiling, tapering onto head plates with suction cups and leads that connected into a computer and holo-screens. Two men sat in the chairs, locked into Turner's machines.

I shuddered anytime I saw those brain sucking devices. I remembered when I had been in one. The experience hadn't been that horrible because I had used it to find Ryan. He had been kidnapped by Elisha who had him strapped into her own version of the machine. But I still remembered the feeling of helplessness.

It wasn't like astral projection or being in an active dream state like I was in now. I had control in those situations. Being attached to one of Turner's machines locked you into your own mind. It was claustrophobic and not something I'd wish on anyone.

Whoever these two men were, they were locked tight in the chairs. I didn't recognize the room either. I wondered whose machines they were: Turner's or Elisha's? Seeing Franklin walking toward the two comatose men made me think the brain machines were Elisha's, but I had no idea or proof either way. Knowing that an I.Q. kid was inside the clone of my dad only made me more worried, since I.Q. kids... well... had astronomical I.Q.s. And did I mention they were sociopaths?

Yeah, not good.

I felt like a spirit floating behind the seven-year-old version of my father, watching as he finally reached the imprisoned men.

The man on the right wore a black suit and appeared to be in his early forties. He must have been around before Age-pro, hardly anyone was visibly that old anymore. Turner was virtually the only 'old-looking' public figure, since he had been fifty when Age-pro was invented. The man on the right was very distinguished looking with an almost regal presence. I couldn't tell how long he'd been locked in the machine: his flushed cheeks and healthy pallor implied that it hadn't been that long, but in contrast his dusty, raggedy black suit looked like it was on its last legs, which made me think it had been a long time.

The man next to him, on the other hand, definitely looked as if he'd been trapped in that machine for centuries. His sallow, sunken in cheeks and eyes made him look as if he was already dead. His black, stringy hair and almost skeletal limbs reminded me of Jill when she went through her anorexic phase. (Okay, that was mean, especially considering Jill would be drop dead gorgeous no matter what state her body was in, but she bullied me most of my high school existence, so I still held a wee bit of resentment!) His suit was worn out as well, but he was much younger than the man next to him – though he still looked to be in his early thirties, which would either make him poor or, like the man next to him, he could have been around before Age-pro was invented.

A strange purple glow wrapped around both their wrists and ankles. The glow looked like a hologram since I could see their skin beneath it.

The Franklin clone began to speak. His words were foreign to me, but I knew a spell when I heard one. Roberta had performed enough magic in my presence for me to recognize what the Franklin clone was doing.

If I hadn't just received a brain-call from a god, I might have written this whole thing off as some kind of nightmare. I'd certainly had enough dreams of Franklin in the last couple of months since I last saw him. Seeing 'my dad' as a kid, an evil kid, a kid who wanted to rule the world with a corpse populace… It was sad and disturbing, and all sorts of confusing emotions ran wild in my head. How could a clone of such a good, decent person be so evil? I guessed it wasn't entirely the clone's fault; he was being puppeteered by an I.Q. psycho, but still. My brain was having a hard time consciously and unconsciously understanding it all.

When the clone finished intoning his spell, the purple glowing manacles dissipated. He reached up to each man's face and touched them with his tiny hands, speaking again in words I couldn't translate. The men's hands began to twitch.

They were waking up.

The younger, sallow man began to spasm in frightening jerks

11

as if having a seizure.

I wanted to wake up. I didn't want to see this. I could feel power, real power, emanating from both men.

Their eyes opened at the exact same time – deep, solid red.

And both sets of eyes looked directly at me.

The older man hissed at Franklin, "Who is *she*?"

***

I woke up holding my chest. I seriously thought I was having a heart attack. I reached for Ryan, but there was only empty bed space.

"Finally, sleepyhead. I think this is the longest I've ever seen you sleep in," Ryan's voice came from in front of me.

My eyes flew up to see him standing in the doorway, looking as beautiful as usual with his swoopy sandy blonde hair, light brown eyes and that face! I couldn't get enough of that face!

At seeing my expression (I probably looked like I had seen a ghost), Ryan rushed to my side, pulling me into his arms. "Are you okay? Elisha didn't turn evil again, did she?"

I shook my head. "I…" I had no idea what to say. How could I explain what happened without sounding as if it had been in my imagination?

Ryan kissed me. Probably to get me to relax, but his kisses never did that. After almost a year of being together, his touch still sent a thrill through me.

Before things got too heavy, I leaned my head back, so our eyes met. "I'm not sure where to start. This is crazy."

"Crazier than heart-stopping assassins and child-clones-I.Q.-brains raising dead armies to rule the world?" Ryan asked with a slight grin.

12

I guess it *didn't* sound any crazier than that.

I smiled back. "Is everyone still here?"

"Yeah, they're downstairs eating the enormous breakfast Nancy's mom made." Ryan tucked a piece of my hair behind my ear. "At least you got to have fun at prom last night, right?"

"Yes, the universe spared me one night of normalcy before it decided to launch me back into… I don't even know. Let's get downstairs so I can tell everyone at once."

Ryan didn't argue, he trusted my judgment, which only made me love him more.

I got dressed, then Ryan took my hand and led me through the door. I lived with Nancy and her parents. They were nice enough to adopt me into their home and lives after my mother was killed by my… grandparents. Yeah, believe me, I know. I'll never forgive them. Ever. But I still held a weird kind of bond with them after everything I'd been through. They'd saved me and my friends on more than one occasion, which accounted for…something. I just wasn't sure *what* though.

I'd learned the hard way that my relationship with my grandparents was full of ups and downs, more downs than ups, but they had proven their loyalty over the last year as demented as that sounded. And trust me, even thinking it felt insane.

Walking down the staircase, Ryan and I hurried through the living room toward the kitchen at the back of the house. I could already hear the sounds of everyone I loved talking and eating breakfast behind the closed door. It made my heart squeeze with guilt. I was about to turn their lives upside down again.

I had long since abandoned the idea of *not* including my friends. The handful of times I had tried they found ways to get involved anyway. At least when they were by my side, I could protect them.

13

And when Fortski made more of his magical immortality serum, they'd be impossible to kill. I couldn't wait for that day. The weight of fear could sometimes be overwhelming at the thought of any of my loved ones dying because of something I brought them into.

As far as my astral projection session last night: I had no idea who those two men were that the Franklin clone released, but I knew they were bad news. Those men were powerful – and they had seen my astral-projected form. Better to be ready than to sit around and wait for something to happen. It probably meant contacting my grandparents, which I wasn't too thrilled about, but I needed all the information I could get.

Ryan turned his head towards me and gripped my hand tighter. "You ready?"

I nodded. "Can we just eat first? So I can enjoy one last breakfast of stress-free awesomeness?"

Ryan leaned down and kissed the top of my head. "Of course." He opened the swinging door, holding it so I could walk in first.

I was greeted by eight heads with eight beaming smiles. Nancy, Bill, Jason, Jill, Eva, Max and Nancy's parents, Vianne and George. My crew.

Nancy stood up from her chair, pancakes abandoned, and hugged me hello. "Good morning. I can't believe you slept in this late," she laughed. I worried about her and Bill the most since they didn't have any super powers besides being eternally loyal. Just thinking of them following me into dangerous situations that elite soldiers had issues with made me short of breath. Seriously, counting down the days until Fortski brought over that serum!

Jason smiled his roguish smile and nodded a hello but had zero intentions of abandoning Vianne's pancakes. The boy loved what he loved and most of all he loved Nancy.

Jason's phone buzzed, as it usually did a million times a day. Now that he was 'The Face' of peace after the whole Elisha/Franklin-clone debacle, the entire planet appeared to only want to rely on Jason for the 'real' news. He glanced at his phone and ran a hand through his curly black hair. After a moment of typing into his phone, he placed it down. "They can't function without me." Ego. Yes. But that was Jason.

Bill ignored Jason and joined in Nancy's teasing me, "Yeah, ten hours isn't enough sleep for you?" He smiled his adorably roguish grin.

Eva sat silent at the table moving her scrambled eggs around nervously but smiling up at me occasionally. The girl was trying to make amends for working with Elisha. A part of me couldn't blame Eva for siding with the previously-evil-witch, since Elisha was essentially the only 'mother' Eva had ever known.

Being an I.Q. kid, Elisha hadn't wanted to remain in a seven-year-old body *forever*, so before she took the permanent immortality serum, she needed to age herself, which meant: Eva and Max – guinea pig time. Elisha had performed the spell that had given my father his powers on the pregnant mothers of Eva and Max, knowing that she had created two more people with the ability to control the dead. Their mothers died from the magic and Elisha took the babies, Eva and Max, which meant they were only seven months old!

Elisha had given Max and Eva experimental aging drugs invented by John Fortski to speed up the aging process. Once they were physically the age of seventeen, Elisha used an upgraded version of Turner's brain machine (possibly the ones in my dream!) and fed Max and Eva a lifetime's worth of information.

Eva had been the first of these trials, resulting in stretch marks everywhere on her body except her face. When Elisha gave Eva the immortality serum all the scars had disappeared, leaving a stunning auburn-haired beauty behind. I still couldn't believe Eva and Max were only seven months old. It boggled my mind!

Max sat next to Jill. He wore his usual all-knowing grin as his dark brown eyes met mine. Max had the ability to jump inside heads and astral project better than I could.

I owed him big time: he had saved my sanity when Elisha and Eva had tortured me.

Max had been in a coma, suffering his own injuries from when Elisha had killed him. (Yes, killed him! The girl wasn't connected to her soul at the time, but still!) My grandfather's doctors brought Max back to life but, compensating for the fact that Elisha had beaten him to death, his body went into a coma to help heal itself.

While I was being tortured, Max's astral form had jumped out of his body and found me. I was able to see him when Elisha and Eva couldn't. Max floated above my wrecked body and reached out his hands, pulling my astral form out of my physical body. I felt no pain after that and was able to come up with a plan for escape. But without Max I probably would have died at the hands of Elisha and Eva.

Now, I could keep anyone out of my head (except gods apparently), but Max's smile faded, and he tilted his head quizzically. "Something's happened."

"What?" Nancy examined my face. "I'm her best friend I would know... what?! You're right." Nancy's face immediately crinkled in concern as she looked at me. "Spill."

I hated that I was so transparent, but secretly relieved I wouldn't have to broach the topic on my own. *Hey guys, wasn't prom great? Pass the scrambled eggs, please. Oh, and I was visited by a*

16

god last night and the last Franklin clone just woke up two guys with some serious mojo. Thanks!

"I don't know how to say this without sounding like a crackpot," I began. I really didn't.

"You're such a conversation tease," Jill rolled her eyes. "Hello?! Look who you're talking to. You made my father explode *with your mind*. Now spit it out."

Leave it to Jill to make me feel all warm and fuzzy about sharing. Ouch. I didn't like to be reminded of the fact that I had made Jill's dad go boom. He had been a walking corpse for the previous five years, controlled by Gramps, but still. Nothing like Jill Forester to remind me that I could seriously suck sometimes.

"Before you start, please sit down and eat." Vianne, always the mom. I let her usher me and Ryan to the two empty seats reserved for us. Vianne and George looked eighteen like the rest of us, but they were a little over a hundred. They still treated us all as if we were their kids though. (Even Jason who was their age!)

Nancy sat down again next to Jason and suddenly all eyes were on me. This time without smiles. Just the normal anticipation-anxiety I had grown used to.

As Vianne scooped out a giant spoonful of scrambled eggs, placing them on my plate, I started at the beginning. "I had a visitor last night." I tapped my head to indicate it had been an astral visitor as opposed to a sneaky-soldier visitor like Isabelle or Dean (another super soldier that had helped us take down Elisha).

"Didn't *that woman* teach you how to keep people out of your head?" Jill questioned. The *that woman* she referred to was my grandmother, Roberta. Seeing as my grandparents killed both her parents, Jill wanted nothing to do with Roberta and Turner. It was only the fact that Turner had saved Max's life that Jill was willing

17

to tolerate their existence. And considering my grandparents were both un-killable (Turner with his serum and Roberta living within a dead clone) Jill didn't have much of an option to do anything about the pair anyway.

"Roberta basically taught me how to build a brick wall around my brain," I confirmed. "But this woman got through."

Everyone stared at me, stunned. Admittedly, it was probably more of a helpless feeling rather than shock. The only ones in the room that could use telepathy or astral projection were Max and Eva, and neither one of them had the power to break past my mental barriers.

Eva shyly spoke up, "So this woman is pretty powerful then. More powerful than Roberta or Elisha?" Eva referred to the two most powerful head-jumpers we knew.

I nodded. "She said she was a god."

No one spoke. Probably for fear of voicing their doubts, as if it might offend me.

I continued forward, "The Titan Atlas, to be exact. But she looked human and she said her name was Kala, so it was kind of confusing. She said she 'became' Atlas, as if she didn't start out as a god, but turned into one. She said she had to do horrible things in order to keep the balance of the planet or it would explode or something." I looked around at everyone's faces and I could tell I was losing some of them.

Nancy tried to give me an out. "Are you sure it wasn't a dream? I mean, you *are* allowed to have those, what with everything you've been through."

"I wish it *was* a dream, but it wasn't. I can tell the difference. This woman was powerful and god or not, she had mojo. She said the world was full of gods, demons, angels and 'Malaks.' Well, technically she said Malaks are angels too. I'm still having trouble wrapping my head around it, but I believe her. When I told her what year it was, she was sucked out of my head and gone."

I paused, not wanting to finish telling them what I saw next. Kala was nothing compared to the Franklin-clone waking up those two men.

Jason spoke, "Interesting. 'Malak' is the Arabic term for angel."

"Really? That's all you got?" I smiled at Jason. Out of everything I confessed, the only thing he brought up was a bit of trivia.

Jason shrugged. "What do you want? I'm a history nerd."

Bill offered his thoughts, "I don't doubt this woman jumped into your head, but couldn't she be lying? Couldn't she just be a scary magic-person like Roberta?"

Ryan nodded. "Bill might be right. This Kala woman might be deranged herself and just *think* she's some kind of god."

I appreciated their logic, but I knew what I knew. I shook my head.

"I know it would be easier to believe that, and I love the fact that you and Bill actually agree on something, but Kala wasn't deranged or anything like that. And when I touched her hand, I saw things that weren't...Earthly. It was like I tapped into her memories or something.

"And I saw places and things that aren't on this planet." I shuddered, thinking about those images. Dark, deep caverns, walls made of spikes, shrieking voices that weren't human, giant dogs the size of houses...

Clearing my head of the memories, I continued, "Guys,

19

Kala isn't why I'm freaked. It was what happened after she left.

"Two men were hooked up to either Turner or Elisha's brain machines. It looked like they had been there a while, locked in place by some kind of magic." I paused, then plunged on, "The last Franklin clone was there too. He performed some kind of spell and freed them. But they were powerful. Very powerful." I could hear the shake in my voice. It wasn't until I shared it out loud that I truly grasped how terrifying the two men had been.

"Who were they?" Max asked gently.

I shook my head. "I don't know. One was older than the other...but...he saw me. *Through the astral projection*, as if I physically stood in front of him. Both their eyes were solid red. He asked Franklin who I was, but I don't think Franklin could see me...Then I woke up."

"We should probably tell your grandparents," Ryan suggested. "They've been around longer than any of us. They might know who those guys are."

I nodded. "Yeah. I was thinking the same thing. But I'm just going to tell them about the Kala part of the dream. I feel like I should tell them about the clone and the two guys escaping in person. Gauge their reaction." Thinking about the two escapees, I shook my head. "It's weird, though. The younger man scared me more than the older one. He was like a living skeleton..."

Abruptly, I stood up. I didn't do that on my own volition. It was as if my legs had a mind of their own. It felt like I had no control over my body.

Worried expressions stared at me.

"What is it?" Nancy exclaimed.

"I don't know!" My voice was louder than I intended. I was scared. I tried moving my hand. It worked fine. So why did I feel like I was being controlled?

Then everything went black.

***

I opened my eyes to see my astral form once again in the room with the brain machines and the two men. And, like before, they could see me as if my physical body was standing in front of them.

The younger man smiled at me. I felt a chill run up and down my spine. Such power. "Little thing. You are the girl from the prophecy: the one who knows death. We can't have you blabbing that we've been awakened. I'm sending you to a place where you'll feel right at home. Lots of dead things for you to play with." He reached out to touch my astral form.

I instinctively backed away. "I don't know who you are, but the only place I'm going is home."

The older man laughed. "You're losing your touch, Hades. She shouldn't be able to move, especially in this form where she's the weakest."

Hades?

Uh, oh.

I knew about as much as anyone who took a history class did about the Greek gods, and Hades was one of the big ones. And kind of up my alley, since he was the God of Death and all.

The older man was right though, I felt like my astral form was encased in mud. I could move, but it was extremely difficult.

Hades appeared frustrated. "Stand still. Trust me, the

21

Underworld will be like a second home for someone like you." He reached out again.

The Underworld?

Uh–no.

As his hand grew closer to my forehead, the terror inside me burst like a balloon filled with too much air.

BOOM!

As if I had broken out of a prison made of stone, I suddenly had the use of all my limbs again. Every part of me felt as light as a feather. I made my astral form fly straight up and toward the ceiling.

As I floated through the ceiling, I could see Hades below me look up with a shocked and confused expression on his face.

***

This time when I opened my eyes, I was back in my own body on the kitchen floor being held by Ryan. Apparently, I had collapsed.

Like a football huddle, the entire gang surrounded me.

Ryan hugged me tighter. "What happened? Are you okay?" How many times had Ryan and my friends asked me those two questions? Too many to count. And probably not the last time they'd be uttered as well.

"The two men. One of them pulled my astral form there, to the room… back to them." I paused, unsure of how to proceed.

"Did you find out who they were?" Nancy asked, but her face revealed she was scared of the answer.

And she should be.

I nodded.

"The Franklin clone just freed… *Hades*."

Chapter Two

31 Years Ago

KALA

Kala sat on her beat-up couch and stared at the screen of her television, feeling a mixture of excitement and dread.

This was it.

The mission Kala had been waiting for.

On the screen, the images weren't horrifying like Kala's Atlas missions normally were. It was simply Kala helping a woman kidnap a child from his parents.

Yes, it would be utter torture for the parents, and it wasn't going to be a picnic living on the run, but this child was special. He was the key to Kala finally being rid of the Atlas curse.

Kala already knew the woman and the boy's name. The boy wasn't a boy, he was almost a hundred years-old, but his parents had started giving him Age-pro around age seven and he'd been 'seven' ever since. And the woman... Her name was Janet. Kala had sent her in as Franklin's nanny.

Franklin Turner. Son of Geoffrey and Roberta Turner, the two most powerful humans on the planet.

Franklin was a part of the prophecy that would free Kala from the Atlas curse forever. In order for him to fulfill his part, though, he needed to stop taking Age-pro and grow up. Franklin's destiny was to become the father of the girl who would save Kala from the nightmare missions she'd had to perform and was still performing.

Years ago, Roberta and Turner had announced to the world that their son had died. They didn't want anyone to know they were keeping him a child.

Knowing that this mission would lead to her own freedom from the Atlas curse, Kala thought the kidnapping would be easy. But it was going to be one of her hardest missions to date. She loved Geoffrey and Roberta. They had become her family. They had her back like only a handful of people ever had in her life. She relied on them. She'd die for them. She loved them.

But if she took Franklin away, their relationship would end.

Geoffrey and Roberta would never forgive her.

Kala knew how long they had tried to have a child, and when Roberta finally got pregnant, Kala was the one to make the toast. She had no idea their child was going to be the one from the prophecy.

The Turners had kept Franklin's powers hidden from Kala for a good fifty years. Kala didn't understand why they kept him a child, but she knew Geoffrey and Roberta were obsessive in their love for their only son, so Kala had rationalized it was the Turners way of keeping him safe.

But Talan had a vision and told Kala the truth. Franklin could control the dead and he was the man from the prophecy. He would have a little girl someday and transfer his powers to her – in his death.

Roberta and Geoffrey knew the prophecy well, so they must have lost their minds when they realized their own son was the one who would die. It made total sense to Kala when Talan found out. Talan was a Grigori angel and could see things in the present and future no human could. Kala had often wondered why the Turners had pulled away from her a little. They were still there for her, but slightly distant. Now she knew: they were terrified Kala would someday do what she was about to do now.

Picking up her phone, Kala called Talan.

Talan materialized in front of her using teleportation.

Kala rolled her eyes. "We *can* use phones, you know."

Talan didn't seem fazed by Kala's attitude at all. "When I hear you need me in your head, I come." He leaned down and kissed Kala gently on the lips. The intense chemistry between them was still strong, even after a couple hundred years. She didn't deserve him. Not after what she had done with Asmodeus.

Kala shook the thought from her head. That was over two hundred years ago. Talan had forgiven her. She still wasn't sure if she forgave herself, but Kala compartmentalized better than anyone, so at this point she was simply grateful Talan was with her.

"Would you like to see my mission?" Kala asked, knowing what Talan's answer would be.

Talan touched her cheek as if she was the most precious thing in the world. His eyes always sparkled when he looked at Kala. She never had to doubt how he felt about her, it was written all over his face.

"I haven't seen you in a while. Can I just bask for a moment?" Talan smiled.

"We saw each other two days ago," Kala laughed.

"Two days is a lifetime."

25

Though Kala knew that Talan was playing, she had to agree. The life she led: committing an act of atrocity every four days so the world could keep spinning, made two days feel like an eternity. She didn't want to talk anymore, though.

Pulling Talan down to the couch, Kala kissed him passionately. Missions could wait a moment longer. Feeling Talan pressed up against her always made her job as the Atlas more bearable.

Kala needed Talan in this moment. Needed to feel how much he loved her. Needed to feel their connection. Kala had never been in love with anyone more than Talan and knew deep in her heart that there was no one else for her. And that was saying a lot considering how much she had loved Jack. But Jack was dead and gone almost three hundred years – by her hand. Happy in the Underworld with Pandora. Kala still loved him, but in a brotherly way.

All thoughts of being Atlas were erased from Kala's mind as she made love to Talan.

Afterwards, as Kala threw her clothes back on and appreciatively watched Talan do the same, (he was a Grigori angel, after all, and that meant he was perfect in every way), she smiled at him. "We're getting too old for doing that on the couch."

"Too old? You're still a baby in immortal terms," Talan teased.

"God, if I'm a baby, I'm not so sure about this whole immortality thing." Kala felt the years, probably harsher than most because of her job description; still, the thought of doing Atlas's job for another three hundred years was excruciating.

Talan finished pulling his t-shirt over his chest, then leaned over and kissed Kala softly. "Once this curse is broken, we can spend our days any way we like, whether it's on this couch or in a big, fluffy bed. Whatever your fragile body can take."

Kala playfully smacked him on the chest with the back of her hand. "What are you, like 8,000? I'll try and keep up."

Talan turned serious as he looked at Kala. "We will break this curse. I promise you. You won't have to live like this forever."

His sincerity made her heart squeeze. Kala had been a soldier before she became Atlas, so she rarely showed vulnerability, but she was safe with Talan. She had cried in his arms at times when her mission had been devastating to complete. That wasn't in her character, but sometimes it had been too much to bear alone and Talan never judged her for it. He had simply held her until she could gather her emotions back together.

Nodding towards the television, Kala raised an eyebrow. "You want to see now?"

Settling in, Talan nodded. "Show me."

It was a complicated process since Kala was the only one who was supposed to see the Atlas visions, but a hundred years ago, Kala figured out how to use telepathy to show Talan the repeating footage of her next missions.

Taking Talan's hand, Kala entered into his mind and opened her own mind at the same time.

Talan watched the television with growing interest. When he saw Janet taking Franklin away, his eyes lit up. "It's finally happening."

Kala nodded. "It was a good call to put Janet in as the nanny."

Talan looked reflective, then spoke. "Kala, I need to tell you something."

"That tone is never good." Kala didn't like it when Talan kept anything from her. It seemed to be the Grigori way of protecting the ones they loved, but Kala hated it.

"Remember the vision I had that told us Franklin would

27

eventually become the man from the prophecy?" Talan asked.

"Yes?" Kala wasn't sure where this was headed.

"That wasn't the whole vision. Janet was in my vision as well. It's why I picked her specifically." He nodded toward the TV. "I knew that the vision on that television was going to come to pass because Janet is going to be the woman Franklin falls in love with. She's the mother of the girl who will break the curse."

Kala found that she wasn't angry at Talan holding this information back from her. She understood immediately that he didn't want to stir her impatience. If she had known that Janet was going to be the mother of the curse-breaker, then Kala would never have been able to wait years for it to happen.

Seeing understanding in Kala's eyes put Talan physically at ease. Kala kissed him one more time then said, "Let's contact Janet."

DAY ONE

Saturday June 4, 2321

KALA

Drinking never helped. As a Titan and daughter of Gaia, the mother of all Titans, I couldn't get drunk. It was annoying. Sometimes I wondered if still being part human had any perks. So far, I hadn't seen any.

I drank the scotch anyway because it still tasted like Heaven.

Minutes ago, I left Talan at Owen's home. I missed him already. We'd been together for so long I couldn't imagine my life without him. I smiled when I thought of how I'd roll my eyes every time he'd say the words 'soul mate.' But now those words felt right. Talan was one of the only true beams of happiness I had in my life.

Having to complete my Atlas missions every four days for the last three hundred years left me numb most of the time. Committing one atrocity after another. I had just finished mission number 27,842. That number was so high it made my head squeeze in agony. Talan helped me through it, though. Sometimes, he'd help with the mission itself. In the end, it was always me, but it gave me a kind of peace to have him there.

Talan and Owen needed to 'handle' some things, which meant I needed to go away. Being Grigori angels made them the most powerful species of angel in existence. The Titans and one of their brothers, Rotoph, had imprisoned the Grigori for thousands of years in the 5th Heaven. Rotoph, feeling guilty, freed a handful of them including Talan and Owen, five hundred or so years ago.

Around the time I first became Atlas we teamed up with Zeus and Hephaestus to free the rest of the Grigori. There would have been a war: Titans versus the Olympians and Grigori, but Talan, Gaia and I trapped Cronus and Hades inside Turner's brain machines for all eternity.

It dissolved the whole feud.

The rest of the Titans disappeared, the Olympians went off to do whatever it was Olympians do, and the Grigori sought out talented humans and helped create the world we lived in today.

Owen had looked overly concerned when he had asked me to leave him and Talan alone. Owen adopted me when I was fifteen and human because he saw something special in me. Turned out that 'specialness' was the fact that I was Gaia's daughter. Unbeknownst to me, being Mother Earth's daughter gave me the innate power to swallow gods and supernatural beings whole, hence why I was Atlas now.

When the true Titan, Atlas, tricked me into doing his job (as he had other humans for centuries), my first task was to kill Jack Norbin. I went to Atlas, begged him to take his job back. I couldn't kill Jack, he was my first love. When Atlas refused, the anger inside me exploded. I consumed him before I knew what I was doing. Atlas died inside of me and I was left with all his memories and

31

powers. By doing so I became Atlas, which meant there was no other alternative: I had to kill Jack, or the world would end. It was painful, but it was the right thing to do.

I stood inside my apartment. It was the same apartment I'd had for three hundred years, only the furniture had changed. It was the last place I lived at as a human and I just couldn't let go of it. I still missed my beat-up green armchair. I kept that thing until it had literally disintegrated onto the wooden floor.

I took my scotch and plopped down on the current plushy green couch. Talan had tried to re-create the exact chair but made it into a couch so he could join me in whatever we chose to do on that couch. It wasn't my green beauty, but it was still darn comfy.

I didn't want to think about what kind of business Talan and Owen needed to discuss without me. It was probably about my kid. Owen knew how much it hurt to talk about him, especially since my child wanted nothing to do with me. Child. He was two-hundred-fifty-seven years old. I raised him, but as an adult he looked to Owen and Talan for guidance.

I had a difficult relationship with his father, Asmodeus. Well, difficult for me. Asmodeus wanted nothing more than to be with me, even after all these years, and especially since we had a child together. Asmodeus was the King of Demons. A creature that looked like a supermodel most days, but when he needed to fight, he could transform into a blue-scaled, flying demon. I was with Asmodeus for three days. Three days of weakness over two-hundred years ago.

The guilt was unbearable at times, cheating on Talan. And then to come away from it pregnant?

Of course, Talan never blamed me, or chastised me, or resented me… he simply said, "Your job as Atlas took away your will to live, but now you have life growing inside you. I hope this helps you see how special you are, Kala Hicks."

I never betrayed Talan again.

And he was right. Feeling my son growing inside me gave me a reason to live. Doing horrible things every four days took a heavy toll on my soul. Creating a child, even from the likes of Asmodeus, was beautiful, magical.

Too bad my son hated me.

The mission always came first but, being a kid, he wanted a mother that would be there for him. My adoptive mom Linda, Owen's wife, was more his mother than I was. Linda was there for him when I couldn't be.

I brushed the thoughts of whatever it was Owen and Talan were up to out of my head.

Holding the remote to my old-school television, I prepared to turn it on. I couldn't believe this flatscreen TV was still working, considering it was two hundred years old. My Atlas missions appeared in the form of visions when I turned on any screen. When holo-TVs first came out, it was like watching a living nightmare in full 3-D color. No thanks! I'd much rather see my visions on good old-fashioned 2-D, where I could still pretend that I was watching some kind of fictional television show and not my actual life.

I turned on the television.

My breath caught in my throat.

The vision was almost identical to my very first one, when I had to kill Jack. But this time, instead of Jack, it was Chelsan's boyfriend, Ryan Vaughn.

Chelsan.

The girl from the prophecy.

I had been watching her since she discovered her powers. She

33

had been a little girl when she killed her stepfather, Bruce, with a black widow spider. But he deserved it. That guy abused too many people to count. His body was untrackable (as in: no device, machine or hunter could find him or anyone near him due to one of Turner's past experiments), thereby keeping Chelsan and Janet safe, so when he died, I worried I'd have to step in to protect them from Roberta and Turner. I was pleasantly surprised when the girl kept Bruce animated which kept his anti-tracer intact. I never understood why Roberta and Turner wanted Chelsan dead. Janet I got: she'd stolen their only son and stopped giving him Age-pro.

I focused back on my vision. The three of us – Chelsan, Ryan and I – were on some kind of plateau in the middle of what looked like a desert. There were shadows everywhere. I was pretty sure those shadows were people, but it was impossible to see any detail beyond that. Bright glowing lights shone from every direction. This was the most distorted vision I'd ever seen. It made me wonder if it was different somehow.

Vision/me stood next to Ryan with a gun pointed to his head. He was begging Chelsan to let vision/me kill him. He said the same words Jack had: "Please, don't let me be responsible for killing billions of lives. I'm not worth that. No one life is."

Vision/me looked at Chelsan, sad. "I'm so sorry, Chelsan."

Vision/me pulled the trigger.

The vision kept repeating after that, like they always did.

Instead of feeling dread or horror, I felt a surge of hope. This had to be it. This had to be the vision that I had been waiting for. The one I could change. That must be the reason it looked different from the others. Zeus had made the mistake of ripping balance from the universe and placing that burden on Atlas as a form of punishment. But Chelsan was destined to take that curse

34

away. I could change this outcome and Chelsan would finally free me. She'd fulfill the prophecy.

I already had a plan.

John Fortski and his immortality serum.

If I made Ryan immortal, not even a gunshot would kill him.

Chelsan would have to find a way to break the curse or the world would end and there was nothing anyone could do about it.

It was risky, but I was so tired.

Kala.

I jumped up from my couch. I hadn't heard that voice in my head in a long time.

Roberta.

Yes? I asked gently.

Last night Chelsan finally experienced the visit you made to her head three hundred years ago. Roberta's voice was cold, straightforward. There was no kindness in it like there used to be. She still hated me. *I think it's time for the prophecy to be fulfilled.*

Roberta always had a knack for timing and, after seeing my vision, I completely agreed.

It had felt as if the day I'd finally meet Chelsan in person would never come.

Of the thousands of horrible things I'd had to do for the last three hundred years, having Janet steal Franklin away from the Turners was still something I hadn't forgiven myself for. Roberta and Turner had been my family. But not anymore. Janet kidnapping Franklin meant I was killing their only son…

I knew Roberta was waiting for my response to her declaration of the prophecy finally coming to pass, so I responded, *Where are you? I'll teleport to you.*

The Population Control Center and Research building. Geoffrey's office.

I felt her leave, out of my head as quickly as she had entered.

I was about to call Talan to come to me for a pep talk, but I didn't want to interrupt whatever he and Owen were discussing. Okay, I *did* want to interrupt, but only because I was sure it involved me and my son.

Here goes nothing.

I took a deep breath and teleported.

In a fraction of a second, I now stood in Vice President of Population Control Geoffrey Turner's office. The décor hadn't changed in three hundred years, still filled with antiques from the early 1900s: a roll-top desk in the corner, a massive mahogany desk in the center with an intricately designed chair to match, thick, heavy curtains with gold tasseled ropes tied loosely to let the sun in.

Turner wasn't there, only Roberta.

She was younger than I'd ever seen her. Talan had said Roberta used one of her clones, killed it, then had Turner cast a spell to house her soul in it.

Playing with fire.

I knew Cronus and Hades were safely locked away beneath the very building I now stood in, but Roberta and Turner relied too heavily on Hades's powers. My Atlas mission three hundred years ago had been to capture the two Titans and strap them into Turner's brain machines, essentially giving Roberta and Turner living magic to control.

They abused Hades's power the most, keeping millions of corpses in their employ. Turner said it was the only way he could ensure loyalty, but I think he simply liked the fact that no one could argue with him.

Roberta was a beautiful woman, even in her late forties when I had known her. Her long, black hair was pulled back in a loose bun. She eyed me with disdain.

"Kala Hicks." She said my name as if spitting the words.

I didn't want this to be harder than it already was, so I got straight to business. "I think you're right about the prophecy. My Atlas mission confirms it."

Roberta paused, thinking, then spoke, "Can you tell me what your mission is?"

I nodded. "I have to kill Ryan Vaughn."

Before I could defend myself, Roberta's eyes turned solid green and a matching fire shot out of her fingers.

Green fire was used for one thing: pain.

It hit me square in the chest, causing every muscle to squeeze in agony.

I was a Titan, so she couldn't kill me, but it didn't mean that I couldn't be hurt. And it hurt.

I used my own magic to wipe away the fire from my body, immediately putting up a protective shell around my skin.

Roberta attacked again, this time with purple fire, which was used to capture, but my shield held strong against it. She might be a powerful human, but Roberta was no god.

The rage in Roberta's face was palpable at her attack being thwarted. She tried again, this time reciting an ancient spell. I recognized it immediately. If she tapped into Cronus, this could get nasty.

I decided to play dirty. Before she had time to finish the spell, I used my combined Gaia and Atlas strength to create white fire, used to control others. Knowing that Roberta would hate me even more, I pushed out the white fire from my hands and surrounded her body with it, leaving only her head free of the flames.

Now all I had to do was speak and she would have to do whatever I asked. "Stop incanting."

Roberta tried to fight the command, but her vocal chords obeyed my voice.

The fire didn't hurt physically, but mentally it must have been agony. Roberta stared at me with unbridled fury. "I can break out of this, you know."

"I have no doubt." I paused, trying to figure out a way to reach her without it ending up in another battle. "I have no intention of killing Ryan."

This made Roberta pause. After a moment her visible rage lessened and she asked, "You think you can stop this one?"

It stung that after all these years, Roberta still knew how my mind worked. It made me miss her. I nodded. "If Fortski can give Ryan the immortality serum…" I left it open for her to finish the thought process.

Roberta didn't disappoint. She nodded with appreciation. "Then he can't be killed."

"Yes." I waved my hand and made the white fire disappear. I hoped Roberta was calm enough now not to attack again, but I was ready for anything regardless. I continued, "We have four days to figure out how Chelsan can break this curse. You have to admit the timing screams that this thing could finally be over. If what you said is true, then last night, she finally experienced what I experienced three hundred years ago, added to me seeing my vision of killing Ryan? It's time."

Roberta sighed heavily, most of her anger gone. I almost caught a glimpse of the woman who used to love me like a mother, but her walls went up when her eyes met mine. "Let's get Forstki's serum and take it to Ryan this instant. I don't want you discussing this with your father or Talan and having them talk you out of it." Roberta straightened her pantsuit. "I won't let you kill Ryan. I will drain all of Cronus and Hades's power to take you down if I have to. Chelsan will never feel the pain of losing Ryan." She pointed a finger at me, threateningly. "Do you understand me?"

"I completely agree." Then I decided to be honest with her, like I used to. "At this point, Roberta, I'd rather see the world end." I couldn't control the slight catch in my voice as I said it.

Roberta shook her head, and her eyes softened slightly. "You must be so tired."

I couldn't speak for fear of breaking down. Yet again she knew my thoughts so well. I usually kept myself cold and reserved. It was the only way to survive the things I had to do every four days. But seeing Roberta again…

It hurt.

A lot.

I wanted to tell her I missed her friendship, but I knew she'd probably try and hit me with green fire again.

Roberta's eyes turned cold again. "We'll go get the serum, then go to Chelsan's *together*."

I didn't argue. It would be better if I didn't randomly show up on Chelsan's doorstep. At least Chelsan trusted Roberta to a certain degree. From my observation, it was hard for the girl having her mother's killers in her life. But Chelsan was strong. She understood that having her grandparents in her life was a necessary evil.

It was funny: Chelsan's feelings for her grandparents had turned from hate to tolerate. Mine had gone from love to tolerate.

We were both in the same place with Turner and Roberta, though I, unlike Chelsan, wished the pair were back in my life. They were good allies to have.

As I followed Roberta through the monstrous building, I wondered if we'd run into Turner. A part of me wanted to. Another part was terrified to see him again. To see the disappointment and hate, but, mostly, to see the hurt in his eyes.

As if reading my mind again, Roberta said, "Geoffrey is busy with more pressing matters. You needn't worry about meeting him today."

I felt relief. I didn't respond, however. Not knowing how Roberta would react, I kept my thoughts to myself. It was safer that way.

After twenty minutes of walking down corridor after corridor, we finally reached our destination: John Fortski's lab.

I saw the doctor at one of his many lab tables, boiling some kind of formula over a Bunsen burner. His labs had looked the same since I first met him. Lots of long tables, each with two or three sinks, beakers, burners and liquids of every color imaginable.

As was his typical modus operandi, Fortski was alone in the giant space. The guy was paranoid. Understandably so. I'd had three missions over the years to stop some kind of project he was working on, the first being to destroy the cure for cancer. It had been my second mission as Atlas. It was pretty devastating for both him and for me. But ultimately, he invented Age-pro, which cured cancer as well as every other disease on the planet, so ultimately it was for the best.

Fortski looked up from his beaker, saw me coming in behind Roberta, and grumbled, "Let me guess, you're here to destroy my regeneration serum?"

I raised my eyebrow in curiosity. "I thought your new immortality serum did that?"

Upon seeing that I wasn't making a move to demolish any of his research or equipment, Fortski answered, "Actually, no. The immortality serum freezes you at the place you are at, like Age-pro. That includes age, organs and limbs. So yes, if you were to lose a limb *after* taking the serum, it would grow back. But anyone who had lost a limb or organ or anything physical on their bodies *before* taking the serum would still be missing that part of themselves."

He stirred the contents of the beaker in front of him. "I'm trying to come up with a way to re-grow or regenerate what was already lost." He tilted his head thoughtfully. "I'd show you by cutting off one of our fingers, but since you're a god, Roberta's body is a clone and I've already taken the immortality serum, it wouldn't be using the scientific method, now would it?"

Roberta had apparently had enough small talk. "We need your immortality serum."

"To destroy?" Fortski asked, looking at me nervously.

I shook my head. "I promise you, I'm not here to destroy any of your research. Apparently, the universe is happy you're helping people re-grow… whatever it is they need to re-grow." As I looked at Fortski sigh with relief, it struck home what a good man he was. His entire life he spent trying to find ways to better human beings. Even after inventing *true immortality*, he was still trying to find a way to help the people who couldn't help themselves.

"Well, that's good," he replied. He walked over to a cabinet with glass doors and opened it wide. "I only have ten vials of the stuff. You don't want all of them, do you?"

"No. Just one dose," I answered.

Fortski nodded and pulled out a small vial with a stopper on top. "One dose it is," he said, starting to hand it over to me – but Roberta snatched it away first.

"I'll take care of this," she said possessively.

She didn't trust that I'd give it to Ryan.

It didn't matter. I wanted Ryan to take the serum and I knew that Roberta would make sure he did.

Fortski glanced at each of us. "If that's all...?"

Roberta answered curtly. "Yes, thank you." She walked out of the room without another word.

I gave Fortski a small wave and he responded with a meager wave of his own. We had a complicated relationship. He respected my job as Atlas now that he had had the last three hundred years to understand it. But, justifiably, it was frustrating for him to have me annihilate some of his best creations. I think a part of him began to take it as a compliment. That his research was so important that a god had to come down and smite it from existence.

I followed Roberta out to the hallway.

She turned to me. "I'm assuming we'll be traveling *your way*?"

I responded with a nod. "Ready?"

Roberta tucked the vial into the inside pocket of her jacket. "Yes."

I touched her arm and we teleported...

...arriving on Chelsan's doorstep.

Without waiting for Roberta's approval, I knocked on the door.

This was it.

I was finally going to meet Chelsan face-to-face.

My heart raced. After all these years. After everything I'd done. Everything I'd been through. The prophecy was finally going to be fulfilled.

The door opened, Chelsan at the front, with eight people behind her.

Chelsan eyed me like she didn't quite believe I was at her doorstep. "It's you."

"It's me," I responded. "Can we come in?"

Chelsan turned for approval from the rest of her crowd.

Interesting.

The girl honestly thought her little gang was a democracy. I could see that Chelsan had no idea that she was the boss. I doubted anyone of them would challenge her. Except for Jill. The way Jill stared down Roberta almost made *me* want to back up.

I inwardly shrugged. The Turners must have done something bad to Jill. Not surprising. It was the only thing I had in common with the Turners nowadays, doing unspeakable things to save the world.

After some invisible confirmation from the crowd, Chelsan turned to me and nodded. "Come on in."

I walked into the nice, suburban house and found that I was a little jealous of Chelsan's life. She obviously had friends and family that loved her and kept her grounded despite what she'd been through. Killing all those Franklin clones…the burden must weigh on her soul.

It was different for me. When I was a sniper before I became Atlas, I had killed bad men to keep my country safe. I had been used to killing. But, even then, it was always difficult taking a life.

Over the last three hundred years I had taken many lives. But Chelsan? Her soul was innocent. Killing would affect her more deeply.

After the door shut, Chelsan ushered everyone into the living room. Everyone sat down on a large wrap-around couch – except

43

for Chelsan, who stood. I knew everyone's name, though Chelsan didn't know that so she went around giving introductions.

Roberta decided to speak first, pulling out the immortality serum. She handed it to Ryan. "Take this, Ryan. It's the immortality serum."

"Um," Ryan was unsure what the implications of this sudden gift meant.

"I don't mean to sound narcissistic," Nancy chimed in. "But why just Ryan?"

I decided I should step in at this point. "Because I'm Atlas and my job in order to keep this world spinning is to do horrible, unspeakable acts every four days. My current mission as of two hours ago is to kill Ryan Vaughn."

Ryan's eyes widened in shock. "Me?" He took a moment to grasp the situation. "You're telling us that killing *me* will prevent the world from ending?"

"If it helps," I tried to explain, "I think I was given this mission more to provoke Chelsan into stopping my curse than anything to do with you personally."

I looked over at Chelsan. Her face was frozen with indecision. She was debating whether or not to attack me. At least she had a little more restraint than Roberta.

"Before you find some dead thing to attack me with or try to tap into my light to control me, I'm *not* going to do it." I made sure Chelsan heard my every word when I said, "You are a part of a prophecy. You're the one who will free me from having to do things every four days, things like killing Ryan – and worse. You are going to put my burden back into the fabric of the universe from where Zeus stole it."

"Oh, is that all?" Jill snapped snarkily.

44

Chelsan's voice was steady despite what I had just told her. "Can you tell me this prophecy?"

Gathering information like a soldier. Good girl. "*One cannot live while the other one exists. A new Atlas shall reign, and the potential must die. A beginning to the end and an end to the beginning. A new paradise shall be born. The Fated One will be the last. The cost will be great, and the immortals will reign. The one that knows death will release the curse of balance. She will be born from the man with the power of death. He will sacrifice his life and his gift to save the balancer. The Fated One is the first. The first of us all. The mother of us all, born into a human.*"

Chelsan was silent, processing what I had said.

Jason took furious notes on his electronic reader. I was sure he'd have a few theories before the day was out. I wished I could throw him a bone and give him more information about the curse and Atlas. It made me think that if Turner and I had been successful all those years ago to transfer my Atlas memories into his brain machine, Jason would be the one to scour through them and possibly find something that might help Chelsan break this curse. But even with Talan's help we hadn't been able to figure out how to transfer the Atlas memories, so they were stuck in my head, hidden behind Talan's brain-blocking magic.

Chelsan interrupted my thoughts, "I'm the *balancer*?" she asked. "And *you're* the Fated One?"

I nodded.

"And the man who sacrificed himself… that was my father?" Chelsan said.

"Yes," I answered.

Then Chelsan turned to Roberta. "That's why you kept my father a kid, isn't it? You knew about this prophecy and didn't want him to have any children."

Instead of being defensive, Roberta gave her a small nod. "Yes."

I was relieved that Roberta's answer was short; I didn't want to explain how Chelsan's mother had been part of an Atlas mission to kidnap Franklin. I knew it would end up in a berating from Roberta and I didn't want to deal with that right now, especially since I'd lost the ability to justify my missions.

I was tired of trying to figure it out. In fact, my pattern for the last couple hundred years was to wait to the last day of my four-day countdown then perform my mission. Once I was done, I'd see what my next mission was, then try and forget about it for the next three days until the fourth day. Those three days were the only way I stayed sane.

Jason interrupted the tension in the room as if he hadn't noticed it was there, addressing us all:

"Let's say best case scenario you're right. Giving Ryan the serum makes him un-killable and as a result Chelsan breaks this 'curse' or whatever and…" his voice was almost mocking — from most probably, disbelief – as he quoted me, *"returns the balance back into the hands of the universe,"* he looked at me directly, trying to make up for his attitude, "taking the missions out of your very capable hands and back into the hands of the Universe. According to that logic, these powers-that-be are still going to want Ryan dead. So how is stopping this whole thing going to keep the world from ending? Because –" He eyed Ryan, "No offense, Ryan," then went back to addressing the group, "I kind of like this planet."

I had thought of this myself, but I was certain that this mission was to force Chelsan's hand. It was time. There was also a part of me that didn't want to care. I wanted to be free. I wanted to be selfish. The toll of my existence was becoming unbearable. In a new, destroyed world, I could still start over. It would be worth it.

My conscience kept gnawing at me though, as I thought those words. Could I let the world be destroyed? After three hundred years of doing unspeakable things? Would it all be for nothing because *I* finally gave up? Because *I* caved? Because *I* was too weak to continue? Even the original Atlas had made sure the missions were still completed by tricking humans into doing his job.

Seeing my indecision, Roberta apparently panicked. She grabbed the vial from Ryan's hands, popped it open and spoke words of magic. Ryan's body immediately froze in place, his mouth opened involuntarily. Before anyone could react, Roberta poured the serum down Ryan's throat, using her magic to force him to swallow it.

It all happened in less than a few seconds.

Roberta released her magical hold on Ryan. He immediately clasped his throat, coughing more from surprise than choking on anything.

"Okay," Bill appeared a little shocked by Roberta's ninja tactics, but then he directed his comment at Chelsan. "I guess Ryan is officially safe now, so let's break this curse before we all die a fiery death."

I almost smiled. I could see why Chelsan kept him around. Bill was good to the core and adapted to situations quickly. He would have made a good soldier. He reminded me of my best friend Derek, an ex-super soldier like me. Derek may not be blood, but he was family and I could tell Chelsan felt the same way about Bill.

Roberta justified her actions, focusing on both Chelsan and Ryan. "I refuse to let either one of you decide to let Ryan die. I don't want my granddaughter to have to choose between the love of her life and the world ending. You both are capable of *anything*.

Chelsan will break this curse as the prophecy says, and the universe will have to get over itself when it comes to killing Ryan."

Chelsan's eyes showed both relief and fear. She nodded her thanks to Roberta, then turned to me. "You wouldn't know *how* I'm supposed to break this curse, would you?"

"Haven't a clue, but we'll figure it out. We have to." I wished I could give her instructions, but I had no idea myself.

Max looked at Chelsan, serious. "I think you should tell them about your dream."

I already knew this was coming, so I set out to relieve Chelsan of any more stress. "That dream was me visiting your head over three hundred years ago. Seeing my vision today and hearing from Roberta that you finally experienced what I experienced all those years back, I knew *now* was the time to break the Atlas curse."

Chelsan shifted her feet, nervous. "Yeah, that wasn't what he was talking about. I didn't tell Roberta the whole dream, only that I dreamt of you."

Roberta's grandmotherly instincts kicked in. "What else did you dream?"

Chelsan scrunched her face as if she were about to rip off a Band-Aid. "It was super weird. But now that you're here, maybe you can make some sense of it." She plowed forward, "I dreamt that the last Franklin clone woke up two dudes that were hooked up to either Elisha or Turner's brain machines. One called the other one 'Hades.' He tried to send my astral form to the 'Underworld' so I wouldn't tell you what I saw, but I zoomed out of there before he could." She half-laughed, nervous. "I know: crazy, right?"

My heart jumped in my throat.

Cronus and Hades.

Awake.

This was bad.

Roberta was immediately on her phone, dialing Geoffrey.

I could feel a shift of nervous energy buzzing in the room at the sight of my stunned reaction and Roberta's frantic one.

Finally, I found my words, "It's not crazy. It *is* Hades – and *Cronus*. If they're awake, we're in trouble."

"Geoffrey! Cronus and Hades have been awoken!" Whatever Turner was saying to Roberta on the other end, made her calm down a little. "You're still tapped in?" she asked.

I knew she was referring to Cronus and Hades's powers. Turner and Roberta had tapped into them the day we imprisoned the two gods in Turner's machines.

"We're coming there now," Roberta told Turner, then hung up.

Roberta spoke to me, "Geoffrey still has access to their power, and he brought up a good point: I'm residing in a dead clone – if Hades had his powers back, we'd have no control over this body. It would just become a rotting corpse."

Turner's reasoning was sound. It gave me a slight sense of relief – and hope. Maybe we could re-capture Cronus and Hades in their weakened state.

"So, there's an *Underworld*?" Jill asked incredulously.

I didn't have time to explain the workings of the afterlife, so I gave her a summed-up version, "When you die, you go to the place you believed in in life. So, Christians go to Heaven. Polytheists go to the Underworld."

Nancy looked spooked, "But no one believes in anything anymore. Where will *we* go?"

Chelsan answered, "Nowhere, because we're getting all you guys Forstki's serum as soon as he makes it."

Roberta, in an act of empathy, added, "You now believe in gods, so if anything were to happen to you, you'd go to the Underworld." She turned to me, "The Fields of Elysium, right? For heroes?"

I could tell Nancy almost liked Roberta in that moment. It was nice seeing Roberta have a moment of kindness. It reminded me of how she used to be.

I confirmed, "Yes, the Fields of Elysium. I've got an 'in' with the man in charge down there and I'll make sure that all of you get a place of honor." This was such an odd conversation to be having, but I could tell it made the lot of them relieved in some way. Except Jill. She still looked like she wanted to punch Roberta in the throat. I knew the feeling.

Roberta stood up. "Let's get back."

And then she froze.

Roberta's skin instantly began to turn gray, decomposing.

Her eyes widened in shock and panic. One last look at Chelsan, Roberta said, "Whatever happens, know that I love you."

Roberta collapsed to the floor, her body beginning to decay rapidly.

Roberta was dead.

Chapter Three

One Month Ago

CHELSAN

Chelsan sat quietly in Mr. Alaster's history class listening to his lecture on the Alice Rose incident from 2143. It still made her skin crawl, no matter how many times she'd heard the story. Alice Rose was the first person (to get caught) giving her baby Age-pro, essentially keeping her child in an infant's body for nineteen years. Her actions were the direct result of why it was illegal to take Age-pro before the age of eighteen.

It had been a month since Chelsan killed all of the Franklin clones in order to save the world from Elisha and her dead army. Though Chelsan knew it was for the right reasons, she still couldn't shake the fact that she had murdered her father over and over again.

Ryan and Max both tried to make Chelsan feel better about what had happened. Tried to share the responsibility. But Chelsan knew it was all her doing. She was the one who had used Ryan's connection to the I.Q. Collective, the Franklin clone's connection to the clone bodies, Max's connection to Elisha and Isabelle's power to stop their hearts in order to kill them all.

What hurt the worst was remembering Ryan saying that the clones didn't want to hurt anyone. They weren't strong enough to fight off the I.Q. kids inhabiting their bodies. So Chelsan had to make a choice.

A choice to kill.

It had all happened so fast. Thousands of people were dying, Chelsan had to stop them.

She had to.

At least that was what she tried to keep telling herself.

The truth was she wondered if there *had* been another way to save the clones but stop the I.Q. Collective.

Could of, would of, should of – it didn't matter. What was done, was done.

The problem was: Chelsan was having trouble living with herself.

Ryan's hand clasped hers and she looked up from her seat.

Evidently, the bell had rung, and everyone was leaving class.

Nancy was next to him with 'worried face.' "You okay?"

Chelsan tried to hide her pain with a smile. "I'm good. Just spacing." She stood up, still holding Ryan's hand.

Apparently, Chelsan was fooling no one.

Ryan gave her hand a supportive squeeze. When Chelsan made eye contact with him, she saw a flash of something she had never seen since everything happened. Ryan looked haunted. It was quickly replaced by a sweet smile, but Chelsan hadn't imagined it. He loved her so much he was swallowing his own agony at what they had done.

Chelsan wanted to vomit.

Nancy shook her head. "Okay, I see that look on your face.

Chelsan, you're freaking me out."

Chelsan found that she had a lump in her throat. Emotions threatened to overtake her. It was so unexpected she didn't know how to hide how she was feeling, so she did what any normal person would do.

She ran out of the room.

Tears streamed down her face as she shoved her way through the crowed halls, hoping to get some distance from Ryan and Nancy. She couldn't take Ryan's anguished eyes at what she had made him do, or Nancy's unconditional love and support. It almost hurt her worse than what she had done.

Chelsan flew down a set of stairs that led to what was once her favorite place, a courtyard that used to be lined with cherry blossom and maple trees – until Elisha blew up the school. Now it was only a few benches and saplings. In time it would be as beautiful as it once was, but right now it just felt deserted and desolate.

Deserted except for one person in the distance sitting on a bench.

Chelsan recognized him immediately.

Max.

Her heart squeezed yet again at seeing him sitting by himself, staring at the brick wall in front of him.

Walking over, Chelsan sat down and wiped the wetness from her face. "I'm sorry."

Max turned to her, slightly surprised, then his face softened. "Why are you sorry?"

"I used your connection with Elisha to murder the clones and I.Q. kids." It made her feel slightly better to say it out loud. Keeping it in made it hurt worse.

Max's kind eyes turned thoughtful. "I don't blame you for that. No one does."

"Well you should. I made the five of us murderers." Chelsan's stomach was still churning with emotion.

"Isabelle is an assassin. She was a killer for three hundred years before you met her, and I'm pretty sure that I.Q. kid that inhabited the Franklin clone had killed long before he met you, too." Max was right, of course, but by trying to make Chelsan feel less guilty it only made her feel worse.

"You and Ryan never asked for any of this." Chelsan didn't want anyone to make her feel better. She just needed to feel bad for a while.

"Neither did you," Max answered softly.

His words hit Chelsan with stunning impact.

The poorly made dam she had created to hold back her emotions shattered into a million pieces. Before she could make another speedy exit, Chelsan choked on her tears.

Max pulled her in for a hug. She clung to him desperately. Max was right. Chelsan had never asked for any of this. She had been forced into this life because her father, Franklin, gave her his powers. And she had done the best she could with them.

Max held her tight as he said, "We saved the world, Chelsan. We saved millions of lives. Don't ever regret that, no matter what the cost."

Chelsan's guilty conscious wanted to deny everything Max said, lash out, anything to stop feeling the pain of killing her father. Yes, the Franklin clones weren't *really* him, but they were made from his DNA, so a part of them *was* him.

Pulling away from Max, she looked at him, searching for any kind of judgment. He was saying all the right things, but did he mean them?

When Chelsan saw only concern and genuine affection there,

54

she knew Max meant every word he said. He didn't blame her. He struggled with the same guilty feelings that she did, but he was able to reconcile his conflicting emotions because he knew what they had done was for the greater good.

Chelsan wasn't there yet, but maybe she could be some day.

"Do you think my grandparents ever feel this bad for all the people they've killed? If they believe it's to save lives?" Chelsan wondered aloud.

Roberta and Geoffrey Turner had murdered thousands of people in the name of Population Control, saving the planet from extinction. How did they live with themselves?

Max sighed heavily, "I don't know."

It was as good an answer as any.

Chelsan sat with Max in the courtyard with her head on his shoulder, and couldn't shake the thought: *Did her grandparents deserve to live after everything that they had done?*

Staring at the newly planted cherry blossom trees, Chelsan honestly didn't know the answer.

Present Time

What in the...

I watched the woman I half-hated/half-cared for rot on the ground in front of me. I was dumbfounded, rooted in place. Ryan was instantly by my side and the chatter in the room became deafening to my ears. It wasn't even that loud, but watching Roberta die in front of me a second time amplified everything.

Kala's hand gently touched my arm and calmly asked, "Can you reanimate her?"

"It wouldn't do any good. It wouldn't be her anymore." The

55

realization of Roberta's death was hitting me much harder this time.

Kala seemed to sense the state I was in, though she remained calm as she said, "Roberta's soul is inside that corpse. If you reanimate her body, she can communicate with us."

Comprehending Kala's words, I instantly connected to Roberta's swirling black hole.

I stumbled back a step. Kala was right. I could feel Roberta's soul trapped inside the rotting clone.

It looked a lot like the white lights I could connect to in live bodies, but not as bright. I made it move to the decaying brain and connected it to the brain stem.

Pieces of flesh slid off Roberta's body. I was losing this corpse fast.

But she spoke. Her voice was gravelly from the rotting windpipe. "We have to get my soul into a live clone. Hades will have control over the dead ones."

Kala acted as if she saw things like this every day. "I don't know the spell you used."

Roberta responded hoarsely, "It's in the Necrotralten."

Kala shook her head, annoyed, then grumbled sarcastically, "Of course it is."

"Geoffrey was able to perform it with the help of Terence last time." Roberta said the name Terence as if it would cause Kala to explode with anger or some kind of emotion.

I watched Kala's reaction. The mention of whoever this Terence was seemed to bother her. It almost looked painful.

Then I remembered...

"*Harry's* Terence? The sniper guy?" I asked.

Kala's eyes were cold as they met mine. "Terence is my son – and he is not, nor will he ever be, *Harry's*. Are we clear?"

Whoa. Her *son*?! Really?! But Terence seemed so boring! Now I wished I had tried to talk to the guy a little more. I didn't want to piss off a god though, so I nodded. "But it's the same guy?"

Roberta stepped in. "Yes, it is. There's more to Terence than being a sniper with 'true aim,' but as I can feel my skin slopping off my body, we have more important issues to deal with. I assume you're starting to lose control of me, yes?"

"Yeah, the less flesh, the less control," I confirmed.

Out of the corner of my eye I saw Jason vomit into a garbage can. You'd think Jason would be used to witnessing rotting corpses, he had certainly seen enough of them, being one of my friends. It was probably the smell. Pretty bad, like a rotted cinnamon aroma.

Jill on the other hand looked quite content at Roberta's current state, and Nancy was taking care of Jason.

Max and Eva stepped forward.

Max offered, "We can help you keep her together."

I nodded and concentrated enough to allow Max and Eva to connect to the black spinning hole, but only just enough for strength. I still controlled Roberta's movements. I knew they were not able to access her light, but at least they could help me move her body.

Kala yelled out to the air. "Talan! I need you NOW!"

A man suddenly popped into the living room. I heard a gasp from Vianne and a whistle of amazement from George. George always loved things he couldn't explain. Part of him being a scientist, I guess.

Talan was a little on the pretty side, to say the least, with brown cropped hair and chiseled features. I wanted to ask who he was, but somehow it seemed inappropriate given the current situation.

Kala turned to the man named Talan with clear and precise

directions. "We need to get her into a live clone ASAP. She said the spell is in the Necrotralten. She said… *Terence* helped Turner the last time."

Understanding and sympathy lined every feature on Talan's face and I kind of wanted to melt. That boy seriously loved Kala. He looked at her as if she were the Queen of Everything. He said gently, "I can do it. We don't need to use Terence."

Kala looked relieved. "Good."

Max shouted, "We're losing our connection!"

I nodded to Kala. "There's not much left to hold on to."

As if to prove my point, Roberta's face slopped off.

Another round of vomit from Jason and this time Jill joined him.

Roberta was silent.

"I'm pretty sure Roberta can't speak anymore either." I felt a surge of panic. "Her light is getting dimmer. I don't think we'll make it to Turner's headquarters in time. Can we transfer her soul into me until we get there?" I didn't *want* to volunteer, but I didn't want Roberta gone forever, either. Not that I didn't trust this Kala/Atlas woman – but, yeah, I *didn't* trust this Kala/Atlas woman. Ryan might be safe from her mission of killing him, but simply *knowing* that murdering my boyfriend *was* her mission made me extremely uneasy. As much as I hated to admit it, Roberta and Turner were there for me, for better or for worse.

It made sense now, knowing why they kept my dad a kid. If he were incapable of having a child, then he would never die transferring his powers to…*me.* I knew they hated my mother and blamed her for killing their son, but this put a whole new layer on it. My mom ruined their carefully laid out plan of keeping my dad safe. And knowing that *my life* meant his death… I could finally catch a glimpse of why they had despised me so much.

There was a lot to that prophecy I wanted to go over in detail. I knew Jason already had it typed into his e-tablet, probably cross-referencing it through every database he had access to (which was pretty much all of them), between bouts of puking.

Kala answered my Roberta-body-vessel offer, shaking her head. "Talan will bring one of Roberta's clones here."

Talan disappeared from thin air like the same way he arrived.

My crew all exchanged amazed looks at seeing Talan pop in and out of the house. It made us a little worried about security; still, I couldn't help but be impressed.

Sweat dripped from Eva's brow and her hands began to shake. Keeping Roberta's body animated was growing more and more difficult. The three of us (me, Max and Eva) had all taken the immortality serum and we all had the power to raise the dead, but for some reason Eva was the only one to suffer side effects. Probably from the growth spurt drugs Elisha had given her. It appeared that Eva's stretch marks weren't the only damage that had been done. Lately, the more Eva used her powers, the weaker she became.

I had to help her, "Eva, Max and I have this. Rest." It wasn't true at all, but I couldn't see her suffer, no matter what our past was.

Eva shook her head. "I may not be as strong as you two, but I can feel Roberta slipping. You need every ounce of power you can get."

She was right, but I wasn't sure what Eva's breaking point would be. I knew she couldn't die, but what if she went into some kind of never-ending coma or was in permanent pain forever, or anything else that might be worse than death. My eyes met Max's and he was on the same page as me.

He gently said, "Eva, please. We have this under control."

Bill got the hint. He carefully walked behind Eva and gently placed her hands in his. "Come on, let's sit down."

Eva was on the verge of arguing, but her body wouldn't let her. She fell into Bill's arms and allowed him to sit her on the couch.

Roberta's grotesque body and the surrounding slops of skin and blood were new to Vianne and George. They had heard the stories of everything we'd been through but never seen it close up. Considering the fact that Jason and Jill who *had* experienced things like this were barfing, I could only imagine what it was like for my foster parents.

I turned to Kala. "Shouldn't we be going to the Population Control building? How long is it going to take Talan to bring one of Roberta's clones here?"

"The same amount of time it took him to arrive and leave," Kala's voice was calm and steady as if pressure situations were her forte. It made me relax a little, though it was taking a lot of concentration trying to keep Roberta's corpse functioning. If we lost control of the dead body, her soul would float away into the ether. Or at least that was what I was afraid of.

Kala continued, "Talan is a Grigori angel, remember? Like I told you about in your dream last night. He's very powerful and will be able to transfer Roberta's soul into a new clone."

I knew she was more telling the group than me. My brain was still trying to process that gods, angels and demons were real. It made me think of Havenville, the Christian Coalition town that Elisha had used as her breeding ground to find Max and Eva. Havenville and towns like it didn't use Age-pro. They believed in one god and that they should live and die as He intended. Immortality was a sin to them. If they knew that not just one god, but many gods existed, plus angels, plus demons, they'd essentially have confirmation that at least some of the stuff they believed was right.

It blew my mind.

I had tuned out Elisha's cuckoo dad, Roland, when he talked about all of it. I had thought it was sad, fantasy fiction. I had felt sorry for the people of Havenville believing imaginary beings were real.

I guess the joke was on me.

Talan appeared suddenly in front of me. He carried an unconscious Roberta clone in his arms.

Barely touching his shoulder was my grandfather, Geoffrey Turner.

I had always thought he looked very old – until I went to Havenville. There, Elisha's sister, Beth, had been in her nineties and she was like one big walking prune. Comparatively, Gramps appeared quite distinguished.

Turner's expression was not one of disgust or repulsion at seeing his wife's juicy corpse, it was full of terror. His eyes went directly to me. "She's still in there? You can feel her?"

I nodded. "I'm holding onto her light. Max and I are trying to keep this corpse in one piece."

Turner didn't look at me like I was a leper-reject anymore; he viewed me with respect and, maybe, even a little love mixed in. It was weird. But I preferred it to the leper variety. I noticed he was carrying a very large book, almost the length of my arm and a width that was half that. The book was dark mahogany, crafted from leather with gold inlay writing on the spine and cover. I couldn't read any of it, but I assumed from the previous panicked conversation it was the Necrotralten.

Nancy ran into the kitchen and came out seconds later with a chair. She hurried over and placed it next to Talan.

"Thank you," Talan gave Nancy a slight smile as he set the Roberta clone onto the seat.

Nancy blushed slightly. The girl loved Jason, but getting any kind of attention from an angel (and a gorgeous one at that) was intimidating. She mumbled, "You're welcome," under her breath then gave me a sideways glance, clearly stating with her eyes: what-the-heck-is-happening-in-our-lives-right-now.

Turner already had the book opened, ready to go. He eyed Kala and with a sentence laced in venom asked, "Where's *Terence*? I need him to do this spell."

Kala slightly twitched at the mention of her son. I was still kind of freaked out by the whole revelation. Terence had been like milquetoast when I had met him. He apparently had what Isabelle had called 'true aim,' which made him an incredibly talented sniper. I felt ripped off that I hadn't gotten to talk to him at any length. He was half-god (and from the intense looks Talan and Kala gave each other), most probably half-angel. Although, if a happy couple like Kala and Talan had a kid, why would there be so much hurt in Kala's expression any time someone mentioned Terence? There was more to the story, but I doubted Kala was the sharing type. She seemed more like Isabelle by the second.

I felt a tug on Roberta's light. She was slipping away.

Max's hands began to shake. This was the longest Max had ever tried to keep a corpse functional. I had kept my abusive stepfather's dead body 'alive' for ten years, but he had only been dead all of thirty seconds before I had animated him. No-rotting equals easy-puppeteering. Roberta's dead clone was a mess. More and more skin and blood kept sliding off her bones. Max and I had almost lost our grip on her entirely.

"Turner!" I yelled. "Do this quick! I'm losing her!"

Turner's face flushed in anger. "I need Terence!"

I gave him a hard look. "You know you don't *need* Terence. You're just saying that to hurt Kala. I know you too well. Now, stop the crap and trust me when I say, Roberta will be dead in less than a minute if you don't transfer her soul into that live clone NOW!"

Any hesitation was immediately erased from Turner's face. He grabbed Talan's hand. "Let's do this, Grigori."

So informal.

More bad history there.

My grandparents had made enemies of angels and gods. Why wasn't I surprised?

But – Talan and Kala didn't look at Turner with anger or hatred. Apparently, the hate-game was one-sided. I knew what it was like to be on the other end of an unfair hate-fest when it came to the grandparents. I was sure Kala and Talan had done something that was necessary, but whatever it was had interfered in Roberta and Turner's lives somehow. Most likely involving my dad. Turner and Roberta only hated deep when it came to Franklin. Either way, I was happy not to be Kala and Talan at the moment.

Talan didn't seem fazed at all by Turner's ire. "Show me the spell."

Turner angled the book so Talan could read. He nodded and the two of them began reciting together what was on the page.

I couldn't understand a word, but I immediately felt the power of the incantation's effect on Roberta's light.

Their words were making her light move.

It scared me. If they took Roberta's light away from me, she could die, and I would feel like it was my fault. I wanted to hang on to it, though logically I knew that would kill her, too.

Max could only connect to the corpse, so he was unable to help me let go of Roberta's light. I felt so alone in that moment. Max's eyes met mine and he looked at me quizzically. He could see I was struggling. His hands shook harder. "Chelsan, there's not much flesh to hold on to. What's happening?"

I was frozen. Frozen in fear and indecision.

Turner shouted angrily, "Why is it taking so long?! It didn't take this long with Terence."

Talan shook his head. "I don't know, I felt us moving Roberta's soul, but now it appears stuck."

"Am I doing that?" I asked in horror, breaking out of my stupor.

A flash of terror in Turner's eyes. "You're not going to kill her, are you?" He said it like he thought it was a possibility. Like I had found the perfect opportunity to 'off' my grandma.

"Of course not!" I yelled defensively. "I can't seem to let her go. I'm afraid she'll die!"

And I was.

Afraid Roberta Turner would die.

It was so conflicting. I hated her so much for killing my mom, and I loved her so much for being there for me in some of my darkest moments. How could I feel two opposite emotions so strongly?

Why was I holding onto her light?

I felt a hand touch my shoulder. I looked behind me to see Kala standing there. "I'll help you."

Kala didn't need to explain. I instantly knew what she meant. I opened my mind and let Kala inside my head.

WHOOSH!

In a blink of an eye my hold on Roberta was lifted. I watched

64

her white light fly out of the rotting corpse. Just as quickly, Kala jumped out of my head. She had done what I couldn't: forced me to release Roberta's soul.

Roberta's live clone gasped and coughed as Talan and Turner had obviously succeeded in placing Roberta's soul into the new clone's body.

My insides felt weak and shaken. I still couldn't comprehend what my momentary brain-fart meant. Roberta's life or death had been entirely up to me – and I had frozen. If Kala hadn't nudged my brain to let go of Roberta's soul, my grandmother would have died. Part of me was horrified at that thought and the other part felt… I didn't know. Maybe I'd never be at peace with choosing to work with the people who killed my mother. On the surface, yes. In the moment of danger, yes. But deep down, where my heart still ached for my mom…

Roberta and Turner had taken her away from me. Forever.

Why all these thoughts and emotions were surging to the surface now was pretty darned inconvenient. I guess when holding my mother's murderer's life in my hands, I choked.

Roberta's clone screamed in agony.

I immediately rushed to her side despite my conflicting emotions. "Is Roberta in there?" I asked Talan. He seemed to be the most knowledgeable in this situation.

He nodded. "The clone's mind and Roberta's are fighting for dominance. Normally, this wouldn't be a contest because Roberta is one of the most powerful humans I've ever met, but she was weakened during the transfer."

Ryan looked at me with concern. "It's like with the Franklin clones. When the I.Q. kids took over their bodies, the clones tried to fight back. My connection with the I.Q. Collective let me see

65

a glimpse of their struggle. It was seriously bad." He eyed Roberta with sympathy.

Kala stepped in. "Talan, can't you separate Roberta's brain from the clone's, like you did with my Atlas memories?"

"I can try, but the clone is a living, breathing entity," Talan explained. "Atlas was dead inside of you after you consumed him. He wasn't competing for dominance. I simply filed all his memories away into another part of your mind. With Roberta it will be trickier. The clone will constantly try to break through and take over its own body. Roberta is the invader in this case."

I tried to follow what he was saying, and for the most part I did, but dang… it made me realize how little I knew about the brain. The supernatural part anyway. The fact that I was learning all these things from someone who wasn't human kind of freaked me out a little. I had to keep reminding myself that Talan was an angel… an angel. Nope, still wasn't registering. He looked too much like a fashion ad to be anything but a super-hot guy.

I decided to stick to the task at hand. "Can I help in any way? I can still connect to Roberta's white light. I could probably connect to the clone's, maybe disconnect it from the brain, like the opposite of what I did to Elisha?" Maybe Talan didn't know who Elisha was, so I explained, "This I.Q. kid, super villain, wasn't connected to her white light and I…"

Talan cut me off with a soft smile. "I know what you did to Elisha, and yes. Let's go in together."

Being that he was an angel, I wasn't sure what he meant by that. Like: go in, go in? Or: *I* go in – and he talks in my brain? Or: he goes in and I go in and we kind of do our own thing? Not wanting to embarrass myself I simply said, "Sure, okay." Yeah, no need for explanation, just send me in, Captain.

Ugh.

I closed my eyes to connect with Roberta's light, then I felt Talan's hand touch my arm.

As if I was in one of my dream-thingies, the scenery swirled around me in a cyclone of colors. Talan was bringing me inside the clone's head, astral projection style, as if I were unconscious. Speaking of which, I was probably unconscious.

"No, you're still awake," Talan's voice sounded next to me. I could barely make out his form through the onslaught of swirling colors. They were giving me an annoying case of vertigo.

I didn't respond to the fact that he had read my mind, for the simple reason that I was trying very hard not to projectile vomit. Not that I could puke inside my head, but who knew what my body was doing while Talan was pulling me inside the clone?

"Here." Talan waved his hand and the colors took shape. We were in Roberta's memory hallway. A long corridor with doors on either side stretched out before us for miles and miles. "You've been here before," Talan observed.

I nodded. "Why are we in Roberta's memories? This isn't exactly what I was talking about when I said I could connect to her light." I didn't feel like strolling down Grandma's memory lane. Literally. I wasn't sure how this was going to help Roberta gain control over the clone's body.

"We're in both Roberta's and the clone's memories," Talan corrected me.

I looked at the scenery in front of me and I was pretty sure we were only in Roberta's. "You're saying they're identical?"

Talan shook his head. "Wait for it."

I waited.

For *it*.

And waited.

Not that I didn't want to be patient, but…

"What are we waiting…"

Talan raised his hand to quiet me, then pointed.

I followed his hand: the hallway in front of us began to blur, then shake violently.

POP!

Black fog exploded in front of us. I closed my eyes and mouth. I didn't want to breathe in or be blinded by supernatural gunk or phlegm or anything.

When I opened my eyes, we were in an entirely different hallway. Twenty doors, ten on each side, all identical, all Turner-lab issue.

I understood. "Now, we're in the clone's memories." I glanced at the measly twenty doors. "Not many."

"It's enough to keep control of this body. The host usually wins in the end." Then he sighed. "But Roberta is strong. She'll be able to keep the clone at bay. We just need to give her a little help." Then he turned and looked me directly in the eye. "Do you *want* to help?"

Yeeks.

The way he said it gave me chills. I knew in that instant that Talan knew I had struggled with letting Roberta live.

"Um." I know, I'm an amazing speaker.

Talan's face relaxed a little. I think it was his way of trying to make me relax, but yeah… angel. Relaxing wasn't in the cards for me. Could he read minds? Did he know my deepest, darkest secrets? Maybe he thought I was evil? Maybe I *was* evil? Did he bring me in here to punish me? I tried to remember any inkling of Roland's long, boring story of angels and demons, but I had zoned out completely while he was telling it. Now I felt like I was in one of my nightmares where I'd show up to class and none of my homework was done, and there was a test, and I was naked... Okay, at least I wasn't naked. Oh man, what if Talan heard that? He'll think I want to be naked with him!

"Are you alright?" Talan asked me.

"No?" My voice was barely a whisper.

I wasn't alright. I was seriously freaking out.

But – at least – from the expression on his face he apparently didn't hear my little *naked* rant. Small favors.

Talan nodded, as if he understood everything. "Roberta took the one person you loved most in the world and not only killed her but made her corpse dance in front of you like a puppet. You want revenge."

My brain couldn't comprehend that he knew what Roberta had done. Only Ryan and I had been in that room when Roberta taunted me with the body of my mother. I had tried to block that memory out. It had been hard enough to accept Roberta and Turner in my life with the knowledge of them murdering my mother and my entire trailer park, not to mention their many attempts to kill me, but Talan's one sentence brought me back to a dark place. A place where I wanted Roberta gone. I had almost killed my grandmother that day by sending a swarm of dead bees to attack her.

But I hadn't.

Because...

Because I wasn't a killer.

Or, at least, I didn't want to be.

I shook my head. "No. I don't want revenge and I don't want to kill Roberta. I'll never forgive my grandparents for what they did, but we've forged a relationship. It may be a complicated one, but I do feel for them. Sometimes it's hate and sometimes it's…" I couldn't say it. It was too painful and felt like too much of a betrayal of Mom.

But Talan finished my sentence for me, "Love."

"Mostly hate but, yes, that other one, too." Still couldn't say it.

Talan seemed to accept this answer. He placed his hand gently on my shoulder. "We are here to help Roberta take control of this clone, but I brought your essence inside the clone so we could talk privately."

'Cause he could do that.

Angels.

"Is this about the prophecy?" I asked.

Talan took his hand away and nodded. "Kala has been waiting a long time for you. She's had to do unspeakable things as Atlas to save the world. She deserves peace."

"I'm not arguing with you, I'm just not sure how I'm supposed to break some curse made by *Zeus*." The thought was a little batty even for me.

"The path is often not clear in the beginning," Talan smiled warmly. "but everything happens the way it's supposed to. You'll fulfill your part, one way or another."

I knew he meant it as comfort, but it still felt like a threat. I immediately became defensive. "Ryan took the serum, so no one is killing him," I said with a note of challenge to my voice. Why I went there, I had no idea, but from the look on Talan's face, he didn't seem to think it was out of left field – which made me more suspicious.

"Ryan is safe," Talan answered. I kept waiting for him to add 'for now' to the end of his sentence or something else sinister like that, but he didn't. Talan seemed to think that those three words would be enough for me.

Ryan is safe.

Shouldn't that be enough?

But it wasn't.

"You're damn right he's safe because I will *never* let anything happen to him." Wow. I was giving serious attitude. Normally, I'd be mortified if I said something like that to anyone, let alone an angel, but it felt right for some reason. Like it needed to be said.

Talan didn't look defensive or threatened. (Apparently humans didn't scare him, and why would they?) He simply smiled. "You'd move the stars and the planets for Ryan. I'd do the same for Kala."

Again, he was saying this for comfort, but my defenses went up again.

But now wasn't the time to get into a debate with an angel. I had to take his words at face value. Talan said Ryan was safe, that he knew how much I loved Ryan, and that he loved Kala just as much. That was it.

And I'd keep telling myself that until I could get my brain to shut up!

Stop!

Another explosion of black fog hit us. This time I kept my eyes open. The hallway switched back to Roberta's memories.

It was fascinating watching the two souls fight for dominance over one body. It was a very strange visual of competing hallways. One, Roberta's with miles of unique and individually made doors, and the clone's with twenty simple, standard metal doors. These hallways were *people*. Was that all we were? Corridors full of memories? What happened if those memories were erased? Would Roberta be the same person? Would she be better? Elisha had threatened to take all of Ryan's memories away and the mere thought of that had almost killed me. Experiences and time spent with the people we loved made us who we were. Sure, I could have created new memories with Ryan, but he would have never remembered our first kiss, or our first laugh... Luckily, Ryan's super brain had prevented Elisha from fulfilling her plan, but the mere thought that she might have been able to succeed still gave me mini heart palpitations.

"Hold my hand," Talan instructed.

I did as I was told, knowing that, whatever we were going to do, it was happening now.

Once our hands touched, I felt a sensation of warmth spread throughout my body. It was powerful and overwhelming. I almost let go of Talan's hand from the sheer enormity of the feeling, but I held on, knowing we had to stick together to help Roberta.

Then I saw it.

Roberta's light.

It crested the hallway like the sun rising in the morning.

It was beautiful.

I had never seen someone's light this close before. It was an entirely different perspective than when connecting to a light or a black hole. At those times there was distance, like casting an invisible fishing pole and the spinning holes were the fish.

But this.

This was a raging ball of blinding, stunning, breathtaking light ... *Alive*.

I was seeing Roberta at her barest essence. I knew now that it wasn't her memories that made her who she was, or that made anyone who they were. It was this.

Her soul.

Glowing in front of me like an orb of magnificence.

"I'm going to put the two souls on the same plane," Talan informed me.

A pulse of energy flowed through me as if someone had turned the bass on too loud. It steadied out to a loud buzz that made my whole body vibrate.

The clone's memory hallway began to take shape over Roberta's. The two existences coming together before my eyes. Both realities blurred from the vibrating.

I turned my face away as the clone's light burst into sight, nearly blinding me as it overlapped Roberta's.

"Connect Roberta's soul to the clone's memories." Talan's voice was calm despite the onslaught of blurred, vibrating imagery.

Did he think I did this kind of thing all the time?

I almost felt it would be easier to try doing this outside the clone body, just so I could get a big picture perspective. Right now, it felt like I'd have to move the sun into another orbit. Too freaking huge!

But I pushed my doubts aside and slammed into Roberta's light.

I was shocked that it was actually easier to control this way. When I moved my hand slightly, Roberta's light moved with me, not sloppy, but precise. I focused on the clone's memory corridor and concentrated on connecting Roberta's soul to the hallway. As I thought about it, bright, white strings of light shot up from the clone's doorways and wrapped themselves around Roberta's light.

"Good," Talan praised.

I felt a surge of pride. I was impressing an angel. Awesome.

"Now connect to the clone's light," he said calmly. "I'm going to open up one of Roberta's doors and you're going to shove it in. Okay?"

"Okay," I replied back, though I had no idea if I could do it.

I kept my hold on Roberta's light for fear of anything happening to her, then connected to the clone's light. Exactly as Roberta's had been, the clone's light was easy to control.

Talan opened up a small, attic-sized door in Roberta's hallway.

Really? Out of the millions of doors, he had to pick the smallest one imaginable?

Before I could get too worked up about it, though, I began to move the clone's light toward the small door.

I felt some serious resistance.

The clone knew. Knew I was going to trap its light inside its own body. Knew that someone else would be at the helm.

Its instinct to survive went into panic mode.

"It's fighting me!" I yelled in the silence. I wanted to jump at the sound. I hadn't realized how quiet everything was.

Talan's voice was soothing in my ear, "You can do it. I can keep the door open as long as you need."

Like a hundred years long? Because that was how long it felt like it was going to take.

But I took a deep breath and focused as intently as I could on moving the clone's light.

Finally, it budged.

I took full advantage of the momentum and mentally almost ripped a muscle pulling it down toward the door.

With a last spurt of strength, I jammed the clone's light

74

into the tiny door. Talan slammed it shut.

I blinked.

***

"You okay?" Ryan was next to me and I was back in my living room where all sets of eyes bored down on me and Talan.

I nodded, then turned to Talan. "Did it work?"

The Roberta clone slumped in the chair, then blinked a few times, straightening herself back up. "I'm good. I'm here. It's me: Roberta."

Looking into her eyes, I knew it was the truth. Despite all my earlier mixed emotions about my grandmother, seeing her alive and well again stirred up feelings I wished didn't exist. But they did.

I hugged her in relief.

Roberta smiled at me affectionately, then noticed the sloppy mess that used to be her. She turned to Vianne. "We'll have a cleaning crew come in immediately." She almost seemed... embarrassed. *Sorry I messed up your floor with my rotting skin and guts!* It was kind of funny.

Turner decided it was his turn as he allowed me to pull away from the embrace only to step in and hold his wife. His face said it all: the man loved her more than life itself.

After he had kissed her sufficiently (and gross!), he turned to Talan. "Take me back to Population Control. Fortski needs to give this clone the immortality serum immediately."

Kala interrupted his order. "Roberta's immortality is going to have to wait. We need to find Cronus and Hades quickly before they gain enough power to become unstoppable."

Turner couldn't hide his anger. "We'll deal with Cronus and Hades *after* I know Roberta is safe."

Sigh.

This argument would last forever unless someone stepped in. Guess that was my role. "Before you guys go at it for another hour, I think you should know that the clone's soul is still inside that body. Talan trapped it in Roberta's brain, but there's still a chance it could break loose. Do you want to trap Roberta in there forever?"

Roberta clasped Turner's hand soothingly. "Chelsan is right. Let's wait before I take any serums. Cronus and Hades are our top priority." Roberta didn't glance at Kala when she said that.

"We still need to get back to Headquarters to examine the machines and figure out how they escaped," Turner spoke directly to Talan, completely ignoring Kala.

Kala didn't seem fazed. She obviously knew the temperament of my grandparents better than anyone.

I filled Turner in, "The last Franklin clone woke them up. I witnessed it."

I could see Turner's brain going a mile a minute, then he said to Talan, "Chelsan, Eva, Max and Ryan are coming. The rest stay here."

An onslaught of protests filled the room, but I had to agree. People with powers and immortality serum only. Ryan didn't have powers, but his brain was a super power unto itself, so he was someone we needed to help figure out what had happened, and Turner knew it.

I addressed the group. "Find out what you can about that prophecy. Jason, keep your ears out with your news contacts about Cronus and Hades. Call us if you hear anything."

Nancy placed her hands on her hips in shock. "You're seriously going to leave us here."

I walked over and hugged her. When I pulled back, I said, "Nancy, until we get you guys that serum there's no way I'm risking any of your lives on insane-o *gods* who would kill you without thinking twice about it. We're talking about Hades. The actual God of Death. He tried to send me to the Underworld while I was in astral projection form. Imagine what he could do with a real, live person in front of him."

Kala added, "All he'd have to do is touch you and you'd be dead. Trust me, he's done it to me. Not fun."

Nancy grumbled for a moment longer, then finally nodded. "Just be careful."

"Always," I reassured her.

Jill gave me a slight nod. "Bill and I will stay here. It's better if we stick together."

Bill seemed to agree with this fully, though he still appeared upset that he wasn't allowed to come. Losing me *and* Eva was hard to accept, still, he handled it like a champ, as always. He hugged Eva first and kissed her gently. So. Cute. Then he walked over to me and embraced me tight. "Take care of her."

"I will, Bill."

I gave Max and Jill some privacy as they kissed goodbye.

After a quick hug with Vianne and George, we were ready to go. I headed for the door.

"Where do you think you're going?" Turner said with some annoyance.

"I thought you said we're going to Headquarters?" I asked with confusion.

Kala motioned for me to come toward her. "We are. We're teleporting. Everyone hold on to me and Talan."

Oh man.

Teleportation.

I was both excited and nervous.

Me, Max, Eva, Ryan, Turner and Roberta all touched a part of either Talan or Kala.

POP!

My world began to spin.

Chapter Four

257 Years Ago

KALA

Kala finished destroying the building just as her vision had told her to do, the screams from the innocent people inside cutting every piece of her soul.

Physically, Kala could feel the countdown clock reset.

She couldn't do this anymore.

Each mission brought Kala closer and closer to letting the whole world end just to save herself from the agony she felt in this moment.

This was her 4,381st Atlas mission.

The thought tormented her.

She had committed one horrible act after the next, every four days, never ending and never any easier.

And like a switch in her brain Kala realized with certainty:

She was done.

She had officially tapped out.

It was time for her to die.

It was time to let this world die.

Because if murdering people inside a burning building was *balance*, then she didn't want to be a part of that world anymore.

Kala felt Ashliel's supportive hand on her shoulder. His voice sounded distant, as if he wasn't there. "We need to get out of here."

She didn't want to leave. She wanted to burn in the fire.

The screams stopped. The people inside were dead now.

Flames threatened to overtake Kala and Ashliel, but Kala was rooted in place.

In a flash of color, Ashliel teleported Kala away from the destruction.

Kala was back in her own apartment. The same apartment she'd had since before... before she became a monster.

Her green comfy chair was on its last legs, but she couldn't part with it. It was the only thing she had left from her past.

"Kala? Are you okay?" Ashliel's voice sounded concerned.

No. She wasn't. But Kala couldn't speak.

Kala was gone.

Only the desire for death remained.

Her will to live had disappeared entirely and Kala wondered how she could have ever had it in the first place.

"Kala?" Ashliel tried again.

Kala didn't budge. She stood in her apartment, no longer able to move, no longer able to communicate. A part of her wanted to fake her well-being to get rid of Ashliel, but she had lost the ability to function.

A moment later, Talan teleported inside the apartment.

"What happened?" Talan rushed to Kala, waving his hand over her eyes, trying to garner some kind of response from her.

For the first time since shutting down, Kala felt a small stirring of emotion.

Destroying the world would destroy Talan.

A seedling of doubt crept up inside her mind.

But it was soon squashed by the echoes of everyone she'd ever had to hurt or kill because of the Atlas curse.

Kala stayed immobile.

Talan turned to Ashliel. "I knew this one would crush her."

"I tried to help, but the curse doesn't let me. All I could do was be there for her. It obviously didn't help," Ashliel responded.

"I should have come. I thought it would be harder for her to do with me there." Talan's voice was laced with anguish. Kala knew he was blaming himself entirely.

She wished she could care, but she didn't.

The more Talan talked about her last mission, the more Kala needed to end it all.

It was for the best.

Talan would try to convince her to complete her Atlas missions, though, like he always managed to do.

She couldn't be around that.

She needed to be alone.

Kala focused on oblivion and teleported.

When her feet hit solid ground, Kala wasn't in a deep, dark, black hole like she had hoped she'd be.

She was in Asmodeus's library.

"Hello, lovely. What brings you to my neck of the woods?" Asmodeus sounded pleasantly surprised to see her.

Kala still couldn't speak. She stood there, not sure what to do.

Why did her mind always take her to Asmodeus whenever her mental stability was in crisis-mode? This wasn't the first time. But she felt worse than she'd ever felt before. In the past she had had hope, now she had nothing. Just desolation and an overwhelming desire for her life to be over.

"Oh boy." Asmodeus seemed to pick up on the fact that Kala hadn't moved or spoken.

He walked over to her, forcing her eyes to meet his. What she saw there was love. Pure and unwavering love. Asmodeus gently held her face in his hands. "What has this done to you?" His eyes were sad, but his expression was fiercely protective.

Kala felt her whole existence shatter.

Standing in front of Asmodeus, a demon who had never wavered in his feelings for her despite how many times she'd rejected him. A demon who hadn't shaken his affection even when Kala made it clear she was with Talan, if anything it only made him more determined.

But most importantly, in this moment, he was the one person in all the universe who would let the world burn. Asmodeus wouldn't stop her. If anything, he'd encourage Kala to blow off her mission. He'd been wanting the Atlas to fail for centuries.

Kala finally found her voice, "I don't want to complete my next mission."

Asmodeus nodded, "Okay."

Hearing that one word sent a thrill of relief so intense through Kala she could barely keep her balance.

Sensing this, Asmodeus held her up with his hands.

"You're not going to fight me?" Kala asked, a part of her still afraid Asmodeus would try and convince her to complete her mission – like Talan most certainly would.

"Me?" Asmodeus laughed. "As long as you give me a front row seat, you can do anything you like." When he was sure Kala could stand on her own, he loosened his grip. "Well, we've got four days to kill. What do you want to do? I stole Zeus's chess set from Olympus. Wanna play?"

Kala felt the overwhelming pressure of duty lift from her shoulders. She had never felt so light. So relieved.

So happy.

It was over.

Being Atlas was over.

She didn't look for a screen to see her next mission because she had no intention of completing it.

Staring at Asmodeus she felt grateful.

Grateful at how he made her feel good about her decision to give up.

Kala was ready to die.

And if she was going to die, she needed to be with Asmodeus. She needed to give in to the desire for him that she had buried deep down because of her love for Talan. Talan was too good. Too good for Kala. She didn't deserve him. She never would.

But Asmodeus?

The King of Demons?

That sounded more like what Kala deserved.

Pulling Asmodeus to her, Kala barely had time to notice his wide, shocked eyes as she kissed him passionately.

Present Time

Things were awkward with Turner and Roberta. Roberta was softening a little; she'd always been the first one to come around when we had our differences in the past. They both seemed to finally be okay with Chelsan though, so maybe there was hope.

Chelsan reminded me so much of Janet, her mother. I tried not to think about the fact that, because of me, both Chelsan's parents were dead. I might not have pulled the trigger, but it was my Atlas missions that had led us all here.

Arriving at Turner's Los Angeles Headquarters felt like either a dream or a nightmare, I couldn't tell which. From the looks on Chelsan and her friends' faces, teleportation obviously impressed them.

Being that the only room Talan and I had ever been to was the room where Cronus and Hades had been kept, it was where we teleported to.

Turner walked directly to the machines and motioned Chelsan to come with. He liked her. I could tell. And Turner didn't like anyone these days.

Turner asked Chelsan, "What did you see the clone do?"

He didn't call the Franklin clone by Franklin's name. Too painful, I'd imagine. Maybe when there were hundreds of them, he could say their names, but now that there was only one left, and an immortal one at that... Turner didn't want to associate his son with an evil I.Q. kid shoved into a clone of Franklin. It didn't matter that Turner had been the one to create the Franklin clones to begin with. Decoys. He thought the clones would be able to fool the gods – or more accurately, *me,* – from kidnapping their son. Or more likely, Turner and Roberta had possibly thought that one of the clones could be a replacement for Franklin, a 'sacrifice' to breaking the Atlas curse. That maybe a clone could fulfill the prophecy and not their son. I never gave them a chance to try. I couldn't risk it.

Once the real Franklin had been taken and later killed, there was no need for the Franklin clones anymore. But I guess they couldn't let any part of their son go. It must have helped them cope in some way.

It was too difficult trying to figure out what was going on in Geoffrey and Roberta Turner's heads. I gave up on that hundreds of years ago.

When Chelsan didn't respond, Turner repeated, "What did you see the clone do?"

Chelsan finally answered Turner's question, "He said some kind of spell. It took off those purple manacle thingies, then woke the two men...er... gods... up."

I could tell that Chelsan was having a hard time with all of this, though she was handling it better than I had. Of course, back when I first found out about the supernatural world, I had been a soldier and gods, angels and demons went so far beyond anything I had ever experienced. Chelsan at least had a super power from birth: Franklin's ability to control the dead. I would have thought Hades would have had a son with powers like that except for the fact that he was locked down in this room. And it was those creepy twins that could control all life in their four-mile radius that had given Franklin his gift. Science met the supernatural. That was the world these days. So different from when I was human.

I walked over to the two of them. "When Cronus and Hades woke up, was there anything else you noticed?"

Chelsan nodded. "Yes. Their eyes were solid red."

Turner and Roberta both looked at me – then we all spoke the same word at the same time, "Resurrection."

Chelsan looked spooked. "Red eyes mean 'resurrection?'"

Roberta answered her granddaughter as if Chelsan was her most precious student, just like how she used to talk to me... "Yes, each color means something different. Take the purple manacles you saw: purple magic is used to capture. Red is used for resurrection." Then she turned to me. "But why resurrection? They weren't dead."

Turner's curiosity for the answer obviously superseded his hatred for me because he looked at me for the answer as well.

"I'm not sure, but it's not good." Eyeing Talan, I asked, "You think it's something like that device Rotoph made? The one that gave Asmodeus and me our powers back when we were in the Underworld?"

"Maybe." Then Talan turned to Chelsan, "Are you sure the clone wasn't holding something in his hand?"

Chelsan shook her head. "I didn't see anything, but I can't be sure. It happened so fast and I wasn't paying attention to every detail." Then she added, "When the older one opened his eyes, he *saw* me. At least, he asked the clone who I was. I woke up after that."

I sighed, shaking my head, fearing the worst. "If the I.Q. kid used that same type of device or if he found a way to accomplish the same thing in spell form, we're in trouble. It wouldn't be a resurrection of life, it would be a resurrection of *power*."

Turner and Roberta looked at each other with terror. Then Turner spoke, "Can we recapture them? Like you did before, with Gaia's help?"

"I honestly don't know, and I haven't seen my mother in couple hundred years, not since Terence was born." That hurt to say. I had thought Gaia was okay with the fact that I had a son with the King of Demons; she had said as much to me. But then Gaia had only stayed around long enough to see f born, then I never saw her again.

Initially, Roberta and Turner were my main support system after Gaia left me. Years later, after I betrayed them, Turner had found pleasure in the pain I felt at my mother leaving me. It took all my patience not to lash out at him, but I had to keep reminding myself that Turner had every reason to hate me. I'd hate me, too. And despite the strained relationship I had with my son, if anyone ever tried to hurt him, I'd tear them to pieces. Literally. So, I let Turner enjoy my pain, then kept us on topic. "I can try and contact Gaia. We might need her again if we're going to recapture them."

I couldn't believe that Cronus and Hades were awake. I mean, I *could*, it was the kind of luck I had in life, but I couldn't help but feel like it had something to do with the prophecy. Everything was connected. This was a lesson I had learned multiple times over the last three hundred years.

Turner headed toward the door. "Let's see if we can locate Hades and Cronus in the surveillance room." He didn't wait for anyone to respond as he took Roberta's hand and left through the door.

Chelsan and her crew quickly followed. I trailed the group about ten feet back with Talan.

His hand wrapped around mine and I instantly felt better. "How you holding up?" he asked gently.

"Never better," I groaned sarcastically.

Talan squeezed my hand supportively. "This could be it, though. Three and a half more days and you'll never have to do another Atlas mission again."

I sighed, wishing it were true, but not being able to release the multitude of knots in my stomach. "I hope I wasn't a complete moron by giving Ryan that serum." I voiced what I feared the most, "If I screwed this up for myself... Forget that. If I screwed this up for the entire planet..."

Talan stopped me in the hallway, letting the group move out

of view. He reached down and held my face in his hands, kissing me gently. When he pulled away, his eyes bored into me with their intensity, his hands still holding my face. "Everything will work out, trust me. The prophecy hasn't been wrong yet, even when we both wished otherwise. Losing Franklin was hard on all of us, especially you. But this is it. Three hundred years and you'll finally be free." Talan kissed me again, this time more passionately.

I pulled away and nodded. "We're going to get lost in this place."

Talan smiled, recaptured my hand and pulled me forward. "Grigori don't get lost."

I smiled back and joked, "Is that right? What about that time we had to break into the Vatican?"

"That was one time." Talan mock-defended himself.

"I'm pretty sure you were arguing with a cardinal about how they had a few things *wrong* in their religion," I countered. It had been amusing: a Grigori angel arguing Christianity with a cardinal. I had been on a mission that day and had no desire to complete it as usual. My mission was to kill a priest. A priest! It made no sense and I was in a deep, dark place contemplating it. Normally, on missions like that I preferred to do it alone, but Talan had said that he knew where I needed to go. I had been in such a depressive state, the thought of studying a map of the Vatican was the last thing I wanted to do, so I agreed to let Talan come as my guide.

And he got us completely lost.

I still think he did it on purpose. It distracted my mind enough to focus on something besides the fact that I had to murder an innocent man. That was my ninety-seventh mission. I had been Atlas for a little over a year and the reality of my future had set in with a furious sadness.

Talan getting us lost and arguing with a cardinal had actually made me laugh. It was the moment I truly knew I was in love with him. That love carried me through for a lot of years. It carried me now. My brief shred of hope that I could finally be done with this curse threatened to overwhelm me.

I couldn't live like this anymore.

I didn't want to.

If Chelsan didn't break the curse I would find a way to end my life.

I knew that with certainty.

"Don't think that," Talan said with worry.

"You're not supposed to read my mind." I wasn't mad. Our connection was so strong sometimes we'd hear each other's thoughts by accident.

"Kala, this curse will be broken in less than four days. I promise you that." His words boomed with power.

I didn't want to argue, especially since I wanted it to be true. "I see them up there."

I nodded toward Turner and the small group. They were a few hundred feet ahead of us, and walking into a new room.

It took Talan and me a few seconds to catch up and enter ourselves. I had to marvel at Turner and Roberta's embracement of technology. They didn't skimp when it came to their toys.

The room was one of the largest I'd ever seen, at least a few hundred yards in each direction. The ceiling and walls were dome-shaped and displayed The Milky Way moving its way slowly across a faux night sky. Though the room depicted nighttime, it was still surprisingly bright. The swirling green marble floor was a nice touch.

Crowded into almost every inch of open space was holo-footage, which I assumed was playing every kind of footage imaginable. Looking around and seeing the other's reactions, I guessed it was as if Roberta and Turner had a camera in every part of the world displayed here in full 3D holographics.

But my curse only allowed me to see my vision of killing Ryan.

A handful of technicians roamed the room, jotting down notes into their e-readers. In the far distance there was a large crowd of people on the other side of the space. Using my Atlas vision, I zoomed in to see why they were gathered together. That was when I saw the stack of dead bodies, corpses ranging from freshly dead, to juicy, to skeletons.

Turner noticed where I was looking. "I had over two thousand dead workers in this building. We're clearing out the bodies now and having them incinerated."

I could see now that the small crowd was hauling the dead bodies away.

Turner's empire had just taken a huge hit.

Losing control of those bodies was half his army. It put him in a vulnerable state instantly. He still had millions of soldiers at his command, but none as loyal as the corpses he controlled.

Then a horrifying thought struck me, "The world leaders! They're dead and you control them, if Hades and Cronus…"

Turner placed his hands up to calm me. "I have a team of warlocks controlling them with spells, and another team ready to go so we can keep control of them twenty-four/seven. Hades won't be able to break through. And to be honest, I don't think us little human-leaders are on Cronus and Hades's radar. The world leaders are too small for them, I think they'd rather take over the world with themselves in the spotlight."

Chelsan appeared scared at the prospect of losing control of the world leaders. "Maybe I could do it? Or Max, or Eva? We have better control than spells, right?"

"You lot have to be within a four-mile radius of the corpse and the leaders are spread throughout the world. The warlocks will be sufficient. We need to focus on finding Cronus and Hades and recapturing them. Let's not get ahead of ourselves." Turner sounded calm despite the circumstances. He was probably just relieved Roberta was in a new body and safe for the moment.

"What about the compound stuff you guys inject in all your metals and corpses? Why didn't that protect your dead workers from Hades?" Chelsan asked.

I knew what she was talking about. Another invention from the scientist, John Fortski. It was a form of anti-matter that prevented supernatural beings from taking over Turner's dead men. In the beginning when Turner first tapped into Hades's power, he had a hell of a time maintaining control over his corpses. Zeus and his cronies found a way to piggyback on Roberta's spell that bound Hades to her and Turner, which meant that the Olympians could take over command of the Turner army at any time. Then when the Titans figured out the secret as well, it was mayhem. All the gods seemed to love the novelty of controlling dead people. And tapping into Roberta's binding spell made it easy for them.

Roberta had tried every magical way she could to stop them, but the gods were too strong for her to fight them off with spells. Science was the only solution. It was the Olympians' and the Titans' weakness. They didn't want to have anything to do with science, probably because they couldn't understand any of it, but mostly because it scared them. Only Cronus had openly voiced his fear of technology and science. He had wanted to end the world to prevent the one we lived in today from coming to pass.

91

Fortski worked for years on a way to stop the gods from taking over Turner's corpse army. Finally, Fortski created a compound that could be injected into the dead bodies and into any material. It not only blocked the gods from tapping into the spell that allowed Turner and Roberta to control corpses, it also blocked the Titans and Olympians from tapping into *any* spell the Turner's controlled. No god could break through. No supernatural being, including Grigori, Malaks and demons, could break through, either. Fortski had successfully found a way to keep true immortals out of Roberta and Turner's magic with the use of science.

Even I was impressed. And I wished I could destroy the compound myself. I couldn't tell you the amount of times the anti-matter almost prevented me from performing my mission.

Roberta answered Chelsan's question, "Hades is the God of Death. No compound or anti-matter would be able to stop him from taking over something dead. He's probably a lot like you. You're the only known being to break through the compound."

It was impressive that Chelsan could break through Fortski's invention, but not surprising to me, having witnessed her capabilities over the last year. The girl might as well be a god. She was truly immortal now and she most likely *could* be a match for Hades. I hoped so at least.

A thought occurred to me. "Why didn't Hades just take over your corpses, kill all your 'live' workers, then control *all* the bodies in the building?"

Turner shook his head as if he had been pondering the same question for a while now. "Maybe he's not powerful enough yet?"

"Maybe you guys had a little help from an angel." The voice came from behind me. My heart stopped in my chest. I hadn't heard his voice in over three hundred years. He had died. Sacrificing himself so we could escape the Titans...

I turned around to face:

Rotoph.

My past with the Grigori had been tentative, to say the least, but seeing him now in front of me filled me with a kind of happiness I didn't expect. He had died to save me and his brothers, fulfilling a prophecy he had been a part of and tried to deny his whole life. So much so he had worked with the Titans thousands of years ago to imprison his Grigori family in the 5th Heaven. But prophecies had a way of coming true no matter how hard we tried to fight them. I was relying on that fact with Chelsan.

"Brother," Talan looked at his brother and I could almost see tears in his eyes. To Rotoph's surprise, Talan embraced him in a tight hug. Rotoph embraced him back, relieved his brother was happy to see him. Seeing as Talan was one of the Grigori that Rotoph had imprisoned, Rotoph probably hadn't been sure if his face would be a welcome one. But when you sacrifice your life, all was forgiven. In my book anyway, and apparently in Talan's as well.

Rotoph and Talan pulled apart and then I hugged him as well. I couldn't explain it. It was so good to see him. I had met him at that time in my life when I had just become Atlas. Everything had been so new and out of control. When he died, I barely had time to mourn, especially since I only knew Rotoph for a little more than a week. But when you were stopping the world from ending, each day felt like an eternity.

I realized we were ignoring everyone else in the group, but I didn't care and neither did they. I could see Chelsan out of the corner of my eye watching Rotoph and me like a hawk.

Talan asked simply, "How?"

Rotoph addressed the entire group. "I was pulled out of Heaven and brought back here through the resurrection spell that awoke Cronus and Hades. The child clone used a piece of the resurrection orbs I created all those years ago. They were destroyed when I died, so I assume all the pieces were at the bottom of the ocean. Oceanus must have collected the pieces and jimmy-rigged a wake-up call for Cronus and Hades." Rotoph shrugged, directing his attention to me. "I forged those orbs with my life's blood, it was how I was able to restore all your powers in the Underworld and after the Grigori blade weakened you. Reactivating the orbs apparently reactivated me," he said with a smile. He was roguishly handsome with his long, crooked nose and angled features, especially when he smiled. "We could probably use a few of those blades for when we find Cronus and Hades, anything to weaken them."

I shook my head. "We had the Grigori blades destroyed a long time ago."

Rotoph nodded and looked a little disappointed, probably because he had helped create the weapons. Sometimes I wished I would have kept one, they were so useful for draining a supernatural being's powers, but the fact that they drained the user as well made them too dangerous to keep around.

Turner joined the conversation. He had known Rotoph as well as anyone, though back then Turner had still been in awe of gods, angels and demons. Now, we supernatural beings were more of a nuisance to him. "How did you stop Hades from taking over the bodies, Rotoph?" he asked.

"Once I popped into existence again, I hid myself from Cronus and Hades. I knew Hades would take over your corpses, so I laid down a barrier spell, similar to my anti-teleportation one. Hades gave up quickly, probably thinking you had figured out a way to stop him from controlling the dead. Unfortunately, my spell wasn't perfect. When you lost your power over Hades, all the corpses went back to their *natural* state." Rotoph nodded toward the mess of bodies in the corner.

"Um," Chelsan looked a little shy, trying to join the conversation.

Roberta immediately touched her granddaughter's arm to encourage her to speak. "What is it, Chelsan?"

"I can still connect to them. They still have their swirling black holes." She said it as if she didn't want to offend anyone.

Rotoph eyed Chelsan, very interested. "This is the girl of the prophecy, isn't it?"

I nodded. "The very one."

Rotoph walked over to Chelsan and kissed her hand. She blushed. He was certainly shoveling out the charm. "Very pleased to meet you. I can see things from Heaven, and you are very impressive."

"Uh, thanks." Chelsan seemed out of her element, as if she was a child in a room full of scary adults.

"I can't connect to them," Max added.

"Neither can I," Eva echoed.

Chelsan appeared even more embarrassed. "Should I disconnect the corpses from their black holes, so Hades can't take them over?"

Rotoph thought for a moment. "It's fascinating that Hades couldn't break through my spell, but you don't seem to have that problem."

Ryan brainstormed, "Could it be because Chelsan's powers were created by science and not magic? Or at least, her father's powers were…"

Rotoph nodded. "That's as good a guess as any." Then he

focused on Chelsan. "So you see swirling black holes on dead bodies? Interesting."

"Anything dead," she answered quietly. "It's how I can control them."

Turner, not waiting for Rotoph to make a decision about the black holes and dead bodies, motioned to Chelsan. "Disconnect them, now," he ordered.

Chelsan nodded and closed her eyes.

"It's done," she said after a moment, then opened her eyes.

And, apparently, that was it. Nothing with the dead bodies seemed to change physically, but according to Chelsan the corpses could no longer be animated again. I couldn't pretend to understand the extent of Chelsan's gifts, but keeping an eye on her for her entire life had given me some insight as to what she could do. Part of me was afraid she had yet to scratch the surface of her abilities. Frightening, considering what she'd managed to do with them so far.

I watched the girl carefully. She'd make a much better ally than enemy.

Looking up at the millions of holo-footage clips playing my vision over and over – killing Ryan – kept me focused and determined not to let his death happen. I knew he had taken the serum, but my vision hadn't changed one frame, so it got me a little worried.

I glanced at the clock: 3d 14h 03m 34s.

2:53 P.M.

Still fourteen hours left in Day One. It both gave me hope and a flash of fear. Cronus and Hades had thrown a wrench into my plans to break this curse once and for all. They felt like a horrible distraction when we should be figuring out how Chelsan would fulfill the prophecy.

Prioritize.

Cronus and Hades first, curse second. We still had time.

Rotoph clapped his hand on Talan's back affectionately. "Well, now that you have me, use me. What can I do?"

Turner addressed all of us. "Take a corner and search. Cronus and Hades have to show up somewhere and, as you can see, we have eyes everywhere on the planet."

Rotoph offered, "Can't Hephaestus tap into your system and find them?"

Awkward.

I stepped in before Roberta or Turner had to explain. "The Turners aren't on speaking terms with the Olympians or the Titans… or Malaks… or demons… or Grigori, really."

Turner's expression was full of venom. "We don't need your kind in my facilities."

"Only when you strap them into your machines and use their powers for yourself," Chelsan said off-handed.

Whoa.

I expected a verbal lashing or worse from Turner or Roberta, but Turner simply shrugged. "I didn't say they didn't have their uses, but I'd rather they not speak."

Rotoph switched gears. "What about Ashliel? I'm sure he'd be happy to help a three-hundred dead brother out."

Turner was on the verge of protest again, when Roberta gently touched his arm to stop him. "We need all the help we can get. If Ashliel will help, we'll take it." Despite her gentle voice and calm tone, Roberta looked like she had chewed nails to utter those two sentences.

Talan seemed skeptical, but I knew Ashliel would help. The last thing Ashliel wanted was Cronus and Hades on the loose.

Before anyone could object, I called to him telepathically.

Ashliel, you better get to Turner's headquarters. One of those I.Q. clones woke up Cronus and Hades and well… you'll have to get here to see the rest.

Really? The Turners? I thought I never had to see those two again.

Afraid so. They'll be good. I hope. Chelsan is here. I know you've always wanted to meet her.

About that… She already knows me.

What?

Before I could respond telepathically, Ashliel popped into view with a large smile. He was handsome as usual, supernatural beings tended to be on the beautiful side.

"Mr. Ash?" Chelsan asked incredulously.

Ashliel gave me a look that said: *I'm sorry, but I couldn't resist.*

I eyed him with annoyance. "*Mr. Ash?*"

"I just had to know her, or at least spend some time with her." Ashliel said with a smile. He wasn't sorry at all.

"Um," Chelsan seemed very surprised. "My freshman Biology teacher was a Grigori angel?"

"Guilty as charged." Ashliel turned to Chelsan with a welcoming smile. "And I'll never forget what you did with those frogs. Brilliant."

Rotoph cleared his throat.

Ashliel turned and his eyes widened in shock. "Rotoph," he whispered.

There was a moment where I couldn't tell if Ashliel was happy or angry to see his brother alive and well. Ashliel had been imprisoned longer than Talan and Owen had been, and I wasn't sure if he was holding a grudge. But his face quickly broke into another large grin as he pulled Rotoph in for a tight embrace.

Chelsan appeared relieved that Ashliel's focus had switched

from her to Rotoph. Finding out one of your old teachers was actually a Grigori couldn't be easy to process. On top of that, it was clear that Chelsan didn't like being the center of attention, though she tended to be in it whether she liked it or not. I knew the feeling. I was something of an anomaly myself with the supernatural beings. They couldn't quite figure me out, either. It had taken me a while to know myself and what I was capable of, and I had no intentions of sharing. Only Talan and my father knew the extent of my powers and I intended to keep it that way.

Ashliel pulled away from Rotoph, his eyes bright with realization. "The resurrection orbs! Oceanus must have found the broken shards. Am I right?"

Rotoph nodded. "I'm sorry it brought back Cronus and Hades, and now you're stuck with me."

Turner had apparently decided he was finished with the family reunions. "Ashliel, can you tap into our holo-system? The sooner we find Cronus and Hades the easier it will be to recapture them."

Ashliel sighed. "Yes. If they're anywhere near a camera I can find them. But they're not going to be weak. Before Kala contacted me, I felt them awaken. I tapped into their brains briefly and..." he glanced at Rotoph sympathetically, "Rotoph did his job too well with the orbs. The child clone was able to use Rotoph's rune-work and restore Cronus and Hades to full power. More than that: It restored them to the strength they were when they were first created." Ashliel turned to me. "You remember how it felt when the runes gave you back your life and powers?"

I did. It had been intoxicating. I answered, "We're in trouble."

Ashliel looked thoughtful. "The only upside is that their power will weaken over time and go back to their 'normal.' So things they can do today, hopefully they won't be able to later on."

I sighed, "We don't have a 'later on.' We'll have to take our chances on them now, super-power-mode or not."

Roberta shook her head. "We can't do *anything* standing here. Ashliel, if you can find them, maybe we can come up with a plan. Chelsan can beat Hades," she added with confidence.

"Uh," Chelsan's face went three shades paler.

"She has us, too," Max offered at seeing his friend's reaction.

I had no idea what Chelsan could do against a fully juiced up God of Death. She might be able to hold her own, or she might fail miserably. But we needed to find Hades first before any of this mattered. "Ashliel?"

The Grigori nodded. "On it."

Ashliel placed his hands in the air, closing his eyes. The holo-images above us began to move: slowly at first, then rapidly, in a circle. In a matter of seconds, the entire room was a whirlwind of flying holo-images moving too fast to differentiate one from the other, although for me, all I saw was Ryan and my gun. The spinning cyclone of images began to spin into a small point that drilled itself into Ashliel's forehead.

Watching as the tornado of footage quickly pounded its way into Ashliel's brain was mesmerizing. Ryan appeared the most impressed, as if he related somehow to the massive in-pouring of information. It must have been a similar experience when he had been trapped inside Elisha's brain machine and bonded with the I.Q. nuts.

I admit, visibly it was impressive.

Ashliel was always a little bit of a show-off, though. He probably could have accomplished the same thing with far less drama. But now that I knew he had been Chelsan's teacher, he was probably trying to impress her a bit. He was also reminding Turner and Roberta that supernatural beings were far stronger than they were. He probably didn't need to rub it in so much, they did just lose their connection to Hades and Cronus. Talk about kicking a couple when they were down.

Every drop of holo-footage disappeared into Ashliel's head.

When he opened his eyes, Ashliel looked at me with a flash of fear.

"Did you find them?" Turner asked coolly. If he had been intimidated by the display of power, he didn't show it.

Ashliel nodded. "They're in this room."

Cronus spoke. "Looking for us?"

I hated that voice.

Three hundred years wasn't long enough.

Cronus and Hades materialized in front of us all.

Both had smug expressions on their smug faces. Did I say smug? Yeah, I still hated them.

"Who's dumb enough to pick a fight with three Grigori and *me*? The one person who could swallow you whole." I had no intention of doing that, but they didn't know that.

Only Hades looked frightened.

Cronus didn't flinch.

"I'm not scared of you." Cronus laughed.

"You should be," I threatened.

"You have no idea what you're up against, do you?" Cronus grinned maliciously.

I didn't like the sound of that. He knew something that I didn't. Maybe if I could keep him talking, he'd slip, like his usual arrogant self used to do.

SLAM!

Every cell of my body was frozen.

Cronus had found a way to stop me from moving!

I was actually embarrassed. One second into this fight and I was already benched.

Chapter Five

Four Years Ago

CHELSAN

Chelsan sat with Nancy at their work station in Biology class. Chelsan was still reeling at how Nancy had put Jill Forester in her place. Chelsan wasn't sure if Nancy would come to her senses and beg Jill-the-queen-bee for forgiveness, but in this moment, Chelsan could at least pretend she had a friend for a little while longer.

Chelsan had just made thirty dead frogs hop out of the windows so Nancy wouldn't have to cut into one. Nancy had confessed to losing her pet frog, Jimmy, and the thought of cutting up a dead frog for biology class had been too much to bear. Chelsan had taken it into her own hands and used her powers to get rid of the frogs.

The only question that scared Chelsan was: Did Nancy figure out Chelsan's powers?

From the expression on Nancy's face, Chelsan could tell that her lab partner knew she was responsible for the sudden luck of not having to dissect a frog, but she was pretty sure Nancy had no idea *how* she did it.

"Thanks for being nice to me and standing up to Jill," Chelsan said before she could think better of it. Inside, she cringed at how pathetic and desperate she sounded. But being completely alone in high school was rough. Not only that: being despised. It hurt more than Chelsan wanted to admit to herself.

Nancy's face fell.

Chelsan had never seen anyone look so ashamed. "I should have done it the day you arrived. I was horrible to you at the beginning of class. I would totally understand if you never wanted to talk to me again," Nancy said in a rush of guilt.

It felt good to hear. Chelsan was too scared to hope Nancy could possibly be her friend, but she decided she was going to risk it.

"Jill makes it hard on everyone. I get why you didn't want to talk to me. And I'd understand if you stop. It's hard being an outcast." Chelsan tried to make Nancy feel better, but from the expression on Nancy's face it only made her feel worse.

"We can be outcasts together. Screw Jill and her cronies. I'd rather be shunned and have a true friend, than be popular and have a friend like *her*." Nancy leaned in to whisper, "Jill Forester is evil incarnate." Then she pulled back and smiled. "And it felt pretty amazing to watch her squirm."

They both glanced over at Jill, who was whispering to her number one lackey, Joan, and staring daggers in their direction.

"So this isn't an elaborate trick to get me to feel like we're friends, then humiliate me later?" Chelsan tried to hide the sound of fear in her voice.

Nancy's eyes widened. "Has Jill done that to you before?"

Chelsan nodded. "She got Alex Adams to ask me out, then when I said 'Yes,' Jill came out of hiding with her crew, laughing at me."

"That's horrible! I had no idea!" Nancy was mortified. "I don't know how to convince you, except to prove it to you every day. I don't know how you made those frogs get up and jump out of this room, but you did that for me. A girl who had been unbelievably rude to you minutes before. That tells me you are a far better human than I am – or anyone else in this school for that matter. I should be asking *you* to be my friend, not the other way around." Nancy sat forward so that Chelsan was forced to meet her intense eyes. "I swear to you, I will be loyal to you to the day I die." Then she smiled, "You're my new best friend whether you like it or not. What do you think of that?"

Chelsan couldn't help herself. She felt a warmth spread through her. Nancy was the real deal, and her words were the first nice things Chelsan had heard since arriving at Geoffrey Turner High. "I think that sounds amazing."

"Now, no arguing, you're coming to my house after school and we're going to binge all of Jason Keroff's greatest moments on my holo-tv. Don't pretend that you don't like the guy. I've seen your e-reader screen saver," Nancy teased.

Chelsan felt a stab of panic. She wasn't sure where Nancy lived and if it was out of her four-mile radius. If she was past the four-mile mark she would lose her hold on Bruce, her dead step-father. She decided to play it safe. "I have to work at Mel's after school. But you could meet me there after I'm off? Maybe we could go to the mall?"

"And buy some shoes! I like the way you think." Nancy nudged Chelsan affectionately with her shoulder. "Deal."

Chelsan had never felt so much happiness in her life. Even if it only lasted a day, she would cherish what happened just now forever. Of course, she didn't have any money for the mall, so Nancy would be doing all the shopping, but it didn't matter. Chelsan wanted to enjoy this moment as long as she could.

When the room quieted down, Nancy made an expression of *we better be quiet*, then started reading the chapters Mr. Ash had assigned to them as he had booked out of the room from shock over the frog incident.

As Chelsan turned on her e-reader to begin reading the chapter, she noticed something outside.

Trying not to be too obvious, Chelsan peered out the window to see Mr. Ash in the distance. To her dismay, he picked up one of the dead frogs, examining it thoroughly. Terror filled Chelsan's bones. What if he knew or suspected she had powers? But no, how would Mr. Ash know that someone could control dead things? Even if he did, he wouldn't know it was her.

But then Mr. Ash did something that surprised her.

Looking at the frog, Mr. Ash smiled, then looked directly at Chelsan and winked.

Present Time

I still couldn't believe Mr. Ash was an angel. And a Grigori angel at that. I remembered that day with the dead frogs and how strange it was how he had smiled at one of the corpses, then winked at me! I had many sleepless nights after that, wondering about that stupid wink! And now to find out it was because he knew everything about me? He had probably found out about Nancy's dead pet and made sure we were lab partners. Suddenly, I felt like a giant lab rat.

Apparently, I had been watched by a lot of supernatural beings my entire life.

It was disturbing.

Speaking of…

Cronus and Hades were way more intimidating in person than floating around in astral projection land.

Cronus appeared to have frozen Kala in place. I wondered if he was using the same type of powers Isabelle used. When I had jumped into Isabelle, I connected to her spinning white hole, which allowed me to control her completely. I was able to see what Isabelle saw when she used her powers: anything moving left small trails of light. Isabelle connected to those trails – and stopped them. She had been trained by Turner and Harry Clifton to be an assassin. Isabelle would connect to the movement of her victim's hearts, then make the beating stop. Every kill looked like a heart attack. Pretty efficient. Pretty terrifying.

When I had used her power, I had made everyone freeze in place like Kala was now.

Maybe I could tap into Cronus's white light (if he had one!) and free Kala?

It was worth a shot.

I concentrated as hard as I could and…

Nothing.

I couldn't see inside the guy.

Note to self: gods aren't human.

Good news was, Cronus was so concentrated on gloating to Kala that he hadn't noticed me trying to tap inside of him. I was now sure he could squash me like a gnat.

For the first time in a fight I felt like I was on the junior varsity team. What could a tiny *human* do against a freaking Titan and an

Olympian? Since meeting Kala and her angel friends, I hadn't been able to shake the feeling that me and my team were the kids while Kala and her team were the adults.

And Adult Number One was frozen in place.

Fire erupted everywhere at once.

Different colored flames – purple, blue, yellow – poured out of the three Grigoris' hands, slamming into Cronus and Hades.

The two enemies must have been made of some kind of fire-retardant skin, because nothing seemed to hurt them.

Cronus only laughed. "We are stronger than we've ever been, Grigori. Your puny fires can't hurt us. I am the Titan of Time, reborn. I freeze you all in this moment." He waved his hands and…

I was frozen.

And so was everyone else.

Wow.

This sucked.

Cronus kept laughing. He was having way too much fun.

Hades, I noticed, wasn't as confident as Cronus. Nevertheless, he had cracked a smile. The God of Death decided it was safe enough for him to step forward to demand, "Where is that girl who escaped my invitation to the Underworld?"

Uh-oh.

It wasn't like I could raise my hand to reveal myself.

I scoured my brain to figure out how I could possibly get out of this situation. Kala had warned me that one touch from Hades and I was on my way to the Underworld, which basically equated to… I don't know…

DYING!

Okay, yes, I had taken the immortality serum, but Kala seemed pretty confident that Hades could get around that. Did that mean he could kill Ryan? Would Kala ask Hades to do that if I couldn't break this curse of hers? It scared me more than having a Titan and an Olympian searching the room for me.

Finally, Hades's eyes met mine. "Ah, there she is."

Hades walked over to me until we were face-to-face. He looked as gaunt as in my dream and his skin was paler, if that were possible. Smiling at me made him more terrifying, though, what with his deeply lined face, beady black eyes and stringy black hair. Gross.

"Can't escape me now, can you?" Hades was pleased with himself.

And, yeah: he was right.

I. Couldn't. Budge.

So frustrating.

If I could have closed my eyes I would have as he reached up and touched my forehead.

But...

Nothing.

A wave of relief flooded through me.

Hades touched me again in disbelief.

Holding my breath...

Nothing.

Okay, feeling safer now.

The God of Death turned to Cronus. "I can't send her to the Underworld. Someone must be protecting her!"

I knew that wasn't true, but since I couldn't speak, I wasn't in a position to correct him. The immortality serum was the true power. Yay, Dr. Fortski – he was a genius! The serum was enough to stop *the* Death God from killing anyone. It meant not only was *I* safe, but so was Ryan and the rest of my crew. Except Roberta,

109

but they had a room full of Roberta clones to remedy that if it happened.

Cronus replied, "That human Alec told us she could be a problem."

Alec?

The Franklin clone.

Alec must be the I.Q. kid consciousness stuck inside the clone. Like Roberta, the *invader* won over control of the body. The clone itself was either working in unison with the I.Q. kid, or Alec had pushed the clone's consciousness so far down inside of him that he might as well be dead.

And thanks, *Alec*. Point me out why don't you?

BOOM!

The room shook violently back and forth, again and again, until the ceiling cracked open. Light poured into the room. It was a beautiful juxtaposition of the fake night sky with its slow-moving Milky Way broken apart by the very real California sunshine outside.

A creature of stunning beauty flew in on giant black leathery wings through the crack in the ceiling. Twenty-feet tall and at least five feet wide, a man with deep blue skin and large shiny scales landed in front of Cronus. He was quite possibly the most beautiful thing I had ever seen.

He almost looked like a human dragon. What in the what was happening in my life right now?!

Before addressing Cronus, the creature turned and winked at Kala, "Hello, lovely. Nothing like the Cavalry, am I right?"

Then the creature screamed. It was the most hideous, high-pitched sound I had ever heard. My whole body shook from the…

Wait a minute.

My body.

It was moving.

SNAP!

When the screeching stopped, I could move.

And so could everyone else.

"Asmodeus," Cronus spat with considerable distaste. "I see you've been delving into those books of yours."

The creature smiled, "I had a little help." He nodded to Roberta. "Time for the fireworks. You ready?"

"With pleasure," Roberta snarled. She was angry. I knew that look. Grams didn't like it when someone got the upper hand on her. I should know, I had done it a few times to the grandparents in the past.

I had no idea what Roberta and this blue-dragon-thingy called 'Asmodeus' were going to do, but I suddenly felt the urgent need to get out of the way.

Kala, apparently, had the same notion. She waved my group over. "Get behind me!"

We didn't need to be told twice. Ryan, Max, Eva and I ran to Kala and the Grigori, standing behind them like the cowards we were. I didn't feel an ounce of guilt about it, either. Seriously, I was staring at the butt of a blue-scaled monster whose screech broke me out of a freezing spell cast by a *Titan!*

Out of Roberta's hands shot a white glowing stream of light, identical to the strings of light I would see when I was astral projecting. It was strange now, seeing it while awake, but exciting as well. Could I do that?

Roberta's light struck the blue creature and he laughed with satisfaction. Energy flowed back and forth between Asmodeus and Roberta within the stream of light. It was some kind of power exchange or enhancer.

Whatever it was, Hades began to back away. Cronus just looked angrier.

The Titan shot out his hands and shards of lightning cracked out of his fingertips, slamming into Asmodeus and Roberta. But their bond didn't break.

Roberta began to incant a spell. I wished I knew whatever language *magic* was. It would help me follow along much better in situations like these.

Cronus waved his hands and I felt myself slowing down. He was trying to freeze us in time again. I didn't know how to fight it. I looked around me and saw that everyone else was slowing down as well.

"You can't keep using the same tricks, old man," Asmodeus mocked Cronus. He screeched his ear-shattering scream and I was instantly mobile again.

"Maybe we should leave this room?" I suggested. I was thinking a good old-fashioned 'RUN!' was in order.

As Roberta finished incanting her spell, a boulder-sized ball of light formed in the air. Asmodeus took this as his cue: with a wave of a finger he directed the giant orb straight into Cronus's chest.

This time, finally, the Titan reacted. His body was thrown back almost halfway across the room, his perfectly coifed suit singed black from the impact of the light ball.

The orb disintegrated into Cronus and he screamed in anguish. His skin began to bubble, melting as if the ball had been made of acid.

But the pain didn't stop him. Within seconds, Cronus stood up and charged Asmodeus. As he ran to battle, I could see his skin already healing. Apparently, being a god meant you had the same advantages as the immortality serum. Healing was a good perk, especially while running.

The blue creature screeched his terrifying scream right before Cronus could tackle him. Cronus stopped in his tracks, falling to his knees and holding his ears in pain.

The Titan yelled over Asmodeus, "Impossible! Your powers should not affect me!"

Turner answered back, "You think my wife and I wouldn't have a plan in place should you two escape? You are as dumb as Kala said you were."

Asmodeus's screaming ended. Thank goodness, I thought my ears would start bleeding if he didn't stop.

Hades spat in disgust, "Letting a *human* tether itself to you, a demon? You disappoint, Asmodeus."

Demon? A freaking *demon* was standing in front of me. And he saved us. And he seemed to be besties with my grandparents. Shocker.

Asmodeus said with a grin, "These humans here? The ones that have been using you and your pops like their very own magic generator? I always side with the winners, you should know that. And, Hades, didn't Cronus put you to sleep for a few thousand years himself by the way?"

I was trying to follow everything that was being exchanged, but it was difficult. Cronus was Hades's dad. Check. Blue-scaled demon tethered his power to Grams. Check. And Cronus apparently put Hades to sleep for a few millennia back who knows when. Check. Didn't know how any of that would help in my current predicament, but it was good to know.

Kala took advantage of the fact that Cronus had fallen to his knees by taking hold of the Titan's suit lapels and tossing him thirty feet in the air.

Whoa.

Super strength. Check.

Cronus came flying down face first, but before he hit the ground the Titan somehow managed to right himself. He pushed green fire straight into Kala's chest.

Screaming in pain, Kala pushed through it and shot a wave of purple flames out of her fingers, trying to wrap the fire around Cronus's body. The three Grigori joined in, all using purple fire as well.

Cronus squirmed and fought, but the fire kept wrapping itself around him, over and over.

Hades, fearing he'd be alone, did something I couldn't comprehend.

With a wave of his arms, a cloud of black fog rippled from his body and flew through the group of humans that had been carrying out the dead bodies.

Instantly, they were dead, falling to the ground, joining the very corpses they had been trying to dispose of.

But unlike the dead bodies I had disconnected from their black holes, these newly killed humans were completely controllable.

But he didn't stop there. He let his black fog travel through the building, murdering each person it touched.

He was going to kill everyone in the building.

I had to stop him.

I turned to Max and Eva. "Try to break Hades's hold on those corpses."

Max and Eva nodded, then focused their attention on the dead bodies running to the scene, controlled by Hades.

He made the cadavers jump into the purple fire that had

partially captured Cronus. Once their bodies blocked direct contact with the Titan, the fire began to lose its tight grip.

I closed my eyes and concentrated on Hades's white light. Unlike Cronus, I could actually see it!

This gave me a thrill of hope. If I could tap in…

Sensing more and more black holes being created in hallways and rooms around me, I had to act fast. I tried to slam into Hades's white light.

My eyes snapped open as I smacked into an invisible barrier. I tried again.

SNAP!

I felt a blood vessel pop in my brain. In my brain! The immortality serum healed it instantly, but still, that flipping hurt!

I had to try again, though. I couldn't let all those innocent people die!

Mentally, I tried to smash into his white light as hard as I could.

POP!

There went another blood vessel. This one in my eye! I momentarily couldn't see when I opened my eyes, but the serum healed it quickly and I was back to 20/20 vision once more.

So far Hades hadn't noticed my lame attempt to control him. He was too busy sending out that deadly fog.

Desperate, I tried another tactic as I saw Max run forward, obviously frustrated he couldn't connect to any of the dead bodies.

Cronus had almost completely rid himself of the purple flames, but when Max shoved one of the dead bodies out of the way, Talan was able to renew the attack of fire.

Hades looked downright shocked that anyone dared touch a dead body that he operated. The Olympian snarled and sent a dose of his black fog at Max and Eva. Hades was more enraged when he witnessed the black fog doing nothing to the pair. Next time I saw Fortski I was giving him a bear hug. Seriously.

I let Max and Eva distract Hades.

I felt Ryan's hand wrap around mine.

"Stay focused," he whispered.

Ryan knew me like no other. He could see that I was attempting something, and he probably was more than a little worried when he saw a blood vessel in my eye bust. I used the calming strength of his hand in mine.

"Deep breaths," Ryan coached.

I did as he instructed, my body instantly calming, my mind focusing.

I concentrated on finding the black fog traveling in the building; more specifically, finding the dust that carried it. Dust essentially consisted of dead skin cells, so it was an easy way to track down the fog.

The fog was about to enter a highly populated lab.

I took one more deep breath and used the dust to grab hold of the fog.

It was a strange sensation, holding a gaseous substance with tiny particles of dead skin cells, but it was working. The fog was on an upper level, so I used the dust to move it up toward the ceiling.

"YOU!" Hades voice roared.

I kind of knew who *you* was.

Really? He didn't feel me trying to break into his *body*, but he noticed when I took charge of his death cloud?

Before he could stop me, I mentally pushed the fog up through the ceiling, letting it dissipate into the air.

Everyone's eyes were on me. Even Cronus — and he was half-covered in purple fire. The Grigori and Kala kept their hold on him as if they were taming a wild horse.

Asmodeus and Roberta had joined in the purple fire party as well.

But Hades's call made their heads turn to focus on…

Me.

Hades had managed to murder at least a hundred people before I was able to stop the black fog. Now they were all on their way to our room.

Out of habit (and, let's face it, security blanket time), I tried to tap into the black holes coming our way. But it was like Fortski's blocking compound times ten. I couldn't wriggle my way in to mentally grab hold of the spinning black holes.

Time to face the music.

Hades's eyes were burning with rage. "You tiny human."

Was I supposed to have some kind of witty comeback? Frankly, I wanted to puke from terror. And calling me a 'tiny human' wasn't much of an insult. For him it must have been though, because he looked like he wanted to disintegrate me on sight.

Good thing he didn't have that kind of power.

Or did he?

I was way out of my element here.

And the look on Roberta's face. She was in the middle of trapping Cronus, but her eyes sparkled at me like I could take down Hades with a snap of my fingers. How could she go from wanting me dead to thinking I was the all-powerful-granddaughter?

"Hey." Yeah. I said that.

The dead bodies Hades controlled ran in from every door in the gigantic room.

They'd be on our little group in seconds.

I didn't have time to chat with the Death God at the moment.

"Max, Eva, try and push through his barriers! We need control of those corpses!" I was telling them to do something not even I could do, but I needed help.

"They're mine, *human*," Hades snarled. "You may have found some magic way to control the dead like Alec has, but I am the God of Death. You're *nothing* in my domain."

Aside from the extreme ouchiness of that statement, it did tell me that he thought I was performing some kind of magic like my grandparents. And he thought that was how Alec controlled dead things as well. Hades was half right. My father first received his powers because John and Samuel Dane (aka the psycho-crazy-twins) tried to kill all life within their four-mile reach. (They connected to the white lights and could disconnect them from the living like I could disconnect the black holes from the dead. They had been born with their powers because their mother had been a guinea pig for a lot of drugs like Age-pro and the such, so their powers came from science, not magic.) When the Dane brothers tried to kill Roberta, she had been pregnant with my father at the time. Not only did it not kill my grandmother, but it was how my dad got his powers. Then later when my dear old grandparents used a spell to kill me and my mom, my father sacrificed himself magically to bring us back – and, inadvertently, transferred his powers to me.

So the origins of my powers were a little science, and a little magic.

It must have only registered as magic to Hades because that was his only experience with the supernatural. It sounded like he'd been asleep during the whole human-technological-advances part of history. He had no practical experience with science.

118

I may not have the kind of skill set Hades had, but I had discovered some impressive things I could do with my powers. I hoped I could do something to get us out of here. I wondered why Kala and Talan didn't just teleport us out of this place?

They were fighters, as in, if there was a fight, they fought. I was a fighter too, but only when I had to. I'd much rather be home, snuggled up with Ryan reading a book or doing other things...

Focus.

I felt Ryan's hand still clasping mine and took strength from it.

The first wave of corpses finally caught up to our group. They surrounded Cronus and took the blows of purple fire for him, blocking the flames instantly.

It was enough.

Cronus broke free and pushed his hands forward. All the air from the room seemed to gather together and push out of his fingertips.

Kala, the three Grigori, Asmodeus, and my grandparents flew across the giant room as if they were falling leaves from a tree.

Cronus laughed in happiness. "None of you can defeat me! I am the first born of Gaia and father of the Olympians!"

Super cheesy.

Eva laughed.

Cronus whirled on her and the smile was wiped from her face.

The dead bodies ran straight toward us.

Oops.

Were we going to die? No, probably not. But there were worse things than dying and something told me Cronus and Hades were masters of the art of torture.

Cronus sent a lightning bolt at Eva. She tried to move out of the way, but a few of the dead bodies held her in place. The bolt smacked her square in the chest, leaving a blackened mark behind.

Eva screamed in pain.

"Never laugh at a Titan, *human*," Cronus sneered.

I really hated the way they said 'human.'

Kala and crew were already on their feet and throwing more colorful fire into the mix.

It wasn't working. It felt more like a light show than a battle.

Asmodeus screamed again, which only added to the chaotic state of the room.

Eva was singed, but otherwise okay, Max began prying the corpses off his sister since he couldn't control them with his power.

Everything was spinning out of control.

Cronus re-focused on Kala.

Hades was using his corpses on the rest of her team, at the same time sending a few of them to hold me and my team back.

Then I realized: neither Hades nor Cronus thought of me, Max or Eva as a threat.

As they had said a number of times, we were just *humans*.

I felt the dead bodies grab hold of my arms; it was such a strange sensation.

Normally, I wouldn't fear anything dead, or think of it as a threat in any way. Even when Turner had used Fortski's compound to keep me out. I had broken through that almost immediately. True, I had motivation: Turner was controlling one of his corpses to inject me with poison.

I shook the thought from my brain before I attacked Turner instead of Cronus and Hades.

Concentrate.

First things first. Get these dang zombies off me.

I kept my eyes open, looking for anything like Fortski's

compound in the dead bodies. I knew there wasn't any science controlling the corpses, it was Hades's magic, but maybe I could see his magic the same way as the compound. My eyes immediately went into dust-mode. Billions of tiny black holes blanketed the entirety of the large room. Anytime a living or dead person moved, I saw them through a swirling fog of dead dust cells. It was almost beautiful the way it ebbed and flowed through the multi-colored fires and the movement of everyone fighting – well, beautiful except for the rather depressing fact we were all being attacked by the King of Titans and his Olympian son.

Okay, next.

Focus on the annoying corpse holding my right arm. I'd deal with dead-guy number two, holding my left arm, later. One corpse at a time.

It was extremely difficult to concentrate, considering everything that was going on all around. Cronus and Hades seemed to be enjoying themselves immensely, fighting with Kala, the Grigoris, the demon and my grandparents. Everyone on our side appeared to be holding their own at the moment, though, so I had a little time.

Through the swirling black fog of dead dust, my eyes met Max's. He spoke through telepathy so no one could hear. *The barriers. I managed to catch a glimpse of them, but I couldn't break through. It looks like a white, almost translucent glow.*

I nodded in thanks. That gave me something. Maybe the reason why I could see Hades's barrier was because the swirling black holes were actually hiding the barrier itself!

This gave me a rush of hope.

I re-focused my eyes, taking them out of dust-mode. All my attention went back to the dead woman grabbing me, on her swirling black hole.

I shut out all the noise and mayhem of the battle raging in front of me. No one seemed to be hurting anyone in any real way. It must be infuriating being gods and never being able to defeat your opponent. I guess that was why they had captured Hades and Cronus to begin with. If they couldn't die, might as well tie them up.

Distractions.

It was so difficult to stay on target when my world was flipped upside down. And somehow, I ended up being a part of *their* world because of some stupid prophecy. Too much.

So back to what I knew.

Dead things.

Couldn't waste time caring about a freaking Death God or a stupid Titan.

I'd been controlling the dead since I was seven and the last year had given me a crash course in what I could do.

I felt like I was in school and it was time to take my final exam.

Pass or fail, I had to try.

I stared as hard as I could at the spinning black hole next to me. Its detail: every swirl, the minute changes in color, the speed of the spin, the black of the hole, the deepness in color…

Is that…?

Yes!

A white, almost see-through glow blending perfectly with the black, just like Max said.

It disappeared as soon as I spotted it.

Focus. Focus.

I stared deeply into the black abyss, deeper, deeper. Come on. I switched my view to dust-mode once again, anything to see the white glow once more.

Swarms of black holes all around me, in front of me, behind me, in my peripheral view.

But I only stared at one.

The woman next to me.

Come on.

I grew dizzy from all the moving black circles fully encompassing every part of me. I could barely hear the fighting surrounding me.

Snap!

And, just like when I had first discovered dust-mode, something switched in my brain. I could now see a layer of glowing white so thin it was well camouflaged by the swirling black holes.

Now that I saw it completely, I couldn't *unsee* it. I knew, as with dust-mode, that now I could adjust my eyes to see the white protective barriers any time I wanted.

I tested my ability to break through the thin white layer of magic.

Major resistance there.

What was I missing?

If Hades was using magic to protect the swirling holes from me, then how was I supposed to break through?

Unless...

Hades didn't know *how* I saw dead things. Maybe this magic shell was *his* way of controlling the dead. If that was the case, then it wouldn't be about breaking *through* his magic barrier, it would be about connecting to the black holes themselves, because that was how *I* controlled the dead.

Okay.

Easier said than done.

The surrealness of having a philosophical debate in my head while gods and angels were tossing each other around like chew toys was palpable. Not to mention the constant waves of black-dust-wind roiling all around me.

But I was on to something, I knew it.

I had to act fast, though.

I was no magician, my powers were innate, so I couldn't fight magic with magic.

But maybe Roberta could.

I called out to her in my mind, hoping she could hear me in her new live clone vessel.

Roberta, are you there?

A few seconds rolled by. I was about to try again when…

My connection to Asmodeus allows him to hear you as well.

Party line, huh? I was a little shy talking to a giant dragon-man. But I didn't have a choice.

Uh, hi. Good one. I should seriously be an ambassador of some kind. *Hades has some sort of magic barrier around the black holes in the corpses. It's thin, but I can't seem to break it. Do you think you could? Or both of you could? Or…*Seriously, such a wordsmith.

Asmodeus's voice sounded in my head. *Hades is using controlling fire to keep hold of the dead bodies.*

Roberta answered, *We can use a shatter spell. It would temporarily break the white fire.*

I interjected shyly, *It doesn't look like fire. It just kind of glows, almost translucent.*

Asmodeus's tone was pretty condescending when he said, *Listen, little necromancer, we know what we're talking about.*

Sorry. Not sure why I apologized, but I didn't want a blue-dragon-demon ripping me to shreds.

Roberta's voice tried to sound encouraging as she instructed me, *Get ready.*

I took a deep breath.

CRACK!

All of the magic white barriers shattered into millions of pieces, then floated out of the corpses like dust.

Mine.

I slammed into every single corpse's black hole in the room.

And made them all freeze in place.

Karma, *Cronus*.

The fighting stopped immediately.

Cronus whirled on Hades, "What are you doing, you fool?!"

Hades's face had turned whiter than it already was. "I…" His eyes turned toward me, "She…"

Cronus eyed me as well. Instead of the fury I expected, he appeared confused. Then he nodded to Hades.

In the blink of an eye, the two gods disappeared.

I switched out of dust-mode so I could see everyone without giant clouds of black swirling dots buzzing like swarms of flies. I quickly disconnected the dead bodies from their black holes so they couldn't be controlled again. I didn't know the temperament of gods yet, but I wanted to make sure Hades couldn't teleport back in with stronger control of the dead bodies and renew his attack.

Kala walked over to me and I could see that she viewed me with respect. She looked at me like I was her equal. I certainly didn't feel that way, but I'd take it.

Then, before my eyes, Asmodeus transformed.

Within seconds, instead of a blue-scaled-dragon-man, there stood a man. A seriously beautiful man. Jeez, what was up with all supernatural beings looking like supermodels?! He was over six feet tall, looked like he spent every minute of every hour in the gym, stupidly chiseled bone structure and perfect hair. And he had somehow managed to magically clothe himself in a t-shirt and jeans since his "dragon" self had been entirely naked.

When his eyes met mine, I was sure my face turned bright red. He was seriously intimidating. Asmodeus smiled as he waved to all the dead bodies around us. "You're welcome."

"Oh, uh, thanks," I stuttered.

With a loud pop, Roberta severed her temporary magical bond with Asmodeus. She said to me, "You don't have to thank, Asmodeus. You were the one who took hold of Hades's dead bodies, just as I knew you would."

I didn't want to contradict her, but without Roberta and Asmodeus smashing apart the magical-white-glowy-thing, I wouldn't have been able to control the corpses.

Apparently, Asmodeus needed everyone to know the truth, though, because he added, "Yes, but Roberta and I broke Hades's white fire so the little necromancer could do her thing. *And* I broke Cronus's time hold on all of you, so, you're welcome."

"You want a medal?" Kala rolled her eyes. She obviously had history with the demon and from the expression on her face, it wasn't all good. There was chemistry there, though. Even I could see that. It almost visibly radiated off of them, something Talan didn't appear to like – but didn't do anything about, either.

"Actually, a medal would be quite nice, thank you." Asmodeus wasn't fazed by Kala's blunt sarcasm.

Kala ignored Asmodeus completely and turned toward me. "Hades was using white fire to control the corpses?"

I answered, "It didn't look like fire, it was kind of see-through."

Kala nodded. "It's probably Hades's innate power as the God of Death to control dead things. It's white because that magic is used by supernatural beings to control."

"Okay." Yeah, words.

"And you couldn't break through yourself?" Kala asked.

Gulp.

Felt like a failure.

"No," I answered honestly. "I'm not a magic person."

That sounded weird.

I felt Ryan's hand re-clasp mine and I instantly felt better.

Roberta was defensive. "We can teach her."

Asmodeus shook his head. "It took our combined powers to shatter Hades's control. The girl doesn't have that kind of strength."

Turner stepped in. "She has more innate power than any god, demon or angel I've ever seen."

Did Gramps just defend me?

I knew we had come to some kind of strange alliance, but he was downright protective.

I wasn't sure how I felt about that.

Turner continued, "Chelsan needs to find out how to access the part of her powers that will allow her to fight magic. Only one person knows more about what you're capable of than anyone else."

Don't say it.

Turner's eyes met mine and there was real sympathy there. He could see that I knew who he was going to name.

I wanted to run away and hide, but I also knew that he was right.

I cringed when he said, "We need to go see Elisha."

Chapter Six

50 Years Ago

KALA

Zeus grumbled, "Why don't you go in there, take the boy and make him have a baby. You humans are too patient. You're part god, act like it."

Kala fought every impulse in her body not to roll her eyes. Instead, she said calmly, "The Atlas visions will tell me when I'm to extract Franklin." A part of her agreed with Zeus, however. Sometimes when a mission was too hard for her to bear, she was tempted to go inside Turner's house herself and grab Franklin. He was still in the body of a little boy, though, so Kala would have to let him grow up before she could pair him up with…

This.

This was why Kala always stopped this line of thinking.

It was perverse and made her feel like a supernatural pimp.

Out of sight, out of mind.

Kala needed to focus on her Atlas missions and hope that someday soon the path to breaking the curse would open up to her. The girl Chelsan, from the prophecy, had said the year was 2321 in her head-sharing dream, which was fifty years from now. Assuming Chelsan wasn't on Age-pro and was actually a teenager, Kala had thirty some-odd years before the girl was to be born.

"I'll never understand you," Zeus raged. "I'm shocked one of your Atlas missions isn't to kill that human couple. They're using our family's life source and magic to fuel their empire." He was complaining about the Turners, Geoffrey and Roberta. He always refrained from calling any human by name. He thought it was beneath him.

"You didn't seem all that bothered by it back when it first happened. In fact, you were all for it. Gloating even." It always annoyed Kala that the gods were so fickle. The amount of flip-flopping that went on among them was worse than any politician Kala had ever met.

"I don't recall ever being behind magic-tapping," Zeus denied – as Kala had expected him to.

"Except when it's using *me* as a battery," Kala retorted, a sharp reminder to Zeus of the time he sucked all her magic dry to repair his broken mind.

Zeus made an expression that proved to Kala how he didn't even remotely see the similarities. Typical narcissist.

"Well, you can at least kill that female child they have locked up," Zeus huffed. "She's tried to take over that couple's hold on Cronus and Hades several times now. I'm surprised you haven't had an Atlas mission to kill her. She's more dangerous than any god."

Elisha.

Kala had been keeping tabs on the *child*. Except of course, Elisha was not a child, just like Franklin wasn't a child. She was

129

in a seven-year-old body, but Elisha was somewhere around fifty years old.

But Zeus was right: Elisha was dangerous.

Elisha aside, Kala didn't feel like explaining the Atlas curse to Zeus one more time. He was the god that gave the curse to Atlas in the first place, but he could never quite remember that the missions were inhuman, terrible acts, not knight-in-shining-armor-that-kills-the-bad-guys deeds.

Killing Elisha would save lives, Kala knew that for a fact since the I.Q. girl killed her fellow I.Q. kids on a daily basis.

Zeus had tried several times to tap into Cronus and Hades, so Kala knew he was simply angry that Geoffrey and Roberta were smarter and more equipped than he was. It must be a hard to accept when humans could out-magic a god, especially a god as powerful as Zeus.

"I can't make up my own missions, Zeus. As much as I'd love to kill Elisha, it's not my job."

Zeus shook his head, annoyed. "Well, it should be. She's trouble."

Kala shrugged. Whether he was right or not, Kala wasn't going to do anything about it. It was hard enough being Atlas as it was, she didn't need to be acting like judge, jury and executioner on top of it.

After a moment, Zeus's face softened, and he sighed heavily. "You won't be seeing me for a while. I need to be away from this plane of existence to think about some things."

"What things?" Kala asked, genuinely curious and not a little bit leery. Zeus thinking was never a good thing.

"Where we gods fit in this world. We're all feeling a bit more useless every day that humans advance," Zeus answered.

130

Kala couldn't help but notice the depressed tone in Zeus's voice. But she thought his leaving Earth for while was a good idea. Maybe some time away would help Zeus lose some of his elitist attitude. She wasn't holding her breath.

"You know how to reach me if you need to." Kala felt a pang of connection to Zeus. He was, after all, her nephew. Still bizarre.

Zeus simply nodded then gave Kala a wistful look. "So long, Kala Hicks."

"Bye, Zeus."

With that, Zeus teleported out of the room and Kala was left feeling that she wasn't going to see the god for a very long time.

Present Time

I could see from the look on Chelsan's face that the last thing she wanted to do was talk to Elisha. I couldn't blame her, I knew the whole story. After Zeus had mentioned it, I was more than a little shocked that Elisha had not been a part of at least one of my Atlas missions to date. But apparently the Universe knew that Chelsan would stop her, or more accurately, reattach Elisha's soul. Maybe Elisha still had a part to play in this world.

After years of doing vile things, I couldn't begin to guess what the Universe's definition of 'keeping the balance' actually meant. None of it made sense anymore. I just wanted to stop being responsible for everything.

Chelsan had been a small lifting of my burden – doing things I knew would have been my Atlas missions if she didn't exist.

"I don't get a 'Thank you for saving my life, Asmodeus. Again.'" Asmodeus joined my side as our large group moved through the hallways of Turner's Headquarters. Talan was on my other side, but

131

he stayed quiet, letting me handle the demon.

I wanted to punch Asmodeus.

And a part of me of me always wanted to hug him.

He *was* the father of my child, after all. I didn't regret those three days with Asmodeus, 257 years ago, but I was always shocked that he still held out hope that we'd be together someday. I was with Talan and I always would be. Part of me hurt for Asmodeus because I knew that would never change. I wondered what would happen on the day when Asmodeus finally accepted the truth. I had to be prepared every time I saw him. My worst fear was that he'd take it out on our son, Terence. Maybe try to kill him…

I didn't like thinking of that possibility, but Asmodeus was a demon, and with him, I had to be ready for anything.

I'd always be bonded with Asmodeus and I'd always love him to a certain degree, but I'd never be with him. Not like that anyway.

"Thank you," Chelsan said quietly.

That girl was way too nice. And probably feeling over her head. I could see how she looked at us, the supernatural beings. It was a mixture of deference and shyness. It completely baffled me. Chelsan could most likely kick any god, angel or demons' butt, or at least dish out some serious pain. She was so humble I almost thought she was faking, but no one could fake the earnestness I saw in her eyes. How could this girl be related to Roberta and Geoffrey Turner?

Then I remembered Janet and Franklin. It still twisted my heart thinking of Chelsan's parents. Two of the kindest, most selfless people I ever met.

"See? The little necromancer knows when to be grateful," Asmodeus said directly to me.

Before I could choose tact, I reverted to my usual defensive self.

132

After three hundred years Asmodeus could still push my buttons. "We had everything under control." Not true, but I just couldn't show gratitude. It was physically impossible for me at the moment.

Asmodeus laughed. "Oh yes, Cronus locking you in time so you couldn't move was all a part of your plan, I'm sure."

I switched our line of bantering. (It could go on for hours, trust me.) "How was he able to do that? He's never done that before. Cronus could have stopped me three hundred years ago with that little trick."

And just like Ashliel had told us, Asmodeus confirmed, "Seems he's got his old mojo back, as in his original, ancient mojo. That resurrection device made him a shiny newborn Titan." He winked sarcastically at Rotoph. "Thanks for that by the way."

Rotoph shrugged. "It saved *you* in the Underworld."

Asmodeus lifted an eyebrow in agreement. "True. But it's going to make our job of imprisoning Cronus and Hades a lot harder."

Talan interjected, "*Our*? You're going to help us again?"

Weirdly, Talan seemed hopeful for the help, though I knew it killed him that I still had a relationship with Asmodeus, he respected it fully. Talan's loyalty and love for me were unwavering, even before I had felt the same for him. My connection with Asmodeus didn't change that.

Asmodeus didn't make eye contact with Talan. He rarely did. I knew it hurt Asmodeus deeply that Terence considered Talan and Owen his father figures and not him. Terence never willingly accepted that he was half-demon. I could only assume he was ashamed by it. Asmodeus acted like he didn't care. He had certainly fathered a number of children throughout his many millennia of living – but Terence was *ours*. That meant something to him, though he only admitted that to me once.

Asmodeus answered Talan's question with a smirk. "After today's theatrics I'm Enemy #1 on their hit list. So yes, Grigori, I'll help when I can." Then he turned to Roberta. "It would be more helpful if you'd take that fancy scientific juice that will make this new body of yours immortal. I can't have my tethered power-witch killed in the middle of battle."

Roberta's hand was locked in Turner's as she responded to Asmodeus, "I'm still fighting with the consciousness of the clone inside of me. Once that issue is resolved permanently, I'll take the serum."

Asmodeus shrugged. "Too complicated for my taste. Let's try to stay out of any fights until then, shall we?"

"When did you guys team up anyway?" I was still in shock that Asmodeus had paired up with a human. Not his style, especially Roberta Turner.

Asmodeus smiled. "I always go where the power is, you know that, buttercup." He moved away from me.

I noticed Max and Eva stealing glances at Asmodeus. Only alive for less than a year it must be hard to comprehend some things. I knew Elisha used her own version of Turner's brain machines to load the two kids up with as much knowledge as possible, but I think even Chelsan sometimes forgot that they had only existed for such a short time. Seeing Asmodeus in his demon form was probably a bigger shock to them than to anyone else in their group.

I surveyed the rest of our merry band of fighters. Ryan and Chelsan were having a private conversation only they could hear, and I didn't want to interrupt. Turner kept his focus on his wife. Rotoph and Ashliel were discussing the finer points of resurrection runes and comparing Heaven #1 to Heaven #5 where the Grigori had been imprisoned for a few thousand years. Talan walked beside me quietly.

Asmodeus...

He felt uncomfortable, I could tell. It was hard for him to be around me when Talan was there. Asmodeus preferred one-on-one. He *had* saved us. I never would have broken out of Cronus's time lock spell without him. And even if I had, it probably would have been too late. Asmodeus deserved a thank you. He deserved my gratitude. I didn't know why it was so hard for me to be thankful to another person, especially Asmodeus. Maybe because he wasn't a person, he was a demon.

I should throw him a bone.

Anything.

I nodded to Talan, not needing to admit my intentions. He nodded back, which essentially equated to his approval. Not that I needed it, but still nice to have.

I walked up to Asmodeus, so we were side-by-side. He seemed almost startled that I had left Talan's side to walk with him. When our eyes met, I said with as much sincerity as I could muster, "Thanks for having my back."

I was pretty sure I short-circuited his brain from the expression on his face. Wow. I had done a number on Asmodeus for the last three hundred years.

But he smiled, genuinely smiled. "Always."

It felt good. It felt right.

Then he added, directing the comment at Talan, "Anything for the mother of my child."

Such a dick.

Asmodeus couldn't help himself. As stubborn as *I* was, he was the same way. It was probably why we had a connection in the first place.

Talan could have been cruel if he had wanted to and thrown his close relationship with Terence in Asmodeus's face. But he didn't. It simply wasn't who he was. Instead he said, "I'll always be grateful for your loyalty to Kala."

Asmodeus hated that. He wanted to get under Talan's skin, make him jealous, anything… But Talan never bit. You'd think Asmodeus would have given up by now. But like I said: stubborn.

I hated it when Terence was brought up in casual conversation, though. Our relationship had never been as healthy as I'd like. My missions always came first. A child couldn't understand that, all he knew was that his mommy was rarely there. I tried giving as much time to Terence as I could, waiting until the fourth day to complete my missions, but it never seemed like enough. It wasn't. Because when I was with Terence, my mind was always thinking of whatever horrible thing I had to do to make him and everyone else safe.

I wish I could have been a better mother.

Terence rarely complained out loud, only his eyes condemned me every time we saw each other. He resented my job, and he resented me for picking the mission over him.

Owen, Talan and Linda were wonderful parental figures for him, though. Owen and Talan were able to help him hone his powers and taught him how to blend in with humans, while Linda, being human herself, let him experience what a real mother should be. Even the Turners were family to Terence. He was like a surrogate son to them before they had Franklin.

It just hurt.

I was proud of Terence. He'd been working undercover for a couple hundred years now, pretending to be on General Clifton's team. Terence reported to Owen and Talan all Clifton's activities, but occasionally he reported to the Turners as well. Not as often as the Turners would like though since their impatience for intel forced them to trick Isabelle into showing her face a few months back when Clifton had tried to start a war with Elisha.

But back in the day when General Clifton managed to turn the whole crew against Turner and proposed that they'd all fake their deaths, Terence decided to stay with General Clifton to keep an eye on him. None of us trusted Clifton. The man was a tyrant and blindly jealous of Turner. He was dangerous and we needed Clifton watched at all times. Since Terence already felt like he had found a family with Isabelle, Dean and Charlie, he had opted to stay. As far as any of them knew, Terence had 'true aim' like me, which made him their sniper, again, like me. The parallels in our lives stung. Our relationship could have been so different if I hadn't been Atlas.

And if Clifton had known what Terence was capable of...?

He'd have tried to use Terence to seize power long before his last failed attempt.

My son's powers were a closely guarded secret. Only Talan, Owen, Derek, Asmodeus and I knew what he could do, and I planned on keeping it that way.

I momentarily turned my thoughts away from Terence to notice that we were heading down deeper into the underbelly of the building. Turner didn't want Elisha escaping, that was obvious. She was harmless at this point, Chelsan having restored her soul, but Elisha was still one of the smartest humans on the planet – second only to Ryan Vaughn. And smart was always dangerous.

I hoped we could get something useful out of Elisha. I had heard she had gone insane since getting her soul back. I wasn't sure

137

what Turner expected Elisha to do for them, but I learned a long time ago never to underestimate the Turners and their opinions on things.

Chelsan suddenly made eye contact with me. From the expression on her face I knew she wanted to talk to me alone. As I joined her side, we let everyone else walk by. Talan was the last to pass, shooting a quick, supportive sideways glance toward me.

Chelsan began timidly, "I'm sure I could ask my grandmother but, honestly, I can't take her encouragement-face right now."

I wanted to laugh at Chelsan's observation, but I kept my cool. It was obvious Roberta now revered her granddaughter. She had been the same way about Franklin. When Roberta and Turner had tried to take out Chelsan, I figured Roberta would always hate her granddaughter, that she'd never stop blaming Chelsan for the death of her only son. But, somehow, Roberta put aside her grief and fury and chose to not only accept Chelsan, but to love and support her as well. That was the problem with the Turners. Their loyalty could flip on a dime depending on how deeply you hurt them. If I wasn't immortal, they would have killed me by now. It wasn't for lack of trying. Spells, weapons, tethering demons and Malaks. They had tried everything. It must frustrate them to no end that I was still alive and kicking.

I looked at Chelsan, encouraging her to continue, "What did you want to ask me?"

The girl paused for a moment, thoughtful. "I'm not sure how much use I can be in this fight. I barely held my head above water back there. I know Roberta and Turner think I can beat Hades, but... I don't know. Death is his domain. I used some of my *tricks* to stop him, but he'll be more prepared next time. Won't he?"

"Listen, you're a force in this world. You battled two of the

138

most powerful supernatural beings to ever exist, and because of *you* they retreated. Don't write yourself off. And, no: Hades is too cocky and stupid to prepare for *next time. We* have the advantage because of our numbers. *You* are one of those numbers, okay?" It was as much of a pep talk as I was capable of. I meant every word, but I wasn't sure how well *any* of us would fare against a fully powered Cronus and Hades. It had taken the joint forces of Talan, my mother, Gaia, and me to capture those two the first time. I was starting to worry that I'd have to consume Cronus and Hades in order to stop them.

I decided to be honest with Chelsan and tell her more about my ability to devour supernatural beings. "There is a way to kill the gods, but I want that to be our last option."

"You mean the way you killed Atlas? You said you ate him or something?" Chelsan asked.

The girl paid attention. I nodded, "The problem is: I'd be stuck with all their memories and the human part of my brain might explode on impact. Or it would feel that way anyway. I can barely stand having Atlas's memories in my mind for the last three hundred years. Sometimes I wish I could erase every ounce of Atlas in my brain. His memories still feel like they're intruding, even after all these years. And he wasn't even one of the stronger gods. I truly believe that if I consumed a god like Cronus or Hades it would kill me, or destroy any semblance of who I am, at least, which equates to the same thing in my book." I paused, reflective. "I hope I never have to do that."

Chelsan looked at me with sympathetic eyes. I could see from her expression that she was furiously thinking of a way for me to avoid the route of consuming the gods. Finally, she said, "If I can do anything to stop that from happening, I will. I promise."

It was sweet and a little naïve, but she was still a teenager. Though she had practically lived three lifetimes already with what she'd been through, there was still an innocence to her that I hoped would never become jaded like me. To be honest, I didn't think I ever had that innocence. Jumping from foster home to foster home, abandoned by my mother in a dumpster… Kind of left me jaded from the start.

But I appreciated her promise. "Thanks. Hopefully, we'll be able to re-capture them before Cronus and Hades get into too much trouble." I wasn't confident of that outcome, but I hoped it would be the case.

Chelsan seemed to take my words of optimism in stride. "I hope so, too, but I wanted you to know that I'm feeling way out of my depth." She paused as if contemplating whether or not to confide in me what she was about to say next, then she plowed forward, "I realized recently that I have the power to connect to people's lights, like I did with Roberta when her clone died, or re-died, you know what I mean. Talan was there, I'm sure he told you, or was going to tell you… or… anyway, I thought *I* should tell you. It's how I was able to control Isabelle and use her powers." She eyed me knowingly. "I'm assuming you know Isabelle, if your son worked with her for a couple hundred years."

I nodded. "I've never met her, but yes, I know of her."

Chelsan continued, "It's how I connected Elisha's soul back to her brain. In fact, I think that's what I'm connecting to – the soul." She shrugged, "Anyway, I couldn't do it with Cronus because I couldn't see his white light. With Hades…I could *see* his white light, but I couldn't go near it. It was completely sealed off from me. But the more that I think about it, the more I think that maybe gods or supernatural beings can protect their lights or souls or whatever. I don't know." Chelsan shook her head. "Am I making any sense?" She sighed, "Maybe if I could practice I could connect to their lights or souls or whatever and control them enough to imprison them again? Maybe using one of those fires? I don't know. Do they even have souls? I'm babbling."

I thought about every word Chelsan had just said. There might be something there. She lacked certain knowledge, though, so I decided to tell her what each fire did.

"As I told you before red is for resurrection and purple is for capturing, but, black is used to blind your opponent or hide something. Green and blue are the nasty fires: green inflicts pain and blue causes paralyses. Yellow is full-on destruction. White fire is for controlling, which is why it makes sense that you'd see Hades's power wrapped around each black hole in the form of a white glow. Maybe the reason you see white swirling holes in people is why you can control them. It may not be their souls, it may be *your* power to control their core being."

"I'm never going to remember all that. I wish Jason was here. He'd be typing everything we say into his e-reader." Chelsan glanced ahead at Ryan's back. "You really can't kill him now?"

I knew how she felt. It was how I had felt when my first mission told me I had to kill Jack. But giving Ryan the immortality serum saved his life. The world might end if I was gambling wrong, but Ryan would still live. Hopefully, I wouldn't be regretting that decision, but of course, I already was. "Fortski's serum is absolute. Ryan is safe."

Chelsan breathed in deep with relief, then looked at me sincerely as she said, "We'll find a way to break your curse."

The cynical part of me wanted to say something snarky like, *You think? It's your boyfriend or the world, so I hope I made the right*

141

decision! Instead all that came out was, "Thanks." I was turning into a softy. What can I say? The girl's earnestness brought it out of me.

Turner called back from his lead position a hundred feet ahead of us. "Elisha is in here."

The announcement was ominous. It felt as if we were going in to see a caged monster. Elisha was as close to a monster as a human could get before Chelsan 'repaired' her. Now we were about to witness what Elisha had become since her soul had been returned to her.

Turner opened the steel door and walked inside. The train of super-beings followed, Chelsan and I being the last to enter.

Elisha was truly stunning to look at. With her black hair and intense purple eyes, Elisha was a unique beauty. She was locked away behind a wall of four-inch plexiglass with one-inch holes lined on the very top for air. An outline in the glass marked the only exit to Elisha's prison and a two-inch by ten-inch slot for food was carved into the center of the door. A toilet and sink rested in the back corner for anyone to see her do her business. It was humiliating.

Elisha appeared to be a young woman of eighteen years, but everyone here knew she was actually in her late nineties. She stood up as our entourage entered the small room, her eyes darting from person to person.

"Are you all real?" Elisha's voice had a slight gravelly tone to it, as if she had been crying.

Chelsan angrily whirled on Turner. "You said you'd move her to a better facility after the last time I came!"

Turner shrugged. "We still have no idea if your little 'fix' will stick. What if Elisha finds a way to disconnect her soul again? We need to keep her well-guarded. I decided that this was still the best place."

Chelsan didn't back down. "I told you there is no way Elisha can disconnect from her soul. It's a done deal. So maybe you should try a little decency for once."

Elisha screamed.

As in blood-curdling-torture scream.

Asmodeus snapped his fingers, immediately rendering Elisha's vocal chords silent.

This only made Elisha panic more. She began slamming her body against the plexiglass with bone crunching impact, holding her throat, trying desperately to regain the ability to speak.

"OPEN THE DOOR!" Eva yelled in terror. Eva obviously cared deeply for Elisha despite everything Elisha had done to her.

With every sickening thud of Elisha's body hitting the glass while her silent screams went unheard, the scene grew more and more difficult to witness.

Turner opened the door and Eva pushed inside. She grabbed hold of Elisha, using all her strength to hold her close.

Nodding to Asmodeus, Turner said, "Give Elisha her voice back."

Asmodeus sighed, "Even I don't sound that bad. Are you sure?"

"Just do it." I gently smacked his arm.

Asmodeus rubbed his arm as if I had hit him harder than I had. "I don't know why everyone is being so sympathetic to the girl. She's worse than any demon or god for that matter."

"Not anymore." Chelsan brushed past Asmodeus toward the cell's open door.

Asmodeus didn't bother to take offense at being shoved aside, he appeared amused by the behavior. Then he snapped his fingers again and the sound of Elisha crying filled the room.

I watched while Chelsan stood awkwardly behind Eva holding Elisha. At this point Elisha was sobbing in Eva's arms, repeating the word 'Beth' over and over. Then she slightly pulled away from Eva, her eyes peering up at Chelsan. Shoving Eva aside, Elisha clawed at Chelsan's legs. "Take it away, please, take it away!"

Everyone in the room knew she was talking about her soul, but no one said a word. Chelsan stared at her, speechless.

Elisha screamed again when Chelsan didn't say or do anything, then she pleaded, "PLEASE, Chelsan. I know you can do it. I can't. I can't. Beth. BETH!" Elisha's eyes darted back and forth wildly as if she were a trapped animal. And she was. Trapped in her own body – with a soul – and the memories of everything she had ever done.

If anyone could understand, it would be me. But at least my evil deeds had a purpose, a meaning. I didn't do my duty out of maliciousness or with an ill-spirited intent. I did it to save the planet. To save people.

Elisha had no such rationale to hold onto. All she had was guilt. Guilt for everything she had ever done. And she had done quite a lot. But obviously killing her sister Beth was the one act she couldn't reconcile with.

"I SLICED MY SISTER'S CHEST WITH AN AXE!" Elisha screamed again, over and over. "She was my TWIN! My TWIN! Twins are connected. We were connected. I tortured her, I tortured her, I watched as she screamed and screamed in pain, but I kept pouring acid on her legs and arms!" Looking at Chelsan, she smiled for a moment, then shook her head in anguish, "You remember the acid? You remember how I tortured you with it? I had tested it out on Beth. I wanted to see if *I* could feel anything.

144

Our bond was so strong. She knew of things that happened to me in the I.Q. farm that she couldn't have known. She knew because we were so connected."

Elisha began to cry. "I kept wiping the acid on her body, waiting to feel something, but I never did." She looked up at Chelsan, wiping her tears. "Beth wasn't like you. She couldn't escape the agony of torture through astral projection, she had to endure the pain and look at me... with those eyes... of terror... of betrayal... of PAIN!" Elisha screamed again. "I can't stop seeing it! My mind keeps playing it over and over and over...*I* did that! *I* didn't care! I just wanted to feel *something*, so I mangled her body. I don't want to care anymore! Please, Chelsan, please: if you can't make it stop, kill me. I deserve it. I deserve to die. Please, Turner! *Anyone?*" Her eyes darted to each face.

Asmodeus stepped forward. "I'll do it."

Elisha tried to shove herself out of the open door toward Asmodeus.

I shook my head at Asmodeus. "You're a prick."

"What?" Asmodeus shrugged. "Everyone was thinking it."

Turning to Talan, I said quietly, "Can you do anything?"

At this point Elisha was clawing her way toward Asmodeus like he was her savior. Eva held her back as best she could, but Chelsan did nothing, still in shell shock at the spectacle of Elisha's tortured soul.

Talan stepped forward and nodded to Ryan and Max. "Help Eva hold Elisha down."

Max and Ryan did as they were asked, all three people clasping onto Elisha's arms, keeping her from tackling Asmodeus to the ground.

Talan placed his hands on Elisha's head.

Within seconds Elisha's body slumped as if he had shot her with a heavy tranquilizer. Ryan and Max were able to let go, while Eva let Elisha fall back into her chest to support Elisha's relaxed body.

Talan's hands stayed glued to Elisha's head, until some kind of invisible moment had been reached. He pulled away and made eye contact with Elisha. "That should help with the pain."

Elisha sat there, saying nothing. I suddenly wondered if Talan had broken her. Though technically she had already been broken. But still. *More* broken, if that was possible.

After a good minute, Elisha slowly began to nod her head, finally answering Talan. "Yes," she paused as if words were difficult for her to speak. "Yes...it's... better."

That seemed to be enough for Turner because, having no sympathy in his voice, he asked, "We're fighting gods, Elisha. I know you knew all about them in the Farm. You tried to communicate with Cronus and Hades several times, don't think it went unnoticed," he chastised.

Weirdly inappropriate, but somehow very in character for Turner.

Elisha didn't deny it, nor did she look particularly fazed by the news. Talan's brain-rearranging may have made the girl too complacent.

Elisha spoke in a steady voice, "They've escaped."

"Since we're fighting them, I'd say that's quite obvious. Alec helped them. He's still occupying the Franklin clone," Turner spat with annoyance. He didn't like the girl, soul or not, and I could tell he wanted Elisha eliminated. But she was too valuable to kill, even Turner couldn't deny that. Though it didn't matter since she had taken Fortski's immortality serum.

146

Elisha didn't respond to Turner's attitude. "Alec was always a little more obsessed about the gods than I ever was." She looked up at Chelsan. "Were you a match for Hades? Your powers are so different, yet so similar. I always wondered what a match-up between you two would look like." It was the first, full, coherent sentences she had spoken since we arrived. Talan had at least bandaged the damage for the time being. I hoped no one would bring up Elisha's sister. I imagined that would be her trigger.

Chelsan appeared a little more relaxed now that Elisha wasn't spouting madness in her face. "I wasn't much of a match." Then she plowed forward, straight to the point. "*Can* my power battle deity magic? You know more about my power than anyone. We thought maybe you'd have some ideas."

Elisha suddenly seemed to realize that her 'chair' was Eva's body. She turned to Eva and her eyes flashed that same insanity as before, but it quickly disappeared and turned into a genuine smile. "Eva," she said quietly and reached back, hugging her. Eva hugged Elisha back. Eva's face revealed an intense relief at seeing Elisha almost *normal,* she had never known Elisha sane *and* having a soul. "Visiting me has helped. I couldn't get my mind right to tell you that, but I want you to know while I have some semblance of sanity. I don't know how long it will last."

Eva simply nodded, too emotional to respond. To Eva, Elisha was essentially her creator.

I could tell Max didn't feel the same reverence. His expression matched Turner's in its visible look of disgust. I couldn't blame him. Elisha *had* killed the boy by beating him to death. Max was cautious and rightfully so.

I'd keep a close eye on Elisha as well. I had known too many entities *with* souls who did horrendous things, myself included.

147

Just because Elisha was dealing with massive amounts of guilt didn't mean that she was now a 'good guy.' I hoped Chelsan would stay wary as well, but one of her flaws was a trusting nature. With the kind of power Chelsan possessed, she needed to have her guard up more than she did. I still couldn't believe that she had an actual relationship with her grandparents after everything they'd done to her. It was admirable, and I understood the advantage to it, but it was probably foolish. Still. She was loyal. And that was something I could always respect.

Elisha finally answered Chelsan's question about her powers. "On paper, Hades should be able to crush you."

I watched Chelsan to gauge her reaction. Most supernatural beings would let Elisha's words ruffle their ego, but I was beginning to learn firsthand of Chelsan's humility. With everything that Chelsan had accomplished in the past year (and considering who her narcissistic grandparents were) I had assumed she had broken down her magic barriers through confidence. But now that I'd spent some time with her, I could see it was through survival and protection of the ones she loved.

Roberta was the one who responded to Elisha, defensive. "I've tapped into Hades's power directly and I've been inside my granddaughter's head. Chelsan is a match for that weasel. She needs to embrace her power."

"I'm right here," Chelsan waved her hand, reminding Roberta she was standing right next to her.

Elisha shook her head, talking to Roberta. "I'm well aware of Chelsan's gifts. That's why I thought a battle between the two would be an interesting match." She focused back on Chelsan. "As I was saying: *on paper* you're no match for him because all we ever knew about your power was through your father and his clones. Even my power pales next to yours, which was why I wanted to repeat the magic transferring spell with you directly. I had seen what you could do, and I was jealous beyond reason. You're practically a god yourself, Chelsan."

I could tell Chelsan didn't like the sound of that, nor did she believe it. But Elisha continued her point, "Think about it. You can control anything dead, but you can control anything living as well, by connecting to their light." Elisha was growing excited by her train of thought. "By connecting to the twins who had the opposite power of you, you were able to figure out how to use their powers through your own!" Her eyes rounded with wonder. "It's stunning."

"Can she recapture Cronus and Hades?" Turner brought Elisha back to the major point of the conversation.

Elisha shrugged. "I have no idea. Right now, I wouldn't say it was likely." She finally stood up, brushing herself off, examining the large crowd in front of her. Eva joined her.

Elisha somehow knew to ask Ashliel, "You must have tapped into the holo-feeds by now. Did you see Alec on any of the cameras?"

Ashliel appeared to be excited about being a part of the action. I knew it had bothered him to sit on the sidelines when Chelsan and Turner had taken down Elisha and Clifton. I could tell he was enjoying this opportunity to work with Chelsan's group. He had been bugging me about meeting the girl the moment Chelsan had been born and received Franklin's powers. I guess I shouldn't be surprised that he had disguised himself as a biology teacher to meet the girl.

Ashliel answered Elisha's query, "No. I didn't see Alec anywhere. He's smart enough to avoid cameras I'd think."

Chelsan asked Elisha, "What more can you tell us of Alec

besides his obsession with the gods?"

Elisha sighed heavily. "Alec Swanson. He was my right-hand man in the I.Q. Farm. He had a knack for keeping all of us together."

Ryan nodded. "I remember him now. He was the one who kept the Collective strong and united when they were swimming in my head."

Elisha agreed, "Yes. I knew he'd be able to lead the I.Q. consciousnesses into the clone bodies. I used the machines, but Alec used his mental abilities, which are strong. Not as strong as Roberta's or mine, but very close." She paused, unsure how to proceed. Finally, she continued, "I thought it was a part of my insanity and guilt, but now I know it was real. I *heard* Alec communicating with Hades and Cronus. He was obviously able to weaken the connection of Turner and Roberta's controlling spell, enough to use the resurrection stones that brought the gods back to consciousness."

Ryan directed his thoughts at Elisha, "Alec couldn't have severed the tie with Turner's brain machines without knowing the programming. He knew those machines better than anyone. It was how he was able to keep the I.Q. Collective together."

Elisha rolled with Ryan's idea. "You're saying he used astral projection to connect with the machine *and* Hades and Cronus's minds?"

Shaking his head, Ryan clarified, "Astral projection would leave his clone body vulnerable. The only thing keeping the Franklin clone from taking over his own body is Alec's strength of mind. If Alec were to mentally leave through astral projection, I don't think the Franklin clone would let him back in. Or it'd be a heck of a fight anyway. No. I think Alec found a way to use telepathy to communicate with both the machine and the gods. It would keep him strong inside the clone's body but allow him to explore outside his body as well."

150

Elisha raised an eyebrow in thought, then turned to Chelsan. "I invented a telepathy blocker. Remember? I used it on you to keep you from communicating when I held you prisoner." She sighed in defeat, looking at Turner, "If only your ego wasn't so big, you might have had the insight to inject the blocker into your power-slaves in the basement."

Turner was on the verge of unleashing a verbal lashing when Roberta entered the conversation. "Yes, an error on our part."

I was shocked she owned up to that one.

Roberta continued, "Is there any way we can use the fact that Alec tapped into the computer and the gods through telepathy to recapture Hades and Cronus?"

Ryan shrugged. "Maybe. We'll have to examine the brain machine to try and see what Alec did to weaken the spell's control over Hades and Cronus."

"*We?*" Chelsan asked apprehensively.

"Elisha and I." Ryan leaned down and kissed Chelsan softly, to reassure her. "We know Alec the best. We also know the machines better than anyone."

I noticed that neither Turner nor Roberta argued the point, which made me realize how much faith they had in Ryan. I suddenly had a flash of jealousy, remembering how it felt having the Turners unwavering trust and loyalty.

Chelsan looked like she wanted to argue the point, but eventually she nodded her agreement.

Ashliel stepped forward. "I'll take them to the machines. I'll be able to help, too."

Turner flashed Ashliel a look that clearly suggested how displeased he was to learn that Ashliel obviously knew the layout of Turner's headquarters, but he didn't object.

151

Elisha motioned for Ashliel to wait a moment as she turned to Chelsan. "Honestly, Chelsan, I've only theorized about your powers. I'm afraid I can't give you the answers you want, only you'll be able to do that. I'm sorry."

I watched Chelsan look both scared and disappointed. The weight on her shoulders was now fully hers.

With a slight nod from Chelsan, Ashliel touched both Ryan and Elisha's arms and the trio disappeared.

Chelsan flinched.

Suddenly, the lights on the walls began flashing and alarms blared.

"Did something happen to Ryan?" Chelsan was immediately terrified.

Turner shrugged. "Ashliel may have set off the alarms by entering Hades and Cronus's prison room. Let me check."

Turner was immediately on his cell phone.

My heart was beating in my chest wondering why the alarms were sounding. I didn't think it had anything to do with Ashliel teleporting to the brain machines.

Roberta stared at her husband, waiting like the rest of us to find out what was going on.

Asmodeus turned to Rotoph. "Could you please?"

Rotoph, being the Grigori that handled protections better than the others, waved his hand slightly. The lights and alarms instantly went silent.

"Thank you," Asmodeus grunted.

He was being annoyingly ornery.

Turner's face went pale and I knew we were in trouble.

"What is it, Geoffrey? Was it Ashliel?" Roberta seemed to be the only one who could speak.

I knew it had something to do with Cronus and Hades. I hoped that whatever it was would be fixable.

Turner focused his attention on me. "Hades took over the world leaders and Cronus killed all my warlocks *and* the back-ups."

"I thought you said Cronus and Hades wouldn't know about the leaders, that they'd take over boldly… in the spotlight," Chelsan said, grasping at straws. I could tell she wanted to go grab Ryan and run home, never having to deal with any of *this* ever again.

Turner didn't snap at her like he was prone to doing. He answered Chelsan calmly, "It seems I was mistaken. A Titan and an Olympian now have full control of the World Government, which means we're in trouble."

"Nothing less than you deserve, human."

I knew that voice.

It was Atlas's father: Iapetus. Considering I had consumed Atlas, in a way he was my father, too, though I felt nothing for the Titan. If anything, I felt loathing.

Iapetus materialized in front of us all, standing next to Turner, but his eyes were on me.

"Son." He nodded in greeting.

Iapetus only saw me as Atlas.

"I'm not your *son*," I snarled.

"No. My son would be too much of coward to fight me, but *you*? You I expect a fight from, which is why…"

I knew what he was going to do.

"ROTOPH!! BLOCK TELEPORTATION!" I screamed.

Too late.

With one hand on Turner's shoulder, Iapetus and Turner were gone.

"Well, that was unexpected." Asmodeus shrugged.

153

Chapter Seven

Two Years Ago

CHELSAN

"**R**eally? There's no one in that school of yours that you like? No one?" Janet smiled at Chelsan from across the kitchen table.

Chelsan knew her mother was coming from a good place, but she was tired of her asking. Aside from her embarrassingly enormous crush on Ryan Vaughn (which she'd never tell her mother about in a million years!), there was no one Chelsan was interested in at school. Because of Jill Forester, Chelsan's only friends were Nancy and Bill. And Bill was just... Bill. He was easy on the eyes, but guys like Bill Merryweather didn't go for girls like Chelsan Derée, so even thinking of the possibility was a bad idea.

And Ryan?

He was her tutor for math, and it wasn't exactly his idea. Mr. Calston had insisted that Ryan help Chelsan, despite Ryan's protests of the match. Chelsan was internally thrilled when it happened, though, and their first five sessions had been amazing. Sure, Chelsan had barely said a word to Ryan except to answer his math questions, but it was the fact that she had kept the embarrassing moments down to a minimum that made the encounters truly wonderful. Her theory was: If she didn't open her big mouth, she'd never embarrass herself. Seemed like a good idea to her.

It wasn't as if Ryan would ever see Chelsan that way anyway. He'd be lynched on the spot by Jill if he ever showed interest. Besides, Ryan was way too brilliant and way too beautiful for Chelsan.

Janet continued playfully, "I'm sure there are a lot of smart boys at that school. None of them have caught your eye?"

Chelsan grumbled, "Mom, you know I only have two friends, Nancy and Bill. You want me to date Bill? Because that's never going to happen. He's too rich and popular to date someone that lives in a place like this." Chelsan motioned to the tidy but dumpy trailer that was their home.

Janet laughed, not remotely offended, and said, "As long as we're safe, I don't care where we live, and neither should anyone else." Then she seemed thoughtful, "Bill, huh? You don't like him like that, I can tell."

"And, apparently, you can tell that I like some mystery guy that I'm not telling you about?"

"Of course I can. I'm your mother. Now, who is it?" Janet raised her eyebrows in anticipation.

A part of Chelsan wanted to confess her crush on Ryan, but she knew it would only get her mom's hopes up for something that could never be. Or, worse, her mother would recognize Ryan's name as the genius child who solved Trilidon's Theorem and wouldn't want her daughter dating a celebrity or something. Either way, Chelsan lost. Better to keep her mouth shut.

"I'm telling you, Mom, there's no one. Now, can we drop it?"

155

Chelsan ate a couple of grapes from the bowl of fruit laid out on the table to distract herself.

Janet shook her head, conceding. "Fine. But if you do ever like someone at that school of yours, make sure he's smart. You deserve someone with a brain in his head, like your father."

Chelsan's heart skipped a beat at the mention of her dad. Janet rarely talked about him. It always seemed too painful for her. Chelsan could see by the way her mother's expression would go from total adoration of his memory, to utter sadness at his loss, that the topic was a sensitive one.

"Dad was smart?" Chelsan asked tentatively.

Janet's mood was good today, so she seemed open to talking freely about Chelsan's father. "Franklin was brilliant. One of the smartest people alive."

Chelsan somehow doubted that, but it was sweet to see how much her mother loved him.

Janet continued, "I know you never got to meet him, but he loved you more than his own life." Her expression was thoughtful. "He'd be very proud of you."

"Of me? I've never done anything special." Chelsan always felt uncomfortable with compliments, but it was nice to hear her mother say nice things about how her father might feel about her. Besides, the only thing that was special about Chelsan was her powers – and she felt those were more of a curse most of the time. Always staying within a four-mile radius so that Bruce wouldn't rot to the ground was Chelsan's own prison. And it was to protect her mother from knowing that she murdered Bruce all those years ago.

Janet reached across the table and held Chelsan's hand tightly. "You are the most important person in this entire universe."

Chelsan rolled her eyes, smiling, "Wow, Mom. That's quite a

statement," she laughed. "You're such a mom."

Janet eyed Bruce sitting in his easy chair watching holo-TV. For a second Chelsan almost thought that her mother knew Chelsan was controlling him. But when Janet turned back to Chelsan she said, "You are the strongest person I know. Bruce almost killed me that day and you saved me."

Chelsan froze. They had never talked about that day, mainly because... Chelsan didn't know how she could explain why Bruce had thousands of black widow spider bites all over his body. Janet didn't seem to want to know, she had been so relieved that Bruce was alive.

Even though he wasn't.

"I didn't do much. That spider had it out for Bruce, I guess. He must have killed its eggs or something."

Wow.

That sounded lamer out loud.

But Janet didn't argue or question, she held on tight to Chelsan's hand. "You have a gift for protecting people, Chelsan. Your father was the same way. You are very special and stronger than you think."

Chelsan felt like this conversation was getting way too dangerous for keeping her powers a secret. Although, for a moment, she wanted to tell her mother everything.

But she didn't want to see her mother look at her with disappointment – or worse, loathing. So she simply nodded, "Thanks, Mom."

Janet let go of Chelsan's hand and smiled, "Are you sure there's no one you like?"

Ugh.

"Mom," Chelsan grumbled.

DAY TWO

Sunday June 5, 2321

CHELSAN

I awoke to the sounds of arguing downstairs. I sighed heavily as I stared at the empty space next to me in bed. After Turner had been taken by another Titan, chaos and arguing ensued that I could barely follow. Ryan decided he needed to stay with Elisha at Headquarters to try and figure out how Alec had manipulated the brain machines. He thought they could figure out a way to recapture Cronus and Hades using the machine. I believed him. One thing the supernatural beings agreed on: Ryan was smart. Smarter than any of them. If anyone would figure it out it would be him. It gave me a surge of pride for my perfect boyfriend, but also a surge of disappointment at having to leave his side.

I came home with Max and Eva, and everyone was still in the living room waiting for us to arrive. They were worried, to say the least, but understanding. I could tell Nancy and Jill were keeping their distance from each other, probably arguing over what they should or shouldn't do. The behavior was so *normal,* though, that it made me feel better about the whole Titans-and-Olympians-taking-over-the-world thing.

Roberta had been a wreck, desperate to figure out what they had done with Gramps. She feared the worst: that they were going to punish him for keeping Cronus and Hades prisoner for all those years. Turner couldn't die, so they could torture him beyond anything imaginable, over and over and over. It made my stomach turn at the thought.

Kala didn't think that was their intention, though. She argued that they took Turner for a different reason: they needed him for something. Kala had tried to get Roberta to think about why they would need Turner. But it just turned into Roberta screaming at Kala.

Kala had been calmer than I ever could be. She listened to every insult and barb Roberta threw at her and calmly answered back, arguing her case and trying to persuade Roberta to think about what information Turner had that would benefit Cronus. At this point, from the way Kala talked about Cronus and Hades, she obviously considered Cronus to be the leader. She acted as if Hades was Cronus's lackey.

It made my face flush with fear. If Hades was just a lackey and I could barely fight the guy, then what possible chance did I have against *Cronus?*

After Roberta calmed down enough (more like her throat was too scratchy to scream anymore), Kala told us that she was going to try and find out where Cronus and Hades were holding Turner and get back to me. Part of me felt like I'd never see her again (maybe secretly wished) but I knew she thought I was going to break this curse of hers.

Yeah, I totally knew how to do that!

After telling everyone the scoop, I was exhausted. I went upstairs to take a nap, but looking outside, I could see I had slept through the whole night. It was morning and the sun was already past the horizon.

Focusing on the arguing voices downstairs, I recognized Jason and… I couldn't make out the second voice. When Nancy chimed in with the furious tone I knew so well, I decided to get my butt up and see what was going on. Dressing quickly in jeans and a t-shirt, I hurried down.

In the living room, Jason and Nancy were heatedly arguing with a live hologram of Jason's boss, Simon Peake. Simon's hologram was solid. I would have thought he was physically standing in front of them if it weren't for the tiny disruptions of holo-signal every time he yelled.

Simon was the head of over 2,500 media outlets, which made him in charge of what the public knew and didn't know. And shocker: Gramps was the man responsible for turning the news into a monopoly. That way my grandfather could do all his dastardly deeds (in the name of saving humanity, ha ha) and keep it quiet. I had never thought about the news all coming from one source before, since I grew up not knowing anything different, but the more I found out what my grandparents did *behind* the scenes, the more I wondered if the public had the right to know, or if keeping them in the dark *was* actually a good thing.

Jason had no such dilemma.

He wanted the public to know *everything*. And apparently that was what this argument was about.

Simon's chubby face snarled in frustration. He looked to be eighteen years old, so he most likely had come from money. His voice was deep and under normal circumstances quite soothing, which was why he'd do the monthly sum-up reports for the entire world. But his voice was pretty jolting right now as he boomed at Jason, "You're lucky I didn't cut all transmissions when you spouted out the Elisha Stearne incident to the ENTIRE WORLD! You could have caused mass panic —"

Jason cut him off angrily, shouting sarcastically, "Because they weren't already panicked when an army of dead people started slaughtering innocents!?"

Nancy chimed in, furious at Simon as well, "The only reason you let Jason broadcast that was because he gave credit to Turner for helping save the day!"

"I don't need to be lectured by a teenager on running my business!" Simon yelled back. "I've been in charge of all world media for over a hundred years now and we've had zero incidents until my star reporter went rogue and started taking over my transmission lines and reporting dangerous ideas that could mean the end of *everything!*"

"Not to be dramatic or anything!" Nancy rolled her eyes.

Jason stepped forward. Though he was talking to a hologram, I could tell he was so angry he was reacting as if arguing with a live person. "We *have* to report this. The world leaders are being controlled by a necromancer *god!* What if they order executions, or destruction of our power sources or food sources? We have to keep the people on guard, or they could die following orders of crazed deities that want them all to die anyway!"

"Now who's being dramatic?!" Simon growled. "You're talking about gods as if they're real! If Mrs. Turner hadn't corroborated your story, I would have had you committed!"

Jason could barely keep his anger in check. "You've known

that Turner has controlled the world leaders through necromancy for over a hundred years, yet you doubt the existence of other supernatural beings? And you think *I'm* crazy?!"

He had a point. Still, to give Simon his due, Jason himself had doubted when he first heard about gods. It was a hard pill to swallow.

Simon apparently was done with this conversation because he said, "I haven't heard a word from Vice President Turner and, until I hear otherwise, I'm keeping you off the airways! Consider yourself suspended."

Nancy looked at Simon as if he were the stupidest human being to walk the Earth. "You haven't heard from him because he's been kidnapped... by gods... the ones that you're now protecting by not letting Jason do his job! And Roberta Turner told you to let Jason do what he wants!"

As angry as they were, it was still kind of cute to see Nancy and Jason yell at someone else and not at each other for once. Their relationship was always a little on the feisty side; I was glad they had a common cause this time. I just wish the cause wasn't fighting the leader of the Titans and the God of Death.

"Roberta Turner is not Geoffrey Turner," he snapped. "And like I said: until I hear from *him*, you're not to set foot in this building!" Simon fumed. "You heard my decision. If I change my mind, I'll contact you." And with that Simon turned off the holo-transmission.

Jason and Nancy stood there, silent, staring at the empty space Simon's hologram had occupied.

"So we can't warn anybody," I summed up the argument as I witnessed it.

Both of them turned around and Nancy walked over to me,

giving me a morning hug. Pulling away, she asked, "Did you hear the whole thing?"

"The highlights, but enough to know we have to settle this thing quick before Cronus and Hades can do any real damage." I wondered if that was possible.

Jason sighed. I could tell he was exhausted. "I'll find a way to take over the airways. Maybe one of those angels could help."

I nodded. "If anyone can, I think it'll be Ashliel. He's the one who basically plugged his mind into Turner's world surveillance feeds to try and find Cronus and Hades. Maybe he can broadcast you or something."

"He's the one helping Ryan and Elisha, right?" Jason asked.

For some reason it stung to hear of Ryan working with Elisha. I knew it shouldn't, he was genuinely trying to help, but I didn't like it.

Nancy seemed to pick up on my feelings, because she smacked Jason in the chest. "Sensitive, much?"

Jason rubbed his chest with an exaggerated 'Ouch!' then proceeded in his own way to try and be sensitive. "You think Elisha is still evil? I thought you fixed that."

"I connected her soul back to her brain. That doesn't mean I trust her." Which was not exactly true: I *did* kind of trust her, but for some reason I didn't want to admit it. I wanted everyone to distrust Elisha. I had no idea why, but it felt right for some reason. Maybe too much of Isabelle and Kala rubbing off on me.

"Well, then we don't trust her either," Nancy stated in perfect BFF form. Then she nudged Jason, "Right?"

"Uh, right," Jason agreed, though I could tell his mind wasn't focused on Elisha at the moment. Proving my point, he switched subjects back to his boss. "The fact that Simon won't listen to

Roberta disturbs me. She told him to give me carte blanche and he's blatantly defying her. Using Turner as an excuse is just that: an excuse." He turned to me, curious. "He wasn't *dead,* was he? I mean, do you think Hades is controlling him like the world leaders?"

"I didn't see any black holes, but honestly, I don't know. Roberta was able to hide corpses from me with that compound stuff at first. I wouldn't be surprised if the God of Death could hide a dead body from me." I hated to admit that fact, but I figured honesty would only help our cause at this point.

Jason plopped down on the couch in a heap. "Doesn't matter either way, I guess. Simon refuses to let the public know the world's about to end."

Nancy sat down next to him, placing her head on his shoulder supportively. "We'll find a way. We always do."

Jason kissed the top of Nancy's head. It was so sweet, I felt like I should sneak out of the room to let them be alone.

"Where is everyone anyway?" I asked, wondering where the gang was.

Nancy answered, "My parents are getting groceries to feed our mini-army, Jill is asleep in my bed upstairs, Bill and Eva went somewhere to be alone, gross, and Max is probably a stalker staring at Jill and making sure she's safe. That about covers it."

"No Kala or Roberta? Or any of the other *beings* or whatever?" I was a little surprised that they had just dropped me off and left me at my house. Maybe my lame performance against Cronus and Hades made them want to keep me out of the way to let the *real* fighters fight. I had barely held my own in that last battle.

"Oh, they're coming, don't you worry your little head," Jason responded with a grunt.

I sat down on the couch next to them. "Don't like them?"

165

"Ehhh…" Jason answered, then leaned back on the sofa cushions, drawing Nancy with him so his arm draped over her. She leaned into his chest comfortably. It made me miss Ryan.

"It's not that I don't 'like' them," Jason elaborated, "it's that I don't *trust* any of them. Their agenda is to kill Ryan. Period. Kala may spout pledges that she won't, that Ryan's safe because he took the immortality serum, but I've seen that look before. You remember our friends Isabelle, Dean and Terence? They all had that look. Killers. The worst kind too: soldiers. They feel they have some sort of justification, which I never understood."

It made my heart squeeze with fear that Jason had the same doubts that I had about Ryan's safety. I sometimes forgot Jason was so much older than us. He'd seen a lot more of the world changing than we had.

I combed my hands through my hair nervously. "Yeah, I'm feeling the same way. But there's no way Kala can kill Ryan. Fortski said anyone that took the serum could be decapitated and still live, so there's no possible way. And Hades touched my head to take me to the Underworld and it didn't work. At all. Logically, if the God of Death can't kill someone with the serum, then no one can." I felt as if I was trying to convince myself more than anyone else.

"But can gods or angels or whatever use some kind of deity magic that could get rid of the serum or something?" Jason asked aloud. Again, tact-boy was at his best.

Nancy closed her eyes, shaking her head, then looked over at me. "Don't listen to him. Kala wouldn't have insisted on the serum if she didn't want to save Ryan."

Jason kept going with his disturbing line of thought. "But she could have given Ryan the serum to make us trust her. If we thought death was off the table, it makes sense that we'd help her willingly. She knows she couldn't get away with an 'I promise I won't kill your boyfriend' deal. We'd never agree knowing that Fortski's serum exists."

Nancy outright smacked Jason in the chest. "You are such a jerk sometimes."

"What?" Jason asked innocently.

"The serum is invulnerable to gods, demons, Malaks and Grigori." Roberta's voice came from behind us. "You saw that in battle, when Hades touched you."

I stood up and turned to see Roberta standing alone in the hallway, the front door slightly ajar behind her. Her words hit me.

"You know that for sure?" I asked.

Roberta walked over to my side and nodded. "I've been around since Kala became Atlas. These beings can't defy science. Believe me, they've tried." Then she placed her hands on my shoulders, forcing eye contact. "I will use every ounce of my powers to stop Kala if she tries to lay a hand on Ryan, do you understand me?"

A knot formed in my throat from emotion. I didn't want to cry, I came close, but I managed to simply nod my thanks.

Roberta took a deep breath, then addressed Jason. "Simon is out of our control. Antel is a Grigori and will teleport you into the main control room where Simon holes up. She can handle whoever is protecting him. Then you'll be in charge of media."

Jason's face lit up. "About time."

Roberta continued, "Antel will be here shortly. Once Simon and *the others* are taken care of, we'll discuss terms."

Kala was suddenly in the living room. "The *others* are Rhea and Theia. Antel should be able to take them, but Owen will be going with you as well."

A beautiful woman with dark skin and even darker eyes

stood on Kala's right and on her left stood a formidable man who positioned himself protectively.

Jason and Nancy jumped to their feet as the room was suddenly becoming full. Jason held his hand out to the newcomers. "I assume you're Antel and you're Owen?" Each of them shook Jason's hand warmly.

Owen spoke first, "We'll need you to stand behind us when we arrive. Rhea and Theia will try to attack you first since you're the most vulnerable."

Kala added, "And they know what a threat you are. They don't want to see you anywhere near a holo-transmitter. The public trusts you too much."

Antel nodded. "Cronus and Hades may be back, but humans are still the power in this world. Cronus may say out loud he's invincible, but inside he knows he's vulnerable to human science. Turner's machine instilled a deep fear in him that maybe we can exploit."

Jason seemed to be taking in their words, processing them and hopefully coming up with a plan.

I still found it strange to hear these supernatural beings refer to people as *humans* when they looked human themselves.

"Are you a *god*?" I asked Owen. Roberta had said Antel was a Grigori, but I wasn't sure about Owen.

Owen turned to me and smiled warmly. "No. I'm Grigori as well. Kala is my daughter."

My face must have revealed my confusion, until Kala clarified, "Owen adopted me –before I turned into Atlas."

"A Grigori angel adopted you *before* you turned supernatural. That's random," Jill said, entering the room with Max, holding hands.

Owen chuckled, "Nothing is random in this world. Grigori can sense beings with power whether it be innate magic or intelligence. We didn't know it at the time, but Kala is the half-daughter of Gaia. I sensed her power and searched her out."

"He saved my life," Kala said with authority. "Gaia abandoned me in a dumpster when I was a baby to hide my presence from any god or angel, so I was stuck in the foster system until Owen found me."

In that moment I knew Kala would do anything for Owen. She watched him with fierce loyalty burning in her eyes. I understood that feeling. I felt the exact same way about my friends and especially about Ryan.

"So why didn't you ever try to adopt or recruit or whatever Chelsan?" Jill asked with a tinge of attitude. "The girl is mad powerful. Were your angel-senses off or something?"

I wasn't sure how to respond to Jill's weirdly phrased compliment to me, slash, sarcastic insult to the Grigori.

Owen glanced briefly at Kala. Upon her nod he answered Jill, "Every supernatural being in existence knew of Chelsan. We follow the prophecies. Chelsan's ties to setting my daughter free made her very special to the Grigori."

Nancy guffawed. "Ha. Yeah, thanks for all your help when Chelsan has almost died like a million times saving the world."

Kala shrugged. "We couldn't interfere."

Owen added defensively, "And Kala has saved this planet every four days for the last three hundred years. She was a little busy."

That shut up Nancy. I felt bad my friends' loyalty to me was causing any kind of tension with… well… with beings that could probably reduce us all to rubble if they wanted.

"Well, I've been reading up on you." Jill didn't seem intimidated at all by the fact that she was addressing angels. "And Gaia is the mother of Cronus. So, you're telling us that Kala is his half-sister *and* nephew? That makes no sense."

Kala shrugged. "I've learned not to think about the inbred nature of my family tree, but yes: I'm his half-sister. A fact which means absolutely nothing to Cronus."

Roberta interjected, "It means that he hates you with all of his being because he's jealous that his mother chose to have another child and not let anyone know."

Owen brought us back on target by turning to Jason, "We should get going. I want to take care of Rhea and Theia before Cronus gathers more support."

Kala nodded in agreement. "You ready, Jason?"

Nancy stepped forward. "I'm going with him."

Jason turned to her. "You know that's not going to happen." Nancy was about to argue – when he kissed her. That always stunned her to silence. (Ryan's kisses did the same for me, so I couldn't blame her.) "Owen and Antel can only keep one of us safe. We're dealing with beings more powerful than we've ever seen before. I wouldn't know how to protect you."

"I can protect myself." Nancy argued, but she knew it wasn't true.

"Nancy, *I* can't protect myself against these guys," I admitted.

"Fine," Nancy grumbled. She got the message. Reaching up she kissed Jason then nodded her acceptance. "Stay safe, okay?"

Antel reassured Nancy, "We'll keep him safe. I promise."

Before Nancy could utter another protest, Jason stepped over to Antel and Owen. With a touch to Jason's shoulder, the trio disappeared from sight.

"I'll never get tired of seeing that," Jill said in astonishment.

"Any news on Turner?" I asked Roberta suddenly. I was surprised I actually wanted to know the answer.

Roberta shook her head, then looked at Kala hopefully.

Kala approached the topic cautiously. "We think Cronus and Hades are holding Turner at the Compound."

"In D.C.?" Roberta seemed surprised. "We've long since moved our operations to Los Angeles. Why would they keep him there?"

Kala answered, "It's a space they're familiar with from before they were captured. Rotoph thinks Cronus and Hades are bound together in some way because of the machines. Since Turner is the expert and helped strap them in, the theory is they need Turner to sever their bond. Cronus can barely stand Hades as it is, but to be *bound* to him? The irony being that it actually makes them stronger, but it could also be a weakness we can exploit."

Instead of panicking and yelling like I assumed Roberta would do, she took this information in stride, processing it. "So we're going back?"

Kala nodded.

Roberta eyed Kala carefully. "You know that's Harry's domain now."

"Yes. We'll need to get General Clifton out of whatever prison you two locked him up in," Kala responded.

"Isabelle and Dean know the place as well as Harry does, but, of course, they left Harry after the Elisha incident. There's always *Terence*." Roberta appeared to be enjoying Kala's pain at the mention of her son.

I decided to step in. "Maybe I should try and contact Isabelle. Like Roberta said, she'd be helpful in this *Compound* place, right? She's been working there for at least a couple hundred years, right?" I kept trying to get Kala's focus back on me, since she seemed as if she was spiraling down a dark hole.

"Harry will do fine. I know the Compound as well. We don't need Isabelle or Dean," Kala said with finality. "Or Terence," she added, her anger directed at Roberta.

"You knew the Compound three hundred years ago. It's changed since then," Roberta gloated.

"How would you know that? You and Turner haven't stepped foot in the place for two hundred years," Kala snapped.

"From Terence, of course." Roberta smiled, wickedly. "He thinks of Geoffrey and I as his second set of parents, you know, since he considers Owen, Talan and Linda his *real parents*. Geoffrey and I were there for him when you never were."

I could tell that *really* stung Kala.

Surprisingly, Jill stepped forward and said to Roberta, "Considering Kala didn't give her son Age-pro for a hundred years when he was a child makes her a better parent than you'll ever be. And remind me how many times you tried to kill your *granddaughter*? Oh, and didn't you kill her mom? *And* both my parents? Yeah, you're the poster child for good parenting."

As far as I was concerned, that would have been enough – but apparently Jill was just getting started as she practically spat at Roberta:

"If Kala wasn't there for her kid maybe it was because, I don't know, *she was saving the world!* Cuz, if she hadn't done that, you, Turner *and* Terence wouldn't be on this planet at all, would you? What were you two doing while Kala was saving your butts twice-a-freaking-week? Stealing powers from gods you were torturing in your basement? Killing world leaders and controlling their bodies? Making a thousand clones of your *precious son* you supposedly care so much about?

"I could go on, but you know who you are. You and *Geoffrey*, gross, are despicable human beings and you don't deserve to live." Jill ignored Roberta's glare and turned to Kala. "I'm on Team Kala by the way." Jill didn't like it when Roberta was smug. Though she didn't know Kala all that well, anyone who was at odds with the Turners was a friend in her book.

Kala seemed amused. "I gathered that."

Jill's words stung me as well. Every single word she said was correct. My grandparents took away my mother, the woman I loved most in this world. Life and world-threatening experiences had brought us together, but the truth would always be there. They *did* murder my mother, they *did* kill Jill's parents, they did all that and so much more. As much as their help comforted me in some ways, it also made me disgusted with myself for having to need it. Most of the time, because of circumstances, I could bury the facts deep down in my subconscious of what Roberta and Turner had done, but truth had a way of growing up through the cracks and before you knew it your brain was full of weeds. And full of regret.

And full of sadness.

Roberta was silent, probably for fear that anything she said would turn my mind against her. I may have mixed feelings about Grams, but she didn't when it came to me. She loved me obsessively and possessively, just as she had with my father.

Finally, Roberta turned to me and asked, "May I speak with you… in private?"

I didn't want to. I could feel Jill's eyes on me, waiting to see how I would respond.

After a moment, I nodded and I walked into the kitchen, Roberta following.

When we were alone, Roberta said, "Chelsan…" she began, then stopped herself.

"What?" Yup. I was defensive. I wasn't going to make this easy. I didn't *want* to make this easy.

"I…" Roberta couldn't seem to form a sentence. She couldn't hide how nervous she was.

"Just say what you're going to say," I prodded, unsure if I wanted to hear anything that came out of her mouth at this moment.

Taking a deep breath, Roberta plowed forward, "I know you can never forgive me, nor should you, but I *am* sorry for what I did to you and… your mother."

I had known as soon as she wanted to talk in private that Roberta would say something to the effect of what she was saying now, but I found that it made me angry.

And to flat-out apologize?

That was too much for my psyche to comprehend.

Roberta took my silence as her cue to continue, "I loved Janet, almost as much as I loved Franklin. Geoffrey and I both did. We trusted her with our only child, and you know how little we trust people. When she took…"

I stopped her right there. "No." My brain felt like it was trembling I was so emotional. "Don't. Taking my father away is not justification for what you did. I will *never* forgive or even understand why you killed her and tortured her dead body. So just don't."

Roberta stopped. I could see the terror in her eyes that her would-be apology may have severed her fragile ties with me. Finally, she nodded. "You're right. There is no excuse for what we did. And we can never make it right. It is our one regret though. Of all the despicable things we've done over our lifetimes, and trust me, there are more than you'll ever know. Hunting down and killing your mother and trying to kill you will haunt us forever." Roberta put her hand up when she saw I was about to retort. "You don't have to say anything. I just… I just wanted you to know in case anything was to happen to us. I *am* sorry, Chelsan. And if your mother was in front of me, I'd beg for her forgiveness on my knees."

Before I could respond to her words, Roberta quickly kissed my cheek and left the kitchen.

She was right to leave. I couldn't process what I had just heard. I wanted to file it away and never think of it again. It was one thing to try and forgive or even reconcile with what they did on my own, but to have Roberta apologize directly to me? It made things more complicated, when it should make it easier. I guess I still wanted the fallback option to loathe them with every fiber of my being whenever I wanted.

The sincerity was real. The emotion was real. The heartbreak in her eyes was real.

That made it so much more difficult.

There was nothing I could do about it now, though, and I needed to focus on the task at hand.

I walked out of the kitchen and back into the living room.

All eyes were on me, but I chose not to look at anyone directly. I wasn't sure what I'd say anyway.

Kala understood what I must be feeling. She acted as if I had just arrived to the meeting. "I was thinking about what you said, and I think you're right about involving Isabelle. You know how to contact her?"

I nodded. Isabelle and I were telepathically connected from everything we'd been through together. It was good to focus on Isabelle and the mission. It kept my mind off of Roberta's words.

Then Kala turned to Roberta. "Get Harry out, okay? We're going to need him."

Roberta didn't argue. "Of course. We'll leave Terence out of this."

I could see a brief glimpse of relief on Kala's face.

Roberta straightened her shirt. "Asmodeus will teleport Harry and me to the Compound. We'll meet you there."

Within seconds, Asmodeus suddenly popped into the living room. "You rang?" he said playfully to Roberta.

"You're seriously her lap dog now?" Kala couldn't seem to resist berating the demon.

There was tension there, although Asmodeus hid his emotions well. He laughed at Kala in a flirtatious way. "Woof, woof." He focused his attention back on Roberta. "You find out where Turner is?"

Nodding, Roberta informed him, "Kala thinks he's at the Compound. But we need Harry to help us navigate. He's built and rebuilt that place a hundred times over since the last time Geoffrey and I set foot there." Roberta reached out and touched Asmodeus's arm. "I'm mentally giving you the coordinates to Harry's cell. Got it?"

"Got it." Asmodeus gave one last wink to Kala, then he and Roberta disappeared.

Talan materialized next to Kala as if he had been waiting for Asmodeus to leave, before appearing himself.

All this teleporting of people popping in and out was making me dizzy.

Talan spoke to Kala, "I can barely sense Turner's life force. It's like it's being blocked from me somehow. We'd better get there quick. Have you decided who's coming?"

Kala eyed me and my friends as if she was putting together a military squad. I guess being a former soldier made her view people differently. I could physically see her weighing the pros and cons of each of us. In the end she went for super powers as she announced, "Chelsan, Max and Eva."

Jill didn't argue, she simply said, "I'll go get Eva. She's with Bill in Nancy's room."

Nancy groaned, "Eew. They better not be doing what I think they're doing."

Jill shrugged. "I could hear the sloppy kissing when I walked by the closed door, so yeah, better wash your sheets."

"I'm going to puke now, thanks," Nancy said, genuinely disgusted.

I had to agree. Eva was clueless when it came to any kind of 'friend-code' since she was new to our gang (and new to existing), but Bill should know better. Hopefully, they had kept it to just kissing and not.... I shuddered. I didn't want to imagine that visual, thank you very much.

Jill disappeared upstairs to go get the couple while Nancy crossed her arms, waiting for them to arrive. In the few minutes that we waited, there was a bit of an awkward silence. Kala and Talan didn't seem too perturbed by it though. Kala always looked as if she was preparing for battle. It seemed like an exhausting way to live, but I guess when you had a job like hers that was the only way to cope.

Nodding at me, Kala asked, "Have you contacted Isabelle?"

Oh. Oops. I forgot.

Embarrassed, I closed my eyes to concentrate and called out Isabelle's name inside my head. I had two ways of contacting Isabelle: one, through astral projection, where I'd jump out of my body and into hers – or two, telepathy. In the past, I'd usually end up using astral projection. Since we were in a time crunch, I figured telepathy would work better.

I had a moment of panic when I heard radio silence on the other end.

Maybe I needed to try astral projection.

I was about to jump out of my body when…

Chelsan, is that you? Isabelle's voice sounded in my head.

Since this was telepathy, I could only hear Isabelle and not see her like I did with astral projection.

Yeah, hi. Um, I kind of need your help, I thought to her awkwardly.

Anything. What do you need? Isabelle didn't hesitate.

Which made my heart feel all warm and fuzzy. We really had made a strong bond.

I asked carefully, *I'm here with Kala Hicks or Atlas or Terence's mom… do you know who I'm talking about?* I didn't know if I'd have to explain the whole thing. I knew that Terence knew who everybody was since he was some sort of super spy, but I wasn't sure if Isabelle knew about who Terence truly was – or who Kala was at all.

I remember a Kala Hicks from years ago. She used to be on the same military team I was, but she moved up or something according to Turner and Harry. She's Terence's mom? Was 'Atlas' her code name?

Okay, she didn't know the truth. I didn't want to get into the mess of telling Isabelle that there were gods and angels and who knew what else. So I tried a different tactic. *I'll have to explain everything when I see you, but some very bad dudes have taken Turner hostage and are keeping him in a place called the Compound. Kala and Roberta think that you know the place pretty well. Can you help*

178

us find him? It's going to be dangerous. The guys that have him have powers stronger than mine and yours combined. I tried to convey the danger without going into too much detail.

Stronger? Isabelle paused, obviously surprised to hear that. *Of course. I can be at your house in less than an hour.* Then she said, *I'm bringing Dean.*

Good. We'll need him too.

Do you want me to contact Terence? He's has been laying low since everything went down with Elisha. He could be useful. With 'true aim' he should be formidable against any enemy, and if they're as powerful as you say, you'll need all the help you can get.

Yeeks. I wasn't sure if Kala was ready to see her son after the conversation, I'd witnessed between her and Roberta. But…

If Terence was part god, part demon, then he probably had a *lot* more powers than Isabelle knew. I figured I'd keep my mouth shut for now. I had no idea what Terence's powers might be, maybe he did only have 'true aim' or whatever. In any case, I'd rather tell Isabelle about all the supernatural stuff in person.

I answered her question about Terence, though, *I think you should let Kala decide whether or not to contact Terence. I'm not clear on the closeness of their relationship and I don't want to spook him… or her.*

Gotcha. We're on our way. Isabelle needed no other explanation. Difficult parent relations came with the territory for people in Isabelle's line of work, especially after she found out that General Clifton had killed her parents, then sent her to an abusive foster dad (a.k.a. my step dad, Bruce) all to trigger and awaken her powers.

I opened my eyes as I felt my connection with Isabelle drop. Looking at Kala I said, "She's on her way here with Dean. It should be less than an hour. You know, cuz, she can't teleport or anything."

179

Kala nodded. "We can wait."

I wasn't sure what bounds I needed to stay within regarding her son, so I treaded carefully. "Isabelle doesn't seem to know anything about gods or angels or anything. She wants to bring Terence to the Compound. She thinks he can help. Isabelle doesn't know much about Terence, does she?"

Kala paused, obviously debating how much information she should tell the room and whether or not she wanted to see her son. "No," she finally answered. "The team and Harry only know that Terence has the ability of 'true aim.' They don't know his true heritage." Then she said hastily, "I'd rather leave Terence out of this. Harry, Isabelle and Dean are more than sufficient for our mission."

I could tell she'd switched into soldier-mode. I got it. Family was a difficult subject for everyone. For everyone with super powers anyway! Ugh!

"I guess we'll have to tell Isabelle about your world, or our world, or the supernatural world – or whatever – when she gets here, right? I don't want her fighting Cronus and Hades without knowing what she's up against." I suddenly felt very protective of Isabelle. I may have held back information during our telepathy session, but I didn't want to do that once she arrived.

Kala nodded in agreement. "Cards on the table. I'm okay with that. Besides, we may be able to use Isabelle's kinetic energy powers against Cronus and Hades."

Kinetic energy? Mind blown. Of course! *That* was why Isabelle could only control things *if* they were moving. It was why she was able to assassinate her victims by stopping their hearts, because hearts were always pumping blood and *moving*. I remembered when I connected to her light and used her powers

180

through her. I had seen trails of light anytime anything moved. I was visually seeing kinetic energy!

I wondered if Isabelle truly knew the nature of her power? I didn't think so: she had been shocked by all the things I had done with her powers that she had never been able to do before by herself. Maybe knowing what her powers connected *with* would help her to use them...?

Maybe Isabelle could be a true force that could help us take down Hades and Cronus!

The nerd side of me was seriously geeking out! I wanted to tell Ryan! He'd flip out too. But he was with Elisha and the stupid brain machines.

Nothing like *that* thought to bring me down.

Since I didn't have Ryan to riff off of, I thought I'd give it up to the room. "*Do* you think Isabelle could stop a supernatural being from moving? They have to use kinetic energy to move, right?"

Max answered first, "It makes sense. I'm pretty sure gods shouldn't be able escape the laws of science."

Talan lifted an eyebrow in thought. "But they could teleport away if they were frozen. It might be a temporary fix, maybe to keep one of them in place long enough for a true attack?"

Kala seemed interested but shook her head. Then she turned to me. "Honestly, Chelsan, only *you* were able to use Isabelle's power to a greater degree. For two hundred years she limited herself to stopping hearts. She didn't know she could broaden her scope, until you showed her differently."

I remembered Isabelle telling me something similar. "But that's my point: if *I* could use Isabelle's powers that way, then she can too. She just needs to practice or something."

181

"Or you could take over her body again, like you did last time," Max suggested.

"No. I don't want to do that. Not to a friend." The thought of violating Isabelle like that again made my stomach turn.

Talan spoke carefully, "But you tried it with Hades, didn't you?"

My nod was small. I was a little ashamed by it, but I hadn't known what else to do. I hated it that my first 'battle' instinct was to jump into an enemy's body and completely take them over. It wasn't okay with my friends, but it *was* okay with enemies?

Kala placed her hand on my shoulder in a comforting manner. "We use whatever skills we have to save ourselves and our team. Don't apologize and don't feel guilty about it. If you can take over Hades or Cronus's bodies, do it. They won't hesitate to do it to you."

Um.

"Okay," I replied. Yeah, total soldier.

Kala tried to ease the tension by saying, "Dean's disappearing trick might work for us, too. I have no idea if Cronus or Hades will be able to see Dean when he's activated his power. It could come in very useful. And since his skin is the equivalent of rubber, I don't think they can harm him physically."

Kala was seriously blowing my mind. Rubber? No wonder he could survive falling from massive heights. I knew it was a part of his power, but jeez! More stuff to tell Ryan!

Jill returned from upstairs with Bill and Eva in tow.

Neither Bill nor Eva looked particularly disheveled, so it was a pretty safe bet that Bill had made sure the 'friend-code' was intact. Even Nancy eyed them with relief.

Bill looked around the room, "What's everyone staring at?"

Jill wrapped her hand around Max's and said, "They all thought you and Eva had sex on Nancy's bed."

Bill's face flushed in embarrassment as his eyes met mine. "We'd never do that *here*."

Eva shrugged, "Not for lack of trying on my part."

"Gross." Nancy shook her head in annoyed disgust. Then she motioned to the couches. "Make yourselves comfortable, we're waiting for Isabelle and Dean."

We didn't have to wait long. Just as Isabelle had said, they arrived in little under an hour. She had a tall, athletic build and her dark brown hair was pulled back in a loose ponytail.

Dean was by her side, a little over six feet and completely ripped. He rubbed his hand over the stubble of his shaved head and turned his eyes toward me. "It took you two months to need our help. My money had been on a week."

I wasn't sure how to respond to that, so I said, "Sorry to disappoint you?"

Dean didn't look like he cared either way, aloof as usual.

Isabelle reached down and gave me a welcoming hug. "Don't listen to Dean. He's still upset we were duped by Harry."

Kala stepped in. "I'm afraid we're going to have to be working with General Clifton to locate Turner. I hope you two can refrain from killing the man?"

Isabelle viewed Kala with interest. Their demeanors were so much alike I would have thought they were sisters. Isabelle stated, "We won't kill him."

"For now," Dean added.

Isabelle addressed Kala and me, "So who are we fighting?"

"Um, you better sit down," I suggested.

Isabelle raised her eyebrow in curiosity.

Ten minutes later, Isabelle and Dean were looking at us all like we were just let out of the looney bin. They had learned a lot about the supernatural world when Elisha and I entered their lives, but the existence of *gods*? It may have been too much to process all at once.

The problem was, we were running out of time.

"You know, Terence joined our crew after he tried to kill me. Turner recruited him. I was angry at first, but Terence and I are family now." She paused, then said flatly, "Whose order was it to kill me? From what you're saying, Turner knew who Terence was before the assassination attempt…"

I saw where she was going. Isabelle wanted to know if Turner had tried to have her killed. She was still dealing with being betrayed by Clifton; now it seemed like she wanted to have a reason to hate Turner again, since she had been doing it for so long.

But Kala shook her head. "Terence missed on purpose. You know this already." She sighed, then answered reluctantly, "My father is a Grigori angel and ordered the missed hit. He wanted Terence on your team to keep an eye on Clifton. Turner was brought in later. He didn't know it was Terence who shot you when it happened."

After a moment, Isabelle finally nodded. I could tell she was disappointed. She wanted to hate Gramps. And after being told that gods were real, Isabelle had only focused on her past. Almost as if she couldn't truly grasp the enormity of what she had just been told.

Kala seemed to pick up on Isabelle's hesitation as well, so she said simply, "Mission first."

This snapped Isabelle out of her doubting stupor.

Isabelle repeated, "Mission first."

With Dean echoing the sentiment, "Mission first."

I kind of wanted to say the words myself, just because, you know, it sounded cool, but I wasn't a part of the 'soldier' club, even if at this moment I wanted to be.

Isabelle directed her next comment to Kala. "D.C. is a long way away. I assume Roberta is waiting for us at the Headquarters air strip?"

"We have a better form of transportation," Kala said as if she was talking about, I don't know, *something normal!*

Turning to Isabelle I explained, "Gods, angels and demons… teleport."

Dean raised an eyebrow in approval. "Really? I've always wanted to teleport."

Isabelle shrugged, still not buying everything Kala was selling, but she willing to move forward. "Let's do it then."

Kala motioned for Max and Eva to come join our little group.

Max and Eva said their goodbyes to Jill and Bill, then stood next to me. They might be a part of this team, but they wanted to make sure everyone knew they were my friends first, soldiers second.

I looked over at Nancy, Jill and Bill, who were now standing together watching us go. I found it hard to swallow from the emotion building up in my throat. They were my family. They might not have super powers, but without them I'd be nothing. I'd have nothing. I knew they'd be too idle to sit by and do nothing though. I hoped that whatever strategy they chose to fight Cronus and Hades didn't involve them putting themselves in the way of any physical harm. I'd learned a long time ago that I couldn't tell them to stay behind for their own safety. They never listened. It wasn't who they were, which made me both terrified for them and proud.

I waved a small goodbye and Nancy rushed up to hug me. It

wasn't in her nature to let a good hug slip by, not when so much was on the line. She gave me one last look of encouragement. "Be. Careful."

Smiling, I said, "I will." Then I eyed her knowingly. "You too."

Nancy hid her guilty look. "We will."

"Promise?" I needed her reassurance.

"Forever and always." Nancy hugged me again and I nodded to Kala.

Kala motioned toward her shoulder. "Everyone hold on. Don't let go until we arrive at the Compound."

I suddenly wondered what would happen to someone who did let go in the middle of teleportation? Would they disappear into the ether? Would they end up in the middle of a mountain? Or in the middle of Kansas? None of those options sounded very appealing so I made sure my grip was secure on Kala's arm.

With one last check that everyone was making physical contact with her, Kala activated her power.

In a blink of an eye we all stood in a huddle in the middle of a giant room that appeared to be a deserted science lab. Row upon row of tables with abandoned beakers and Bunsen burners were covered in layers of dust.

The group separated and I could tell Isabelle and Dean were having a turn-around in the *believing* department. Nothing like having physical proof to persuade a person, and teleporting was a pretty convincing argument.

Kala spoke to Talan, "I'm glad Fortski's old lab is still intact. I was afraid we were going to teleport into a construction zone." She looked around more carefully. "Which way should we head?"

"Let's wait for Roberta to arrive with Clifton and Asmodeus," Talan suggested. "They can confer with Isabelle and Dean about where's the most likely place Cronus is holding Turner."

"We can *confer* right now without them." Isabelle walked over to Kala and Talan, followed by Dean. "This part of the Compound hasn't been touched in over a hundred years. Harry always referred to it as 'Geoffrey's space.' If Cronus and… Hades…" It seemed hard for Isabelle to say their names, as if repeating them out loud somehow made the situation more 'real,' but she continued, "The most remote place to keep Turner would be ten floors down on the Red Level. It's the highest security. Not sure if you can teleport us there, but if I were to bet, Turner's there."

"I agree," Harry Clifton's voice sounded from behind us.

Isabelle turned at the sound of his voice and, as her eyes scanned him over, she made an expression of disgust. If looks could kill, Harry would be dead where he stood. Nope, she hadn't forgiven him yet.

I didn't think she ever would. This was the man that killed her parents, sent her to abusive foster parents then lied about it, telling her it was all Turner.

Dean didn't look as upset, but I could tell his protective side was up. He cared more about Isabelle than about his own anger toward Clifton. Honorable, but Dean was still a jerk. He had a signature move of becoming invisible, sneaking up behind a person and snapping their neck. I still didn't trust him, but I trusted Isabelle, so that would have to be good enough for now.

The demon, Asmodeus, stood next to Clifton and Roberta trying his best not to make direct eye contact with Kala. I felt like I was in class watching some guy crushing on some girl, acting all cool like he didn't care, but it was obvious to everyone in that room that he totally did! I kind of felt sorry for him. I wasn't sure if I should be feeling sympathy for demons, but the guy looked like an abused love-sick puppy. It was hard not to feel some kind of empathy for the demon.

Roberta walked over to me, Max and Eva. "You three okay?"

"Uh, sure," I said, awkwardly. "Thanks."

Eva and Max said nothing, but Roberta didn't seem to mind our lack of enthusiasm. Her mind was obviously focused on getting her husband back.

Clifton joined Isabelle and the others, ignoring Isabelle's death stare. He looked like he expected as much. He also appeared much thinner than he was the last time I saw him, and a lot older. I mean, the guy was fifty when Age-pro was invented so he always looked old, but Clifton had a kind of strength and power to him that defied his age. Now, after a couple months in 'Turner prison,' he seemed weak and frail. It made me wonder if Turner had stopped giving him Age-pro.

Kala viewed the General with an expression of resignation. She had worked with him and Gramps three hundred years ago. What had the three of them been like back then? I could tell she had no love for Clifton, but she didn't seem to despise him like Isabelle did either.

Leading the team, Kala took charge. To Clifton, Isabelle and Dean, she commanded, "You three take the lead. We'll search the Red Level first."

I could tell Isabelle liked taking orders. Her demeanor changed from Clifton-rage to I-have-a-mission-get-out-of-my-way contentment.

Dean made himself invisible while Isabelle took the lead. She didn't need a gun since her power could stop hearts. Did gods have hearts? I guess we'd find out. I needed to tell her about the kinetic energy thing too. I had no idea if she had been working on her powers or not. Isabelle had said she couldn't do on her own the things I had done with her powers, but maybe in the couple months we'd been apart she had learned a thing or two.

Clifton followed a few paces behind Isabelle, careful to keep his distance. I kept expecting Dean to suddenly materialize and snap Clifton's neck, but thankfully it never happened.

Walking through clouds of dust as our feet hit the floor was an experience I wasn't used to. I felt a tickle in the back of my throat and almost sneezed, but we were quickly out of the giant, abandoned science lab before I turned into an allergy mess.

The outside hallways appeared as long deserted as the lab, but miraculously with less dust. If Ryan were here he'd probably have some explanation for it, like there was more access to the outside air in the lab, or the room was bigger so there was more dust, or something brilliant, but he wasn't. He was being brilliant at another compound like this one. It was kind of creepy that Gramps had been making facilities like these for three hundred years.

The only good thing about the dust was the fact that I could control it. Normally, I could weaponize dust that couldn't even be seen, just the normal amounts floating around in the air, but having it visible and in front of me? It could prove useful. Although, do gods have lungs? The whole concept of beings that looked human, but weren't, still boggled my mind. I had a lot of figuring out to do. I hated feeling helpless. You'd think having powers would fix that feeling, but it didn't. I constantly felt like I was swimming in deep water and I could barely dog paddle.

My position in the group was in the middle with Eva and Max. Kala, Talan, Roberta and Asmodeus trailed behind. Despite being in such a large group, I still felt wary. Our last encounter with Cronus and Hades hadn't gone so well and there had been more Grigori with us. I hoped that, this time, somehow Isabelle and Dean's powers might be unique enough to make a difference.

We traveled for what felt like hours. To be honest, it could have been. I had no concept of time down there, walking through hallway after hallway made of some kind of matte black metal on the walls, ceiling and floor. Each hallway led to more and more abandoned rooms with dusty desks covered in outdated screens and electrical boxes that used to pass for computers. It became monotonous after a while. It amazed me that this place existed and only Harry's team had occupied it for the last two hundred years.

It was quiet. So quiet that only the sound of our footsteps made any noise in the place. I became distinctly aware of the embarrassing fact that my Chuck Taylors squeaked every time I walked. Eva kept looking at me whenever a squeak became a little too unruly for her taste, but she didn't say anything.

No one did.

We just walked.

And walked.

And walked.

We came to a stairwell and an elevator, no different than a few dozen others we'd passed, but Isabelle motioned for the group to stop. "We'll take these stairs in case the elevators are being guarded."

Kala nodded her approval from behind me. She was still in charge. Isabelle didn't know her personally, but I could tell that she respected Kala. Maybe it was the way Kala carried herself, or maybe it was simply because Kala was Terence's mom, but either way, Isabelle had no problem deferring to Kala.

Which weirdly seemed to upset Clifton. I knew he had history with Kala since she used to work with him and Gramps, but obviously they weren't on the best of terms. And to have Isabelle listen to Kala and not him anymore, probably hurt him more than he thought it would.

Isabelle opened the door to the stairwell, and we all headed down, deeper into the Compound.

At least Turner's Headquarters had people in it. Trudging through there had been a pain as well, but it somehow didn't feel like we were traveling into an empty tomb like the Compound did.

More and more stairs made me feel like we were eventually going to hit the center of the Earth. At least we weren't going up them though. I think I would have felt like dying! Not that that was possible!

Finally, we reached a door on a level that looked like all the other levels, though the stairs still went down farther than I could see. Apparently, this was our stop.

Isabelle opened the door and led us all through.

I realized why they called it the 'Red Level.' The walls, ceiling and floors were a deep, dark color of red. When Isabelle had said *Red Level*, I had assumed it was more symbolic like an emergency level or some other thing that is associated with the color red. But no, just literally – red.

The 'red' soon lost its novelty as yet again we traveled through hallway after hallway and room after room. I was beginning to think Isabelle might be wrong and Turner was nowhere near this place when –

Hades and Cronus suddenly appeared before us.

They stood at the end of the hallway we were currently in, blocking us from entering the room behind them.

I tried to peer around Clifton and Isabelle to see if Turner was inside that room, but I couldn't see much since the opening was completely covered by Cronus and Hades.

Dean kept himself invisible. I had no idea if he planned to attack or not.

I had no idea if any of us were going to attack or not.

I wasn't sure of anything anymore. I was so out of my element it was ridiculous.

And Hades scared me.

As in: really, really scared me.

Cronus spoke first, "You found us. Not surprising. I always had a thing for this place. I'm surprised your newly found *Rotoph* didn't try and block us out like last time."

Kala addressed him from the back of the group, "He was busy."

"And not powerful enough," Cronus mocked. "He couldn't have stopped us, even if he had tried. We're stronger now than we ever were."

I think Cronus wanted credit for beating Rotoph or something. Like he thought he had the upper hand against the Grigori this time. It was like watching a five-year-old. It weirded me out.

Kala rolled her eyes. "Yeah, yeah, you told us this the last time. Now hand over Turner before I end this all and consume you."

I knew Kala was bluffing since she had confided in me that consuming another god might be the end of her. Or, the end of her mind anyway. She was good at faking confidence, though, because if I hadn't known any better, I would have thought she'd eat these two gods up right now.

Surprisingly, Cronus didn't seem fazed at all by Kala's warning. "You always say that, but you never do it. When you bluff too many times, it takes all the bite out of your threats."

Kala didn't argue the point, which made me nervous. Did that mean we should start fighting?

No one made a move.

It was getting a bit awkward.

No one wanted to fight. At least that was what it seemed like.

Finally, Kala walked ahead of the group to stand about ten feet away from Cronus and Hades.

Cronus *said* he wasn't scared of Kala consuming him, but he still took a step or two back at her approach.

Hades squirmed.

It made me realize that Kala was the only one they were intimidated by. Probably because she was the only one who truly had a way of killing them. They had grown so used to being immortal that finding out there was a way of dying must be terrifying.

Kala leveled her gaze at Cronus. "Give us Turner *now.*"

"You couldn't defeat us before. You can't defeat us now," Cronus snarled – then his face suddenly contorted in pain. He clutched his chest. "What's... happening?"

I'd seen that action before. I guess gods *did* have hearts. And Isabelle was making Cronus's stop beating. There was no swirling black hole, so Cronus wouldn't die from it, but it sure looked like it hurt.

Isabelle, on the other hand, thought she was killing him. She stepped forward with confidence.

Cronus yanked his hand away from his chest angrily and pointed at Isabelle. "Are you doing this?"

Isabelle didn't answer and concentrated harder.

Cringing in pain, Cronus waved his hand lightly and Isabelle flew through the air, tumbling into Clifton, both of them falling in a heap on the floor.

Cronus bellowed, "I don't need my heart to beat, you annoying bug," he rubbed his chest again, "but that hurts." He sounded offended.

Dean suddenly appeared behind Cronus, reaching up to snap his neck. I almost thought he'd succeed but...

Cronus reached back in one fluid motion, grabbed Dean by the head and threw him onto the Isabelle-Clifton pile on the floor. "Is that the best you have? Two humans with peon powers?"

Hades grunted. "I'm bored." He turned to Kala. "You're not getting your human. We need him. You should all leave now."

"We're not going anywhere." Kala nodded to Talan behind her.

Talan sent black fire out of his hands, straight over our heads and directly into Cronus's chest. Cronus's eyes instantly turned black. He tried to back away, fumbling on his feet, the black fire making him blind.

Hades looked shocked, then perplexed.

Kala sent her own purple fire toward Hades, but Hades blocked it with his own white fire.

It was a battle between Kala's fire and Hades's fire.

Talan and Asmodeus pushed ahead of us to attack Cronus: Talan with purple fire, and Asmodeus with his scream.

A white stream of light swarmed out of Roberta and tied itself to Asmodeus. They were exchanging energy again. Roberta began incanting a spell.

Isabelle and Dean were still stunned at being thrown around like rag dolls, their powers apparently useless against gods.

And Max, Eva and I were frozen in indecision. We had no idea how to help or what to do. It was a horrible feeling.

Desperately, I tried tapping into Hades's light. Maybe I could do it. Maybe I could control him and make him imprison himself again. But his light was still cloaked by some kind of magic. I could see that it wasn't the same translucent white stuff he had used to control dead things. So, what was he using to protect his light? I concentrated as hard as I could to break through – but I couldn't see what I was trying to break through. The whole attempt felt useless. I was way out of my element here.

Hades suddenly turned to me. His white fire was being held back by Kala's purple flames, but he smiled at me with confidence.

"I have an army of dead in that room, can you sense them?!" he yelled over the battle, fighting Kala's fire but ignoring her completely. His eyes were only on me.

I couldn't sense any dead bodies. Was he lying? Was he trying to make me prove my powers to him? I didn't know what to say, so I said nothing.

"You can't, can you?" he laughed, then glanced at Max and Eva. "What about you two?" They shook their heads.

Kala renewed her purple fire with a fury, but Hades held it back with his white fire. "I am the God of Death. Every servant of the dead belongs to *me*."

I didn't like where this was going.

Then my heart dropped as Hades focused all his attention on me. "Every necromancer is *mine* to control." Smiling, he said to Kala, "Time to put your favorite little pets to use."

Uh, oh.

I knew no one else could see it, but a wave of displaced air rushed toward me, Max and Eva.

Hades was going to take over our bodies.

Over our minds.

Over our souls.

I quickly grabbed Eva and Max's hands.

No!

Chapter Eight
257 Years Ago

KALA

Kala pushed.

She had never felt so much pain in her life and her cells had fused with a gods', so that was saying something. But she had also never felt more alive.

Kala was giving birth to a child.

Resting on a bed in Roberta and Geoffrey Turner's guest room in their mansion wasn't where she imagined having her baby, but there was nowhere else she'd rather be. Looking around the room, Kala saw all the people she loved most in this world: Talan, Derek, Gaia, Owen, Linda, Roberta and Geoffrey.

Talan held her hand tightly, allowing her to squeeze his fingers until she was sure they would snap. But Talan showed no signs of pain, just pure joy that he was about to be a father. Derek stood behind him, waiting in case Talan needed a break. He looked the most nervous of them all. Kala felt a surge of love for her best friend. Derek could handle fighting gods, but watching his best friend give birth? The boy was a wreck.

Kala looked at Talan and tried to give him a smile that said she was doing fine, but she felt like her insides were being attacked with lightning bolts. She was still amazed at Talan's ability to forgive her. She had told him everything about her time with Asmodeus. And since she was Gaia's daughter, Kala knew the second she had conceived. It was her third day with Asmodeus and Day Three of her mission. Kala had thought she was going to let the world burn back then. She was going to ride it out with a demon and fail her Atlas mission on purpose.

But the tingling woke her up in the middle of the night.

The sensation swept through her like a storm of emotion and she knew…

She was pregnant.

And, like a snap of the fingers, Kala was back on target.

She knew she'd do anything for the baby inside of her – and that included the mission. Her baby would live in this world, so Kala had to keep it spinning.

Kala told Asmodeus. She didn't want there to be any secrets, any miscommunications, any misunderstandings. She was having his baby, but Talan would be the father, if Talan still wanted her after being with Asmodeus for three days.

The demon was surprisingly okay with it. At least, he didn't argue. He made some flippant comment about the grandson of Gaia being raised by a Grigori, but that was it. He let Kala go without an argument.

Talan had taken the news with a mixture of joy at seeing life in Kala's eyes again and a deep sadness that he hadn't been the one to give it to her. He forgave her instantly, which only made Kala feel worse, but she was relieved as well. She didn't want to raise this baby with anyone else but Talan. He was her soul mate.

He was the man who deserved so much more than Kala Hicks.

And now, nine months later…

Gaia stood in front of her and was the acting *doctor* in this situation as no one was sure what kind of birth this would be. The baby was part god, part human and most unpredictably, part demon. On the chance the child would come out looking *less than human* (Asmodeus's true form was a blue-human-dragon for example) Kala decided to give birth in a private location. When Roberta insisted that Kala have the baby at their house, she had gladly accepted.

Kala felt a pang of guilt that Asmodeus wasn't there with her, but it was too complicated to have him there; and besides, he'd made it very clear that he didn't want to come anyway. Inside, Kala knew that was a lie, she saw the hurt in Asmodeus's eyes when she made her wishes clear that she didn't want him there for the birth, but Kala chose to take Asmodeus's words at face value.

Roberta was on Kala's other side, wiping her forehead with a cool, wet cloth. "Are you sure you don't want me to conjure a spell to get rid of the pain? It won't hurt the baby."

"No, I'm good. Thanks though," Kala said through clenched teeth.

She wondered if Talan wanted her to accept Roberta's offer since it was his hand she was crushing, but he didn't say a word. He simply smiled at Kala like he was the happiest man alive.

Another pang of guilt.

How could Talan be so happy, knowing the baby wasn't his? Knowing it was Kala's betrayal that caused the pregnancy in the first place?

Kala pushed those thoughts aside. Without becoming

pregnant, Kala would have died nine months ago, taking the world with her. This baby saved her. Saved everyone. Talan may have been hurt by the method, but he was happy with the result. And Kala chose *him*. She could have chosen Asmodeus and Talan would have accepted that, but she chose Talan.

And, apparently, that was enough.

"I can see the head," Gaia announced, and Kala almost laughed at the excited gasps from the room.

No one was sure what to expect, but they all agreed on the fact that this baby would be loved like no other. Everyone in that room was going to be some kind of parent figure to the child. Kala would still have to do her Atlas missions, and these were the people who were going to help her raise a child when she had to go.

Speaking of which, Kala checked her internal countdown. Labor had taken longer than anyone expected, and she only had two hours to complete her next mission. It was going to be a doozy, both physically and mentally. Landfills had grown out of control in the last seventy years and her Atlas task was to uncover a particularly nasty one that was butted up against a reservoir, releasing its toxins into the water. The chemicals alone would do serious damage to the locals that drank water from the reservoir. At first Kala couldn't see how this would help *balance* the world, so she had asked Talan to show her the future to see why poisoning potentially thousands of people was important. Kala needed him to do this from time to time, to help her cope with what she had to do.

Talan had showed her what digging up the landfill would lead to. In four years, because of this tragedy, a world law would be put into effect. All paper, packaging and dumping would be illegal and punishable with life without Age-pro.

Talan's visions were a great comfort at times. It was nice to see how everything balanced out eventually. By doing this horrible deed, the world would heal and never have to suffer from pollution and landfills ever again.

But that wasn't going to happen unless this baby came out.

And just like that the pain was gone and the cries of Kala's newborn filled the room.

Tears streamed down Gaia's face as she held Kala's baby in her arms, her voice was filled with joy when she said, "It's a boy, and he's the most beautiful baby I've ever seen."

"Not that you're biased or anything," Owen laughed as he looked at Kala's son in wonder, "but I have to agree. He's pretty darn perfect."

"Takes after his mother," Geoffrey smiled at Kala, affection beaming in his eyes.

Talan's hand squeezed Kala's supportively as joyful tears fell down his cheeks as well. "Let's meet our son."

Gaia and Linda wrapped the boy in a soft blanket, then handed him over to Kala.

Kala wasn't a crier, but she practically sobbed when she held her son for the first time. She had never felt so connected to life as she did in that moment. She had never felt so much love washing through her like a liquid rainbow come to life.

Kala was truly happy. Deep, inside every cell, happy. She wanted this feeling to last forever.

"Terence. His name is Terence." Kala gazed into the eyes of her little boy and in that moment knew true bliss.

Present Time

I positioned myself so I could fight Hades and at the same time confront Chelsan and her two necromancer friends. With Hades taking over their bodies, I wasn't sure how we could win this fight. I had never considered the fact that Hades could take control of Chelsan. He didn't use that power at our last confrontation, so it didn't occur to me that it was a possibility. It should have. It was sloppy of me.

When I looked over at Chelsan I nearly stopped my fire attack from surprise.

Instead of facing three very powerful necromancers: Chelsan, Max and Eva dropped to the floor, convulsing.

Turning to Hades, his white fire grew dimmer and his expression was one of shock as well. "I really hate that girl."

I felt a surge of hope. Hades wasn't as strong as he thought he was. Or, more importantly, Chelsan may be stronger. I wouldn't know until I talked to Chelsan. Right now, though, she and her two friends were having full-blown seizures on the floor.

In a rage, Roberta stopped incanting and like before, a ball of light burst from her and Asmodeus, hitting Hades.

The Olympian was thrown back and crashed violently against the wall. Hurriedly, Hades rushed up to stand, white fire flooding out of his hands before my purple fire could take him over.

Roberta rushed to her granddaughter's side, calling to Chelsan, trying to get her to snap out of her current state of convulsing.

I couldn't focus on them right now, I had to take down Hades before he and his dad could cause more trouble. With Hades controlling all the world leaders, Cronus could take over this planet or destroy it pretty easily.

The problem was: they were too strong to capture.

I needed the help of my mother, Gaia. The last time we captured Cronus was right after he had fought an ocean battle that resulted in massive injury from Rotoph's suicide Titan bomb. So he had been weak. And even in his weakened state, I had still needed my mother's help. And because of the Franklin clone using the resurrection magic from Rotoph's said bomb, Cronus and Hades were stronger than ever.

I still didn't know how a clone could have gained that much power and know-how to break two gods out of Turner's brain machines. Sure, he had an I.Q. kid's soul and power inside him, but that only happened a few months ago. This I.Q. kid, Alec, had to have had this planned long before he took over the clone's body.

But how did he know about Rotoph's bomb at the bottom of the ocean? How did he collect the broken shards?

The answer was: he couldn't have.

He had help. Oceanus? Iapetus? Any one of the Titans? My brain needed to work this out, but it also needed to focus!

Hades's white fire threatened to overtake my purple fire. White fire was used to control, purple fire was used to capture. I would have loved to use green fire to cause Hades some pain, but it wouldn't help matters any, only make me feel good. Luckily, Talan's black fire had kept Cronus blind this entire fight.

Cronus was fighting back viciously, though, using his strength and lightning bolts to strong effect. Asmodeus had already been hit twice by Cronus's lightning. Strangely, Cronus hadn't attempted to use his time-freezing power again. It made me remember Ashliel saying their power would weaken over time. I hoped so anyway.

The battle brought us all out of the hallway and into the large room that we had seen behind Cronus and Hades. I couldn't get a good look at my surroundings as the dark red walls were not lit and made it difficult to see anything at all. There were shadows and shapes in the back of the room, but I couldn't tell if it was furniture or the army of dead Hades had threatened us with.

Isabelle and Dean were back up from their momentary daze of disappointment.

In spite of knowing it wouldn't kill Hades, Isabelle still focused all her power on his heart.

"Damn it, that does hurt." Hades cringed in pain.

His fire weakened from Isabelle's attack.

My purple fire almost reached his skin.

BOOM!

Hades threw back my fire with a large sweep of his hands, extinguishing it instantly.

Whoa.

Hades's smile was both confident and surprised. He may have been powerful enough to throw off my fire, but he wasn't powerful enough to take control of three necromancers.

Hades didn't see it that way, though. From the look in his eyes, he wanted to crush me.

Well, the undefined shadows in the back of the room were not furniture. As promised, an army of rotted corpses marched toward us.

I could have used Chelsan right about now. She had said it had been difficult to take over the dead bodies from Hades, but it would have been easier to have her try and keep these corpses away from us. I wasn't worried about winning a fight with dead things; it was more of a nuisance that kept me from obliterating Hades and Cronus.

Turning to Roberta and Asmodeus I yelled, "Can't you guys destroy Hades's white control fire, like the last time?! It might make the dead bodies collapse!"

Roberta and Asmodeus nodded and focused on the sea of corpses.

Like before, a cloud of dust fell from the bodies as the barriers had been broken.

But other than that nothing happened.

Roberta shook her head as she said to me, "We destroyed the barriers but we still need Chelsan to control the bodies!"

It also appeared that even though the white control fire was gone, Hades could still control the dead people.

I did the only thing I could do and sent yellow destroying fire into the dead bodies' ranks, lighting them up like funeral pyres. I had to admit, it gave the room some much needed illumination.

"Pretty brutal way to light up a room, wouldn't you say, Kala?"

That voice made my heart and mind sing with complete and utter joy.

I turned around, hoping my ears weren't playing tricks on me.

Derek.

My very best friend in the entire world, galaxy, universe!

His smile welcomed me, and I wanted to stop fighting immediately to give him a giant hug, but yeah – army of dead and Hades breathing down my neck made that particular gesture impossible for the moment.

Plus the fact that Derek held a weapon in his hands. It was shaped like an old bazooka: a large black metal tube, shoulder rest and trigger. But I knew Derek too well: this was going to do some damage.

Sure enough, Derek placed the contraption over his left shoulder and pulled the trigger. A beam of blue light shot out of the black tube and straight into Hades's face.

To me, it looked like a very bright spotlight, not even a solid, thick laser beam, so I wasn't sure what Derek had expected to happen...

Hades screamed.

The Olympian clawed at his face as if he had cockroaches crawling under his skin. All his magic spells dropped, his white fire and his hold on the army of corpses, the bodies falling to the floor in a smelly, burning heap.

Cronus had regained his eyesight as he momentarily stared at Hades screaming. Talan snuck in a blast of purple fire to try and gain control over Cronus, but the Titan answered back with another lightning bolt.

Derek aimed his light canon at Cronus and hit the Titan in the chest with the same strange blue light. Cronus reacted the same as Hades, screaming in anguish.

Cronus barely had enough gumption to move, let alone fight. Despite his pain, he leapt across the room and grabbed Hades's arm.

The two gods vanished, teleporting to safety.

I was relieved and disappointed all at once. Relieved because I knew we were about to have our butts handed to us by Cronus and Hades. Disappointed because we still had no idea where Turner was, failing our mission to save him. At least Derek had actually hurt Cronus and Hades.

Speaking of…

I turned to Derek, who now had his supernatural bazooka strapped over one shoulder. Pulling him in for a hug was the best thing I'd felt in a long time. Derek knew me better than anyone. He was one of my original crew when I was human and working in Turner and Clifton's elite military team. He had been with me through my entire transition of turning into Atlas, something I couldn't have done without him. Loyalty was more important to Derek than breathing. It was something we both lived our lives by.

He was immortal as well, thanks to me. Derek had been severely injured, and I had used my powers to heal him before I knew how to use them properly. The result was essentially the equivalent of John Fortski's immortality serum. Derek had been decapitated once on one of my Atlas missions. Sure enough, his whole body regenerated from his head right before my eyes. With Age-pro being invented only a few years after I gave him the ability to live forever, he didn't have to hide his immortality from his family, which was a great relief to him. I had dinners with Mama Echols and the rest of his family the first Sunday of every month for the last three hundred years. I'd do anything for Derek and his family. I considered them my family too.

Derek pulled back from the hug with a smile. "Good to see you too."

Derek's eyes always seemed to be smiling, like he had an eternal sparkle at all times. He was a tall, muscular drink of water, with dark skin, full lips and a shaved head.

"What are you doing here?" I asked Derek, grateful, but not sure why he was in the Compound in the first place. "And what kind of weapon is that?"

"One of your own inventions?" Talan walked over to Derek, embracing him in welcome.

Derek lifted the weapon off his shoulder and showed it to Talan and me. "Yeah. This one is simple: I managed to recreate ultraviolet C and project it with this bazooka. Skin is skin, whether you're a god or a mere mortal and UVC is the highest form of sun radiation. UVC can't get past the Earth's ozone, so no one ever feels the damage down here. But being hit directly… Basically, I gave the both of them a bad sunburn, or a mild case of melanoma," he chuckled.

I was always amazed at how resourceful Derek had become over the last three hundred years. He had started out like me as a military grunt serving our country, but with everything supernatural that had happened to him, he dedicated a lot of his time to inventing and science. It had always been a fascination for him back in the day, but now he was an expert. And a damn good inventor. The soldier in him still only made weapons, but old habits died hard.

"So this weapon could hurt everyone in this room?" Asmodeus asked, making sure to stand out of Derek's line of sight behind me.

Derek looked as if he'd like to try it on Asmodeus, knowing our history, but he simply shrugged. "Pretty much." Then he looked at me warily. I had known him long enough that I could tell he wasn't sure if he should continue.

I prodded, "Spit it out. What?"

Derek sighed. "I've been working with Terence on a few things. He's the one who came up with the idea for using UVC rays. He knew the damage it could do to supernaturals like the gods."

I hated that my own son was a sore spot for me and that my best friend was closer to Terence than I was. But it was Derek. And I could appreciate the fact that Terence loved Derek as much as I did.

"Wow, the whole family is here."

I closed my eyes.

Terence.

He was here.

Opening my eyes, I saw my son walk towards us. My breath caught in my throat. I couldn't help it. He was my boy. My son. My heart burst every time I saw him, filled with so much love and pride I thought my head would explode. Of course, I never felt comfortable saying any of those things to him. Probably why he rarely spoke to me. His scruffy close-shaved blonde hair and bright blue eyes… he looked so much like Asmodeus… It must be difficult every time Talan laid eyes on him.

Terence nodded toward Chelsan and her two friends, still writhing on the floor. "You guys just going to ignore the grand mal seizures going on? Or are you too busy enjoying your reunion. It's not like you don't see Uncle Derek every month."

Attitude.

But… also correct.

I hurried over to Chelsan and the others.

Roberta had disconnected from Asmodeus and was now holding Chelsan's head in her lap. She had let Max and Eva spasm on the floor without comfort. Typical.

Motioning for Derek and Talan to hold Max and Eva, I asked Roberta, "What happened to them? Did Hades fry their brains?" All I knew was the fact that Hades had wanted to take control of these three and failed. I hoped Roberta might have some answers.

Roberta shook her head. "I don't think so. I've been trying to enter into Chelsan's head to see what's happening, but her blocks are so deep I can't get through." Her eyes shone with pride. "Chelsan was somehow able to put up a shield in her brain… and Max and Eva's. She protected them and herself from Hades. I told you she was powerful. *I* wouldn't be able to do that."

"Impressive," Asmodeus commented from a few feet away. He stood apart from everyone, his eyes darting occasionally in Terence's direction. They didn't have the greatest of relationships, worse than my own with Terence, and I couldn't imagine seeing our son was too comfortable for him, especially with Talan there.

"Hades is gone now, though. Shouldn't Chelsan be snapping out of it?" I asked.

Roberta shook her head. "No. Hades is still trying to get inside their heads. I can feel his essence surrounding their entire brains. I've been tapping into Hades's power for hundreds of years, I know his signature better than anyone's."

"Is there any way to get him out of there?" Looking at Chelsan and the others spasming I found their odds were greatly diminishing at keeping Hades at bay for long, especially if Chelsan was doing all the work.

Roberta's expression showed she was at a loss. It was new territory for her as well and that was scary in itself. Roberta answered, "We have to hope Chelsan will be able to keep Hades out for good."

"She's strong enough. If anyone can, it's Chelsan." Isabelle walked over, watching Chelsan with concern.

Asmodeus rolled his eyes. "Well, if Kala-lite says it's so, then it's so."

Terence eyed his father with disdain. "Kala-lite? Isabelle is twice the soldier *mother* ever was."

I didn't say a word. I was hurt, but I knew anything I said would provoke him and I didn't want a fight right now.

Unfortunately, Derek didn't see it that way. He gave Terence an angry look. "Kala has been saving our collective asses for three hundred years. Take your mommy issues somewhere else."

Terence answered with a grunt. Only Derek could get away with scolding him like that. Terence respected and loved him as much as I did. I could tell he wasn't mad at Derek, he just wanted to get in his barb to hurt me.

Asmodeus kept his mouth shut after that.

Isabelle appeared curious at Terence's outburst. She obviously wasn't used to him acting out like that. And from the looks of it both Isabelle and Dean were surprised that Terence had this other side to him. Not only did they find out right before they got here that Terence's fealty hadn't been to Clifton, but that his mother was a god and his father was a demon. To say that this was a shock would be a massive understatement.

Like a pro, however, Isabelle didn't confront Terence or ask him where his allegiances lay. She didn't have to. I could see Terence's radiating loyalty to her and Dean. They truly were his family, just like Derek and Jack had been to me when I was a soldier. I felt a pang of jealousy.

I focused back on Chelsan, telling Roberta, "We should get these three to one of the med bays on this floor. At least let them seize in peace."

Roberta nodded, worried. "I should stay with her, but I need to find Geoffrey."

Obviously conflicted, I set her mind at ease. "We'll keep searching for Turner. But you're probably the only one who can break through to Chelsan, if that's possible. I think your granddaughter needs you more right now." I was being manipulative, by emphasizing the fact that Chelsan was her granddaughter, but I needed Roberta out of the way. I didn't like her and Asmodeus working with each other or that they were magically bound. I daresay Asmodeus *liked* Roberta. I couldn't blame him. I had too, once. I still did, but there would be no forgiveness on Roberta Turner's end for me. So yet again, I was acting from jealousy. Being Atlas had taken its toll on all of my relationships. I was lucky I had a select few who stuck by me, but I understood why some like Roberta and Turner couldn't. If Chelsan truly broke my curse, I'd need another three hundred years of therapy.

If Roberta knew I was manipulating her, she didn't show it. She simply nodded. "I won't leave her side." She turned to Asmodeus, her expression pleading. "Get Geoffrey back."

I wasn't used to seeing Asmodeus show a soft side. He rarely showed it to me, and I knew I was the one person he cared about most in this world. But the look he gave Roberta was sincere, and he said, "We'll find him."

After that, no one spoke.

Derek carried Eva and Talan carried Max, but it was Isabelle who carried Chelsan. She was bonded to the girl and obviously didn't trust anyone else with Chelsan's care.

Only the grunts and sounds of the necromancers' arms and legs slapping against the people carrying them could be heard. It was eerie, especially walking through the deep, red-colored hallways.

Finally, we reached a medical bay where there was a line of beds on metal frames against the wall. Chelsan and the others were set down on the three middle ones.

Roberta only had eyes for Chelsan, though. It was as if Max and Eva didn't exist. It probably made no difference in terms of snapping them out of their seizure fits. Chelsan was the one holding Hades back. I wondered if Max or Eva knew what was going on.

"Can't you make them stop convulsing?" Roberta asked Talan with a slight edge to her voice.

Talan shook his head. "If I accidentally break whatever shield Chelsan's thrown up to block out Hades, we'll be dealing with the most powerful necromancer I've ever seen controlled by Hades. It's not worth the risk."

Terence nodded in agreement. "You know better than anyone what Chelsan is capable of, Roberta. It's next level god-powers."

Roberta kept her eyes on Chelsan and didn't argue. I could tell Terence's words were the ones that convinced her and not Talan's, which only showed that she trusted Terence.

Woosh!

A powerful, short burst of air almost knocked our entire party over from its sudden blast. Then it was gone as soon as it hit.

Chelsan, Max and Eva all stopped spasming. They now rested peacefully on their beds as if asleep for the night.

Roberta's eyes lit up with hope. She gently shook Chelsan's arm to wake her.

Nothing.

Closing her eyes, Roberta kept her hold on Chelsan, reaching out with her magic to sense what was happening. After a moment she opened her eyes and said, "Chelsan is still fighting off Hades, but she was able to move all their minds to a place where their bodies wouldn't have to fight."

Isabelle asked, "That's why they were seizing? Because their bodies were fighting Hades's hold as well?"

I could tell she was trying to work things out. Isabelle was still new to the supernatural world. She had always thought of 'powers' as a form of genetic science, never knowing that magic was real.

Roberta corrected Isabelle, "Not *they*. Chelsan. She's protecting all three of them. She's getting stronger though. I can feel it."

I didn't know if that was true or wishful thinking. Either way, I hoped Roberta was right.

In the meantime...

"Derek, how long have you been at the Compound? Do you know if Turner is being held here or not?" Now that we weren't fighting gods and dead things, we could have a conversation about the mission.

"Terence and I have been here a couple of weeks, working on some projects," Derek answered cautiously, always trying to be careful of my feelings. "If Cronus and Hades brought Turner here, we didn't know about it. But, Kala, this is a big place. They could have put him a mile deep and we'd never be the wiser."

I braved the attitude I knew I would get and asked Terence, "We need to know if Turner is here." Only Owen, Talan, Derek, Asmodeus and I knew the extent of Terence's powers – unless, of course, Terence had decided to share. But considering Isabelle and Dean (his closest allies) only thought he had 'true aim,' it was a safe bet that they were in the dark when it came to Terence's 'other' talents.

Terence gave me an annoyed look, but seeing the desperation in Roberta's face softened him. He placed a reassuring hand on Roberta's shoulder then said, "If Geoffrey is here, I'll be able to find him."

Roberta clasped his hand, gratefully not questioning how Terence would be able to do it. Roberta had always been greedy for power and new spells. The fact that she was so overwhelmed with worry for both her granddaughter and her husband enough to not be curious about Terence's powers was almost alarming.

Terence had many abilities, his most valuable gift was shape-shifting. He could transform himself into any living creature, be anyone. If Turner or Clifton had ever known about this, who knows what they would have tried to make Terence do? But the skill I wanted him to use now was his ability to astral project. Terence's astral projection was much more sophisticated than what humans could do. Terence could project his mind almost like a bomb with a blast radius. We still had no idea how far his radius extended but it was at least a few miles. In one flash of projection, Terence would be able to see inside every room, hallway, nook and cranny of the Compound all at once.

Terence stood back a few feet from everyone. Isabelle and Dean watched with curiosity, seeing a side to their comrade they'd never witnessed before.

Closing his eyes, in less than a few seconds, they were open again, Terence charged with energy. "Turner is here. He's three floors down and guarded by Themis and Iapetus. Cronus and Hades are there as well." I was shocked when he addressed me directly, real concern in his expression. "Turner is encased in a Metlod."

Great.

Talan, Asmodeus, Roberta and even Derek knew what a Metlod was and what it meant, but Clifton, Isabelle and Dean were in the dark.

It was Clifton who asked though. "What is a *Metlod*?" His eyes barely met Terence's. I could see how betrayed Clifton felt toward my son. Learning of Terence's true loyalties before he got here must have been a shock, but as a soldier Clifton adapted quickly. It still didn't take away his butt-hurt expression, though.

I answered, "A Metlod is a magic encasement that keeps all spells and magic out and is impenetrable as far as I know. You can't defeat it with magic because it neutralizes it on contact. And the surface might as well be titanium-reinforced steel, there's no human tool that can break through it."

Isabelle said incredulously, "If you guys were so scared of Cronus and Hades escaping, why didn't you put them in this *Metlod* thing?"

Fair question. I had suggested the same thing over two hundred years ago when Roberta had first discovered the spell that could create a Metlod in the Necrotralten.

I didn't have to answer Isabelle's question though, because Roberta said honestly, "We needed their powers. The Metlod

214

would have taken that from us."

Roberta and Turner had been too reliant on Cronus and Hades's powers. By encasing Cronus and Hades into a Metlod, it would have cut them off from the gods' powers. Just controlling the dead world leaders alone would have been a difficult issue to resolve. The Turners would have had to employ a battalion of warlocks to keep the leaders animated, like they had before Cronus and Hades took them over. Not to mention the fact that Turner and Roberta simply loved power. And Cronus and Hades had given them an endless supply of it. It must be gut-wrenching to lose it all now that they were no longer connected to the gods.

"I need the Necrotralten. Maybe there's a spell that can break the Metlod," Roberta suggested.

"You've been through every inch of that book for over two hundred years. There was nothing about breaking the Metlod." I tried not to sound as dismissive as I felt, but I failed miserably.

Roberta yelled, "We have to try something!"

I was at a loss.

None of this was getting me closer to Chelsan breaking the curse. Looking at her comatose form, I scolded myself for being such a fool. I never should have given Ryan that serum. I should have waited first to see if Chelsan could break the curse. Now I was on Day Two of my Atlas countdown and if Ryan didn't die at the end of it, the world would end. Cronus would finally get his wish and he didn't even know it.

The problem was: I didn't want to complete my mission. The thought of killing Ryan somehow seemed worse than most of the things I'd done over the years. It was too brutally close to when I had had to kill Jack. Chelsan and Ryan deserved to have a life together, a future.

I couldn't go down that rabbit hole.

I had to have faith that Chelsan would somehow fight Hades off and snap out of her coma.

If the countdown ran out, it ran out. There was nothing I could do about that now.

Rescuing Turner had to be the priority simply because Cronus and Hades needed him. If Rotoph was correct, the gods wanted Turner to sever their bond. It made sense. Years of being locked into the brain machines, their powers being drained by Roberta and Turner... Rotoph thought that it had fused their souls in some way. I didn't think Turner would be able to break this bond, but Cronus and Hades didn't need to know that. As long as they thought Turner had value, they'd keep him safe. It wasn't as if they could kill him, since he had taken Fortski's immortality serum, but they could certainly make Turner wish he were dead.

I realized everyone was staring at me. I was the unofficial leader of this group and I could tell they looked to me for answers. Or at least for a plan of action.

But I had no clue of what to do.

A thought suddenly occurred to me. "Maybe Poseidon can help? Or Zeus? I haven't heard from them in a while, but they have to know Cronus and Hades have escaped by now. Maybe they have a solution to the Metlod." In truth, I hadn't talked to or seen any Olympian in at least fifty years. And before that it had been a hundred. I didn't get along well with most of my supernatural family, if you could call them family. Since Gaia was my mother, I was technically Aunt to all the Olympians and sister to the Titans. Poseidon was the only one I had any kind of connection to. He had helped me through Gaia's abandonment and genuinely cared for Terence. I certainly didn't feel any kind of familial bond with the rest of them, but there was a tiny part of me that would like to think that a dysfunctional family was still family.

From the expressions on the faces of the people who knew the Olympians, no one seemed too keen on the idea.

Asmodeus pointed out, "Poseidon maybe. He's always a bit more apt to listen, but Zeus? I thought you said it's been over a hundred years since you saw that idiot."

"Fifty, but still. It wasn't like we had anything to say to each other, so there was no reason. Now there's a reason," I rationalized, more to convince myself than anyone else.

Talan lightly touched my hand supportively. "You're the only one here who can make contact with the Olympians. It's worth a shot."

I squeezed his hand in thanks. I never said it was a good idea, it was just an idea. But either way, Talan had my back.

Concentrating, I reached out telepathically to Poseidon first. If anyone would listen, it would be him. It had been so long, though, I wasn't sure if I was reaching him. After a few more minutes of trying, I figured Poseidon must be deep in the ocean unable to hear me or was ignoring me completely. I hoped it wasn't the latter, but it had been a long while since we talked. The sea god might have taken offense.

I switched to reaching out to Zeus. I was about to give up when his booming voice filled my head.

Kala. I assume you're contacting me because my father and brother escaped that prison of yours? Zeus's tone was laced with an I-told-you-so attitude.

I answered back, *Yeah. They have Turner and we're trying to get him back, but they put him in a Metlod. Any ideas how to break it?*

Zeus answered quickly, *You know, if it weren't for that pet human of yours, Metlods would have stayed where they belonged in that damned book of Asmodeus's. Technically, this is all your fault. You locked Cronus and Hades into those machines, you gave that infernal woman the Necrotralten, so you have to figure it out! Leave me and my family out of it!*

And with that last scolding, Zeus was gone.

Despite what Zeus said about keeping *his family* out of it, I reached out to Hephaestus and Hera as well.

Nothing but radio silence.

"Well, no help there," I announced with a groan. "Poseidon wouldn't answer, and Zeus made it clear he doesn't want us to involve him or the rest of his clan. And apparently, they all got the message too, because none of them responded to my call." It was no surprise that Zeus and the Olympians had no desire to get involved. It was also no surprise that Zeus didn't remotely consider me family. I was pretty sure he didn't believe I was Gaia's daughter.

"What a surprise. No one in your family wants to help you," Terence grumbled under his breath.

Derek snapped at him, "You ungrateful punk."

"Derek, don't. It's fine." I stopped Derek from defending me.

Terence knew he could push the boundaries of Derek's temper without fear of Derek ever truly being mad at him. Terence obviously risked angering Derek just to throw another jab at me.

A quick check of my internal countdown: 2d 01h 20m 32s. Two hours left of Day Two.

We were running out of time.

"Terence isn't wrong." I shook my head. "And I have no idea what to do next."

Chapter Nine

Two Weeks Ago

CHELSAN

"Why do I keep losing strength?!" Eva yelled in frustration.

Chelsan had no idea, but she didn't want to upset Eva for what felt like the millionth time, so she said, "Let's try something new. See if we can keep your strength steady."

Eva looked like she was about to have another outburst when Max placed a comforting hand on his sister's arm. "We're trying to help you. I know you're frustrated, but you have to calm down in order for this to work."

Eva slowly nodded.

Only Max could calm her like that. Not even Bill had that kind of power, and Eva was head over heels with him.

Chelsan surveyed her surroundings. It was a beautiful four-bedroom condominium overlooking Lake Franklin. Fifteen floors up, the apartment had floor to ceiling windows that surrounded the entire open living area and kitchen, giving the illusion of being outside. The décor was simple and elegant, highlighted by dark wooden floors, and furniture in varying shades of gray and white. It was Max and Eva's condo and it was only a few miles from Geoffrey Turner High.

Turner had gone above and beyond Chelsan's expectations when he took it on himself to make sure Max and Eva had a nice place to live. The apartment was completely paid for. Turner had a chef come over and make all their meals with groceries delivered every Sunday, plus he sent cleaners in twice a week to keep everything neat and orderly. Chelsan was a little jealous – though she was sure Roberta would do the same for her – but the less time Chelsan spent with her grandparents the better, so Chelsan just appreciated the gift they'd given Max and Eva.

Chelsan was there now because, since the Elisha incident, Max and Eva wanted to know more about their powers and Chelsan was the only one who could teach them. One hiccup they had discovered, though: ever since Eva took the immortality serum, she started running low on energy when she used her powers.

Really low. As in, Eva had passed out a handful of times.

"Here." Chelsan held out her hands for Eva and Max to take.

Max took her right hand and Eva, begrudgingly, took Chelsan's left.

"I don't know what holding hands is going to do. It's not like we can combine powers or anything." Eva wasn't making this easy.

Chelsan breathed deeply to calm herself before answering. "We can connect if we concentrate hard enough, just like Max, Ryan, Isabelle, the Franklin clone and I did when we... killed the clones." Chelsan still found it hard to say it out loud, but at least she felt she was finally coping with what happened. Max had been a huge help. Even Eva had tried in her own way to be supportive.

Though at the moment, Eva was just being annoying.

220

Max stepped in again. "You need to concentrate, Eva."

Eva appeared to gather herself together and nodded in agreement. "I'm frustrated. I'll be good, I promise."

Sometimes it struck Chelsan hard that Eva and Max were only alive for less than a year. It made sense why Eva's emotions could be all over the map. She had been forced to grow from a baby to a teenager in less than a month, then one of Turner's brain machines loaded her brain up with language and knowledge of a lifetime. The two of them were chosen by Elisha because they had certain 'markers' in their DNA similar to I.Q. kids, which meant that their intelligence was off the charts. The downside being that I.Q. kids had no connection to their souls, which ultimately made them psychopaths. (Like Elisha had once been, until Chelsan had re-connected it back to Elisha's brain.) Lucky for Chelsan, Max and Eva were indeed connected to their souls, so Elisha had to deal with that disappointment. But only being alive for a short time and having to deal with everything they'd had to deal with? No wonder it was so hard for Eva to process.

Max handled it all much better considering he'd been through the same ordeal. But there was something very special about Max. He possessed a certain grace and quiet confidence that Chelsan admired. Jill was one lucky girl.

Chelsan tightened her grip with both Max and Eva and concentrated as hard as she could on uniting the three of them together.

Immediately, Chelsan felt Max's astral form connected to hers. Then...

Chelsan felt Eva's astral form tugging to break loose.

"That's it, Eva. I can feel you there. Just focus on Max, then me, in that order," Chelsan said calmly.

221

Eva didn't verbally respond, but Chelsan could physically feel Eva's astral form separating from her body more and more, then connecting to Max and her, then…

SWOOSH!

Suddenly, the three of them were floating above their bodies, still holding each other's hands in astral form.

Eva's eyes were round with shock and wonder. "We did it!"

Chelsan had to smile. "I think this is the first time I've done this when we haven't been in some kind of life-threatening danger."

Eva looked like a whole new person, full of excitement and radiating with a sense of accomplishment. "Can we fly?"

Chelsan and Max exchanged amused glances, but it was Chelsan who responded, "Baby steps. But we can at least go out over the lake. We have to stick together though, or the bond will break."

Eva nodded happily and Chelsan and Max led the way, flying through the window and out over Lake Franklin.

Though the scenery was breathtaking, Chelsan couldn't keep her eyes off Eva.

She had never seen Eva this happy before. So joyful and… so childlike. Eva was experiencing something new and exciting that didn't involve death, or mayhem, or any other horror her short life had handed to her.

As much as Chelsan's feelings about Eva were conflicted, in this moment watching Eva was a pure delight.

Because for the first time, Eva was finally free.

Present Time

"Seriously, Chelsan, what is happening?" Eva asked for the hundredth time.

"I told you: I'm not sure. I just know that *that,*" I pointed up to the swirling white and blue sky, "is Hades trying to take over our brains."

"And *you're* holding him back?" Eva still seemed incredulous even after explaining everything that I knew to her.

Which, admittedly, wasn't much.

"Can we help?" Max offered again.

Our conversation cycle had been going round and round like this for the last ten minutes.

Shaking my head, I made sure I locked eyes with Max. "I don't think so. I don't know how I'm holding Hades back, I just know that I am."

Eva viewed our surroundings in fear, "So we're safe on a whim. Your protection could fall apart at any moment." She didn't phrase it as a question.

And she didn't need to. My protection *could* fall apart at any moment.

"Yeah," I acknowledged.

Not sure what to say next, I searched the area where we were. We stood on the edge of an enormous canyon. Actually, to say it was enormous was underselling it. Two Grand Canyons could fit inside of its walls; so much so, I could barely see the other side. The canyon, ground and rocks were all reddish-orange in color, going on for miles and miles in every direction with no vegetation or anything manmade in sight. Up above us was Hades in the form of a giant swirling sky, like a tornado about to hit ground.

I knew this place was created by my imagination, but I had no idea why my brain decided to invent a giant canyon in the middle of nowhere. Usually, my mind took me to places like this when I was physically or mentally in danger. I knew the mental part was Hades trying to get inside my head, but I had no idea if my actual body was in any kind of trouble or not. Why didn't I go to my 'happy' place of an oak forest that always calmed me down? Or a spa?

Nope.

A rock desert with nothing around us, and a chasm that was impossible to cross. It had to be some kind of metaphor or symbol that my mind wanted me to recognize but, honestly, all I could do was stare at that swirling vortex and hope it wouldn't consume us all. The thought of being controlled by Hades (or anyone for that matter) was terrifying, especially when I was guilty of it myself. Geez, *I* had tried to take over *Hades's* body. Total hypocrite, I know. But it didn't change the fact that I didn't want Hades to use me to hurt anyone I cared about.

And I certainly didn't want him controlling Max or Eva either. They could cause as much damage as I could in Hades's hands. When Hades sent his essence toward us, I could see it. Acting only on instinct, I somehow threw up a mental shield for the three of us. I wish I knew how I did it. It would probably help me push Hades out for good. Once I had somewhat stabilized the Hades-get-out-of-my-head shield, I used astral projection to bring Max and Eva into my head.

But every second I could feel him tapping against my protective barrier, trying to take over our minds. They had both assured me that they couldn't sense any of Hades's magic or presence. Which made it all the more difficult to keep him out. I was on my own on this one, no matter how much Max and Eva wanted to help.

"Maybe if we held hands and concentrated, we could figure

224

this out?" I suggested. I was at a loss and wanted to do *something*.

"I'm willing to try anything. I feel more useless than I normally do." Eva looked defeated. She did have a rough time of it lately. We still weren't sure why she'd lose some of her juice while using her powers, but in astral-projection-land hopefully that wouldn't be the case.

"You know I'm down," Max said as he took each of our hands, ready to go.

I closed the circle by taking Eva's free hand and looked up at the sky. "Let's concentrate on Hades's essence above us. See if we can move it or something. Or maybe attack it in some way."

A moment later, I felt energy surge through each of my hands, traveling in a circle, and then that the energy began to pulse as it moved through us. It was slow and steady at first, coursing through my right, then my left hand. The harder I concentrated on Hades, the faster the pulse beats hit.

"I think I can see the entity," Max exclaimed. "Not just the swirling visual from your dreamscape, but the actual entity of Hades."

I could see the god, too: more than spinning lights, but as an actual blob of energy, trying to push its way through…

…my shield. I could see flickers of the barrier I had mentally made.

Eva smiled with excitement, "I see it, too! It looks like water trying to get inside a piece of glass!"

"Yes," I confirmed, though I wasn't sure what any of this meant, or if it was progress. But it was more than we had a few minutes ago, so I'd take it.

My shield became clearer and clearer to see, as if someone had poured liquid over it to give it a shape. And the more we could see it, the stronger my bond to it felt.

Hades's essence tried to push through it in desperation, as if it sensed he was being cut off more strongly this time. But I could tell Max and Eva were gaining in strength at being able to physically see what was guarding them.

WHOOSH!

I felt a sudden calmness flow through me.

"Whoa," Eva said what I was feeling.

"Right?" I answered. "What was that?"

"I think we've made the barrier stronger and it somehow made our physical bodies not have to fight as hard," Max suggested.

That felt right to me, too. "Yeah, it's like we were all clenched up and now we're more relaxed."

"But what does that mean?" Eva asked, wanting answers I couldn't give her.

Shaking my head, I peered up at the semi-transparent bubble above us that kept Hades out. "I'm not sure, but we need to try and contact the others now. We're probably in some kind of coma to them. I bet Roberta is trying to get in here to tell us what's happening. The problem is, I don't know how to let her in without giving Hades access to our brains."

We all let our hands go from each other.

Max replied, "Not worth the risk. We'll have to try and see what we can outside our bodies. Your shield will hold if we astral project out of here, right?"

"I wish I knew. But you're right, we need to figure out what's happening, maybe find a way to block Hades off permanently," I agreed with Max.

Eva sighed heavily. "You guys go. I'll stay here to make sure the shield holds. If it starts to break, I'll yank you back in with our connection."

Max didn't like the idea of leaving Eva. "No, you go. I'll stay."

Eva shook her head. "Max, you and Chelsan have done this before, joint astral projection in dangerous situations. I haven't." She smiled supportively, "I'm as safe as I can possibly be. I'm literally standing inside Chelsan's brain. It'll be very easy to pull you guys back if this barrier begins to crack."

I added, "She's right. You and I will have a better chance at staying locked together because our bond is stronger." I didn't want to offend Eva, but I knew she agreed with me. Max and I had been through a lot and most of that was through astral projection. We had the best shot at success.

Max gave one last look to Eva, whose expression was one of resoluteness. Max finally nodded, turning to me.

"Let's do it," he said, determined.

Before either one of us could think about it, I grabbed his hand and leapt into the canyon.

Max almost let go of me, the move shocked him so much, but it was the only way I could think of to get us out of there. Truth be told, I had no idea how I created this place, so it was a good bet that literally jumping out of it would get us to freedom.

As Max's grip tightened, I knew he understood my plan.

The rush of air felt so real, my heart raced in a sudden panic.

We were falling.

And we were falling fast.

Could we die in astral form?

Would our souls be crushed from the force and our bodies be in limbo for all eternity because we took Fortski's serum?

I couldn't stop the terrifying thoughts from entering my brain, all while we plummeted down into the seemingly endless canyon.

The ground suddenly came into view.

And we were going to hit it.

Hard.

Max's arms pulled me toward him, wrapping me close. Taking his lead, I enfolded my arms around him as well.

I closed my eyes in terror as the ground was inches away...

But there was no impact.

I opened my eyes.

We were floating above our bodies that were lying in some kind of infirmary. Roberta hovered over mine in particular, her face crinkled with worry.

The others from our party were standing close, watching, obviously unsure of what to do. I suddenly noticed that Terence was there, too, standing next to a rather intimidating man – with a *bazooka* in his hands? Kala was trying very hard not to look at her son as she talked with bazooka man. Derek. Kala called him Derek. From the way they communicated with each other I could tell they'd known each other a long time.

Max and I pulled ourselves apart from each other, but kept our hands held tight. And like when I'd been tortured by Elisha, Max and I became our tethers. The most interesting part was the fact that I could still mentally feel Eva tied to us as well. And I was fully aware of my protective shield. I couldn't physically see it, but I could sense it as if it were another limb of my body.

"How can we get them to hear us?" I asked Max. I didn't want to take over someone's body. Now, having personal experience of how invasive the act was, I felt even more reluctant to use that particular skill of mine.

Max, on the other hand, was more practical. "We should jump into Isabelle and control her body."

"Max," I said, a slight quaver in my voice. "Please don't make me do that."

Max's expression was one of understanding. "I know. It's unethical and a horrible thing to do, but Chelsan, of all people here, Isabelle will understand, and she'll be the easiest for you to take over, since you've done it so many times with her already."

Rub it in.

I had built a friendship and trust with Isabelle. Taking over her body made me feel like I was using her anytime anything went bad.

Max continued, "Isabelle is a soldier. She'll understand."

Floating over our bodies, watching everyone in that room, Max was right. I just hated myself for it.

Terence started to pick a fight with Kala about tactics and apparently Kala's incompetence. That was when I realized Kala's view of their relationship was no exaggeration. It was more words than I'd ever heard from the guy, so it was very strange, but I didn't like him attacking Kala like that. For better or worse, I liked her, and Terence seemed to be trying to hurt her just to hurt her. Reminded me of my grandparents.

"Okay," I said to Max. "Keep your hand tied to mine and let me do the work."

Max had already experienced this type of ride when we hijacked John Fortski's body. It was during my torture session and we needed to make Fortski hide the immortality serum from Elisha.

Man, I was such a jerk.

With one last squeeze of the hand, we jumped inside Isabelle.

I instantly saw her light and connected to it.

I felt the familiar flush of adrenaline of connecting to Isabelle's life source. It was so hard to stay focused at first because the power rush was so strong. After a few moments, the familiarity of controlling Isabelle took over.

Isabelle's voice was loud and clear. *Chelsan! We were so worried!*

I was hoping you'd find your way out!

I hate that I'm using you like this, I wasn't sure... I began.

But Isabelle cut me off, *Chelsan, I'm good. It's fine. You need a body that's not currently fighting off Hades. I'm glad I can help.*

I hated that she was fine with this, but I appreciated it as well. It made the guilt factor slightly less, but I still felt like an a-hole.

Situating myself inside Isabelle, I tapped into her sight and vocal chords.

I'd never get used to this. At least I hoped I never would. It was like having an out-of-body experience *inside* a body. I *was* Isabelle down to my fingers and toes, but my mind was mine. Isabelle was here too, of course, but it was almost as if I had shoved her consciousness aside so I could take over, like what Talan and I had done with the clone's light so Roberta could control its body.

"Guys, it's me, Chelsan," I spoke through Isabelle.

That silenced the room.

Roberta leapt to her feet and immediately hugged Isabelle. "Are you okay? What happened? I still feel Hades trying to take control of you," Grams rambled in concern.

"He is. I made a protective barrier for all three of us, though, that seems to be holding. Honestly, I have no idea how I did it, so I'm not sure how long it will last. You guys should probably put our bodies in some kind of prison that will prevent us from using anything dead to hurt you. If Hades takes over..." Saying it out loud made me realize how terrified I was of what the consequences might be if Hades took us over. It was the first time I was grateful Ryan wasn't there.

"We can't leave without Turner," Kala joined the conversation. "We want to extract him before Cronus and Hades can sever their bond."

"Did you guys find out where he is?" I asked.

"He's a few floors down in a magic encasing called a Metlod. No magic can penetrate it and no weapon that I know of can break it," Kala admitted.

I could tell it was killing her to confess that she was at a loss over what to do.

"Max and I can use our astral forms and take a look. Maybe I can at least communicate with him. Best case scenario: I can possibly take over his body and maybe help him escape?" I phrased it as a question because I had no idea what this 'Metlod' was or how powerful it could be. From the expressions on everyone's faces, I could tell the confidence level in the success of my idea was slim.

But no one had any other ideas, either, so Kala gave me a nod of approval. "Do it. We'll seal your bodies in this room and meet you down there. The room is guarded by Iapetus and Themis. Cronus and Hades are there too. We'll keep our distance as long as we can, but we'll need to strike fast. If you can give us a signal, great, but we can't wait for it."

Oh crap.

"Um, I just remembered Cronus and Hades can see me in my astral form." I could still feel the terror of having two gods staring me down when I was only there in spirit.

Kala paused, then shook her head. "You'll have to stick to the ceiling and corners. Let's just hope they're too concerned with themselves to notice you."

I made Isabelle nod. "Okay. I'll try and get you word as fast as I can." It had to be done. I was more on edge than before, but I knew that backing down wasn't an option.

Kala added, "We'll fight until we can bring out Turner fully

231

encased in the Metlod, or if you can find some way to help him escape. Either way, Turner is coming with us." She said it with such confidence I felt a surge of inspiration.

"Max and I will communicate through Isabelle," I said.

Dean's face met mine, anger in his eyes. "Why don't you *communicate* through me. Isabelle is tired of being your slave."

It was like a slap in the face because I felt the same way.

Don't listen to him. He's just being protective. Isabelle tried to make me feel better.

He's right, though. I didn't want to do this to you again. I was at a loss for words. I had no defense for what I was doing.

Dean will be fine. Stick to the mission. Isabelle tried to salve my guilt.

Dean's words still hurt, though, like I was evil incarnate.

But it was Terence who spoke to Dean, "Isabelle is fine. I can hear her. It makes her feel like she's contributing."

That's very true, Isabelle conceded.

Dean barely glanced at Terence. "I don't care. I'm tired of Isabelle being abused by the Turners."

Ouch.

I was a *Turner* now to him too.

I wanted to crawl into a hole and die.

Please don't listen to him, Chelsan, Isabelle said. *He's speaking from love, not as a soldier. Trust me, I'm fine. Go and see what you can find out about this Metlod. The sooner you two leave, the better. I'll talk to Dean.*

I wanted to leave, so I said, *I promise, after we're done with this mission, I will never do this to you again.*

Don't be sorry, and don't make any promises. If you can use me to save the world like we did last time, I'm all for it. Now go.

232

I squeezed Max's hand tight and the two of us jumped out of Isabelle's body.

As we floated toward the floor to go find Turner, I could hear Kala forming up the troops. They would be down with us soon. I hoped we'd be of some help.

"This Metlod thing sounds fascinating," Max mused.

"Yeah. I'm not real keen on the magic. I kind of wish Elisha was here. Weird?" I looked over at Max as we passed through another floor.

Max shrugged, "With a soul, Elisha may be of some use to us. And yes, her experience in not only your powers but magic would serve us pretty well against the magic/steel casing thing." His eyes met mine with conviction. "But I'd always put my money down on you no matter what your experience is. You'll figure it out and I hope I'll be able to help you."

I wish I had as much confidence in myself as everyone else seemed to have. If I wasn't in astral form, I'd probably vomit right about now. So much pressure. I was the kind of person that hoped all the bad stuff would go away and not keep resurfacing like it had over the last year. Sure, I'd had my powers my whole life, but I had only used them for things like… keeping my abusive step-dad alive… and making my neighbor, Katie, think her dog hadn't died… and… pretty horrific stuff if looking on the outside, but compared to the last year of my life? Bruce and zombie-dog were nothing.

Passing through another floor, Max pulled me back with his hand.

We were there.

In the room with three Titans, one Olympian and… the Franklin clone.

233

He must have just arrived, since Kala hadn't mentioned him before. I hoped he wasn't hiding some kind of spell up his sleeve that would stop the team from rescuing Turner. I had to warn them before they attacked. Max and I floated as close to the ceiling as we could, hoping no one could see us.

The clone's eyes glanced in our direction.

Max and I froze.

"Do you think he can see us?" Max asked what I was dreading.

"I'm pretty sure only Cronus and Hades were able to see me in astral form last time. So I don't think so."

I watched the clone carefully. It still gave me pangs to see the child version of my dad. I knew the I.Q. kid Alec Swanson was running the show in this Franklin clone's little brain, but knowing that there was a tiny piece of my dad still in that body always gave me an irrational hope that I'd somehow get to know him through the clone somehow. I'd need to kick Alec out first. Even though I was assured by Roberta and Turner that the clones were in no way like my father, a part of me didn't want to believe it.

"Elisha couldn't see us when you helped me escape from my body. She knew I was gone, but she couldn't see me," I rationalized, hoping I wasn't about to have the clone's eyes suddenly meet mine all horror-style. "It's the gods we have to worry about."

Hades looked in our direction. I was about to take Max and go, when...

Nothing.

Cronus glanced over at us as well... No recognition either.

I waved slightly, just to check, terrified they'd be alerted.

More nothing.

How could they have seen me before, but not now? Maybe they *were* losing strength? They had just been fully resurrected when they saw my astral form before. Was this the proof that they were losing their powers bit-by-bit like Ashliel suspected? I needed to tell Kala. Maybe there was a chance of capturing them now.

After a few moments had passed, and being sure they couldn't see me, I began to relax. It was obvious no one in that room knew there were two floaty ghosts hovering over their heads.

Weirdly, they were all standing around like they were in a break room or something. It was almost funny. But mostly, from what I could tell, egotistical. They were not worried one iota. I felt like I was watching some kind of reality show. There was so much confidence mixed in with a little bit of narcissism in the way they spoke to each other. Cronus was the biggest peacock and the others showed deference to him, but I could see the flashes of hatred in their eyes. I wasn't so sure they were thrilled that he was back, but they weren't trying to overthrow him either.

"Is that the Metlod thing?" Max pointed with his free hand to a large silver oval leaning against the back wall. The surface looked like it was made of shiny steel with no openings or grooves, a man-sized metal egg.

"Yeah, it's got to be."

It was actually quite beautiful. The surface was smooth and unblemished by fingerprints or smudges, its reflective exterior almost looked like liquid it was so shiny.

But it was solid.

And I had no idea how to break it open.

"That thing looks pretty impenetrable," Max observed as well.

"Yeah," I agreed. "I guess they're going to have to carry it out."

"But that means fighting these guys. Our guys could barely handle Hades and Cronus and that was *with* us."

I could tell Max wasn't trying to be negative, it was simply his way of thinking through a problem. Unfortunately, all I heard was the fact that we had no chance. Did we really *need* Gramps? I hated that my brain went there, but I couldn't help it. We were going through an awful lot to rescue him, but shouldn't we be focused on recapturing Cronus and Hades? One didn't exclude the other, I guess, but I was beginning to feel like we were saving Turner because everyone knew we had no shot at taking down Cronus and Hades. It was disheartening to say the least.

Kala seemed to think that Turner's machines somehow linked Cronus and Hades together and that they needed Turner to break it. But wouldn't it be better if Cronus and Hades were unlinked? Right now, together, they were undefeatable – maybe separated they'd be more manageable. I didn't want to question someone like Kala, though. She knew what she was doing.

Besides, here I was holding hands with Max, floating above four gods and an I.Q. kid inhabiting a clone of my dead father. What did I know anyway? I felt more helpless than anything else.

"Hey, Chelsan?" Max's voice sounded quizzical. I noticed he was staring at the Metlod. "I think I see something… different about that thing."

"Different how?" I turned my attention back to the magical shell.

"It's like you described when you were stuck in that coffin. You said that Fortski's compound looked like little worms, right?" Max referred to the anti-matter compound that Fortski invented to keep necromancers like me from using my powers.

So, if this Metlod was similar… in terms of keeping magic out… maybe I could see it in the same way as I did with the compound.

I nodded. "Yeah, I could see the anti-matter doing its job to stop me from using my powers." I squeezed Max's hand for support. "Let me see if this is similar."

I concentrated on the Metlod as hard as I possibly could while in astral form. It was a lot harder than I expected. I wasn't used to dealing with giant 'magic' devices. I had a hard enough time with manmade ones!

"Do you see it?" Max prodded.

"Not yet. It looks solid." I felt frustrated. "If you can see it, maybe you can push past it like I've been able to do with anti-matter."

Max shook his head. "I can only see it in flashes, not enough to see it fully. I'm not sure if what I'm seeing is real. We *are* in astral form. My mind could be playing tricks on me."

I didn't believe that. I wished I could see what Max was seeing.

I flipped on my dust-mode, but that simply made the whole room a black fog of swirling dead cells. Flipping back to 'normal' vision, I tried to mentally bring myself back to when Elisha helped me reverse the polarity of a magnet from a Clean-Up hover truck that was trying to capture us. She had said it was similar to what I could do with dust. I remembered completely losing my eyesight for a few minutes as a result. I didn't want to repeat that, but I had a feeling if I was going to see anything inside this Metlod, Elisha's method was the only way to do it.

"Wait, Alec is talking about you." Max broke my concentration.

I took a moment away from trying to break into the Metlod to listen in.

The Franklin clone/Alec spoke to Cronus, "Chelsan can't break into the Metlod. If my powers are useless against it, then so are hers."

Cronus grumbled, "She's more powerful than you. I've seen

it." He nodded disapprovingly toward Hades. "*He* can't even take over that girl's body. *That* should be impossible."

Hades rolled his eyes, but I could see he was embarrassed. "I'll get into that brain of hers. She's only human. No one can beat me when it comes to the power of death…"

Iapetus cut off Hades, "Well, that girl did. And my son is working with her."

Cronus snapped back, irritated, "Would you stop calling Kala Hicks your 'son?' She's our sister, though I hate to utter those words. But it's the truth. The sooner we stop underestimating her, the sooner we can grind her into the dirt."

Alec, in his creepy child form, appeared calm in front of the immature god storm. "From what I know of Kala Hicks, she shouldn't be an issue. As long as she doesn't consume any of you, she has limited power. And you provoked her as I instructed, yet she still didn't devour you, like I had said she wouldn't."

From the expression on his face, Cronus obviously didn't like it that a human had told him to do anything. "Yes, you're very smart," he said sarcastically. Then he sighed, "Kala is coming for us as we speak. She's going to take that Metlod whether she can break her human out of it or not."

I noticed how, except for Alec, none of the gods liked to refer to humans by their names. We were just *girl* or *human*. I also noticed that Alec had not yet used Turner to break the bond between Cronus and Hades, if that was even their plan. If it was, how did they expect Turner to break any bonds when he was stuck in a magical prison? It made no sense, until…

"The machine is almost ready," Alec said with confidence. "Once it's up and running, I can sedate Turner and place him in it. We'll find out everything we need to know."

238

Cronus perked up at this. "I can't wait to strap that nasty human into his own machine. Three hundred years in that thing! Being drained of my magic, of my being, of *everything*. I'll make sure I return the favor once we get what we need from him."

Cronus was livid, and I almost felt sorry for Gramps. A Titan and an Olympian were about to get their revenge-on. How many people had fantasized about exacting vengeance on Turner? Too many to count. But it looked like the gods were going to succeed.

I was about to grab Max and go. If we could plan the timing where Cronus released Turner from the Metlod in order to attach him to the brain machine, that would be the best time to attack. We wouldn't need to break into the Metlod.

But as I was about to fly away, I saw a flash of what Max had seen surrounding the Metlod.

Max had obviously had the same idea I had when he said, "We have to get back. We can attack when they take Turner out for the brain machine."

I turned to him, "Wait. I saw it, too. For an instant, like you said."

Max nodded, knowing I wanted to stay and try to see what I could accomplish.

Focusing back on the Metlod, I placed my mind in the same state I did when reversing the polarity of a magnet. It felt like I was going three levels deeper than dust-mode.

Blindness.

I took a deep breath so I wouldn't panic. It was difficult, but I had experienced this before, I could do it again. I reminded myself that I was blind because what I was seeing was so thick. When carefully examined, the blackness before me consisted of trillions of tiny black dots, moving and dancing everywhere around us.

Maneuvering my way through the mass of shifting black dots, I led Max closer to the Metlod. Max didn't argue or say a word at all, allowing me to keep my focus.

As we neared the Metlod, the tiny black dots grew more concentrated as if they had stuck together to form the Metlod itself.

Interesting.

It wasn't the worm-like structure of Fortski's anti-matter compound, but I could see why both Max and I got confused in the quick flashes we saw before I switched into super-crazy-dust-mode. Though the tiny dots were positioned tightly together, the way they moved around the pod had an almost slithering effect.

It was so thick.

I didn't know how I could penetrate it.

At least with the compound, there was enough space between 'worms' that I could move beyond them to use my powers. 'Thick tar' was the only way I could describe this.

I decided to let Max in on my insight. Maybe he could help me come up with an idea.

"I see what the Metlod is made of, but it's so thick. I don't know if I can use my powers beyond it." I could hear the frustration in my own voice.

I was still blind, so hearing Max close to me was comforting. "Can you move through it? I'm touching the Metlod now and it's solid for me. You try."

There was so much certainty in Max's voice. Taking my cue from that, I reached forward.

And my hand moved through the thick substance. I nearly yelped from excitement. "You're right. I can move through it!"

"This should just be a shell. Keep holding my hand but try going through. See if you can communicate with Turner." Max's voice was energized with excitement.

"I'll squeeze your hand if I need you to pull me back out."

With that, I stuck my head in first. It felt like a thick gel against my astral form, but I could move through it. Max was right, this thickness was only a six-inch wall. My face burst through the surface and I could suddenly see again.

And right before me was my grandfather. He was fully awake and feeling the walls, trying to find a way out. When his hands brushed through my head, he stopped.

Looking around frantically, he said, "Chelsan? Is that you?"

I had no idea if he'd be able to hear me, but I thought I'd try since we were in an unexplainable magic bubble anyway. "I'm here. Can you hear me?"

From the look on his face, I could tell he absolutely could not. But that didn't deter his faith that I was there. "I know you're here. I could feel your essence. But you obviously can't communicate with me." He patted the walls once more, trying to find me.

I decided to try one more thing. I took my free hand and touched his head. "Can you hear me now?"

Relief and exultation flooded his features. "Yes. Yes, I can hear you. How did you…? Never mind. Nothing you do should surprise me. Your astral form can enter, but can you pull me out?"

"I don't see how," I answered honestly.

"Tell me how your astral form entered." Turner was in sleuth mode.

"Remember when I reversed the polarity of the Clean-Up magnet? I made my vision go into that mode and the Metlod is a bunch of teeny tiny swirling dots clustered super close together like tar. I pushed my way through and… here I am." That sounded lame even to me.

But Turner was thrilled. "Fascinating." He thought for a moment. "Do you think you could move it? Like you did to get in here? Or what you did with the corpse's boiling blood for the plexiglass when you helped Elisha escape?"

I remembered melting the plexiglass: heating a corpse's blood up to boiling level so it could melt the glass.

This time I didn't have a corpse or my own physical body to try and move the particles. And yet... I *had* moved them to get inside. Maybe I could *only* move them in astral form. "I can try. Cronus and his crew are right outside. They'd kind of notice if the Metlod opened. *If* the Metlod opened. Let me go back to Kala and tell her we need her to break in."

"Go. Hurry."

I pulled out of the Metlod.

I adjusted my view to see normally once again.

I nearly gasped when I saw a dent in the Metlod. Luckily, it was on the side opposite the gods, but it still made me paranoid. I had definitely changed the surface of the Metlod which gave me slightly more confidence that I could do this.

"He's in there and I think I can get him out," I said to Max. "We need a distraction."

"Gods, demons and angels make the best distractions," Max smiled.

"Just what I was thinking." Keeping our hands held tight, we soared through the floors toward Kala.

Chapter Ten

247 Years Ago

KALA

Kala watched Talan playing with Terence in the park outside their house. This was their home, located outside of Seattle, Washington. Kala and Terence had over fifty residences around the world, for ease of completing her Atlas missions. Roberta had insisted that Kala had comfort no matter where she needed be to complete her tasks. The Turners had bought every single one of the homes. They probably would have bought more if Kala hadn't put her foot down. She had trouble remembering the addresses, there were so many, but Kala appreciated their generosity more than she could express. Roberta and Geoffrey loved Kala like their own; now they doted on Terence like he was their grandchild.

Talan and Kala had decided to make the Seattle home where they'd raise Terence. They figured they'd need a place where Terence could grow up that felt 'normal.' Not that his life was anywhere near normal. At ten-years-old Terence's powers had started to show. Kala knew her son would have some kind of special abilities, being that his grandmother was the goddess of all life and his parents were a demon and a human who devoured a god. Still, Kala had no idea what to expect.

Right now, Talan was throwing a Frisbee to Terence. Kala could tell Talan was being very careful to throw the toy directly toward Terence. He made the mistake of throwing it too high once and Terence had jumped fifty feet in the air to the shock of the other visitors of the park.

It struck Kala as funny watching a Grigori angel playing something so 'human' like Frisbee, but Terence loved it.

And Terence loved Talan.

He just didn't like Kala very much.

With a sigh, Kala interrupted their playtime.

"Terence! Come here for a minute. I need to talk to you," she shouted.

He was getting so big: Kala couldn't help but feel she was missing his entire childhood. Completing an Atlas mission every four days kept her on the move and traveling all over the world to all those empty houses the Turners bought for her. Not to mention the mental strain. It was difficult for Kala to switch it off, but she had to force herself to be present whenever she was with Terence. She knew she was already screwing him up enough as it was, she didn't need to add 'brooding mother' to a long list of grievances Terence would hold against her someday.

Terence raced over with the Frisbee in hand. His face was flushed from playing, but he gave her a rare smile. "Did you see how far I can throw? Talan went back half a mile before!"

He still called Talan by his name and not 'Dad.' Kala wasn't sure how she felt about that but didn't want to push the issue. Asmodeus was Terence's actual father and it was apparent that

Terence only wanted to call the demon 'Dad,' though Asmodeus rarely saw Terence or spent any time with him. She imagined it was too painful for the demon. Then again, maybe Asmodeus didn't care. Terence wasn't his first child. According to Talan, he was Asmodeus's seventy-fourth. So maybe Terence was just one of the many neglected offspring in Asmodeus's long immortal life.

"A half a mile? That's amazing!" Kala praised her son, though she wasn't surprised. One of the first gifts they discovered about Terence was his 'true aim,' something he inherited from Kala. He could hit any target, or apparently, throw a frisbee directly to another person at far distances. Kala had used this gift for her soldier duties as a sniper, back when she thought she was only human, but she didn't want that for Terence. She wanted to keep him far away from anything violent. It was bad enough being raised by a mom that had to do horrendous things every four days to keep the world spinning; she desperately didn't want Terence to follow in her footsteps and feel like he had to fight the fight. It would be difficult though seeing how every figure of authority in Terence's life was always in some kind of feud against evil. Not really evil, just annoying family that constantly tried to take over the world, but Olympians and Titans might as well be evil the way they disregarded and discarded human life. On the other side, the Grigori, the Turners, the Malaks, the demons, all fought to keep this planet spinning.

The gods either showed indifference or wanted an all-out battle to take control.

Either way, these were the people who surrounded Terence.

Feeling resigned, Kala knew that it was probably only a matter of time before Terence decided to join the fight. She hoped it wouldn't be against her, just to spite her for not being there for him like a real mom would.

Terence's smile faded quickly as he saw the duffel bag thrown over Kala's shoulder. "You're leaving?"

"You know I have to," Kala tried to make her voice sound as calming as possible.

"Why do you bother coming home? You don't stay long enough for anything anyway." Terence lashed out.

Talan stepped in. "Terence. There would be no home to live in and no park to play in if it wasn't for your mother. You owe her your gratitude."

"I'm sorry, Mother." Terence said the words, but his eyes showed defiance.

He was a boy who wanted his mom.

But soon he wouldn't want her at all. Kala could see the resentment growing inside Terence like a plague. There was nothing she could do about it, though. The missions had to be completed.

"I know you hate me, but hopefully someday you'll understand." Kala was never much for words, and she was reasonably sure those were the wrong ones to say, but she didn't know what else to do.

"He doesn't hate you, Kala," Talan interjected.

But Terence looked at her with anger. "How can I hate someone I barely know?"

With that, Terence ran off toward the house.

Talan's hand touched Kala's softly. "He doesn't mean it."

"Yes, he does," Kala answered with a solemn expression. "But there's nothing I can do about it."

Talan didn't argue. He didn't have to. There was no solution. No cure. No way out of being Atlas. Kala had to bide her time for the next two-hundred-fifty years until the girl from the prophecy would break the curse for good. Maybe then Kala could be a good mother to Terence.

Kala hoped it wouldn't be too late.

Present Time

Derek and Terence led us down a side staircase he was sure Cronus didn't know about. If the Titan *did* have knowledge of the stairwell, Kala didn't think Cronus cared one way or another. He didn't see them as a threat. At all. I could see it in Cronus's eyes. He knew I wouldn't consume him and therefore my one tiny shred of power I had over him was gone.

Over the last three hundred years I had had a lot of time to reflect on what I'd done to Atlas. I killed him. Swallowed him whole. All his thoughts and memories were alive inside of me though. Talan had performed his magic brain-reorganizing technique to keep me from blacking out every time I had an Atlas flashback, but I decided a long time ago I didn't want to experience devouring a god again. The integration process was extremely painful. I only survived because Gaia was my mother, though we didn't know that at the time. It meant I'd survive consuming any god, demon or angel, but *surviving* didn't mean living. From the depth of my soul, I knew if I ever did it again, I'd be lost forever.

It was more terrifying than I could describe. To lose your mind... Maybe it was because I had almost lost my mind countless times in the three hundred years as Atlas. Doing the unthinkable. Murdering innocents. Destroying lives. Creating chaos to bring peace. All things I had no control over. If I didn't do them, the world would end. So why would I invite insanity by my own will? I couldn't.

247

And Cronus knew it.

Our party was light four people, because Roberta decided to stay with Chelsan, Max and Eva. I didn't like that the only weapons I had against Hades were comatose and being nursed by the closest link I had to the God of Death. It also was very telling on how much Roberta loved Chelsan if she was willing to stay behind while we attempted a rescue of Turner. It was as if Roberta had her son, Franklin, back.

Focusing back on the mission, I walked behind Derek and Terence, Talan and Asmodeus right behind me. Isabelle, Dean and Harry took up the rear. I hated to admit it but, since they were the least effective, I wanted to give them a better chance to retreat if needed. Keeping them in back was the best way I knew how to do that.

I kept my eyes on Derek, not wanting to stare at Terence like I wanted to. I couldn't help it. He was my son. I loved him more than life itself and he hated my guts. Welcome to parenthood.

Terence, as usual, ignored me completely and kept his focus on Derek as well. I couldn't show Terence how much I loved the fact that he was so close to Derek. I was afraid if he knew how I felt he'd break ties with Derek just to spite me. My son was as stubborn as his mother, so this was an actual possibility.

Turning to Derek, Terence announced, "This is the floor. Turner and the Metlod are three doors down from this stairwell, headed north."

Derek turned to me, "Should we attack? Or wait for word from Chelsan?"

I shrugged. "I don't think we can wait. We don't know what her situation is. If Hades takes over her body, we'll just be sitting here in a stairwell for the next three hours."

"True. I can hit them with my UVC gun, but it won't kill them. After a while they'll build up a resistance to the pain. I've noticed you supernatural beings tend to do that." Derek placed his UVC bazooka in his hands, ready to fire.

I shook my head. "Your weapon has more of an effect on them then anything *we've* been able to do. Maybe if you burn them, we can get some shots in."

"And if we use controlling fire, maybe we can keep them subdued long enough to recapture them – or at least take the Metlod," Talan added.

I motioned Isabelle, Dean and Harry forward. "The Metlod will be up to you three. We'll keep the gods distracted while you guys carry it out."

Isabelle nodded and opened her mouth to say something, when she stumbled as if an invisible wind had pushed only her.

"It's me, Chelsan." The voice and body were Isabelle's, but the tone and words were Chelsan's.

I asked her quickly, "What did you find out?"

"I might have a way to free Turner, but I need you guys to distract everyone in the room," Chelsan said.

"Do you need Isabelle's body? Should we find a way for her to get to the Metlod first?" I didn't need to know the full details, but I did need to know some logistics.

Isabelle shook her head. "No. I'm pretty sure the only way I can get Turner out is through astral form. I can't explain it, and I'm not sure it'll work, but if I can't do it, I'll jump into Isabelle and tell you. And Cronus and Hades can't see me anymore in astral form. I think they're getting weaker. Or at least weaker than when they were first resurrected."

I nodded, processing what that might mean. "Good to know.

The power of the resurrection stones is fading back to their 'normal.' Let's not get too cocky, but maybe we can catch a break."

Talan interjected, looking at Isabelle/Chelsan. "We'll get the Metlod out of the room if you can't break it."

"Also," Chelsan added, "the Franklin clone is in there with them. He seems to be the one with the plans. I'd bet he's the one who told them to take Turner."

"Interesting, but not surprising," I said aloud. "We'll try and take him out, maybe capture him for information."

It was an extremely volatile plan that relied on a lot of things going our way, but it was all we had. Besides, I had been in worse situations and succeeded, so I wasn't about to give up now. I eyed Isabelle and gave a small salute. "Let's do it."

With that, Isabelle's body jerked slightly. She shook her head, and when her eyes met mine, I knew she was Isabelle again.

Terence opened the door, motioning to me, and we were off, heading down the hall and toward a fight.

Chelsan hadn't instilled too much confidence in me of her ability to release Turner from the Metlod, but I wanted to give her as much time as we could to let her try. Either way, that Metlod was coming with us.

About half-way to the door Derek took the lead, his UVC gun already propped on his shoulder.

Terence, next in line, directed his attention to Isabelle, Dean and Harry. "Dean, we need you to disappear and keep Isabelle and Harry guarded while they grab the Metlod." Dean immediately vanished from sight. All business, Terence revealed to his former team, "I have more than 'true aim' and astral projection bombing." He nodded to Asmodeus, "That's a demon and he's my father, so I have another *talent*."

Harry looked both annoyed and fascinated at the prospect of Terence having yet another power. Isabelle only looked pleased by the idea of having an additional weapon to help them.

Terence turned to me and asked, "Rhea?"

I nodded. Shape-shifting. It was the edge we needed. I was relieved Terence had decided to use his power himself. If I had suggested it, he never would have agreed.

To the shock of Harry and Isabelle (and quite possibly Dean, though I couldn't see him), Terence's body shifted before our eyes until the Titan Rhea stood before us, down to the ice blue eyes and long black hair.

Harry muttered, "It would have been nice to know about this particular... skill."

Terence/Rhea ignored Harry, then looked at Isabelle. "We good?" It was always strange how Terence's shape-shifting ability was all encompassing; even his voice was Rhea's.

Isabelle's face was still frozen in surprise, but she nodded shortly. "We're good."

Terence/Rhea focused back on me. Logically, I knew it was my son, but seeing Rhea stare back at me was disconcerting, to say the least. "Do we know Rhea's current whereabouts?"

I nodded. "She's at the Media Station with Theia. Owen and Antel are there to take them down, so Rhea may or may not join Cronus here, depending on how the fight is going."

"I'll teleport in and tell them I need help with Owen and Antel. I'll try and get as many of them as I can to come with me," Terence said.

Asmodeus asked, "Where are you going to teleport them to?"

Terence/Rhea answered, though I could see he still felt uncomfortable talking to his father in a civilized manner. Anger was much easier for Terence. "I was going to take them to a different part of the Compound. You have another place in mind?"

Asmodeus reached out and touched Terence/Rhea's arm before Terence could pull away. Asmodeus must have passed a location to our son telepathically because Terence actually smiled. "Wasn't that Zeus's prison in the 5th Level of Hell?"

"The very one," Asmodeus grinned back, genuinely loving that he was having a moment with Terence. "It won't hold them permanently, but it should keep them there for a few days, long enough for us to pull this off."

Terence/Rhea nodded appreciatively, then turned to Talan. "You adjust your hearing?"

Talan nodded. "I can hear everything."

"I'll try and get them out as quickly as possible." With that, I watched my son who looked like Rhea teleport out of the hallway.

Keeping my eyes on Talan, I waited with the others for our cue to bust in. Knowing my worry for Terence, Talan whispered what was happening, smiling at the apparent success of the ruse, "Terence has them riled up. Looks like Iapetus and Themis are going with him."

"We're still left with Hades, Cronus and Alec." Two Titans were better than four. I didn't know what the clone could do without any dead bodies, but I didn't want to count him out as a threat. Following Chelsan as closely as I had for the last eighteen years, people with her powers were not to be underestimated.

To Derek I said, "Get that hand cannon ready, we're going in blazing."

Derek positioned the bazooka, ready to go.

We all watched Talan for our cue.

"Done. Let's go." Talan touched the door and it exploded

inward, blasting its way inside the room.

Derek took the lead and beamed his UVC gun directly into Cronus's face. Cronus screamed in torment as the blue light engulfed his entire head.

Hades appeared downright befuddled, even though he had to be expecting an attack. I'd learned a lot about gods over my tenure as Atlas, and they were arrogant to the point of stupidity. I honestly think Hades thought we'd given up because of our last two battle failures. We needed to trap Cronus and Hades again. This time we'd make sure they couldn't escape.

I let purple fire loose from my fingertips, engulfing Hades in a cocoon of flames. Talan did the same with Cronus while the Titan was still reeling from Derek's UVC blast.

For a second, I thought we had them. It felt as if we had finally caught them off guard enough to chain them down once more. Maybe they were growing weaker faster than we thought they would.

But as before, both Cronus and Hades flew back the fire simultaneously, snuffing it out as if their bodies were made of wind. Without a doubt, they were connected. I still couldn't decide if their being connected was a good or bad thing for us, but it certainly made it easier for them to fight off an attack.

I noticed Alec had taken a few steps back, not wanting to participate in the battle. Seeing Alec in a child's body made it difficult to view him as a threat, but I had too much experience with I.Q. kids. They were sociopaths and wouldn't think twice about killing *anyone*. Maybe we could use that later on in terms of convincing him to turn against Cronus, but for now, I kept my side eye on the kid, not wanting any unpleasant surprises.

A wave of green fire from Cronus hit me before I could duck

out of the way. Every nerve in my body surged in anguish. Trillions of tiny explosions detonated in my veins, feeling as if my blood cells had all popped inside of me. I couldn't focus on anything. I tried to push back the pain, but it was so intense it was hard to think of anything else but the torment.

Asmodeus ran to my side and deflected the green fire, redirecting it to his own body. Instantly, he grunted from the pain, but seemed to be handling it better than I had. Or at least he wanted me to believe that.

Derek launched another UVC attack, but as he predicted, the gun's beams seemed to have less and less effect on either god.

Talan sent another round of purple fire toward Cronus and Hades both. They swatted it away like it was nothing, though it was enough to end the green fire attack on Asmodeus.

This was more than frustrating.

I could see Isabelle trying her best to use her powers, as she and Harry made their way to the Metlod. I could only assume Dean was with them.

There was nothing left to do.

We would die there or be seriously maimed if I didn't do something quick.

I was terrified, but we had no choice.

I had to consume them both.

Reaching out, I attached myself to both Cronus and Hades's auras.

And then… I saw it.

Confirmation.

The bond.

They were indeed connected with an intertwining chain of light. I yanked on that chain and drew it toward me.

Everything sounded as if we were in a giant tunnel. I could hear Cronus and Hades shrieking in terror. Talan and Asmodeus screamed at me to stop. But I had to. We couldn't win. I needed to do this.

The chain of light drew closer to me.

And the closer it came, the more I knew that this would be the end of me.

I'd lose myself if I absorbed their essences.

I was terrified.

I wished I could say good-bye to Terence.

One more breath and Cronus and Hades would become a part of me.

My eyes met Talan's, so full of anguish and horror.

I was about to lose myself forever.

As I was about to pull their light into my body…

The whole room stopped.

Frozen. As if someone had hit pause on a holo-TV. The magic fire from both sides froze in the air. No one moved. No one spoke. No one screamed.

Did Cronus stop time again?

No. Cronus and Hades were statues, their mouths and eyes opened wide in primal fear.

When I dropped my arm, I realized I was the only one of my team that was still mobile.

"You can let go of their lights now, Kala. They can't move. You don't have to consume them." It was Isabelle's voice.

I whirled around to see Isabelle standing next to Turner and a melted Metlod parked behind them. He was looking at Isabelle with a kind of awe and I knew in that moment that it was Chelsan who was speaking.

"What did you do?" I asked her.

"Isabelle doesn't know how to use her powers yet, but I do." Chelsan/Isabelle smiled. "I guess science wins. Even magic uses kinetic energy. I'm not sure how long I can hold *gods* though."

As if in answer to that question, Cronus and Hades teleported out of the room.

Chelsan/Isabelle frowned. "Talan was right: teleportation is their loop-hole. Check." Then she turned to me. "I'm going to release everyone except Alec and those fire beams. As soon as you guys secure Alec and clear the room I'm going back to my own body."

Clifton left first in a hurry like the rat he was. Talan, Asmodeus and Derek ducked under frozen fire beams as they exited the room as well.

Dean suddenly became visible again directly behind Alec, then snapped the clone's neck. Dean shrugged, "He'll live." Dean tossed Alec over his shoulder, moving toward the open door, then eyed Isabelle with disdain. "Now get out of Isabelle's body."

I followed Turner, Isabelle and Dean out of the room. As soon as we were clear, Isabelle stumbled forward slightly as Chelsan left her body. The frozen fire shook the hallway slightly as it hit the walls.

Isabelle's eyes were focused as she turned to face me. "I really wish Chelsan would show me how to use my powers like that."

I nodded. "Let's get back up to the infirmary."

Isabelle shook her head. "I'll go with Turner, Dean and Harry. You four need to go to the Media Station. That's where Cronus and Hades think our fake Rhea took the others, so they probably teleported there. Kala, the *real* Rhea is there. Terence will be in big trouble if they find out he can change into any one of them."

I couldn't believe I hadn't thought of that. I knew she was right, and I appreciated how even through the chaos of the last hour, Isabelle's thoughts were of her fellow soldier, my son.

Thinking of the possibilities made my skin crawl. "If Cronus shows up at the Media Station and sees the real Rhea there – and Iapetus and Themis missing – he might figure out we have a shape-shifter on our side. It wouldn't be that much of deduction to figure out that Terence is the culprit."

I knew what I needed to do to save my son. "I have to take Rhea down before she has a chance to tell Cronus the truth. He might still wonder where Iapetus and Themis are, but I'll worry about that later."

My eyes met Asmodeus's. He was thinking the same thing. Our son was in danger and we had to act fast.

It was Talan that spoke first, though. "Let's go now."

We all nodded in agreement. Motioning for the others to hold onto me, Derek, Asmodeus and Talan obliged. In a flash I teleported us all to the Media Station.

Immediately, I was pushed back by Owen as green fire almost exploded into my chest. Instead it hit with a jolting force on the wall behind me.

Derek fired his UVC gun into Rhea's back with no hesitation. He knew the stakes: protect Terence at all costs.

Rhea shrieked from the pain. She hadn't yet built a tolerance like Cronus and Hades had.

Cronus and Hades were there, though, engaged in battle with Antel and Rotoph. I guess Rotoph had been summoned to join the party.

Theia was crumpled in a corner, not moving. At least the good guys had so far managed to debilitate one of the Titans. Luckily, the battle was going full force, so it didn't appear as if Cronus had had time to confer with Rhea.

Fire of all colors raced across the room, slamming into walls, each party barely missing the other. I turned to Owen, "Has Cronus talked to Rhea at all? Think. It's important."

Owen could tell by my expression that my question was vital. He shook his head. "Cronus and Hades teleported in and started fighting when we took down Theia. Why? What happened?"

"Dad. We need to focus on Rhea, only Rhea. We can't let Cronus talk to her." I eyed him knowingly, hoping he'd fill in the dots.

Owen knew me better than anyone. "Terence?"

"Yeah," I responded. I watched as Owen's whole demeanor changed.

We were on the same page.

Rhea was the target.

I almost felt sorry for her when the might of two Grigori angels, the King of Demons, an immortal human and Gaia's daughter attacked from all sides.

Antel and Rotoph deduced our intention of a complete Rhea take-down and threw the force of their powers into Cronus and Hades to hold them back from defending Rhea.

Rhea barely had time to recover from the UVC bazooka when a concentrated blast of yellow fire surrounded the Titan's body. Yellow fire was used to destroy. A Titan could never die permanently, but they could be torn apart for centuries. No one had ever gone that far before, but the five of us were united in our common goal: protect Terence. If Cronus ever found out what Terence could do, he'd either kill him – or find a way to control Terence to use his powers to serve him. Neither choice was acceptable. So if it meant putting Rhea on ice for a few hundred years, so be it. I never liked her anyway.

Through the yellow flames, I could see Rhea's wide, desperate eyes. She screamed for Cronus to help her, but Antel and Rotoph were doing their job well. Cronus and Hades couldn't break through to save her.

With a giant POP Rhea's body broke into a million pieces and shattered to the ground.

I had never seen a god destroyed like that before. Talan once described it to me in great detail, having witnessed it himself only a handful of times, but nothing could prepare me for the suddenness and release of power. We had defeated a Titan.

Cronus roared in anger. "HOW DARE YOU!" His body was being plowed by purple fire at this point, but it was as if he felt nothing. "SHE WAS MY WIFE!"

"And technically our sister, but she needed to go down, Cronus. And so do you." I used my Gaia powers to make the ground shake. It was one of the powers I inherited from her and my favorite perk. I could see the jealously in Cronus's face. He hated the fact that I was more like our mother than any Titan or Olympian. And me, being me, I had to rub it in a little more. "At least I didn't consume her."

Cronus flinched through the purple fire. He was scared now. Afraid I'd try to consume him again.

I played on that. "Now, where were we before Chelsan rudely interrupted us at the Compound."

Hades was gone. Teleported away before I could utter another word. Cronus gave me once last glance, then teleported away as well.

And that was that.

We all stood there in the destroyed room surrounded by broken holo-monitors and holo-TVs fizzling in and out of picture surrounding us. Theia was still a crumpled mess in the corner but with one last glance at me, she teleported away.

All that was left were the tiny shards of Rhea that covered the floor like broken glass.

Rotoph was the first to walk over to the remains of Rhea. "This will only hold her down for a few years. She's strong. I can already feel her trying to rejoin her body."

"A few years? Damn," I voiced my disappointment. "I was hoping for a few hundred."

"Well, she's out of the picture for your current mission anyway," Derek added.

"And most importantly, Cronus has no idea Terence pretended to be Rhea," I sighed in relief. "With Iapetus and Themis trapped in the 5th Level of Hell for a few days, that's three Titans down."

"So we're facing nine now. That seems more doable." Derek grunted.

I couldn't tell if he was being sarcastic or not. Either way, their numbers were down. It was only a slight advantage, but still an advantage.

"How do we get word to Terence?" I asked Asmodeus. "He has human blood in him, the 5th won't be kind to him." I remembered the first time I had gone to the 5th Level of Hell. Talan had to infuse me with some of his Grigori magic so that I could breathe.

Owen tried to be delicate as he said, "He secured the Titans in the 5th. He's at the Compound with the others now. He contacted me moments ago."

I tried to hide my emotions, but Owen could see right through me. I didn't think I'd ever accept Terence not wanting to have anything to do with me. I hoped that things would change if Chelsan could finally break this curse. I vowed I'd make Terence my top priority after the Atlas curse was behind me. "Is he safe?"

Owen placed his hand on my shoulder, supportively. "He is. He said he's going to stay with his team until we need him."

His team: Isabelle and Dean. I shook my emotions from my thoughts and focused back on the mission. "What next? Is the Media Station secure?"

"Um… not yet." From behind a solid metal desk, Jason Keroff crawled into view. He stood up, straightening his clothes, gathering himself. I could see a slight shake in his hands. Watching gods fight in front of him wasn't something he could adjust to that easily.

Antel walked over to Jason. "What do you mean? Can't we access the proper channels here? We need you on the air to tell the humans about their dead world leaders being controlled by Hades and Cronus. If they start ordering them to do things…"

Jason sighed, frustrated. "Yeah, I know. I've been trying since we got here. I was even going to show the public some of your fire fighting to prove to them it's all real." Jason shook his head. "I can't access the port that lets me speak to… well, to basically everyone." Jason shrugged, "When I couldn't access that, I was hoping I could at least put up the necessary blocks to keep Cronus or Alec or whoever out of the system. I figured if I can't go on the air, then at least they won't be able to, either – but there's some kind of firewall keeping me from doing that too." His face was pale. "I've never seen anything like it. It's either supernatural or Alec-the-super-clone has figured out a way to bogart the media servers. Either way, it doesn't look good for our future."

Rotoph turned to Antel. "We need to get Ashliel in here. Maybe he can break through."

"He's with Elisha and Ryan examining the machines," I informed them.

"I'll pull Ashliel away until we can sort this out," Antel said.

"In the meantime, keep trying," I urged Jason.

He immediately went to work, typing at the only working holo-computer in the room. The battle had done a real number on the room.

A few minutes later, Antel arrived with not only Ashliel, but Elisha and Ryan as well.

Antel announced, "The boy found something in Turner's machines."

I didn't know how Ryan felt about being called 'the boy,' but from the intense expression on his face, I don't think he noticed.

Jason's eyes met Ryan's. "What is it, Ryan?"

Ryan joined Jason's side and typed a few commands into the holo-computer while explaining, "Elisha, Ashliel and I have been scouring Turner's brain machines, searching for anything that might tell us how Cronus and Hades escaped." He typed a few more commands, then stepped away. A holo-image of a glowing sphere rotated in front of them. "This is how."

Jason examined the bright yellow ball of light rotating in front of him. "What are we looking at?"

Ryan looked deeply troubled. "It's the I.Q. Collective, or at least a part of it."

"I thought they were destroyed when, you guys... well... you know... killed them all." Jason didn't try to word that delicately.

Ryan was used to Jason's insensitivity, though, and continued, "We did, but Alec had been the one keeping us all together before the I.Q. kids were transferred into the Franklin clones. We thought that the Franklin clone Alec inhabited was in control of its own body when we killed all the I.Q. kids and their clones, but I think he used that moment to take them all back inside of himself."

I stepped in at this point. "Wait a minute. Slower. What are you saying?"

Ryan gathered his thoughts, then said, "The day that we – Chelsan, me, Isabelle, Max and the Franklin clone, aka Alec were connected – we thought we had killed the I.Q. Collective and their respective bodies. But Alec was using us. Tricking us. When Chelsan used me and Alec to connect with all the I.Q. kids and the clones, Alec used the moment Chelsan killed the clones' bodies and took the I.Q. Collective's souls inside his brain."

Jason sat back, eyes wide. "So we're not just dealing with Alec, we're dealing with the whole I.Q. Collective?"

Elisha nodded, joining the conversation. "The most powerful minds in the world, all inside one completely immortal body."

Ashliel stared directly at me. "Their power is something I've never seen before. I think they freed Cronus and Hades to find a way to take over their bodies. The Titans are too arrogant to realize what they're up against."

"Is that possible? Can these I.Q. kids take over a god's body?" I asked incredulously.

Elisha shrugged. "I'd bet anything that they're going to try." She nodded toward the glowing holo-light. "Part of the Collective is guarding the computers, the brain machines, anything with a network. It's why we can't access the terminals, and it's also *how* they were able to wake Cronus and Hades."

"We have the clone in custody at the Compound. I'll telepathically tell Roberta about our discoveries," I offered.

Elisha nodded, "Thank you. It's better if it comes from you. Roberta has me blocked from her."

I concentrated and connected to Roberta, relaying the news. I didn't wait for a response. I knew I had to keep it brief. She didn't want me in her head, but Roberta also knew that she had to keep the lines open. If the team at the Compound needed me, Roberta would telepathically call me, or Chelsan would when she was up to it, or *if* she was ever up to it. Her condition still remained in limbo.

"Done," I announced.

Jason shook his head, visibly shaken by the news of the I.Q. Collective. "We have to warn the planet. We have to break through, if just for a few minutes."

Ashliel leaned next to Ryan and placed his hands on the holo-computer terminal. "I'm going to try and get you a window, get ready…"

Jason waited for his moment, hands on the computer, ready to speak. He knew he'd have to be quick.

As Ashliel closed his eyes for a deeper connection to the computer system, his body suddenly seized, then completely froze in place.

Jason stood up, taking his hands off the computer for fear of the same thing happening to him.

"What happened?" I hurried over to Ashliel's stiff body.

With a quick touch from Talan, Ashliel was released from whatever had trapped him in place, but Ashliel was bent over, panting from the attack.

Suddenly, all the working holo-monitors flipped on, despite their broken condition.

Cronus's face appeared on every single monitor as if a hundred of his heads were floating in the room around us.

"This can't be good," Asmodeus said under his breath.

I had to agree.

Using a supernatural force to take over the humans' source of news made me unnerved. Cronus hated humans. He wanted to the world to end so it could be reborn with Titans ruling the Earth once more. Little did he know that Alec, the one human he trusted was an entire army of the most demented psychopaths ever to exist on Earth, and they probably planned to hijack the Titans and most likely any god or demon they could possess, leaving Cronus for a helpless fool.

On the holo-monitors, Cronus laughed. "I address all humans on this planet. I am Cronus, King of the Titans." The holo-view zoomed out so that Cronus now stood in front of a line of men and women, with Hades at the end. "These are your world leaders."

Oh man.

"Every single one of them is dead and controlled by the *human* you revere as your hero." A floating holo of Turner rotated around Cronus's head.

Cronus spat out in disgust. "My son Hades is the ruler of the Dead and will not allow anyone in his domain!"

Hades waved his hand dramatically: the world leaders' bodies dropped to the ground, rotting instantly, until all that was left were bones and blood.

The camera view focused back on Cronus, until only his head was visible again. It felt like he was looking right at me when he said, "I am your god now."

Chapter Eleven

Two Months Ago

CHELSAN

"**A**re you nervous?" Nancy asked Chelsan as they walked down the long hallway leading to Elisha's prison.

"Does wanting to projectile vomit all over the floor count?" Chelsan kept practicing breathing exercises to calm herself, but nothing seemed to work. Her heart raced and her hands were clammy and wet from sweat.

Chelsan was seeing Elisha for the first time since...

...Since Chelsan gave Elisha back her soul.

Turner had warned Chelsan that Elisha was practically incoherent and that it was a waste of her time to visit, but Chelsan needed to see Elisha. Chelsan's action of connecting Elisha's soul back to her brain was the right thing to do, but she still felt guilty that by doing so Chelsan had rendered Elisha insane. Worthy trade, but it still stung.

Chelsan knew she should feel nothing but hatred and loathing for Elisha, but knowing that the girl hadn't been connected to her soul... it made Chelsan realize that this new Elisha wasn't the same person. This newly-souled woman had to deal with what she had done: killing thousands of innocent people. The punishment should fall on the disconnected-soul-Elisha, not this new version. Let the old version of Elisha feel every ounce of pain that she had inflicted on others so ruthlessly.

Not sure why she had come, Chelsan almost turned to Nancy to back out.

But Nancy gave her a look of encouragement and said, "You can do this. Hopefully, it'll make your nightmares stop finally."

The nightmares.

Chelsan couldn't sleep anymore without being tortured by seeing herself murder all of the Franklin clones. Her father. Hundreds of them. And Elisha's eyes... those purple eyes, so beautiful and so full of anguish... The images were seared into Chelsan's brain and she couldn't escape them in waking life or in sleep.

So she finally gave into Nancy's theory: see Elisha and confront the nightmare.

It wasn't a rock-solid theory, but at this point, Chelsan would try anything.

Chelsan nodded. "I just need a minute before we go in there."

Nancy nodded back and placed her arm over Chelsan's shoulders for comfort. "It's weird that there are no guards down here."

"Roberta knew they'd make me more nervous, so she sent them away." Chelsan sighed at her grandmother's obvious belief in her ability to take care of herself should danger arise.

Nancy reiterated Chelsan's thoughts, "Your grandma thinks you're the strongest person alive. Not that I disagree."

"I could take the guards with dust or something, but Elisha? I'm a little scared about confronting her. She knows way more about my powers than I do. Supposedly her powers aren't as strong as mine, but I wouldn't put it past her to figure out some way to even the playing field."

"But she's good now. She won't hurt you." Nancy almost sounded like she was trying to convince herself.

"Unless she blames me for everything." Chelsan took Nancy's arm from her shoulder and held both her hands. "Listen, maybe you should wait out here. I don't want her to hurt you."

Nancy shook her head. "No way. When it comes to my faith in you, I'm Roberta times a million. You won't let Elisha hurt me and I'm not leaving you alone with her, so forget it."

"Nancy…" Chelsan began.

But Nancy cut her off, "No. I'm coming in, so let's get in there and do this, okay?"

Chelsan knew there was no arguing with her best friend and, frankly, she didn't want to face Elisha alone. Chelsan hoped that Elisha couldn't use her powers to harm them in any way. Turner had assured Chelsan that Elisha's cell was a clean zone, which meant nothing dead inside, not even dust. There was nothing he could do about skin cells, however, and Chelsan had remembered drilling Elisha and Eva's dead skin cells deep within their skin…

The horrible things Chelsan had done…

She wondered sometimes if she was really a bad guy. Maybe she was more like her grandparents than she cared to acknowledge.

Walking a few doors down, they finally arrived at Elisha's cell. There was a keypad in front where Chelsan typed in the code, then placed her eye next to it for a retinal scan. Again, she didn't know how to feel about the fact that her grandparents trusted her so much that they were giving her access to pretty much everywhere in the building.

The door opened with a loud SHUNK and the girls stepped inside.

Plexiglass walls greeted them, and Chelsan was brought back to Elisha's I.Q. Farm prison where Elisha had tricked Chelsan into helping her escape. It was sadistic for her grandparents to choose the same prison, although it wasn't surprising.

Elisha was huddled in a ball in the corner of the square cell. She looked as if she hadn't showered since she arrived, her hair matted and skin grimy with sweat.

"I'm glad we can't smell through that." Nancy never could hold back her tongue, but Chelsan had to agree. Elisha probably smelled ripe from the looks of her.

At Nancy's voice, Elisha sprang out of the corner and jumped to the plexiglass wall, flattening her hands against its smooth surface and staring directly at Chelsan.

Chelsan and Nancy jumped back from the sudden and extreme creepiness of the situation, but after realizing that Elisha was truly locked in, they relaxed slightly.

"Are you God, coming to take my soul?" Elisha's voice was raw, as if she'd been crying or screaming.

Chelsan remembered that before Elisha was taken to the I.Q. Farm, she had lived in a Christian Coalition town where they didn't take Age-pro because they believed in God and wanted to go to Heaven or something when they died. Chelsan never paid much attention to religions. There were no such things as gods and other mythological creatures, only people like Elisha and Isabelle, where science and magic had gone wrong and created what they were.

Elisha had been taken at the age of seven, but she obviously

269

still had some of her religious beliefs ingrained in her head.

"Elisha, it's me, Chelsan." Chelsan's heart squeezed with a guilt she knew she shouldn't feel but couldn't control. This girl before them, who looked seventeen but was in her nineties, was broken.

A flicker of recognition in Elisha's wild eyes. "My savior and destroyer."

Nancy grumbled, "That's not ominous at all." But Nancy's mother-bear instincts kicked in as she said to Elisha accusingly, "Listen, you almost destroyed the world, and you tortured Chelsan until she almost died, not to mention beating Max *to death*, and killed thousands of other innocent people including your own twin freaking sister! Remember Beth?!" Nancy fumed.

What did that say about Chelsan? She never forgot, either, but she let things slide a lot more than her friends did. Having a civil conversation with her grandparents was something Chelsan knew Nancy could never do if their roles were reversed. Did that make Chelsan a monster? Was she more like Elisha than she was like Nancy?

It took a few moments for Elisha to respond, but once Nancy's words registered in her brain, she began to scream uncontrollably.

Chelsan yelled over Elisha's screams, "Elisha! Stop! You need to stop!"

When Elisha showed no sign of abating, Chelsan pounded on the plexiglass until Elisha regained her composure and went back to staring at Chelsan like she was both in awe and disgusted by her.

Then, in a flashing moment of sudden lucidity, Elisha lashed out, "What are you doing here?! Come to gloat?!"

Chelsan decided to come straight to the point, "I'm having nightmares... I thought seeing you..." Chelsan grabbed Nancy's arm and turned toward the door. "This was a mistake. Let's go."

Elisha slammed her hands against the plexiglass, eyes alight with fire and madness, making Chelsan turn to face her. "Not Hades himself could best the all-powerful Chelsan Derée! Believe me, I tried! I tried to match you! I tried to best you! Not even your father had an ounce of your power and he's the one who gave it to you! What are you, Chelsan! Are you a god? Are you Hades? Did you escape and find some way to jump inside this mortal girl's body?!"

Chelsan shook her head in response to hearing Elisha's ramblings. If Chelsan recalled rightly from Mr. Alaster's history class, the time when they covered mythology, Hades was the God of Death. It made sense that Elisha would compare her to a mythological god that had power over dead things. But the intensity with which Elisha was spouting her nonsense felt so *real* to Chelsan, as if Elisha truly believed what she was saying.

"I'm no god, Elisha. I'm just me." Chelsan had no defense.

Elisha laughed hysterically. "Yes. Those are the truest words you've ever spoken."

As Elisha kept laughing, Nancy tugged on Chelsan's sleeve. "I think we should go."

Chelsan nodded slowly, not sure why she had come in the first place. What had she expected? Peace? Closure? Now that she thought about it logically, how did she expect Elisha to quell her nightmares? If anything, today probably would create more bad dreams.

As Chelsan opened the door to leave, Elisha stopped laughing. In a voice small and broken she said, "No one can beat you, Chelsan. Not even the gods themselves. You saw inside me when you connected me back to my soul... but I saw you, too."

Chelsan turned, eyes meeting Elisha's.

271

Tears rolled down Elisha's face as she continued, "You don't know how much power you hold. You've only scratched the surface. I'm terrified of the day you tap into your gifts fully." Elisha began to sob.

Through choked tears Elisha finished, "The world will end that day, and you will become a god."

DAY THREE

Monday June 6, 2321

CHELSAN

It was a much easier trip for Max and me to return to the room holding our bodies. I knew it would take Isabelle and the others a bit longer, but at least they didn't have to fight their way back this time.

Helping Turner escape was weirdly easier than I thought it would be. It almost felt as if the Metlod *wanted* me to open it, as if I was connected to it somehow. Since Max and I had needed to keep our hands clasped together, I could only use one hand. Once my fingers tried to pry it open, the surface became malleable like clay. It was strange to have any physical sensation while in astral form, but I could feel the walls of the Metlod as if I were corporeal. The Metlod was supposed to block all magic, but when I'd started pulling the tiny particles apart it felt as if I was tearing through something solid, not something made from a spell. Magic still confused me. I knew my power was innate and maybe it was a type of magic, but it never felt that way to me. When I watched Roberta or Turner perform actual spells, that was magic. Or the bizarre fire pouring out of Kala and the other supernatural beings, that was magic. But me? What I did, felt like an extension of my own body. Maybe magic felt that way to the gods, angels and demons too, though. It made no sense whatsoever, but connecting to dead things and controlling them always felt *real* to me whereas magic seemed like an out-of-reach power I'd never truly understand. I'd seen it with my own eyes, but it was still some intangible thing to me.

So seeing the Metlod as a giant pod of tiny slithering dots made it seem more like an actual physical object, not something made entirely of magic. If I could see it in its most basic form, as a thick tar of squiggling worms, I could shape it into anything I wanted. And that was what I did.

Instead of passing through the Metlod, I pulled my hand down, smearing the walls until I created a hole. I knew Turner couldn't see my form, but he could see the hole. He smiled from ear-to-ear as I clawed at the Metlod's walls with my astral arm, until the entire top and middle of the pod were on the floor in a gooey mess. Turner crawled out of the Metlod like a baby chic breaking out of an egg.

I'd never forget when Turner's eyes focused on the battle that was happening in front of us. That was when he told me to take over Isabelle's body. He said Kala was in trouble and I needed to stop her from consuming Cronus and Hades. For a moment I had seen real concern, then it was replaced by his 'business' face. I knew that face well. He had used it a lot with me whenever he didn't want to *feel* anything.

But he had been right. Kala was in the process of sucking

in Cronus and Hades's lights. It had been terrifying. It was one thing for me to jump into a body and control a person's light; it was entirely another for Kala to pull the light out of the bodies themselves and swallow them whole.

I had to remind myself not to get on Kala's bad side.

Before jumping into Isabelle, Turner told me he knew how to keep Hades out of my head, but I had to hurry.

With that, I had jumped into Isabelle. I needed to stop all movement in the room to stop Kala. I hadn't exactly mastered Isabelle's powers yet, but I'd used them enough in the past to know what to do.

Kala's face had shown such relief. I had remembered our conversation about how she was terrified by the prospect of consuming another god or supernatural being. She was afraid of losing herself entirely.

I knew that feeling well.

The two times I had tapped into hundreds of people's lights. First, with the pregnant women at Havenville, then with the Franklin clones. Both times I was filled with so much power and light that I started to forget who I was. It had been as if my soul was breaking apart into a million pieces so that I could join with the hundreds of lights. It was a terrifying feeling. Even taking over one person like Isabelle, I still had to fight the sensation of power flooding through me, especially when using her powers.

I was grateful when Dean ordered me out of Isabelle. I hated that feeling.

I could only imagine how Kala felt after she'd consumed Atlas.

I turned to Max, floating next to me, holding my hand. "Shall we?"

Max nodded and we jumped back into our bodies, flying

through the thin layer of Hades's magic that still tried to take us over and through my dome that kept him out.

The vision of the canyon formed in front of us, then we landed next to Eva, who stood up when she saw us land. Her eyes lit up. "Did you find anything?" Eva glanced at the barrier above us. "Not a single hole or crack. That thing is strong."

"We got Turner out. He said he might have a way to keep Hades out for good," I told Eva.

Eva eyed the two of us. "I can tell you two had quite an adventure."

Max smiled. "Turner was in some magical barrier thing called a Metlod. It's supposed to be unbreakable, but this one..." Then he turned to me. "Chelsan, I know you won't believe me, but you seem a lot more powerful than any of the gods."

I dismissed that notion immediately. "Max, when I watched Kala pull in Cronus and Hades's souls... I could never do anything like that. I'm just a human."

Max shook his head, adamant. "You are more than human, Chelsan. We all are, to a certain degree, but you are something more."

Terence suddenly appeared in front of us.

I'd never been so happy to be interrupted in my life, though it was a bit of a surprise to see the guy... or demon... or god... or whatever Terence was.

Max wanted me to be more than I was. I had been lucky so far and that was all there was to it. I was no god. My brief encounter with Cronus and Hades (especially Hades) was enough proof of that for me! Hades could squash me like a bug if he wanted to. What could I do against *the* God of Death? I was just a minion or servant or whatever. I wasn't a god and that was all there was to it.

And–Hello! That flimsy dome over us was barely holding Hades back as it was. Which made me wonder...

"How did you get in here?" I asked Terence.

As far as I knew, we didn't have a strong connection. I thought that if anyone would be able to break through my defenses it would have been Roberta.

Terence viewed his surroundings with an interested expression. "Roberta opened a space for me to push my consciousness in. She was afraid if she had tried to come herself, your protection zone may break. The hole is sealed now, and Hades was too stupid to notice." He raised an eyebrow. "Which isn't all that surprising. From everything I've heard, he's not the smartest one of the bunch."

Terence was talking to me like we were friends. The guy had probably spoken two words since I met him, and he had seemed to be Team Harry all the way. Now, despite knowing Terence had been a double agent, that knowledge didn't help me much. I still barely knew him. And he was a freaking shapeshifter! (Which was kind of incredible.) More importantly, he was Kala and Asmodeus's son. That alone made Terence an asset. But it also made him dangerous.

I decided to take control of the conversation. "Turner said he had an idea of how we can keep Hades out of my head for good. Is that why you're here?"

"Right to the point. I like it." Terence peered up at the protective dome. "Yes. I'm here to make *that* permanent."

"How?" Eva stared at Terence with slight annoyance. Since Eva had been Elisha's right hand woman, she'd spent way more time with Terence than I ever had. Elisha had struck a deal with Clifton to start another world war and Terence was a part of that package. From the expressions on Eva and Terence's faces, they didn't like each other very much.

Terence ignored Eva and directed his attention to me. "We need a little privacy."

Waving his hand, Eva and Max popped out of existence. I immediately panicked. "What did you do? I was protecting them!"

"Calm down. You're still protecting them. That dome of yours encompasses all three of your brains." He nodded with respect. "Nice job, by the way." Then Terence gestured to where Max and Eva had been standing. "I placed their consciousnesses back in their own bodies *where they belong*. It'll help with what I'm about to do next." He shrugged. "They don't like me much anyway. I wasn't a barrel of laughs when I had dealings with Elisha. I'm afraid I treated Eva rather poorly. In my defense, she rivaled a demon's temperament."

I couldn't argue with that. Eva had enjoyed torturing me. Yeah. I definitively couldn't blame Terence for giving Eva the cold shoulder, especially knowing he was really on the 'good' side, whatever that meant. The line between good and evil was becoming more and more blurred every day. But Max?

"Max has always been on my side though," I said a little defensively. When working with Elisha, Max knew right from wrong. He had helped me and my gang try to take down Elisha and Elisha had repaid Max by *killing him*.

Terence raised his eyebrow in agreement. "Max is a good kid, I'll give you that, but he's highly protective of Eva and I don't want either of them to get in the way. What we're about to do takes an enormous amount of concentration."

I felt like gulping. Yup. Gulping felt like the right thing to do. "What are we going to do?"

Terence smiled and the guy almost looked normal. "I bet you could guess." He looked at me like we were best buds again. I was

279

finding it more contagious and less strange this time. "Come on. What have you come across lately that has an impenetrable surface that no magic can break through…?"

"A Metlod?" I asked with surprise. "Like around our brains? Like metal?"

Terence shook his head. "No. A Metlod is a magic barrier. It takes on its form by what it needs to protect. So if we succeed it'll be similar to what you already have now, just impenetrable."

"Won't that block out our powers?" I asked.

"Honestly? I have no idea. I'm only thinking of you right now, though. Max and Eva will most likely be out of commission if we do this. But you're different." Terence looked thoughtful. "Listen, if your powers came solely from spells or innate magic like a supernatural being, then, yes, the Metlod would probably block you from using them. But your father's original power was created by mutated science when the twins tried to kill everyone in their radius."

He paused, working it through. "But *you* got your powers from a spell your father performed to bring you back to life–and his powers transferred to you *magically*. So, it could go either way."

Shaking his head with awe, he continued, "All I know is you are the only human or otherwise to ever break through a Metlod." Terence smiled appreciatively. "Still don't know how you pulled that one off. I bet it'll drive Cronus mad when he finds out what you did. How a human can do something a god can't."

"It was difficult," I interjected, not liking where this was heading. I hated to admit it, but I was afraid of losing my powers. I would do it if it meant protecting the people that I love from… well… from *me*, but it scared me to be without any kind of defensive magic against *gods*.

"That's why I'm here. If you can tell me how you did it, maybe we can find a way for you to not only block Hades out for good, but also keep your arsenal in play. Let's see if we can make science win over magic. I know my *mother* would disagree but, knowing Turner like I do, I believe technology will be the only way to defeat the Titans," Terence said with a slight hint of disdain when he mentioned Kala.

I wasn't going to touch that with a ten-foot pole, so I focused on the Metlod. "It's hard to explain. Somehow, I managed to see the Metlod as super small dots, like dust or atoms, I guess. Once I was able to do that, I could move it around like a thick custard."

"Interesting." Terence responded with a frown. "If you did that inside your head, it would open a hole, allowing Hades to stroll right in. So the only way to access your powers, if they are indeed *magical*, and not scientific, would be to destroy the Metlod – which, at that point, what's the point?"

I sighed. "The point would be to keep me and two other necromancers out of Hades's reach. Look, I barely know what I'm capable of, but Hades won't have that problem no matter how *stupid* you think he is. I could do some damage, maybe to the people that I love, and I'll never be able to live with myself if I do anything to hurt them."

Terence stared at me with sympathy. "You're not a killer. And you're not much of a soldier, either. I mean that in a good way." He confided, "When your mom is a mission-based machine that used to be a Navy Seal… let's just say I was destined to be a fighter." He sighed and his face softened more. I was seeing a side to Terence that I wasn't sure many people had ever seen.

He continued, "I've been watching you since you were a little girl." Smiling, he clarified, "Not in a creepy way, but every supernatural being knows about the prophecy. Me especially, because it could mean that my mom could stop doing Atlas's job and finally rest. I know it seems like I hate my mother, but I don't. I love her more than she'll ever know, or at least, more than I'll ever *let* her know. It sucks that she always had to choose the mission over her own son. Yes, logically, I know I wouldn't exist if she didn't complete her missions—because the world would end as we know it. I guess I just wanted my mom and not a soldier every once in a while." Terence ran his fingers over the stubble on top of his head. "And whenever I'm around her, I can't seem to stop myself from lashing out. My head tells me to shut up, but my mouth doesn't listen. I can see how it hurts her, yet I do it anyway. So what kind of person does that make me?"

"A normal one. Most people in pain lash out at the people they love. I should introduce you to Jill. She couldn't stop her mouth from making my life a living hell, either. But it was only because she was miserable. She had no idea her father had been killed years ago to be Turner's puppet. Imagine trying to connect to an empty vessel you thought was alive?" I still shuddered thinking of how that must have felt for Jill.

Plus, I didn't know my boundaries with Terence.

But he had shared so much of himself, I wanted to say something to try and relate. I had no idea why Terence was sharing, but I appreciated it. I felt for the guy. I was lucky. My mom was always there for me no matter what. I knew in my heart of hearts Kala would die for Terence, but she didn't strike me as the kind of person who could express her emotions very well.

Terence had a far-off expression on his face. "At least when Jill found out her father was dead it gave a reason for his behavior. She could cope and get better, which I'm assuming she did since she's a part of your little gang now." Terence shook his head. "I tried for so many years to connect with my mother, but she always kept me at a distance, as if I was a nuisance, shoving me off on my grandparents, but let's face it, Owen and Linda are my *real* parents. And I consider Talan more of a father than my real father. But Talan looks at me like I'm the physical embodiment of my mom's betrayal of him." Terence laughed. "I can't win, so I'm a dick." Smiling, Terence looked at me with curious eyes. "Why am I confessing my soul to '*The one who knows death?*'"

I answered Terence's question. "It always helps to confess to a stranger." I looked around at the scenery. "Especially when you're inside that stranger's head, protected by a psychic bubble where no one can overhear you."

Terence laughed. "Very true." Then his tone turned thoughtful, "I know I'm a stranger to you, but I do feel like I know you. You're the girl who's going to give me my mother back, which basically makes you the most important person I'll ever meet."

Okay. Sweet. But stress intensified. I had no idea how I was going to break that curse. It was bad enough feeling the pressure from Kala, who had to do these horrendous acts every four days, but to see the hope in Terence's eyes at finally getting his mom back? It was soul-crushing. I wasn't sure what to say, so I nodded up to the bubble. "Should we try this Metlod thing?"

Terence rubbed his hands together to gain his focus. "Yes. Let's do this. Hold my hands." I placed my hands in his. Instantly I felt a surge of energy.

"Whoa…" I mumbled aloud.

Terence was amused at my reaction. "I have a lot more power than most supernatural beings. My mom's Atlas, my grandma is Gaia and my dad is the King of Demons." He closed his eyes to

283

concentrate. "Keep your bond strong with Max and Eva and let me create the Metlod."

That sounded like a good plan, considering I had no earthly clue about how to make a Metlod. With each second, a pulse of magic jolted through me and I found it hard to keep my focus. But I knew if I didn't, Max and Eva would be the first to succumb to Hades's rule, so I made myself think only of them and the protective shell that bound us at the moment.

Terence began speaking words I couldn't understand. I was used to this from my grandparents, but it always ranked high on the ominous factor. With each word, the pulses grew more and more powerful, almost jolting me to my knees. Terence's hands gripped tighter, keeping me up on my feet. I felt the intensity of his power wash through me. My brain still couldn't comprehend the enormity of connecting with a true supernatural being. It was such an all-encompassing force, I couldn't imagine the fact that these gods, demons and angels carried around that feeling all the time and were still able to function normally. Just five minutes of that kind of power and my head felt like exploding.

Terence stood strong, though. He was so different from the man I met a couple of months ago. I never thought much of him at all. To me he was all military. A human with an ability like mine and Isabelle's that gave him perfect aim. If I would have known how much mojo this guy was packing, I probably would have asked for his help. The fact that he never offered it wasn't lost on me either. Supernatural beings only seemed to do things if they thought it would serve themselves or their mission.

The pulses of energy sped up. I had to hold on tight at that point. It almost felt as if my body would fly off the cliff. (This time not on purpose!) Terence's words gained in volume, though he didn't seem to raise his voice; it came from deep inside of him. I knew my body wasn't standing on a real canyon edge, that I was just a projection of myself, but it didn't stop my hands from shaking.

At this point, though, Terence was in the depths of the Metlod spell. I could tell he hadn't noticed my discomfort or my terror.

I was way out of my league. A peon in the face of hundred-foot monsters. A tiny speck of light in a bolt of lightning. Basically, a human.

I tried to keep my mind steady, though feeling the strength of Terence's power was frightening beyond measure. There was no logic to it, especially since I had my own gifts, but I couldn't shake the fear. I felt helpless.

Then I saw it.

Black ooze formed in the center of the bubble above me as a small circle, then began to spread across the dome as if some giant entity was pouring tar over my protective barrier. The black substance surrounded the entire landscape, this time gushing down the sides and into the canyon, quickly filling it up.

I was going to drown if I stayed in here, though I knew that was impossible.

Terence stopped reciting the spell, and the pulses of energy stopped.

As the black ooze gathered at our feet and began to rise, he smiled at me. "Time to wake up."

***

Gasping for air, I jolted upright in the small bed I had been lying on. Next to me, Max and Eva did the same.

I was surrounded by a group of relieved faces. Though, if I was being honest, Harry and Dean seemed indifferent. Roberta and Isabelle were the most ecstatic at my regaining consciousness.

I tried to give them a smile of assurance, but my attention was drawn to Terence, who stood at the foot of my bed with a pleasant grin. "I don't feel Hades anymore. He's gone."

"What about your powers? You feel them?" Terence asked as if we were the only two in the room, just as it had been inside my head.

I tried to sense anything dead around me: dust, bugs, anything. Nothing.

"Unless this is a sealed floor for dust or dead things, then no. I can't see anything dead," I answered.

Terence held out a dead fly, his expression showing his sympathy for me. "This floor is as dusty as they come. Give it some time. You may just have to adjust to the Metlod."

My heart sank. I should be happy. I should be relieved. I both hated and loved my powers. It was because of my powers that I lost both my parents, but it was also because of my powers that I had saved the world. I hated to admit that I was crushed. I didn't know how to hide it from all the staring eyes. I distracted myself by turning to Max and Eva. "What about you guys? Anything?" I already knew the answer.

Max and Eva shook their heads in the negative.

Roberta tried to look supportive. "You'll figure out a way. Don't worry. You've overcome bigger odds than these. And if we need to, we'll take the Metlod out of the three of you."

"No!" I snapped, startling Roberta – and myself as well. "Sorry, but no. We can't risk Hades taking us over."

Max interjected, "Chelsan is right. The three of us are too dangerous in the hands of Hades."

I looked over at the corner of the room and I felt like my eyes were playing tricks on me. A man stood there quietly. I didn't recognize him. He wore a suit and tie and had pure white hair. I was about to ask who he was, thinking we may have added some kind of supernatural soldier to our ranks, when the man reached out and grabbed the unconscious form of the Franklin clone.

I stood up. "Hey!"

All heads turned to the man holding Alec's small body in his arms.

"Hyperion!" Terence yelled at the man.

If my Greek history was correct, I was relatively sure that Hyperion was another Titan.

Hyperion smiled at Terence. "Tell your mother, she's going to lose this time."

"You can tell me yourself, you little weasel," Kala was suddenly inside the small room. She brought ten other people with her as well, making it a tight fit for the already crowded space. All I saw were bodies in front of me. "You're not taking that clone," Kala said.

Hyperion went from *cocky-face* to *I'm-going-to-run-now-face* in less than a second. Talan was the closest to the Titan, reaching out to grab Alec from Hyperion's grasp. Hyperion leapt back a step, eluding his grasp and slamming up against a wall.

Before Talan could try again, Hyperion vanished from the room, taking Alec with him.

"We need that clone!" Elisha's voice rang shrill over the crowd. The room erupted in heated conversations that, frankly, I couldn't follow.

My heart sang for the possibility… If Elisha was here, then…

Suddenly the most wondrous thing I could possibly imagine

happened. Ryan was in front of me!

He pulled me in for the best hug I could ask for and when he finally pulled away Ryan kissed me gently, holding my face in his hands.

We ignored the noise of all the voices around us and took each other in, enjoying the moment while we could.

Finally, Ryan asked, "Are you okay? They told me what happened. Are you still fighting Hades's control?"

I shook my head. "Terence sealed the three of us with something called a Metlod. It's like a magic barrier that protects any magic from going in, or any magic from going out. Hades can't take control of us anymore." I could see from the expression on Ryan's face that he understood the implications of what that meant. He pulled me in for another embrace.

"When Kala imprisons these gods again, you'll get your powers back," Ryan said soothingly.

I looked up at his beautiful face. "I'm okay. Really. It might be nice to have a little break for a while."

"Take down the Metlod now." Kala's voice rang above the rest.

The room quieted down as Kala's orders reached our ears. I spoke up first, "We can't. Hades *will* take us over and then we'll be a liability."

"How are you going to break the curse if you're hog-tied by a magic suppresser?" Kala asked as if I was supposed to know what 'hog-tied' meant, but from her tone, I got the gist.

"How do you know that having the Metlod isn't the way I break the curse?" I countered. "The point is, you have no idea how I break the curse, and frankly, *I* have no idea how to break the curse and we have way more to worry about than your stupid curse." I was frustrated and obviously still upset at the Metlod rolling around in my head. Part of me wanted Kala to get her way and have Terence take the thing down, but I knew I was on the right side of things, so I stood my ground.

Kala's nostrils flared, which is more terrifying than you'd think. She steadied her voice as she spoke: "With my mission now impossible to complete thanks to Fortski's serum, the world *will* end if you don't break the curse. So I'd say it's high on the priority list." She whirled on Terence. "Now break the Metlod."

"No," Terence said.

"No?" Kala stared at her son intently.

"No," he answered back.

Kala looked like she was about to kill someone. Literally. Finally, Owen's hand touched his daughter's arm. "Kala, Chelsan is right. The prophecy isn't clear on whether or not she will use her powers to break the curse. Maybe the Metlod *is* what is needed."

"I think we should be worrying about what just happened, not about whatever this is," Elisha said, waving in Kala's direction. "The clone was taken by the Titans, which means if the Collective is going to make a grab for their bodies, it's going to be soon."

Wait. What?

"The Collective? As in: the I.Q. Collective?" I was pretty sure my eyes were saucers at this point.

Ryan nodded his head. "Alec must have sucked their souls into his body when you killed the Franklin clones, like he did to me when the I.Q. kids' bodies were killed the first time. Remember, I had the entire Collective in my brain… like Alec probably does now." Ryan held both my hands as he recalled, "Alec didn't say a thing after you stopped the Franklin army, then he disappeared. We didn't think about it, since Turner said he was tracking the clone down. But apparently, Alec used the Collective to take over Turner's network of computers and brain machines. They have all that power and now, we're pretty sure they want god suits for their psychopathic brains."

Kala apparently was back in mission mode as she added. "Cronus went on International holo-tv and let all the dead leaders rot in front of the world."

Jason chimed in. "Then he said he was 'our God.' It was a thing."

Ashliel added, "We should warn Zeus and the other Olympians. This I.Q. Collective will most certainly want their bodies as well. Does anyone know how many of them there are?"

Elisha answered, "Sixty-five."

Asmodeus raised his eyebrow in thought. "With all of Zeus's brood and the non-stop deity inbreeding, there are more than enough gods for this Collective to possess."

"Is this possible? How in the world would I.Q. kids take over the gods' bodies?" I felt like everyone was having way too much faith in Alec and his buzzing lights.

Elisha's purple eyes met mine. "If they could harness an enormous amount of energy, then, yes, they could use Turner's network to hijack the deities."

"Where would they get this energy?" I realized that I was asking questions that no one knew the answers to, but I didn't know what else to do. And now that I was chained down with the Metlod, I felt even more useless.

Elisha shook her head. "I don't know. It could be anything. But without access to Turner's network, we're completely blind."

Then a thought occurred to me. "If the lights that Alec is keeping in his brain are truly souls, couldn't I connect them to their consciences, like I did with Elisha? Maybe it'll make Alec stop completely."

It was Elisha who shot my idea down. "If the Collective were actually in their own bodies, then yes, you could probably do that, but Alec is in a clone and if the Collective is successful they'll be in the bodies of other beings. Their souls will never match. It'd be like putting a circle into a rectangle. They'll never be able to connect to a conscience again."

That was dire.

Before I had time to truly process the ramifications of what Elisha said, everyone in the room was suddenly choking. I looked around, searching for the cause, when a cloud full of dust went up my nostrils and down into my lungs. The more I coughed the worse it was. I couldn't gasp to breathe in air.

Only Elisha was immune, standing in the middle of the room with a glazed expression on her face. Then she began to laugh. When she spoke, it was her voice, but it was Hades who spoke through her. "At least I have control of one of you! A Metlod around your brains. Clever. But stupid. Now there's nothing you can do to stop me."

No one could escape the dust swirling around in our lungs. Hades's words stung. He was right. There was nothing I could do to stop him. The choking was unbearable. I immediately felt guilty for all the times I had inflicted this particular move on people, particularly on Jill. I felt myself starting to pass out from lack of air. All the humans dropped to the ground unconscious. The supernatural beings may have been susceptible to the cough, but they obviously didn't need to breathe to stay awake. But it also didn't look like they could hold their breath to stop the choking.

Hades spoke through Elisha once again, "This body was always jealous of this little trick of yours, human. I had to make a few tweaks in this girl's powers for her to be able to do it, but her memory was ripe with envy. In fact, there are a lot of things I can enable her to do. I'll have my own super-powered necromancer soon."

And to give Elisha all that power? Even with a soul I wasn't sure she'd be able to resist using it for her own gains. Hades was right: when Elisha was evil, she coveted my powers more than anything. She had tried to kill me in order to get the full use of what I could do. If Hades gave that to her and he controlled her...

We were in serious trouble.

Thank goodness the Metlod kept me protected from Hades, it would be much worse if my team had to confront Elisha and me both. Now I needed to take Elisha out of play *now* before Hades could make her indestructible.

So how was I going to do that without my powers?

Seeing Ryan's unconscious form next to me only fueled my anger, and watching Kala and the other beings hack away made me frustrated. Weren't they gods? Angels? Demons? Hades was besting them with choking on dust? Dust? Really? From what I'd heard they could hold their breath under water indefinitely, with no need of breathing, but Elisha/Hades must be swirling the dust around and pushing it in and out of their airways to make them cough like this.

Coughing myself, I couldn't get any air. I was going to join Ryan soon and – then what? Hades would win? He must know he couldn't make Kala and the others pass out, so why was he doing this to them? To annoy them? For his own entertainment? Yes. All of the above. It was sinking home that these Titans and Olympians were as immature as they come.

Less than a minute had gone by, but it felt like an eternity. Kala and Talan were already trying to move forward to reach Elisha. Asmodeus began to scream and choke at the same time. The scream was as vicious as before, though, despite the hacking. But Hades only intensified the amount of dust being pushed down the supernatural beings' throats, causing them to stop in their tracks once more.

Elisha laughed. I remembered that wicked laugh. I knew it was Hades, but it brought back the memory of her burying me alive, torturing me with acid as I hung from chains, killing thousands of innocent lives to build her dead army…

Something snapped in me.

And I could see the dust.

I could see the tiny black swirling holes.

Just as fast, they disappeared.

I had a flash of fear that I might have punctured a hole through the Metlod, but there was no sign of Hades so I figured I was okay. I knew that if there had beeen an opportunity to control me, Hades would have taken it instantly.

My powers were half science, half magic: I needed the science part to win.

I held onto that shred of hope. I could do it again. I had to.

Closing my eyes I concentrated harder than I ever had in my life.

I opened my eyes.

Black swirling dust filled the room like fog and still no feeling of Hades. I was tapping into my power without opening a hole in the Metlod.

I saw the swarms of tiny particles swirling around everyone's lungs. (Way more than I ever put in anyone's lungs by the way!) I reached out and tried to connect with the dust.

Almost.

It felt as if I were just touching the surface of the black dots.

I needed to wrap my power around each particle. The air was slipping away from me. I had to stay awake.

Instead of connecting with all the dust in everyone's lungs, I tried to connect with mine first.

Yes.

It was instant.

Maybe because it was inside me. I wasn't sure. I wasn't going to argue. I yanked the dust out of my lungs as quickly as I could.

Air poured into my lungs with delicious speed. It never felt so good to gulp oxygen down like candy. It was the most wondrous feeling and it gave me a rush of adrenaline. Though I knew I couldn't die, choking like that had made me feel like I would. Suddenly having life surge back through me gave me a strength I only tapped into in extreme situations.

And this was one of them.

My mind remembered the sensation of grabbing hold of the black swirling holes that had been in my lungs. I used that to connect to every single piece of dust inside everyone's lungs.

I yanked all of it out.

Used to battle, Kala recovered first. "Terence! Metlod! Now!"

Elisha's eyes went wide with fear, staring at me with disbelief. Through her voice, Hades croaked, "You *can't* use your power through a Metlod. That's not possible!"

I looked at her with as much confidence as I had in me, knowing that Hades was staring back. "My power was made with science, not magic. It's what you gods fear and it *will* defeat you." I was making that part up, but I had learned one lesson from my battles with Turner and Elisha: making them *believe* I was more powerful than I was always seemed to keep them off guard.

Terence grabbed Elisha's arm.

I could feel the dust swirl again, Hades trying to retake control. The dust was the only thing dead in the room, though it was impossible to know for sure since I didn't quite have my powers back.

But I had enough strength to keep the dust at bay.

Terence began chanting the spell that would create a Metlod in Elisha's brain. It was much less frightening as an observer rather than when being the receiver. Within seconds, Elisha dropped to her knees while Terence finished the incantation.

"It's done," Terence announced to the silent room.

Now that the dust was out of Ryan's lungs, I knelt down next to him and gently shook him awake. His eyes slowly opened, and he smiled when he saw me. "You okay?" I asked.

Ryan massaged his chest from the pain of such severe coughing. "I'll be fine. What about you?" He touched my cheek gently, his eyes full of worry.

I nodded. "I'm good." I helped him to his feet as the other humans began waking up on their own.

I turned to Jason first. "You alright?"

Jason cleared his throat, his voice rough as he said, "That was probably the most horrible thing I've ever experienced." He looked around. "What stopped Elisha? Are we going to have to keep her locked up again? Because I'm down with that."

Elisha stood up herself, visibly shaken. "I... I couldn't stop Hades."

Terence walked away from Elisha without an explanation. He didn't care that her soul was back in place. I was realizing more and more that Terence wasn't the forgiving type.

Eva answered Elisha though. "There was nothing you could do."

Elisha nodded. "I'm sorry." Then she turned to me. "How did you do it? How did you connect to the dust through the Metlod?"

All heads turned toward me.

Jason gave me an impressed nod. "*You* saved us? Through a magic barrier you're not supposed to be able to break through?" He looked at Kala and the other supernaturals proudly. "That's my girl."

I noticed Terence trying to hide a smile at that. We had bonded when he jumped in my head to create the Metlod. I didn't know where that bond would lead, but I was starting to feel the inklings of fondness for the guy. I figured if Isabelle trusted him, I should too.

"Before any more of you ask me how I did it, I have no idea," I said.

Roberta looked at me with the reverent pride that always made me squirm. "I knew you'd be able to gain your powers back."

"Whoa. I don't have my powers back." I wanted to stop that train before it left the station. "I don't know what I have. I was barely able to connect to that dust. I did it out of panic. I'm not sure I can do it again." I pointed to a dead fly on the ground. "Like that fly? I can't see its black hole." I concentrated on the fly. After a few seconds I saw glimpses of the black swirling hole. "If I focus hard enough, I can see it, but it takes a lot of concentration."

Turner shrugged. "It's a start, anyway. And you did it without opening a hole in the Metlod for Hades to jump in. Now we *know* there's the possibility to use your powers while keeping the Metlod intact."

Kala turned to Eva and Max. "What about you two?

Anything?"

Both shook their heads.

Max added, "We'll keep trying as well. Now that we know Chelsan was able to use her powers through the Metlod, maybe we can too."

Kala took control of the room once more, turning to Derek. "Let's get everything we can from your lab, anything you think might work against a Titan." Then she focused on Terence. "I know you're not going to like this, but you and I have to tell Zeus about the I.Q. Collective. The other Olympians still see Zeus as the god in charge, so if he listens, they'll all listen. And if Alec found a way to transfer their consciousnesses into gods, Zeus and the others will be in trouble."

Terence said flatly, "Zeus wants nothing to do with you."

Kala didn't seem perturbed. "Which is why I want you to come with me. He likes you more than me and maybe he'll listen to you. We have to warn him and the others."

Asmodeus interjected, "What if you're wrong and Zeus decides he wants to try and end Terence…"

Kala cut him off. "He won't. But either way, Terence has got this. I trust his abilities over Zeus's any day."

Asmodeus didn't cave. "I agree, but that doesn't mean he can't be hurt by an Olympian."

Terence held his mother's gaze a moment longer before glancing at Talan. "Nothing to say?"

Talan was trying to give Terence a look of support, but it came out more as a forced smile. "You should do whatever you're comfortable with."

I could tell Terence didn't like that answer. I could also tell that Asmodeus didn't like that he had been ignored in Terence's decision-making process. But the demon didn't say a word.

Finally, Owen placed a hand on Terence's shoulder. "You can do this, but just remember, Zeus might be your family, but he's not to be trusted. Be careful. Warn him, then leave."

Terence shrugged at Kala. "Why are you coming? I can go by myself. Zeus won't listen to a word you have to say."

"Zeus hates me, but he'll listen." Kala didn't offer any other explanation.

"So what? We're supposed to sit here and wait for you two to come back?" Asmodeus did not appear pleased.

"Not here," Turner interjected. "We'll go back to the L.A. headquarters."

It seemed like we were all about to do the whole teleportation thing again. I was just relieved Kala hadn't wanted me to come with them to see Zeus. I wasn't sure how many gods my brain could comprehend at this point.

That was when I sensed it.

"Um, guys?" I said to the others – while looking at Elisha. If any other necromancer was strong enough to use their powers through the Metlod it would be her. "Do you sense that?"

Elisha tilted her head, concentrating. "I don't feel or see anything."

Kala asked, "What is it?"

"I'm not sure," I confessed. "But I…" I closed my eyes to make sure I wasn't imagining it. When I did, the image grew stronger. "Uh, oh."

"What?!" Asmodeus rolled his eyes with annoyance. "*Humans* and their lack of communication skills."

"*Demons* and their lack of patience," Jason mumbled in retaliation. (I realized his mumbling was because he was probably afraid of being burned to a crisp for talking back to the King of Demons.)

Asmodeus let it slide. He shrugged as if he agreed with that statement.

I decided to continue before Asmodeus changed his mind. "It's a bit fuzzy since I don't have full use of my powers, but a few miles north from here I can see thousands of black swirling holes in the ground."

"A graveyard?" Ryan asked.

"These bodies are deep," I explained. "Way deeper than six feet. Like three or four miles deep. They're on the edge of my sensor radius."

All eyes turned to Turner, but he shook his head. "No. I didn't bury thousands of people three miles into the ground. And the Compound ends a mile north from here so I'm not *storing* dead bodies near here, either." He almost appeared offended at the silent accusation. "Besides, I haven't stepped foot in this place for years," he waved in Clifton's direction. "Harry's the one who uses this area, why don't you ask him?"

Ryan stated, "Because until a couple months ago, Clifton had no idea dead bodies could be controlled by a necromancer, and you've had him locked up the entire two months."

Turner didn't respond right away. Finally, he threw up his hands. "It's not me. I don't know why there are bodies three miles under."

I brought everyone's attention back to me. "Um, those black holes are moving, super slowly, but they are moving."

Talan asked gently. "Do you have enough use of your power to control them?"

I concentrated on the dead bodies. It was a strange sensation:

seeing the black holes, but not being able to connect to them. After a moment or two of trying, I shook my head. "I'm sorry. I can only see them." I had never felt so defeated in my life. As much as I thought people's praise of me was completely overblown, I never realized how much I appreciated it. And now I missed it.

Ryan's hand wrapped around mine and he kissed the top of my head. From the look in his eyes, I could tell he knew I felt helpless.

Kala was all business, though. "Maybe you can control them if you're right above them. We'll take a couple of hover-jeeps over to where the bodies are buried. I don't want to teleport if we don't know the area."

Derek took control after that. "I'll take us up. Follow me."

After what felt like miles of walking, we finally reached the surface.

It was still morning. A fresh cool breeze was circulating, a welcome sensation after being cooped up in an underground complex. The landscape wasn't what I imagined it would be. An abandoned warehouse was a few hundred feet away, but everything else was dirt and shrubs. A few outcroppings of trees smattered the landscape. Otherwise, we might as well have been in a desert.

Derek headed towards the dilapidated warehouse. "The hover-jeeps are in there."

Clifton seemed perturbed. "I thought those had been abandoned and were non-functional."

Derek had no love for Clifton, I could tell by the way he barely acknowledged his existence. "I let you believe what I wanted you to believe."

Clifton didn't argue. From the expression on his face, though, it was clear that he didn't care much for Derek either. I knew Kala must have left the squad because she had turned into Atlas, but it made me curious as to why Derek had to leave. Was it loyalty to Kala? Or did Clifton do something to Derek? I'd probably never know. Soldiers didn't like to talk about themselves.

Walking inside the warehouse I could see why Clifton assumed the holo-jeeps had been abandoned. There were five of them and they looked like piles of junk covered with dirty sheets in the far corner of the empty building. When Derek pulled off the first cover, though, the damage wasn't as bad as it looked from a distance. The jeeps were beat-up and dingy, but otherwise seemed like they were in working order.

Piling into four of the five jeeps, our eclectic entourage took to the air. Being in the lead jeep, I sat next to Derek and gave him directions as we all flew low to the ground.

Being only a few miles away, we arrived at the spot in a couple of minutes. I motioned for Derek to stop the hover-jeep.

Stepping out of the vehicle, the ground was hard and cracked by the sun. A few bushes were scattered around the area, but their leaves were brown and, as I could see from the black swirling holes, very dead. At least I could now *see* dead things without concentrating, even if I could only barely control them. That was strangely comforting. And there were a lot of dead things scattered across the ground. Mainly bugs and vegetation, but the bodies deep underground overwhelmed my vision.

The bodies were below, thousands of them, inching their way up to the surface. At this rate, though, it would take them hours to get here. If Hades was controlling them, he was taking his time about it. It could only be Hades, but a tiny part of me suspected Elisha. I mean, maybe that was why the corpses were moving so slow because she was fighting through the Metlod. I trusted Max and, though I didn't trust Eva, I knew she wasn't powerful enough

301

to do something like this *before* she had the Metlod, so I was reasonably sure it wasn't her either.

But how could I test Elisha without her being suspicious?

My mind was pulled away from Elisha when the corpses suddenly disappeared.

"They just went away," I declared.

"Maybe it's the Metlod blocking you from seeing the dead again?" Owen suggested.

I shook my head. "There are thousands of dead things all around us and I still see them. It's just the bodies that disappeared."

Owen took the lead at this point, walking to my side and talking in a calm, soothing voice. "Let's see if you can connect to any of the dead things around you. Try to connect to what was easiest for you before the Metlod." I could see why the others looked up to him. He had a fatherly way about him even if you weren't his kid. He reminded me of Mr. Alaster: patient and happy to help a student learn.

"It was always easiest for me to connect to plants. I kept my mother's garden 'alive' for years without her knowing it," I admitted.

Owen nodded and we walked over to a dead bush. "Let's try this little guy then."

Unlike the other bushes, it didn't have brown leaves attached to its body; it was all black, cracked, empty branches.

I focused all of my attention on the bush. I tried to remember what it felt like to connect to the dust through the Metlod, but this was a much larger scale.

Nothing.

I was so frustrated inside I wanted to scream, but I knew that would worry Ryan, so I held myself in check.

It felt as if Owen and I were on an island all to ourselves, our backs to the large ragtag group of super beings and humans.

Owen seemed to sense my frustration at not being able to control the plant, placing a comforting hand on my shoulder. "Don't push too hard. Stay relaxed and think only of the bush. Have you ever mediated before?"

I shook my head. I had always wanted to, but never quite got around to it.

"I think you have, you probably didn't realize it. Think about when you've had to use your powers to a greater scale, like you did when connecting with the twins or when you connect to Isabelle and her light. It takes a lot of focus, right?"

I nodded in agreement.

Owen continued, "That's a form of mediation. It's second nature to you so your brain doesn't know how to get those results while the Metlod is in place. You're going to have to teach it a whole new system. A new way that doesn't involve magic or puncture a hole in the Metlod for Hades to have access to. Your power to control dead things comes from an accumulation of science experiments. I don't know if you know this, but the twins got their powers because of drug testing on their mothers. It's how Isabelle and Dean got their powers as well. The only piece of magic that's attached to your powers is the way in which you received them: the spell your father used to bring you back to life that transferred his powers to you."

I did know all that, but for some reason the way Owen said it made me want to listen to him for hours. He could tell me my whole life story as if I'd never heard it and I'd enjoy myself.

Owen stopped and took a beat. "I'm not sure if you'll have full use of your powers, but most of them should still be intact." He smiled at me. "You're starting from scratch. You didn't connect and control the first dead thing you saw as a child, did you?"

I remembered Larry the goldfish: my first swirling black hole that I ever saw. I didn't do anything but stare at him. It was years later when Bruce was beating my mom and me that I connected to the black widow spider that ultimately I made kill him.

I answered Owen's question, "No. I didn't connect to anything dead for a couple of years. I didn't know I could. I just saw black swirling holes everywhere."

"Like now?" Owen looked at me knowingly.

He was right. It was like the beginning when I only saw dead things but didn't know I could control them. I was able to connect to the dust without busting a hole in the Metlod, so I should be able to connect to anything. It would take practice. I would need to re-learn how I used my powers.

But my fears overwhelmed me. "I'm afraid I won't be able to learn how in time with the Metlod there. And what if I rip it open by accident."

"What you accomplished with the dust was nothing short of a miracle. And I'm an angel: I can say that. You didn't open a hole then, so there's no reason to believe you will now." He smiled warmly at me. "That was a life or death situation and your brain simply reacted, like it did with the black widow spider, when you defended your mother against Bruce."

I noticed he worded it in a way that refrained from calling me a killer, which was untrue, I had killed Bruce that day – but I appreciated Owen's kindness.

Owen continued, "Try to hold onto the exact sensations you feel when connecting to the dust."

I nodded. An actual angel was standing next to me, helping me regain my powers. I knew Roberta was probably chomping at the bit. Normally, she'd be the one to help me, but I was glad it was Owen and not Roberta. It was nice having a genuinely decent teacher with zero baggage help me out instead of a grandmother with questionable motives.

I turned back to the dead bush and took a deep breath. Calm. Focus. Remember connecting to the dust.

I could see it.

A path in front of me.

Owen had been right, it was very different from how I connected to the dead pre-Metlod, but the path *was* there. I could see it. There was a blurry wall in front of each hole, almost like the compound Turner used to inject into his dead lackeys to keep me from taking them over. But this was stronger, thicker, somehow more 'real' (though I knew that didn't make any sense). I needed to break through it with the Metlod intact.

It was only a stupid bush, but it felt like climbing Mount Everest at this point!

The path was clear, though, so I just had to get to the black hole. I needed to reach it with my mind. Push past the blurred shell that kept me from my power.

It almost felt like it had felt when I was smearing the walls of the Metlod. Instead of slicing open a hole with my hands, though, now I let my mind move through the wall as if it was made of water instead of tar. Liquid, unbreakable, still intact, no tears, no holes. Because I realized that what my brain chose to see as a blurry shield around dead things was, in fact, the Metlod itself.

And… I was through.

Unlike the compound that shattered when I busted through it, this time, the shield was still intact around the black swirling hole. I was simply through to the other side of it.

Once inside the bubble, I connected to the bush as easily as I could before the Metlod.

Instantly, bright, fluorescent green leaves sprang out of the branches of the shrub. Within seconds we stood before a thick-leaved bush that had probably never looked this good in its entire existence.

"Nice," I heard Asmodeus say under his breath from behind me. I had impressed the King of Demons.

Owen's hand squeezed my shoulder and when I gazed up at him his eyes sparkled with pride. I never had a real father growing up, but I always imagined that this would have been the way my own father would have looked at me. Owen would never know how much I appreciated that moment.

The dead bodies suddenly reappeared, slightly closer than before. "I can see the bodies again. Let me try to connect to them now that I know how."

I didn't wait for permission, but no one said a word to stop me, either. I concentrated on the corpses. I saw the Metlod bubble around each body and slid through the surface of each shield.

So far, so good.

I then connected to each black hole.

"That's weird," I said aloud.

"What are you seeing?" Owen asked.

"I'm connected to the corpses, but I can't control them. It's almost like they're not there. It must be the Metlod." I couldn't think of any other explanation. I was fully connected to the bodies' black holes, but it felt as if their limbs belonged to themselves. As if they were still alive.

Owen asked gently, "May I use my powers to connect to you. I need to see what you see."

I nodded my approval. It would help to have another set of eyes.

Owen kept his hand on my shoulder, and I could feel a warmth spread down my arm.

Without warning, the bodies popped out of existence again.

"They're gone again." I felt like an idiot at this point. Owen must think that I was a liar. "I don't know what's happening. It's like they're going somewhere else, then coming back here. I swear I didn't make it up."

I looked up at Owen and his face was white. Turing to Kala he said, "Hades is opening the Underworld."

Um, excuse me?

Kala focused on Owen. "Are you sure?"

"Positive. I saw the corpses shift out of our dimension." Owen addressed the awaiting group. Owen spoke to Antel, "You and Talan need to go to the Levels of Hell. I sensed a breach there, too. Hades has more than Titans working on this. I fear the Olympians may have switched sides." To Kala and Terence he said, "You two still need to go to Zeus – but Terence, please, shape-shift and go as another Olympian, not yourself. If the Olympians truly have switched sides, they'll attack you as soon as you arrive. Kala, you need to stay hidden. Do not let any of the Olympians see you unless you're sure you can talk to them. I hope I'm wrong, but I don't think Cronus can pull this off without the Olympians to help."

Elisha pushed forward so she could be heard. "This is it. This is the kind of power that Alec needs to send the Collective into the gods' bodies. He probably convinced them that this would give Cronus and the others ultimate power, but he's tricking them into becoming god puppets for the Collective. Alec will use the brain machines to connect them all. The gods will be helpless to prevent it."

I knew she was right.

And, apparently, so did everyone else.

Kala gave one last hug to Owen, then turned to Terence. "Let's go."

Like a flash, Kala and Terence were gone, off to see Zeus.

Chapter Twelve

152 Years Ago

KALA

Kala looked out over the ocean and felt a strange kind of peace. After completing her Atlas mission, she had teleported to one of her favorite places on Earth: the Giant's Causeway in Ireland, one of the few places where Kala could go to forget temporarily who she was and what she had to do. She stood on one of the many jutting rocks that were crammed together to look like a platform of mismatched rectangular-shaped pedestals. She had brought Terence here once as a child and he had said that it looked like a bunch of stairs leading to everywhere and nowhere. It was a sweet sentiment at the time. Now, as Kala reflected on her life, it felt more true than a simple child's observation.

Terence was over a hundred now and barely spoke to Kala anymore. He made a point of spending plenty of time with everyone close to Kala, but not with her directly. His form of punishment for neglecting him as a child. Kala had tried to be a good mother, but it wasn't in the cards. Being Atlas prevented her from ever truly being present with Terence.

Her son had now been working undercover for Owen and Talan for decades. Terence considered his crew more of a family than she was.

Kala couldn't blame him. She had similar feelings toward her own mother, Gaia. Abandoned as a baby in a dumpster, forced to live in foster care until she was a teenager, then as soon as Terence was born… gone. Took off like she always did.

Kala hadn't heard from her since.

"Thinking of grandmother?"

Turning at the familiar voice, Kala embraced Poseidon tightly. He was the only god who gave a damn about her. He was also the only one that didn't act like a spoiled, petty child. He had helped Kala through the years with her missions, but also with the feelings of betrayal she felt toward Gaia.

Gaia was Poseidon's grandmother. He well knew the bite of her abandonment.

Kala pulled away and the two of them stood on a rock pedestal of their own, staring out at the ocean instead of each other.

"I thought I was different," Kala admitted. "I honestly thought she loved me."

"She does in her own way, but grandmother never stays around for anyone. Not even ones she loves," Poseidon answered over the roar of the waves. He paused for a moment then replied sadly, "We all thought we were different. It's how she makes us feel special."

The words hurt more deeply than Kala would have imagined. She had thought she was numb to her feelings of rejection but hearing that she was no different from any of Gaia's other kids or grandkids stung. It wasn't that Kala felt she was better than any of them, but Gaia had acted so differently with her. She had promised

Kala that she'd never leave her again.

"I don't know why I'm thinking about this now." Kala was used to shutting down her emotions, so it was always a shock when they bubbled to the surface.

Poseidon lightly touched Kala's arm to bring her around to face him. When their eyes met, he confessed, "You're thinking of her because it probably means she's thinking of you. It's all any of us have of her and we've learned to appreciate those moments."

"So, when I'm thinking of dear old Mom, I should feel good about it because it means she's thinking of me? Screw that. She's not worth it," Kala said with a twinge of hate in her voice. And why shouldn't she hate her mother? Gaia gave her fifty years of love and acceptance, then left her...again.

Fifty years.

Kala hadn't fully appreciated those decades. She had fallen into a deep hole of despair during that time. So much so, she had almost let the world destroy itself.

And Gaia was the embodiment of the planet. Mother Earth herself.

Maybe that was why Gaia had decided to leave.

Because Kala had almost destroyed her own mother by letting the world burn.

Only becoming pregnant with Terence had saved Kala, had saved the Earth, had saved Gaia.

It made a strange kind of sense that Gaia would leave right after Terence was born.

Poseidon interrupted her thoughts, "It's no use trying to figure out grandmother's motives, Kala. This has been Gaia's way since the dawn of time. You're lucky you had the time you did."

Slowly, Kala nodded.

Poseidon stared out at the ocean again and Kala followed his gaze. "It's beautiful, isn't it?" he said.

"I know Zeus and the rest of you hate Geoffrey Turner, but he's the reason the oceans are clean again." Kala could never get the god-side of her family to see all the good the Turners had done for the planet. In fact, almost all the Olympians had completely turned against the Grigori and the humans, as if Cronus was influencing them from the basement of Turner's Headquarters.

"I know you care for your humans, Kala," was Poseidon's answer.

"I'm part human, too, Poseidon."

"Yes," he paused as if struggling with that thought, then said, "but you're more god than human now, Kala Hicks."

Though it was a true statement, it still bothered Kala to hear. Instead of arguing, Kala decided to change the subject. "Why did you come to me, Poseidon?"

"I simply wanted to check in on my aunt. I missed you," Poseidon responded honestly.

It filled Kala with a calming happiness. Poseidon was a true friend. She had never thought she'd grow close to any of the Olympians or Titans. But Poseidon had been kind from the start, and he was strong enough that the others didn't judge him for his relationship with Kala.

"I missed you, too," Kala answered warmly.

"Do you know your next mission yet?" Poseidon asked gently.

Kala shook her head. "I'm going to wait a couple of days. I want to see Terence."

"Are you sure that's a good idea?" Poseidon proceeded carefully, knowing the subject was sensitive.

Kala looked up at the ocean god and there was determination

in her voice. "I'll never be like Gaia, Poseidon. My son may hate me, but I won't abandon him even if he begs me to."

Poseidon nodded his head as if that decided the matter. "He's in Gibraltar."

Of course Poseidon knew where her son was located. It felt like everyone knew more about Terence than Kala ever did.

"Thank you, Poseidon. You've always been there for me and Terence. I can never repay you for that."

"You're family. No debt is owed." Poseidon gave Kala a rare smile. "I'll see you later, *Aunt* Kala."

Kala smiled back. "See you later."

And with that, Poseidon teleported away.

Kala continued to gaze out at the ocean, enjoying the last few moments of peace before she saw her son.

Present Time

I looked around the room, and it appeared to be empty.

Terence had his usual disapproving glare focused in my direction. "I thought you said this is where Zeus was."

I ignored his attitude like I always did and responded, "I teleported us a few hundred feet to where I last communicated with him. About fifty years ago I had a mission where I needed to track someone so I had Talan activate a spell that can find anyone I telepathically link to. It's come in handy many times." I didn't tell Terence that I had used it several times on him before. If he found out, he'd never contact me telepathically again. Of course, now that I admitted this, he probably never would anyway. When it came to my son, *distance* was his way of punishing me.

"Where are we anyway?" Terence said, examining the room we were in.

It was small, with two sealed windows overlooking a river surrounded by trees, which in my estimate, put us on the fourth or fifth floor of some kind of office building. I had no idea where we were in the *world* though. We were lucky we hadn't teleported into a rock, but I had made a lucky guess that Zeus was holing himself up in civilization. Only Poseidon had stayed true to who he was, living mostly in the oceans with only rare appearances on land.

"I'm not sure where we are. Let's check out the other rooms. You lead, in case you need to shape-shift." I wished that had come out less authoritative. I had no idea how to be a 'mom' to Terence. I only knew how to treat him like a soldier.

Terence didn't flinch at my command, though, which made it that much worse. It meant he expected me to act this way. He had probably given up on me being any kind of normal mother a long time ago.

I followed him into the next room after he gave the All-Clear. This building didn't appear to have any humans working in it, which most likely meant that Zeus had used his powers to empty it out so he could have it as a base of operations. By the same token, this could simply be a way station, a decoy, just in case I had the ability to find him.

Terence whispered, "Kind of odd, using an office building for a hideout?"

"Yeah, I'm wondering if he's still here at all." I expressed my doubts aloud.

Terence suddenly held up his hand for a halt. "I hear voices." He cocked his head to the side. "I'll use my astral projection blast, see what I can find."

Terence closed his eyes. In mere moments, they were open again and he didn't look happy. "Zeus is here. Bottom floor. Not alone."

"Who's with him?"

"Cronus and Hades and ten Olympians. My blast didn't let me stay long, but they seemed pretty cozy with each other."

Owen's fears were right: the Olympians were working with Cronus.

"We have to make sure. Maybe this is a preliminary meeting of the minds." I hoped it wasn't as bad as I suspected. "Anyone missing you could pretend to be?" I asked.

"Hephaestus and Hera weren't there," Terence answered. "I have no idea where Hera is, but I overheard Zeus say Hephaestus was 'checking the system,' whatever that means. I can work with that, since it probably means he'll be gone for a while."

"Good call. Hera is never far from Zeus's side. She may be back a lot sooner." My heart began to race. I didn't like the thought of Terence going into the lion's den alone, but we needed to know what we were up against.

Terence nodded and transformed in front of me. After a moment of what always looked painful to me, but obviously wasn't to Terence, 'Hephaestus' stood before me, a few inches taller than Terence and a foot broader in shoulder. It was as if I was staring at the god himself, his voice matching the god's, "I should teleport in, right?"

Nodding, I offered an idea. "Maybe you should rough yourself up, make them think you were attacked by me and the Grigori?"

Terence smiled at the plan, which filled me with happiness. It was the first time in years he hadn't looked at me with disdain. "Yeah, I've got just the thing." After another moment of shape-shifting, he

315

mimicked burns on his forearms and face. "Uncle Derek's UVC gun on full blast. Cronus and Hades know how that feels. Hopefully, it'll catch them off guard enough that they won't notice the fact that I know absolutely nothing." He raised his eyebrow in amusement.

Then I did something I hardly ever did, I clasped his arm with my hand. "Please, be careful. And teleport out of there at the first sign of trouble."

Even though he looked like Hephaestus, his eyes appeared both surprised and pleased at my concern. The expression was quickly gone, however, as his defensive walls went up like clockwork. "I'll teleport back to the LA headquarters." He pointed down at the ground. "They are in the room two over from this one on the bottom floor. If you hide in the room next door, you should be able to hear everything."

Before I could respond, Terence popped out of view.

Exiting the room, I located the stairwell and hurried down the steps trying to make as little noise as possible until I reached the bottom floor. Carefully opening the door, I saw the hallway was clear. I slipped into the closest room and as cautiously as I could, I traveled through each room using adjoining doors until I was at the door that led to the 'god conference.'

Terence was right. I could hear everything. The door was cracked slightly open as well, so I was able to see everything, too.

Terence was already into his story and I could tell Zeus and Cronus were eating it up. Zeus wrapped his arm around Terence, who played the part of Hephaestus beautifully. I knew the god, and *I* would have never known the difference. When Terence transformed into someone, it was almost as if he took a part of their brain with him, as he was able to imitate the smallest idiosyncrasies with perfect accuracy.

The room was full of Olympians and a handful of Zeus's children. From my vantage point I could see: On the Olympian side: Demeter, Hestia, Eos and Selene. And on Zeus's kid side: Ares, Prometheus, Apollo and Artemis. Some heavy hitters. I had only had brief encounters with Artemis and Apollo; they helped me out on one of my Atlas missions a couple hundred years ago. The others I only knew from reputation. There were a few others in the back I couldn't see because of my limited view. This many Olympians in a room with Cronus was not a good sign.

"The first thing we do when we reach ascension is get rid of that damned *human*," Cronus said. "No one should be able to invent things that hurt gods. Anyone who does will be executed. Forever." He was obviously still a little upset with Derek and his toys.

Zeus spoke to Hephaestus. "Did you find out if the machines were safe? We don't want to end up like you two, trapped in those damned things and used as power sources. We're not getting duped by this *clone*, are we?"

As Hephaestus, Terence answered, "I couldn't tell for certain. The clone knows the machines better than I do."

Smart. Fishing without sounding like he was fishing.

Cronus's tone was dismissive. "Hades and I have been in that *human*'s machines for three hundred years. We were only trapped there because of Mother and her mutant human spawn. It won't happen again." He nodded to the corner of the room, but there was nothing there.

I assumed that *mutant human spawn* was in reference to me. Nothing like family to make you feel wanted.

Cronus continued, "I'm telling you, there's nothing this clone Alec can do to hurt us. I felt it. Only Mother was powerful enough

317

to do that and, as you can see, she won't be a problem anymore." Cronus glanced at the same corner again and I was suddenly filled with a sense of dread. There was nothing there, but he kept looking over there as if there was.

Hades interrupted my thoughts when he added, "Alec needs everyone to sit in the machine so he can bind us. We can't break open the portals to the Hells and Heavens if we don't. I've been working on opening the gateway to the Underworld since my connection is the strongest with that dimension. And it's working. It's slow going, but it's going. Once all of you and your children connect with us through the machine, we'll be unstoppable. We'll be able to crack open the Heavens and Hells and finally rule all of existence."

"Besides," Cronus interjected. "We'll be going one at a time, so Alec can't pull anything with the rest of us standing there. We'd destroy him."

"We're in." A familiar voice came from the back of the room.

It was Poseidon.

I knew I shouldn't be surprised. But I was. Of all the Olympians, Poseidon was my friend. He was cool, calm, collected and, above all, reasonable and intelligent. Poseidon was the only god I had spent a lot of time with in the past. Some of the talks we had meant a lot to me. He had helped me reconcile my feelings for Jack and helped me embrace Talan. I owed him. He was there for me when I had felt completely isolated and alone. It was painful to see him here. I hadn't seen him in over a hundred years, but we hadn't parted on bad terms.

So why would he consider this madness? Family obligation? Brainwashing? What? I couldn't think of a reason he'd agree to destroying the world. Maybe in my time as a human I might have understood why he'd consider it, we humans had dumped a lot of our waste into the ocean, slowly choking its life away. But Turner had changed all that. With his giant incinerators and paper/packaging laws, Turner had made garbage a thing of the past. What garbage people did create, Turner used in the incinerators to power half the world. The ocean was cleaner than it had ever been. So why would Poseidon want that destroyed?

Terence almost broke his cover when he turned to see Poseidon. My son's eyes showed the same shock and disappointment that I felt inside. Poseidon had been a part of his life as well. He took Terence to places in the ocean that no human had set foot in. Poseidon had been the adventurous uncle that somehow seemed separate from Zeus and his cronies. And that was the crux of it: Poseidon had considered us family, when no other god did.

Luckily, Poseidon knew nothing of Terence's shape-shifting ability, otherwise he may have seen through the disguise. Terence immediately hid his feelings and turned away as Poseidon approached him, Cronus, Hades and Zeus.

Zeus placed a hand on Poseidon's shoulder. "I'm glad you've finally came to your senses, brother."

Poseidon gently pushed off Zeus's hand. A gesture that gave me a slight pang of hope. Maybe there was a still a chance to change his mind.

But when he spoke, all hopes were dashed. "I don't do this for you or anyone else. I do this because the humans don't deserve to have this planet anymore. They are a plague and need to be eradicated. No matter how many of them their leader exterminates, there are millions to take their place. In time they will choke every bit of life out of this planet and there will be nothing left for any of us."

I never took Poseidon to be a gloom and doom kind of guy. He had always filled me with hope and faith of the future. Something must have happened to turn his mind. I wish I knew what it was so I could try and turn it back.

The scary part was the fact that the I.Q. Collective and the gods' goals were the same: bust open the gates of the Heavens, Hells and the Underworld, which basically equated to the end of the world as we knew it. I could hardly fathom the idea of ending the world without it being because I failed an Atlas mission. But how could I stop them?

I took a deep breath. I'd have to tell the gods the I.Q. Collective's plans. It might be the only way to prevent any of this from happening. Alec needed the power from opening the portals to all the dimensions to take over the gods' bodies. If the gods knew that was the reason, they'd never do it. Yes, Zeus hated me, but he was also paranoid – and if I left a seed of doubt in his head, he wouldn't step foot near that brain machine.

I had no idea if they'd try to kill me on the spot, but I had to open this door and tell them the truth.

I was about to swing the door wide when Cronus nodded to the empty corner of the room again. "Do you think her prison will hold?"

Her? There was nothing there.

Zeus seemed rather pleased with himself. "She's been there for over two-hundred and fifty years, ever since that abomination was born, so yes, this Metlod has worked perfectly."

Poseidon looked angry at Zeus's gloating. "Keeping her prisoner was a necessity, not something we enjoyed doing."

Cronus shrugged. "I don't care what you do to her. She's dead to me as far as I'm concerned. It's vital that we keep her out of the way. That death-girl broke that annoying human out of a Metlod. We can't risk her doing the same here."

Metlod? I didn't see any Metlod. And *abomination*...

Two-hundred and fifty-seven years ago, Terence was born.

Who had a connection with Terence that Cronus despised...

Gaia.

My mother.

She hadn't abandoned me.

She had been captured and imprisoned by the Olympians. My insecurities about Gaia had been so powerful it had never occurred to me that she might be in danger. I'd let her sit in a prison for hundreds of years because I self-centeredly believed she didn't want me. The guilt washed over me, threatening to drown me.

I tried to keep my mind focused, but it was difficult. Hate seethed inside of me. Zeus, him I expected something like this from. But Poseidon? It made me despise him. Thinking back on all our conversations about Gaia and how she was always distant with all her children and grandchildren... Meanwhile he was holding her captive. Poseidon let me believe she had left me. It was better for him that way, because then I couldn't help her escape. It was a betrayal on such a basic level, it made me embarrassed and ashamed that I had fallen for it.

I wanted them all to burn.

I almost considered letting the I.Q. Collective have their way and wipe off the gods' smug faces for good, but considering it required an apocalypse that combined the Heavens and the Hells on Earth... not an option.

All I knew was that I wasn't leaving here without Gaia.

That was a promise.

My problem though was that I needed to be able to *see* the

Metlod in order to *take* the Metlod. The Olympians had obviously hidden it from this reality, which probably meant it was slightly out of phase...

Turner's dimension displacement technology.

Even Elisha had used it to hide her soldiers from Chelsan on the day Chelsan took down her army. Zeus must have found a way to use the same technology to hide the Metlod that held my mother. He couldn't have used magic because of the nature of a Metlod.

I needed to contact Roberta. I knew nothing about dimension displacement technology, but between Turner and/or Elisha maybe they'd have a way for me to bring the Metlod into our dimension.

Zeus laughed, "Catching grandmother was easier than I thought it would be. She was so obsessed with seeing her grandchild I was able to trick her into coming here. I told her that Kala had to keep Terence hidden and that this was the secret location. When she got here, Poseidon, Hera and my twins performed the spell." Zeus nodded toward Apollo and Artemis.

I was surprised at the silence of the room. None of the other gods were speaking except for Zeus, Cronus, Poseidon and Hades. It was eerie in a way. Blind obedience? Or just wanting to stay out of it.

Though I knew she'd hate it, I made contact with Roberta.

We've got a problem.

Roberta's voice was instantly in my head. Her tone was cold though. *What is it?*

Gaia's been in a Metlod for 257 years and the Metlod is being held in another dimension. I'm pretty sure it was your dimension displacement technology, since magic wouldn't work on a Metlod. Do you have anything that can bring the Metlod back, so I can get her out of here?

There was a pause. My guess was that she was asking Turner and Elisha for advice. Finally, she answered, *Do you know where the Metlod is located in our dimension?*

Yes. Cronus keeps nodding toward a corner of the room.

Another pause, then: *Elisha has a device. You'll have to be accurate, but it'll work like a displacement bomb of sorts. Do you think you can do that?*

I viewed the room full of super deities, knowing that I was outnumbered.

Yeah. I can do that. Time to be a super soldier. My son and I were expert snipers, but we'd both have to rely on our magic and hand-to-hand fighting ability for this one.

Talan is coming with the device.

I felt a surge of relief at hearing Talan's name. My rock. We'd fought gods before and won. Just not this many at once.

Terence hadn't said a word since he had given his fake report to Cronus and Zeus. He was waiting for me. By not teleporting out, he was telling me that he'd follow my lead. I may not have had the privilege of spending a lot of time with my son, but it didn't mean I didn't know him well.

I tested out my telepathy toward Terence. *We're taking that Metlod,* I said.

I figured, he answered back. *It's Turner's displacement technology, isn't it? They got anything that will defuse it?*

I was both proud and amused that Terence had figured out everything on his own. He had become such an amazing man, it made my heart squeeze with pain that we couldn't have a better relationship. But, of course, I kept my answer brief. *Yeah. Talan is bringing it.*

Better hurry. I'm sensing this meeting is about to break up and we can't let them near those machines. You're going to have to tell them about the Collective.

I know. I'll come in as soon as Talan gets here.

A plan began to form in my brain.

Talan popped in next to me. We knew each other's essences so well we could find each other anywhere in the world. His soft smile gave me instant comfort. Talan held out a small circular device the size of a quarter. As I took it, I squeezed his hand and he squeezed back.

We were really doing this.

Placing the device in my front pants pocket, I walked into the room, Talan close behind.

We both held our hands up in supplication, though I was prepared to get hit with a blast of fire or lightning.

As soon as Cronus saw me green fire used for causing pain balled up in his hand.

As Hephaestus, Terence gently touched Cronus's arm. "Let her speak. We can kill her if we don't like what she has to say."

Surprisingly, Cronus listened. He let the fire snuff out.

I felt the entire room stare at me. No one seemed to care that Talan was right behind me. It was strange. Only Hades and Cronus looked at me with hatred and venom. Most of the others either looked curious or indifferent. Zeus couldn't disguise his annoyance, but he kept quiet. It was only Poseidon who couldn't meet my eyes. He was ashamed. Good.

"I'm not here to fight," I began slowly. "I'm here to warn you."

"Why should we believe anything you say?" Cronus snapped back. "You've been attacking me from the moment I escaped the prison *you* helped put me in."

I slowly put my hands down, keeping one hand next to my

pocket where the displacement device rested. "*You two,*" I nodded toward Cronus and Hades, "are probably a lost cause, since you've already been in Turner's machine." I eyed the other gods in the room. "But the rest of you are still safe… for now."

I paused. When I was sure I had their full attention, I continued, "The clone you have been dealing with is playing you all for fools. Alec is holding the entire I.Q. Collective in his brain. He intends to use the machines to connect all of you. Then, when you tear the walls down between dimensions, he's going to use that power so that the souls of the Collective can hijack your bodies. You can't go into the machines."

As I looked at their faces, I could see the distrust of my words in their eyes. Honestly, I wouldn't trust me either if I were them. Being Atlas for the last three hundred years hadn't gained me many friends. I had lied a lot to get what I needed from them. They knew I'd say or do anything to complete my missions. I had to try to convince them otherwise. Curse or not, the world was going to end.

Apollo stepped forward, his expression curious. "What is an I.Q. Collective?"

Zeus brushed his son off with annoyance, but answered, "That damned purple-eyed girl and that army of clones a few months back. She almost took over the planet with that little stunt." He focused his attention on me. "I thought all the I.Q. souls died when the clone bodies died."

"That's what we thought, too, but that 'purple-eyed girl' and Ashliel figured out that Alec pulled the Collective's souls inside of himself, just like he had done before with Ryan Vaughn." I tried to keep my voice as reassuringly neutral as possible.

At the mention of Ashliel, from their reaction I could tell that

Apollo and Artemis respected the Grigori enough to take my words more seriously. The others, however, still stared skeptically at me.

Zeus didn't like that his children were wavering however. He barked at me dismissively, "You're just trying to save this annoying little planet of yours. You'll say anything to try and stop us."

"She's telling the truth," Talan said with authority.

Poseidon's eyes met Talan's and he replied gently, "Talan, we know you would do anything for Kala, including backing her up if she intended to trick us."

"So your mind is set on tearing down the walls between the dimensions?" I asked incredulously. "So much so that you'd risk being possessed by a bunch of psychopathic humans?"

Cronus laughed, "Please. Humans aren't strong enough to take over a deity's mind. Not even these so-called 'geniuses.' Your little pet necromancer has tried how many times now to take over Hades's body? And that little clone reveres her like she's some kind of god herself. What chance does *he* have if she can't do it? Zero." The Titan was very sure of himself. After being imprisoned for a few hundred years, he was still cocky.

I couldn't hide my sarcasm as I snapped back, "And how did trying to control this necromancer go for Hades? Even with your so-called super-strength the machine gave you two? Oh, right: he couldn't do it. A measly little human was too powerful for a *god* to possess. A *human* necromancer." I turned to Hades. "That should be nothing for you, Hades, but you couldn't deliver, could you?"

Hades looked embarrassed, while Zeus's children shifted uncomfortably. I grabbed onto the hope that I could sway them. "Hades didn't tell you that, did he?"

Zeus paused to think for a moment.

I continued, "Chelsan Derée. The girl who stopped Elisha *and* her army of clones *and* the dead. *Hades* couldn't take over her body. She was *stronger* than him. She was *better* than him. And she's *human*. Alec and the I.Q. Collective are no joke. They will possess you if you let them. Be smart for once in your eternity of existence and don't set yourselves up like dominos to be knocked over with a single push!" I was angry now at their obvious ignorance.

I was also inching closer to where I knew they were hiding the Metlod. I had no faith in the Titan and Olympians' judgment. Their thought process came from a place of selfishness, fear and power-hungry motives.

And, like clockwork, Cronus shook his head. "The fact that you're so desperate to keep the gods away from the machines only confirms that we should do it. You have Atlas's job and, if I'm being honest about it, you're better at it than he ever was. Your sole purpose in life is to keep this world intact and maintain the balance. If we tear down the walls of the dimensions, your world will end. You'll say anything to stop us. Everything out of your mouth is a lie."

The stab in my heart though, came from Poseidon, "In fact, you'll say the very thing that would stop us from moving forward with our plans. But, Kala, what you don't understand is that playing on our fears and paranoia of humans only makes us want to destroy them more."

"I'm not *playing* on anything. I'm telling you the truth. If you hook into those machines, the I.Q. Collective *will* take over your bodies when you tear down the walls of reality. Period." Man, gods were frustrating.

"It comes down to one simple fact," Zeus said, eyeing me with disgust. "We don't believe you."

Talan stepped in a second time. "We won't let you destroy the world."

327

Not good. Especially since they would think this was confirmation that I was lying to save the planet.

Olympians and Titans didn't like a hint of a threat.

Cronus laughed, "And how do you plan on stopping us? United, the Olympians and Titans will crush the Grigori and any other Malak or demon that stands in our way." He sneered in my direction. "Including that lover of yours who likes to call himself *King*."

Reading the room, I saw that the doubters were no longer doubting.

"So you're choosing to be idiots. Again." Probably not a smart thing to say in a room full of gods, but their willful ignorance was infuriating.

"Insulting us only proves your lies." Poseidon was sure of himself now. And the more confidence he exuded, the more the others puffed up in agreement.

This was it.

An attack was imminent.

It was the usual way of things when dealing with my family of deities. Talking escalated to arguing which then escalated to some kind of fire match. I needed to stop them from falling into Alec's trap, but I wasn't sure how that was possible at this point.

Guilt pushed aside, I was getting Gaia out of here. If anyone could fix this situation, it would be her. My siblings, nieces and nephews were airing on the side of stupidity yet again. They would never see that humans could be smarter than them, stronger. You'd think, after thousands of years of learning the same lesson over and over – never underestimate your opponent – that they'd have a better sense of when they were being duped. But their naivety was the worst kind, because it came from a place of narcissism – and from fear. A deadly combination.

Terence's voice sounded in my head, *Time for that displacement device.*

I could see from the look in Talan's eyes that he had received the message as well. I discreetly placed my hand in my pocket.

Zeus's eyes began to glow yellow, the color of fire used to destroy. He planned on trying to kill me and Talan. No time to feel hurt or betrayed, I had to act fast.

I'll take Zeus, Terence announced after seeing the yellow fire grow in Zeus's eyes.

I'll try and keep everyone off of you, Kala, Talan said, *focus on unmasking the Metlod.*

I didn't want to think about what we'd do after that. I acknowledged the plan, then immediately ducked and rolled just before yellow fire burst from Zeus's eyes and hands. I landed in the spot where the Metlod was supposedly being kept.

Cronus's eyes widened. "She knows! This was her plan all along! Kill her!"

Terence as Hephaestus picked Zeus up like the god weighed nothing and threw him into Apollo and Artemis. I sometimes forgot that Terence inherited his super-strength from Asmodeus, and it certainly came in handy now, especially since the room now believed that Hephaestus had turned on them.

The expression on Zeus's face was full of anguish and betrayal. I had to give it to Terence, he played Hephaestus well when he said, "I side with what's right, *father.*"

Zeus lay there, entangled with Apollo and Artemis, but there was no disguising that he was butt-hurt.

Taking advantage of the momentary confusion of *Hephaestus's* betrayal, I pulled out the displacement device and activated it.

With a loud POP, a Metlod appeared in the room.

Cronus screamed, "I said KILL HER!" A blast of yellow fire poured out of Cronus's hands directly toward me.

Soon every god in that room was throwing yellow fire my way. I leaped over the Metlod to hide, hoping its anti-magic properties would protect me.

I wasn't wrong.

The onslaught of fire hit the Metlod, lighting up the room as if we were standing outside in the bright sunlight. Thankfully, the strange magical cocoon absorbed it all.

Talan jumped over to my position while calling out to Terence in his head, *Now, Terence!*

Terence pushed Poseidon as hard as he could, sending the ocean god flying across the room, his body slamming into a wall. I could tell by the look on Terence's face that it had been therapeutic. Never breaking cover as Hephaestus, Terence quickly joined Talan and me.

Population Control building! Turner's office! I yelled in my head.

We all grabbed each other's arms and touched the Metlod.

In a flash we teleported away, leaving my idiot family behind.

Chapter Thirteen

Two Years Ago

CHELSAN

Chelsan waited patiently at an empty desk in the Geoffrey Turner High School library. E-readers lined the walls, organized by genre. The school replaced the readers every few years or so, because a school named after the most powerful man on Earth deserved the best technology had to offer.

No one was in the library at this particular moment, not that anyone ever was. The library and the cherry blossom courtyard were Chelsan's favorite places to go at her school, since in those places she didn't have to deal with… humans. Mainly, Jill Forester. At least Chelsan had Nancy and Bill. They made high school life tolerable.

Looking at the clock on the wall, Chelsan wondered when Ryan Vaughn would arrive. He was already ten minutes late. Just thinking about him made her palms sweat. He had been forced to tutor Chelsan in Math, Trigonometry to be exact. Chelsan wasn't behind in the class, she had a solid 'B,' but she couldn't afford to get anything lower or she'd lose her scholarship. And Geoffrey Turner High was the only high school within her four-mile radius, so Chelsan had to make sure her grades were up so she could stay. Mr. Calston was a solid supporter of Chelsan, so he wanted her to have the very best tutor, which is why he talked Ryan into saying 'Yes.'

Right now, though, Chelsan was beginning to feel like Ryan wasn't going to show. She couldn't blame him. Jill had made it very clear in class that Ryan should blow Chelsan off and that he'd be socially rewarded for it. Chelsan still wasn't sure what she had done to earn Jill's never ending ire, but that was the way things were and Chelsan had to accept it.

Ten more minutes. That was all she was going to give Ryan, then Chelsan would pack it up and leave. Maybe she hadn't looked hard enough on the holo-net for Trig tutorials. She had watched all the holo-videos she could find and they helped, just not enough to get her that 'A' she needed. And definitely not enough to truly make Trig 'click' in her brain. Ryan was her last hope for that, especially since he was probably the smartest person on the planet.

Chelsan swallowed hard thinking about it.

Not intimidating at all.

Why had she agreed to this?

Now she secretly wanted Ryan to flake. Thinking of that option made her instantly relieved.

Just as Chelsan was about to pack up and go, Ryan entered the library.

Chelsan's heart stuck in her throat.

There was no way she could do this! What had she been thinking?!

Ryan Vaughn saw Chelsan and gave her a quick head nod of

greeting as he made his way toward her.

He even walked cute, Chelsan noticed immediately, his tall, lanky body sauntered over and his sandy-blonde hair looked extra perfectly messy today. Chelsan tried hard not to stare too intensely. She didn't want Ryan to think she was more of freak than he probably already did.

After arriving at the table, Ryan sat down across from Chelsan, laying his e-reader in front of him. He pulled out a stylus from the side of his reader and Chelsan realized that she didn't have hers. Already feeling her face burn from embarrassment, Chelsan chastised herself internally for not thinking about the fact that she'd actually need to write math problems down in order to learn anything!

Ryan seemed to notice the problem. "No stylus?"

Speechless, Chelsan simply shook her head in the negative.

Ryan sighed.

Chelsan wanted to throw up.

He picked up his reader and walked around the table to sit next to Chelsan.

Next to her!

Now she really wanted to throw up!

"We'll use mine today. It's probably better that way, anyway, so I can show you how to work through a couple of sample equations." Ryan's smile was brief – but it was there!

Chelsan knew he was probably simply being nice, but he had no reason to be. In fact, being nice was probably a social death sentence. It had been that way for Nancy. Bill was relatively unscathed, but that was because he was stinking rich. Chelsan guessed that Ryan had a reasonable amount of protection, too, considering he was famous for solving Trilidon's Theorem, but she wasn't sure that would be enough for *this* school. For Jill Forester.

Anyway, the smile was nice. Chelsan would take anything she could get.

Chelsan tried to smile back, but knew her face had contorted in ways that she hadn't wanted it to. Better stick to Trig.

Pointing at the practice equations, Chelsan asked, "Do you want me to try and do these, then you can tell me what I did wrong?" Wow. She was impressed with herself. She had got out a full sentence without stuttering or fainting.

"Yeah, that sounds like a plan. Here." Ryan handed Chelsan his stylus.

Chelsan's hands shook as she took the stylus. Stupid hands!

Ryan obviously noticed, but he didn't say anything, didn't do anything. He ignored it. Which only made Chelsan more nervous. Which only made her hands tremble more.

At this point Chelsan wanted to chop off her hands and bleed to death. It would be easier than what she was currently feeling.

Ryan wasn't going to be able to ignore this for long. He probably thought she had some kind of disease or that she was having a seizure or worse: Ryan Vaughn knew that Chelsan Derée had a raging crush on him and he was disgusted.

Discreetly, Chelsan tried to take a few calming breaths. Her hands steadied a bit, but they were still kind of vibrating like she was some kind of freakazoid.

Why me? Seriously?

Chelsan focused on the equations in front of her, trying to ignore the fact that since her hands were shaking, the numbers she wrote were a little on the jittery side. She hoped Ryan would be able to read her writing.

"You cold?" Ryan asked.

Chelsan wanted to leap for joy at that. Ryan was giving her an out for her crippling shyness.

She answered softly (because Chelsan had learned over the years that she could hide the shake from her voice if she talked quietly), "Yeah, it's pretty cold."

It was seventy-five degrees, but Chelsan was going to take that excuse and run it into the ground.

"I didn't bring my coat, but we could go to my house. It's warmer there and I have an extra stylus." Ryan suggested. His voice was quiet as well, though Chelsan didn't dare read into it. He was probably mortified at her behavior.

Then what he had actually said hit her and she froze. Ryan Vaughn has just asked her to come over to his house? His house! An open invitation to his freaking house!

But just as fast as her heart soared with the thought, it quickly smashed to pieces. Chelsan knew from Nancy that Ryan lived a few houses down and across the street from her.

And Nancy was five miles away from Bruce, which meant, so was Ryan.

"I'll be okay. We should probably stay here in the library," Chelsan managed to say.

Was that *disappointment* in Ryan's eyes?

The thought both pleased and mortified her. Maybe Ryan...

No.

Chelsan shook the thought from her head.

Who was she kidding? Ryan Vaughn would never be interested in someone like her.

Never.

Her hands stopped shaking and a sadness filled her chest.

It was better that way.

Looking back at the reader, Chelsan continued her work on the trigonometry equations.

At least she could enjoy being this close to the boy she liked.

That was something.

DAY FOUR

Tuesday June 7, 2321

CHELSAN

I felt like I was in prison. I had figured out a way to use my powers through the Metlod, but I could still feel it surrounding my brain like it was wrapped in rubber. But I also felt like I was in prison because... well... I kind of was. The whole gang of us did that teleportation thing and were currently at the Population Control Center. Luckily, Grams thought I needed some rest, so she let Ryan and me take one of the bedrooms. There was no way I was sleeping, though – my adrenaline prevented me from escape – instead, Ryan and I caught each other up on everything that had happened while we were separated.

Ryan said that Elisha had been mostly normal, except for a handful of times he thought Talan's 'brain wipe' almost fizzled out. Elisha's face would go slack for a few seconds, then she'd look up at him as if nothing happened. He said it was on the weird side, but he'd take it over screaming-unhinged-Elisha.

We had fully geeked out when I told him about Isabelle's powers – the ability to control kinetic energy – and how Dean's powers apparently made him as resilient as rubber. I could see the wheels turning in Ryan's head going over every implication that controlling kinetic energy and having skin that was impenetrable could mean. We both still found it strange that only *I* seemed to be able to use Isabelle's powers to the fullest. I tried explaining it to Isabelle, but she couldn't seem to see her powers the way I did. She claimed she could still only see the movement around peoples' hearts. I promised her that if the world was still spinning in a few days, I'd try my hardest to show her everything she could do.

Ryan gently kissed my neck as he wrapped his arms around me. We were lying in a giant bed full of fluffy pillows and the softest comforter I'd ever felt in my life. Roberta wasn't kidding around when she wanted to give her granddaughter comfort.

I pulled Ryan in closer as we lay on the bed, holding each other. His lips pressed against mine and all thoughts of my grandparents and death washed away. It amazed me that Ryan still gave me butterflies every time he touched me, each time he kissed me. I wondered if those sensations would go away eventually. I couldn't imagine that they ever would. With everything that had happened in our lives, I wanted to be in the moment and truly appreciate the fact that somehow through this screwy, bizarre world we had found each other. What were the odds of that? I felt so lucky I thought my heart would burst.

As Ryan's hands grasped me tighter, I could feel how much he loved me, how much he needed me in that moment. Our kisses became more fevered as if we hadn't seen each other in months, as if we were trying to erase all the chaos surrounding us. Ever since

Ryan took the immortality serum, I knew he couldn't die, but a part of me was still terrified. Killing Ryan was Kala's mission.

And, yet again, I was somehow the only person who could stop it by breaking her curse.

Pressure, anyone?

Before I knew it, our clothes were off. Feeling Ryan's skin against mine made me push aside my terror of losing the love of my life. My soul mate. I let myself give into this one piece of time, a moment that erased all fears and doubts. It was just us. Two souls in the eye of the storm, hoping that the madness would somehow pass us by. I'd never be this close to anyone for the rest of my life. And taking the serum, that meant eternity. And eternity sounded really good right now.

***

I guess I finally did end up sleeping. I woke up next to Ryan, who was resting peacefully next to me. I didn't think Roberta had intended her only granddaughter to be making love to her boyfriend when she gave us this room, but if anyone understood it would probably be her. No one could argue that, horrible as my grandparents were, they loved each other to terrifying lengths.

I stared at Ryan, trying not to be too stalkery. I couldn't help it. He was so perfect. He even snored quietly. I tried to memorize every line, every curve of his face, then stopped myself.

What was I doing?

I was acting as if this was the last time I'd ever see Ryan.

My brain couldn't relax. Couldn't let go of the fact that the death of Ryan was Kala's mission.

The cycle of thoughts kept repeating in my head. Over and over.

Ryan and I would still live forever. What did the end of the world really mean?

Right now, it looked like the world was going to end anyway if Alec succeeded in opening up these portals or whatever. I still wasn't clear on that either. The fact that the Underworld and Heavens and Hells existed was a little too much for me to comprehend. What would opening up the walls to these places do? Were there demons and monsters, or more angels and *Malaks* (I think that's what Kala called them?) It already sounded like a complete apocalypse was going to destroy the world *before* Kala's four-day timer ran out.

At least I made Gramps bring the gang here for protection, then gave them the immortality serum as soon as they arrived (yes, Jill too). But was that a cruel and selfish thing to do? *Here guys, drink this serum so you can live forever in a world that's about to implode on itself. You're welcome.*

And if we did manage to foil Alec and the gods' plans to break down the dimensions, the world would still end because I'd never let Ryan die. Serum or not, *I'd never let Ryan die.* That was a fact. I had no idea how I could stop a god, but I'd find a way. I'd have to. Losing Ryan wasn't something I could recover from. In that way, I was exactly like my grandparents.

Somehow, all these supernatural beings thought I was part of a prophecy. There was no mistaking that I was the one the prophecy was referring to. I had memorized the thing in the vain hope I could get out of it somehow. Or convince them it was about someone else. But the passage: *The one that knows death will release the curse*

341

of balance. She will be born from the man with the power of death. He will sacrifice his life and his gift to save the balancer.

Me: without a doubt.

Apparently, I was *the balancer*, whatever that meant. I wasn't used to mythology and religion and things like that. I barely knew what anyone was talking about when we had been stuck in Havenville.

I mean, really: how was I supposed to break some ancient curse? I wasn't a magic user. I had powers over the dead, but so did Hades. Why couldn't *he* break this stupid thing?

I knew I shouldn't be worrying about any of this right now. We had to stop Alec and the gods first, but my brain couldn't help going over every single possible scenario. If I was being honest, nine out of ten of them ended badly. The odds weren't looking that great for a happy future.

I jumped slightly when I heard a knocking on the door.

Ryan stirred awake, his eyes sleepy. "Tell them to go away."

I smiled and leaned down, kissing him on the cheek. Quickly grabbing my clothes, I threw them on as fast as I could. Ryan yanked me down on top of him before I could leave the bed. "Don't get it. We can ignore them."

I kissed him again. "If we were home, I'd be tempted, but we're in my grandparents' lair. Privacy is off limits."

Ryan sighed heavily, but his eyes were amused. "Lair, huh? I like the sound of that. It fits them."

I threw Ryan's t-shirt in his face playfully and walked over to the door, opening it.

It was Owen.

I felt warm fuzzies when I saw him. I had no idea how he felt about me, but I knew he was a friend.

The worried expression on his face pulled me out of warm fuzzy mode though. "You're probably sick to death of hearing the word Metlod, but you're the only one who's ever been able to break one."

"Another one?" I asked.

Owen nodded. "It seems Gaia's been kept in one by Zeus for a couple hundred years."

I couldn't fathom the kind of mental anguish of being stuck in what equated to a magical coffin for two-hundred years would cause. I had been buried alive by Elisha and had barely lasted a few days mentally. Maybe being the Mother of All Gods gave her a built-in coping mechanism, but I highly doubted it.

"Show me where she is." I wasn't sure if I could repeat what I had done with Turner, especially with a Metlod of my own in my brain, but I had to try. I wished I had never heard of the word 'Metlod'.

Ryan quickly joined me, fully dressed, and Owen led us down the hallway.

This seemed like a different wing of Population Control. I wasn't sure if I'd been here before. It was similar to the section of rooms we had stayed in when the whole Elisha thing went down. I could use an epic food fight with Bill right about now. I wondered where the Turners were holding my friends. I fully planned on seeing them after I hopefully helped out Gaia.

Gaia.

Jeez. My life was cuckoo. I was using Gaia in a sentence and it was real. I suddenly realized this was how it must have felt for my friends to find out I had the power to control dead things. Totally out of their realm of reality. Still, they'd adjusted fast. I, apparently, did too. Yay me.

Ryan's hand clasped mine. There was a desperation there that was growing stronger with each moment. No matter how much I tried to ignore it, the feelings grew more intense. I was sure Kala knew where we were on the whole countdown clock, but all I knew is that we were on Day Three and it was sometime in the evening. I think it was nighttime anyway. Or maybe it was early morning and we were already on Day Four! It wasn't as if there were any windows this far down in Population Control. I knew the sun had been about to go down right when we arrived and who knew how many hours had passed since then.

Ugh.

I never used to care this much about what time it was. Amazing how finding out my boyfriend's life was on some kind of a god-curse-countdown could make me hyper-aware of every second.

Really, Life? This was what you had in store for me when you planned out my destiny? Thanks. No seriously, thanks a bunch.

Owen's voice cut through my self-tirade, "She's in here." He opened a door and held it for us to walk through.

Inside, Kala, Terence, Talan and my grandparents stood around an identical Metlod to the one that had held Turner, a smooth metal-like surface formed into a perfect oval. This one lay on its back, unlike Turner's, which had been leaning against a wall. Seeing the Metlod this way, definitely made it look more like a coffin and less like a sci-fi hibernation egg like the one at the Compound.

Kala motioned me to her. I let go of Ryan's hand and walked over to the shiny prison that held the Mother of All Gods.

Kala's eyes met mine, and for the first time I saw desperation reflected there. "Can you get her out?"

I wanted to be more confident, but with a Metlod of my own to

344

deal with I wasn't sure. "I'll try."

Kala simply nodded. She'd take any strand of hope at this point.

"I thought she had abandoned me," Kala admitted, so softly only I could hear. "She was locked in this *thing* for centuries because I never bothered to look for her."

I could feel the guilt radiating off her body. I wasn't sure what to say. The fact that Kala had assumed her own mother would leave without a word for hundreds of years was somehow her first line of thinking, only made me realize how distrustful she was. Kala must have been burned badly for her to think Gaia would cut her off like that. Then again, Gaia did abandon Kala in a dumpster, so maybe Kala had a reason to distrust her mother so deeply.

I finally responded, "I'm sure she'll understand." Wow. I was really bad at the whole *comforting* thing. I was glad I didn't add, *That is, of course, if I can get her out.*

Kala's response was a slight smile, which was the equivalent of telling me not to bother trying to make her feel better. Before I'd need to insert my foot in my mouth, I turned to the Metlod and placed my hands on its surface.

"I'm not sure I can break out of my own Metlod," I admitted.

The surface of Gaia's Metlod felt like solid metal, but that really didn't matter. I had to be in astral form to break through it anyway.

I was worried though, now that the protective Metlod was firmly in place inside my head, that going into astral form might break it somehow.

I wanted to groan in frustration, but I didn't want Kala to feel any worse, so I closed my eyes to concentrate harder. I had to defeat two Metlods here, but the one around my brain needed to stay intact.

Before, with Owen, I had been trying to slide through my Metlod to reach the black holes of the dead, like water, so it couldn't break. This was so much different because I wasn't trying to break through to a black hole, I had to escape my body in astral form by breaking through *my* Metlod, then reach over and tear apart *Gaia's* Metlod. I didn't want my brain to mistake Gaia's Metlod for my own, so how was I to tell the difference? Yes, logically, I knew the Metlods were separate, one in my head, the other in the form of a metal egg front of me, but I didn't know how to move through mine to get to hers. They blended together in a way that I couldn't seem to separate. I was terrified I'd melt a hole in the Metlod in my head before I knew what I was doing.

Bottom line: I was in way over my head.

Magic and ancient prisons and gods were completely out of my wheelhouse. I didn't know why I was somehow able to do these impossible things, and I was frustrated that everyone expected me to be some kind of expert at everything I accidentally accomplished.

I made a decision. I needed help.

Opening my eyes, I turned to Owen, "I can't tell the difference between my Metlod and Gaia's. I'm afraid of breaking mine open by accident." Honesty. It needed to be said. I couldn't look at Kala, though; I was afraid I'd be welcomed with a whole lot of disappointment.

Owen was instantly by my side, always the teacher, which gave me a small sense of relief. I was still nervous of what I had to do though. "Let me help you." He reached out his hand to hold mine, "May I?"

I clasped his hand, trusting him implicitly. I felt a warm flush travel through my body, and I knew Owen was getting the lowdown on what was going on in my head. "I'm going to surround your Metlod with white fire, which is used to control. I won't be able to control you because the Metlod will extinguish the power of the fire, but maybe we can create a visual placeholder for you to see your own Metlod more clearly. But I won't do it without your permission."

I appreciated Owen asking for my blessing, but this kind of magic was on a whole other level for me. Having a Grigori angel tell me he was going to wrap my magical-brain-casing with another magical-brain-casing made of 'white fire' was absolute gibberish to me. So I did what anyone in my position would do and said, "Uh, sure, okay." Eloquent as usual.

Owen answered with a small smile.

Then I saw it.

This was the strangest sensation I had ever felt. It seemed as if there was a layer of white fire sitting behind my eyes, and I guess there literally was. It was as if Owen had amplified the Metlod, making it glow with pearly white flames. The downside to the situation was that I could barely see in front of me. I was officially in 'fire-vision.'

But now there was a problem.

I could tell the two Metlods apart, which was good. The fire acted, like Owen had said it would: a visual separator for the two magic-blocker encasements, but I couldn't mentally move through my own Metlod anymore, which was obviously bad.

"Um," I uttered.

Owen finished my sentence, "You can't move through your Metlod at all now."

"Yeah," I answered.

Owen's voice was firm and commanding as he said, "This is very important, Chelsan. The Metlod is protecting you from my fire so no supernatural being can control you or hurt you with their fire, but it is blocking you from using your powers through the

Metlod." He eyed me carefully, "I want you to try to break through the white fire. I'm going to use all my power to stop you, so it won't be easy, I want to see how much control you have. The gods might try to surround your Metlod with fire to stop you from using your power since you can, against all odds, use your powers despite the Metlod. The gods won't understand you. Using powers through a Metlod will scare them and they'll want to destroy you more than they already do."

Hearing a word like *destroy* in reference to gods and how they felt about me left a knot in my stomach. But I did as Owen asked and tried to push through the Metlod and the white fire.

Nope.

The white flames actually hurt. Not physically, but mentally. It was hard to describe, but it felt as if I burned my brain whenever I tried to get through the fire. How could I break through something as powerful as Grigori fire anyway? It seemed impossible.

But I had managed to freeze the fire when I had use of Isabelle's powers. It *was* possible to control. I never thought of being able to do it with my own power, since it only worked with dead things, but maybe if I could break the fire down to its simplest form. What did fire do? It burned. It destroyed. But did magic fire do that? Would there be anything in it that was dead? Like ashes? I was probably overthinking this, but I didn't know what else to do. I instinctively knew I was onto something.

First things first, push through my protective Metlod and get as close as I could to the white fire with my mind without tearing a hole in the Metlod. When I had my focus back I was shocked that my mind slid through the Metlod with ease, as if it was made of water like before. No hole. No breach for Hades to exploit. I almost immediately jumped backed into the safety of my brain from the intense burning, but I managed to keep my thoughts focused just outside the Metlod. My brain was caught between the fire and the magical encasing. I was sure I'd have some kind of seizure at any moment.

I closed my eyes, hoping this would help me see things more clearly.

It did.

I could see the Metlod behind me and the white fire in front of me burning like a wall of impenetrable flames.

Break it down to its smallest form…

I concentrated on the fire as hard as I could, ignoring the pain. I stared into the flames as if in a trance, trying to see something beyond the fire itself. After a while flashes of brighter white appeared, almost like the lights I saw in people. The ones that I could connect to and control. I wasn't sure if this was because of the fact that the fire was white or if what I was seeing was something new so I decided to ask, "Can you change the fire? I mean make it red or some other color?"

Owen's responded, "We'll have to skip the fire magic that causes pain. Only purple, black and white are painless. White is to control, purple is to capture, and black is to blind. So: capture or blindness? Which one would help you?"

I thought about it for a moment, then expressed my opinion. "Capture seems similar to the control one, so purple, I guess."

"Capture it is," Owen said.

For someone who was messing with my head, I was surprised at how comforted I was by his voice. It wasn't like me to trust someone so quickly, but I did. For some reason I trusted Owen more than Kala or any one of her entourage. I had no idea if it was the right thing to do, but I had to trust my gut. It was the only thing I could do at this point.

The white fire washed away before me and was replaced by deep, dark purple flames. I refocused my energy and stared at the flames as I had done with the white fire.

Sure enough, the same flashes of white appeared.

Okay. Good. Now what?

There was nothing else for it but to give it a try. I focused on connecting to one of the flashing lights.

Whoa.

I was *inside* the purple fire. Flames flowed all around me. It felt as if just my thoughts were inside the fire. Not thoughts. My energy. Yes. My energy source, the thing that made me, me. The source of all my power.

My soul.

It was something I knew from the times I'd connected to others' white lights, especially Elisha when I reattached her light to her brain. But it wasn't that I had connected to their souls, I already knew that, it was that *my own soul* was connected to theirs. It somehow made me feel more guilty for hijacking Isabelle's body. I had been using my soul to basically override hers, controlling her like a puppet. It was horrifying.

I pushed away any negative thoughts and tried to figure out what it meant that my soul was now connecting to a part of the purple fire. Could I control it?

I was about to find out.

I used the same thought process that I did while controlling people. I didn't feel flushed with power like I usually did; instead, it felt more like when I connected to dead things.

I realized then that everything had its own power source, even dead things.

My powers allowed me to connect and control the dead by attaching myself to the black swirling holes. But things that were alive? It was like when I controlled the twins. They saw *everything* alive with swirling white holes, not just people. So did I have that power now too? Did I always have it, but was simply never able to tap into it? Or did connecting to the twins open up that part of my brain and give me that power. I didn't see swirling white holes in everything, only in people. But maybe like with my dead-dust-mode all I'd have to do would be to adjust my vision to see the white holes in all living things?

This was getting way too complicated for me. I needed to test my theory out.

Starting with the purple fire.

I connected to the white flashing lights in the flames and pushed them with all the mental might I could muster.

And the fire was gone.

Completely absent from my brain.

"Hold him down!" I heard Kala scream. "What did you do?!"

I opened my eyes to see Owen collapsed on the floor, flailing his arms and legs in a full-blown seizure.

I was horrified. My eyes met Kala's: she was seriously pissed.

"I don't know," I muttered. "I don't know what I did. I pushed out the fire, like he wanted me to."

Kala knelt down, holding her father's head in her lap, trying to calm him down.

Talan had been analyzing the situation, apparently, because he said, "Chelsan pushed Owen's purple fire back into Owen. He's fighting off his own fire. His body doesn't know how to respond, so it's fighting back."

Uh-oh.

"Fix it!" Kala shouted at me.

"I…" I was about to say, *I don't know how*, but I thought if I did that, Kala would clock me, so I decided to nod and close my eyes to concentrate.

I immediately jumped inside Owen's body and landed…

…directly in the purple flames. They were everywhere. In his head, arms, legs, anywhere I looked, his insides were burning with the purple fire. I felt like screaming from the horror that I felt.

But I had to do something!

I instantly connected to the flashes of white within the fire once more and pushed again. This time with a destination.

I opened my eyes to see Owen looking up at me, exhausted, but smiling. He was okay. My shoulders collapsed in relief. I hadn't realized how I'd been tensing them up this whole time.

Kala helped Owen to his feet, her expression concerned, but relieved.

Owen nodded behind me.

I whirled around to see the purple fire precisely where I had imagined sending it: the center of the room. It looked like a strange purple campfire, its flames almost touching the ceiling.

With a wave of his hand, Owen snuffed out the fire and placed his hand on my shoulder. "That was very good, Chelsan."

"Good?!" I exclaimed. "I literally tortured you with your own magic!" I couldn't believe he was acting like I was his prize pupil after I had done such a horrible thing to him.

But, shockingly, it was Kala who explained. (I thought she was going to kick my butt for what I did to Owen) "I'm sorry I panicked. I do that when it comes to my dad, but Chelsan, Owen is right. What you did was amazing. I've never seen a deity, demon or angel take another's magic and use it against them." She turned to Talan, "Unprecedented, right?"

Talan nodded. "It's never happened before."

That seemed to be my special talent in life: doing things that no one had ever done before. It still didn't make me feel any better for torturing poor Owen despite the glowing comments.

"Can you tell me how you did it?" Owen asked gently. He almost seemed like he'd be okay if I decided not to tell him. Or maybe he wasn't sure if I knew how I did it. Why did I always feel like such a failure despite the fact that everyone kept telling me I was some kind of super-anomaly, full of powers no one else had access to?

"I'm not sure if it's because of my connecting to the twins' brains or not, but I could see the white light that made your fire magic alive. I connected to it like I did when I controlled the twins. They saw all living things the way I see all dead things, except all dead things have black holes and all living things have white holes." I was so great at explaining things. Yeah.

But everyone in the room seemed to get the gist. "Very good," Owen praised me again. "Do you think you could do it again, if one of the gods tried to surround your Metlod with fire?"

I nodded. "Yes. Once I do something, my mind pretty much remembers it instinctively." Then I remembered why we had started this whole thing in the first place. "I still need you to surround my Metlod with fire so I can tell my Metlod from Gaia's. I can get through the fire with no problem now. I just need it as a reminder, so I don't break mine by accident."

I could sense that Owen wanted to pick my brain some more on how I was able to use his own magic against him, but he knew releasing Gaia was a higher priority. He nodded in agreement.

He used the white fire this time. It was beautiful now that I knew how to move through it. It worked perfectly as a guide to keep me from breaking my own Metlod. I couldn't wait until we defeated Hades and I could get rid of the thing. *If* we defeated Hades. On second thought, I should probably get used to the magic-shell around my brain.

My astral self moved through the white fire and toward the shiny black Metlod that held Gaia. I still couldn't believe all this was real.

As I did with Turner's Metlod, in my astral form I began to push through the surface of the magical prison as if it were made of liquid. It was easier this time, as I had said to Owen, once my brain remembered how to do something, it was easier for me to do it again. After shoving through what felt like twenty feet of tar (probably only a few inches!) I finally made it to the other side.

And there she was.

A beautiful older looking woman.

I had expected the Mother of All Gods to be... I don't know... bigger? Glowy? Something. But she looked like a regular old human, similar to all her other deity children. She was old, too. I mean, I knew she was like thousands of years old, possibly millions, but she appeared as if she was a fifty-year old lady. Pretty freaking old, especially when the rest of this world either looked eighteen or thirty. But, dang, she was stunning. Giant eyes opened to see me as clearly as if my actual body was standing in front of her. Considering I was probably a ball of light or something, having Gaia look directly at me was disconcerting.

"The one that knows death," Gaia said with a note of wonder in her tone.

I spoke in my astral form as I had with Turner, though I wasn't sure if she'd be able to hear me. I didn't have the same kind of connection with her that I had with Gramps. Yuck. But I tried anyway. "From the prophecy."

Gaia nodded.

Okay, she could hear me. I guess that shouldn't have surprised me, considering who she was, but I had to admit, talking to her, even in ghost form, was intimidating.

"I knew you would come for me," Gaia replied.

"You did? But you were imprisoned a couple hundred years ago. I wasn't born yet."

"You're the one that will free my daughter from the curse. I would know you like I know my children." Gaia's face was solemn and peaceful.

I couldn't understand it. I had barely been able to function when being buried alive for only a short time (I still had nightmares about it and get me into an elevator: forget it!), but Gaia, who had been locked in this Metlod for hundreds of years, seemed perfectly content.

I had to ask, "How are you sane? Being locked in here for so long?"

Gaia's face broke into a smile. "Gods experience time differently than humans. The Metlod may block my magic so I cannot escape, but it doesn't block my mind from leaving this place. I am able to travel between dimensions." She eyed me knowingly. "I have learned a lot about you."

I suddenly felt self-conscious. The way Gaia said it made me wonder which parts of my life she knew about. Could she read my mind? I immediately remembered killing Bruce with a black widow spider, then all the clones of my dad I had to kill to stop Elisha from murdering more people. Events that tormented me every day. Was

355

she going to smite me? Or at least smite my ghost form? Could she do that? She kept looking at me with kind, smiling eyes, but maybe that was a cover and she planned on punishing me somehow?

Gaia explained, "The Underworld is open to me in my spirit form. I spent a lot of time there."

She said this, looking at me as if I should know what she was talking about, as if that would answer all my questions.

"I met some people there who told me about you." Gaia was trying to make me guess who it was…

Who would be in the Underworld?

Then it hit me.

My parents.

"My parents are in the Underworld?" I asked, scared I had jumped to conclusions.

Gaia nodded. "I can take you there if you want?" Gaia seemed in no hurry to escape the Metlod. She genuinely appeared to care more about me reuniting with my parents than leaving her two-hundred-year prison.

Though I was in corporeal form, my voice shook, "You can do that?"

Gaia nodded. "My children and grandchildren are attempting to open up the gates to the Underworld and all the Heavens and Hells as we speak. I don't know what will happen to the souls of the Underworld after that happens, so now is the only time I can guarantee you'll have with your family."

Panic surged through me at the thought of something happening to my mom and dad. I never thought much about the afterlife, but now that I knew it existed and my parents were in it, it made me want to stop Hades and Cronus even more. If my parents were happy and the gods could potentially ruin that, I'd do anything to stop them. "Yes. Take me to them. Please." I couldn't hide the desperation in my voice.

Gaia reached out and touched my ghost form and the blackness of the Metlod swirled with color until we both stood on solid ground.

It was like with astral projection when I would feel and see my own body though I knew I was only there with my mind. Gaia stood next to me, beautiful and ancient. We stood at the top of a small hill of the greenest grass I'd ever seen. I could feel the soft blades underneath my bare feet, and I would swear I was actually there. For what seemed like miles and miles, soft rolling hills of the same vibrant green stretched out before us. There was no one to be seen. We were completely alone.

Gaia's expression was one of worry, "Hours ago these fields were filled with people. Hades must be closer to breaking open the Underworld than we thought. The humans must have seen the way to come back to Earth and their base instincts took over."

"My parents, too?" I asked, not bothering to hide the catch in my throat.

"I'm afraid so." Gaia didn't seem all that pleased by the prospect.

I was almost too scared to ask for fear the answer would be no. "Does that mean they'll be coming back to life?"

Gaia's eyes told me what I didn't want to hear. She shook her head. "Your parents are dead, Chelsan. Breaking out of the Underworld doesn't change that. As soon as Janet and Franklin and all the other souls leave the afterlife, I don't know what will happen." She sighed as if she didn't want to tell me something, but finally she continued, "They could end up gone forever."

"We have to stop them!" I exclaimed in horror.

Gaia nodded. "Get me out of the Metlod. We have to stop Hades and the others before it's too late."

Gaia grabbed my hand and we were back in the darkness of the Metlod.

There was a fire in me like I had never known. I needed to save my parents. I was technically saving their afterlife or souls rather than their living, breathing lives, but the possibility of them not existing at all was too excruciating. It was strange because I never believed in an afterlife before. Now, knowing that it existed, knowing that my parents were happy and safe, I'd do anything to keep them in that place. Anything.

As I did with Turner's Metlod, I used my astral form to grab onto the teeny tiny worm-like substance and pulled it down as if we were in an egg made of thick mud. Within seconds, I had torn down the entire top of the Metlod and Gaia crawled out with little trouble.

I rushed back into my body and opened my eyes.

Chapter Fourteen

268 Years Ago

KALA

"You're not doing too well. I can see it in your eyes, your body... your soul." Gaia's voice was laced with concern as she looked at Kala with sad eyes.

Kala had no response to that. She had no response to much of anything lately. The role of Atlas was taking its toll and Kala wasn't sure how to handle it. It did help seeing her mother look like she gave a damn, though. Before Owen and Linda, Kala hadn't had that experience at all. She had always wondered who her mother was. Who would be willing to abandon a baby in a dumpster? Later realizing that Gaia had done it to hide her scent on Kala made sense, but Kala was still scarred by her foster-care childhood.

They stood in Kala's apartment, looking out the window. Kala had come home to find her mother had been waiting for her. Kala had no idea how long Gaia had been waiting – she hadn't been to her apartment herself for the last three days. But Gaia didn't seem to mind. Kala guessed that when you'd been alive as long as her mother had, a few days were like seconds to her.

Gaia's arms wrapped around Kala as she pulled her daughter in for a tight embrace. Kala let her, though she barely hugged her mother back. She just didn't have it in her.

Mentally preparing to perform the Atlas mission took a lot out of Kala and she had two hours left to complete her current task.

Serial killers.

Her mission was to make Geoffrey Turner sanction serial killers.

The Atlas vision was clear: she has a simple conversation with Geoffrey where he agrees to secretly use serial killers as a way to control the population.

Disgusting.

Evil would be allowed to live and hunt the innocent.

How was this balancing the world?

The little voice inside her head answered like it always did: *Because this world will choke on itself if the population isn't culled.*

Kala hated that she thought that way now. It came from performing thousands and thousands of missions. Horrible, horrible acts that ultimately made the world go round.

And though this one was technically 'easy,' it still made her stomach churn with disgust.

Gaia pulled out of the limp hug. "Tell me about your mission."

Kala shook her head. "I don't want to think about it. Don't worry about it. This one is a cake walk compared to my last one." Which was the truth. Only four days ago, Kala had to drown a woman in a vat of liquid rubber. Whenever she closed her eyes Kala could still hear the woman's screams. The reason for that act was one that Kala didn't want to know. If she thought hard enough, she could probably figure it out, or get one of Talan's future visions, but she didn't want to. Like a robotic assassin, Kala had watched with no emotion as she threw the woman into the scalding liquid rubber.

"What was the last one?" Gaia asked gently.

Anger and rage flushed through Kala. "I said I don't want to talk about it! Why do you keep prying! My job sucks! I hate it with every fiber of my soul and I'm not sure I have one of those anymore. Not after what I've done!" The last sentence came as a cry.

Gaia didn't take offense at Kala's outburst. She simply took Kala's hands in hers. "Zeus gave this curse to Atlas as punishment. It wasn't meant to be easy or Atlas would have done it himself and not tricked humans to do it for him."

Kala yanked her hands away and answered with words that were laced with snark, "You think? I never would have guessed. Thanks for clearing that up for me."

No matter how mean Kala was to Gaia, her mother was still unfazed by her spite. "I fear that you are going to lose who you are because of these missions."

Kala's gut reaction was to lash out again, but she took a moment to stop herself, then said, "I fear that, too."

"You need an anchor. Do you think Talan could be that for you? Someone to pull you out of the darkness?" Gaia's face radiated warmth that spread to Kala's chest.

Kala wondered if that was some kind of power of her mother's, especially since it seemed to be working on her. "I love Talan," was all that Kala could say.

"But is he your anchor?" Gaia persisted.

"Yes. I can't imagine my life without him," Kala admitted.

"That's not the same thing." Gaia stepped closer to Kala and placed her hand on her daughter's cheek. "I will be your anchor."

361

Tears came to Gaia's eyes. "I will be the one who saves you from yourself. I will always be here for you. I will never leave again."

Gaia's words sounded like a prayer or magical spell, rhythmic and full of power. But Kala felt every word was a life raft for her soul.

"You promise?" Kala asked quietly.

Gaia's eyes sparkled with a love that filled Kala with a sense of wonder and happiness.

"I promise," Gaia said.

And Kala believed her.

Present Time

I didn't normally show my emotions around other people, but seeing Gaia crawl out of the Metlod, I couldn't control myself. I helped Gaia out the rest of the way and pulled her toward me, embracing my mother tightly.

Whispering in my ear, Gaia said, "I missed you."

It stung like nothing else could. The guilt was almost too much to bear. I had abandoned her in this prison, assuming she had abandoned me. My own personal baggage didn't allow my brain to consider the thought that my mother might be in trouble. I hated myself in that moment.

As if reading my thoughts, Gaia looked me in the eye with a serious expression. "Don't blame yourself. There's no way you could have known."

Then her eyes left mine to rest on Terence. Joy exuded from every part of Gaia's body. "Terence."

To my surprise, Terence returned her gaze with equal affection, which gave me a pang of jealousy. I knew I had no right to feel that way, but I wasn't skilled at controlling my emotions. Hence the reason my mother was stuck in a Metlod for two hundred years.

As Terence rushed to greet her, Gaia pulled away from me to embrace my son. And then something happened I wasn't expecting: a rush of warmth flooded through me at seeing my mother and my son hugging each other. It was a feeling I couldn't describe. The envy and pain washed away and for a brief second, I felt whole.

Turner cleared his throat. "We're on a time crunch here. Aren't you on Day Four now?"

My heart stuck in my throat.

I didn't need to look at a clock to know Turner was correct. I'd been Atlas too long and felt every second of every minute pounding in my head like a hammer on nails. We were well into Day Four. I hadn't noticed because I was too distracted by everything that had been going on. Only mere hours left, and the world would end if I didn't kill Ryan Vaughn.

Not enough time!

Gaia stepped into action. "He's right. We have to go to the portals. My children and grandchildren are fools and we have to stop them."

Roberta asked, "Portals? We thought the dimensions would open and collide with this world."

Owen added, "Chelsan could see the dead crawling through the ground outside the Compound."

Gaia seemed to see Owen and Talan for the first time. "Owen, Talan." Just in the way she said their names I could feel the affection there. Gaia rounded back to Owen's observation though. "What Chelsan saw is the fabric of the dimensions colliding. She'd be able to see that everywhere on Earth if she concentrated, but the gods need to create actual gateways for the worlds to collide. Once the portals are made, it'll be about expanding them until there's nothing left of this world."

Ryan stepped forward. "So when these gateways are in 'portal form,' can we destroy them before they take over Earth?"

Owen and Talan exchanged looks, then Owen answered, nodding, "When we opened a portal to the 5th Heaven, we destroyed it after we brought the Grigori through."

Talan added, "I'll bring the Grigori together and we'll try to take down as many portals as we can."

"It took most our power to take down the one." Owen tried to hide the fear from his voice.

Gaia shook her head. "I'll be able to help."

"Um," Chelsan interrupted in her usual shy way, "Speaking of the underground dead bodies, I can feel them getting closer. We should probably hurry." Her eyes flashed at Gaia with a kind of desperation. Something more personal was motivating Chelsan than simply the dimension gates opening.

Gaia gave Chelsan a reassuring smile, then turned to me. "We need to make sure Chelsan's parents do not cross over into the living world. I'm not sure if we can return the souls back to their afterlife once the portals are closed." Gaia had obviously promised Chelsan the chance to see her parents again but had also told her what might happen to them if they escaped the Underworld.

It made me worried: not that Chelsan might not get the chance to meet her parents, but that Chelsan obviously wanted little else. It told me she was like her grandparents in that regards. I could see in her expression that Chelsan cared more for seeing her parents than she did for the world potentially ending.

Which ultimately meant if I had to kill Ryan to complete my mission, Chelsan would do anything to stop me. I envied her in a way. To have that unwavering loyalty and love that would allow millions of people to die to save the one person she loved. I didn't have it in me. I killed Jack, the man I loved.

And the sad thing was: I'd do it again.

It was a relief that I wouldn't have to see if my theory was true or not. Ryan was immortal now. Impossible to kill. Chelsan would have to find a way to break this curse before the world ended.

Yeah, no problem.

In the meantime, our missions coincided. I decided not to comment on my observation. Instead, I looked at everyone in the room briefly. "Let's do this. We'll meet up where the portals open. I'll give you the coordinates telepathically once Chelsan, Gaia and I get there."

"And me. I'm going with you three," Terence interrupted.

"We should bring Elisha too," Chelsan added. "If anyone can use her powers through a Metlod like me, she'll be able to. I'm pretty sure I could walk her through it."

I turned to Terence. "Go get Elisha. I'll use my telepathic link to Zeus again. He'll be where the action is at."

Terence popped out of view, then quickly materialized with Elisha next to him. The ex-psychopath looked curious as she examined the melted Metlod. Chelsan waved her over and began speaking with her in hushed tones, explaining to Elisha how to use her powers through the Metlod.

I motioned my group toward me, then turned to Talan and Owen. "Be careful. Zeus has probably had eyes on all the Grigori for a while. He could stage an attack to prevent you from interfering with the portals." As I said it, I knew they'd have already thought of that, but they both nodded their agreement anyway.

Turner cleared his throat.

I had almost forgotten about the Turners.

Turner addressed me, "We'll work with Ashliel on figuring out a way to sever the link with the I.Q. Collective and Alec and the brain machines. Maybe prevent the entities from taking over the gods' bodies."

Probably the most important task. Gods I could deal with. The I.Q. Collective? They were much more unpredictable.

"I'll send Ashliel the coordinates as well. Good luck." My eyes lingered on Roberta's, hoping to find some kind of rekindled friendship there, but I was met with a cold stare.

My group stood next to me: Terence, Gaia, Chelsan, Ryan and Elisha. Quite an age range: from the Mother of All Gods to a teenage girl. "Everyone hold on to me."

I felt each one of their hands touch a part of my arm. Focusing on Zeus, I teleported us all…

…to the most terrifying spectacle I'd ever seen.

We were somewhere in the middle of a desert with giant red rock structures looming all around creating shadows under the moonlight.

It was the place of my vision. The place where I had seen myself killing Ryan Vaughn.

Every god I'd ever known – and some I'd never met – stood in a circle. Six open gateways surrounded them, glowing against the darkness of night. Dead center in the circle was Alec's silhouette, looking like a harmless child walled in by deities. The boy who was about to unleash the I.Q. Collective straight into the gods.

The air crackled and boomed as the Titans and Olympians attempted to open the rest of the portals. The noise was almost deafening, a stark contrast to the serene landscape around us. Thousands of corpses ranging from skeleton to freshly killed stumbled out of the six gateways, looking around at their surroundings as if seeing the world for the first time. Out of the six portals, I didn't know which Hells or Heavens had been opened yet. I honestly couldn't tell just from the corpses, but either way we needed to shut them all closed.

I remembered being in the Underworld where everything was a shade of gray, so seeing the lack of color through one of the opened gateways indicated that the Underworld was now open. Recalling back when I was in the Land of Death, going from monotone to full-color brightness was jarring, and to the corpses walking out onto Earth? It must have felt like a new kind of Heaven. Some of them looked starved and vicious, while others simply looked confused.

Chelsan scanned the scene, obviously searching for her parents and probably hoping she wouldn't find them for fear of them losing a spot in the after-life. I could only imagine what was going on in her head and the conflict she struggled with.

Cronus and Hades stood out as the leaders of this giant circle of at least a hundred gods. Even when they had been in their brain-machine-coma, they'd obviously managed to gather deities to their cause. Thinking of Zeus and his imprisonment of Gaia, I still couldn't believe I hadn't noticed any of it. I didn't want to, I guess. I was too busy focusing on my missions to worry about Zeus and his cohorts. Speaking of: Zeus stood next to his father, Cronus, hand-in-hand. I knew it would be bad when the two of them were on the same side, but seeing it in person made it real.

Six gates open.

Five more to go.

I immediately sent the coordinates to Talan, Owen and Ashliel through telepathy then added, *And guys, six portals are open, we don't have much time.*

Talan responded for the group, *We're on our way.*

I turned to Gaia, "You take Chelsan inside the Underworld and get back here as fast as you can. The Grigori are on their way, but I'm going to try one more time to convince Cronus he's walking into Alec's trap." I knew it would be a waste of breath, but I had to try.

Chelsan said something to Ryan and they kissed, then Gaia teleported the girl away.

"Elisha, can you control any of these dead?" I asked, not expecting a favorable answer.

"Some, but not all. Chelsan told me how to work through the Metlod, but I'm not as powerful as she is." Elisha didn't seem bothered at all to admit that.

I nodded. "If you can use some of the corpses, it may be useful. Just get ready for my orders. I may need you to create a distraction."

Elisha nodded without argument. Whatever Talan did to take out 'the crazy' in Elisha seemed to still be working. Besides controlling the dead, I needed Elisha and Ryan because of their connection to the I.Q. Collective. Ryan especially. He once had all their souls roaming around inside of him; it was his connection that allowed Chelsan to kill all the Franklin clones. Maybe with Talan or Owen's help Ryan could do...

Something...

I had no plan.

Sometimes that was a good thing. Plans could be overrated. But mostly they could go wrong. I had thousands of Atlas missions that I accomplished on a wing and a prayer with no plan in sight.

Time to stop this thing.

The three of us walked until we were about twenty feet away

from the circle of doom. We had to pass hundreds of corpses running, shambling, or walking away from the gateways. They didn't seem to have any purposeful direction, only to escape their respective afterlives. Hades wasn't controlling them, and it didn't seem like he was going to, either. A few months ago the world had seen an army of dead almost take over the planet; once these wandering dead people made the news, there would be a whole other nightmare to deal with.

When we were close enough to attract the gods' attention, but far enough to run and get lost in the sea of corpses, I stopped.

"Cronus!" I yelled.

The circle didn't break, the gods' intent on opening up the last five portals, but Cronus's eyes searched until he found mine. He looked more irritated than angry. "Go away, half-breed!"

The dead suddenly parted like a river before us and I noticed Elisha's eyes were closed in concentration. From the expression on Cronus's face, the action surprised him greatly. More importantly, it disturbed Hades. One good thing about Elisha: she had a flare for the dramatic.

I took advantage of the moment and yelled above the noise, "If you open up those last gates, the I.Q. Collective will have enough power to take over you all!"

Alec looked over at me, curiosity and understanding twinkled in his eyes.

If only Cronus wasn't an egomaniacal narcissist, he might have had an inkling of suspicion from the expression on Alec's face. But Alec knew what I knew: he had the gods duped. They would never see a human as a real threat, even when it was staring them in the face. Literally.

"You speak lies to stop us! But we will take this world again.

A new world with all the lands of dead and demons side-by-side with the living!" Cronus spat.

Cronus couldn't separate from the circle to fight me, in fact, none of the gods could. It kept me safe for the moment.

Then it hit me.

Demons.

I hadn't seen any coming from the portals.

They had only managed to open up the Underworld and the gateways to the Heavens. That was why none of the dead were aggressive or attacking. The Hell dimensions would be much harder to break open, and when they did, creatures of unimaginable power and destruction would pour through.

There was no way I was letting that happen.

I needed to break the circle.

"If you choose to stay idiots, then so be it!" I screamed – then sent green fire straight into Cronus's chest.

It bounced off some kind of invisible barrier.

I tried again and again.

Nothing.

Their magic shield was stronger than any I'd ever seen.

"You think we wouldn't protect ourselves from you and the Grigori?" Cronus laughed.

Zeus couldn't help himself as he laughed with his father, "Who's the idiot now?"

I looked at Alec: he kept my gaze and smiled. He was getting ready and he knew there was nothing I could do about it.

"That would still be you," I declared, but I was out of ideas, so stalling seemed like the best option until the Grigori arrived. "Let me guess: Alec, here, made this magic barrier by connecting you all in Turner's machine?"

A flicker of concern crossed Cronus's features, quickly replaced by his usual bravado. "Gods will always be more powerful than humans. Alec is no threat. He simply knows which side to be on."

I shrugged. "If you're so powerful, why do you need a mere human's help?"

The circle seemed to waver and shudder slightly. I was reaching some of them and their connection was weakening. Maybe I could stop this by convincing a few gods to break the circle.

Alec appeared to sense this as well, because with a loud CLAP another portal opened.

And I saw something that chilled me to the bone.

Alec opened that gateway himself with a wave of his hand. It was discreet, so the gods wouldn't pay too much attention. Feeding into their egos was easy. Alec made them believe it was their magical skills and powers that were opening each portal.

But it wasn't.

It was Alec and the I.Q. Collective.

The gods were nothing but a battery.

I knew the feeling. Zeus had done the same thing to me a while ago to regain his strength and mind back. But this was different. Instead of draining the gods of power like Zeus had done or like the Grigori blades, Alec had found a way to give the gods more power the more he siphoned from them. It was the perfect illusion. Alec was fattening the gods up like trussed pigs for the I.Q. Collective, so that when he transferred all the Collective's souls into the vessels, they'd be at max capacity.

"I can't control the newbies," Elisha said through exerted breath.

"That's because they're not dead," I sighed in annoyance. Things were about to get a whole lot worse.

To a human eye, it looked as if more dead people were pouring out of the new gateway, but to my supernatural eyes, I saw that they were all demons. No creature-features yet, only the kind that passed for human, but they were demons all the same. The 1st Level of Hell had just been opened.

Wait.

Scratch that.

It wasn't the 1st Level, it was the 5th, Cronus's home for thousands of years before he and Hades were captured. The Titans' connection was strongest with this dimension so it made sense it was the first Hell to open.

The 5th Level of Hell.

I knew this for certain because Terence had taken Iapetus and Themis there when we battled at the Compound – and now those two Titans had just walked out of the 5th to join the circle of their brethren. And they were followed by...

Rhea and Theia.

Rhea, fully formed (though she should still be in a million pieces), and Theia, recovered fully from her injuries at the News Station.

Cronus stared at me with venom, "We know you have a shifter among you. First imitating Rhea to trick my brother and sister into Zeus's prison in the 5th Level of Hell, then pretending to be Hephaestus trying to tell us lies about our human ally." He eyed Rhea with pride and love. "You see what the human's machine has done? It has restored my Rhea to me and healed Theia, and with the power of the 5th Level of Hell they are fully cured."

I didn't turn to Terence in fear that they'd guess he was the shifter.

Cronus roared with laughter. With all the Titans in the circle, he felt invincible. And, I feared, maybe he was.

Suddenly, over a thousand Grigori angels all teleported in and surrounded the circle of Titans and Olympians. Their chants were in complete unison, their voices loud and overpowering.

So much power all in one place. I could feel it deep in my bones.

Reacting to their incantation, the magic barrier protecting the gods began to visibly reveal itself in a soft, fuzzy glow. Soon the tones of the Grigori chants began to create small fractures through the protective bubble.

Alec understood the situation before the gods, his condescending demeanor quickly switching to focused concentration. He knew he was running out of time.

A loud screeching filled the air.

It filled me with intense pride and happiness.

Asmodeus had arrived, in full demon form, flying above the circle, wings outstretched majestically, a humanlike, brilliant, blue-scaled dragon ready to take on the Titans and Olympians. His sleek form dove toward them. Using his large black talons, he chipped away at the magic shielding, helping the Grigori break it down.

Terence transformed into an almost identical humanlike, deep-blue dragon and flew up to help his father. My son in his true form was beautiful, his scales shimmering in the eerie light of battle. And by the way Asmodeus flew by his son's side, I could tell he was happy.

BOOM!

Another portal opened.

Another Hell unleashed.

Demons larger than Asmodeus shambled out, roaring their pleasure at finally being free to wreak havoc on Earth. 'Living nightmares' were the only words I could use to describe them. Some with blackened spikes for skin, others with popping liquid boils for eyes, all unique in their grotesqueness. But with one screech from Asmodeus the demons slowed down and awaited orders.

Asmodeus always boasted he was the King of Demons, but for some reason I figured it was a title he gave to himself. Now, seeing how these misshapen and distorted creatures revered Asmodeus made me realize he truly was their King. And they were ready for *his* commands.

With another loud screech from Asmodeus, all the demons pouring out of the two Hell dimensions attacked the protective barrier.

Demons and angels united against the gods.

I knew we were witnessing something that had never happened before. The two men in my life: Talan, the Grigori angel that was my soul mate, and Asmodeus, the demon and father of my only child, fighting together.

My heart almost stopped when out of the gateway from the Underworld walked Jack and Penny, followed by thousands of corpses, all armed with swords and axes. Jack saw me from afar, knowing where I was and shouted, "Where do you need us?!"

"Take down that protective barrier and break that circle!" I shouted back.

Jack, all soldier, even after three hundred years, nodded, and barked orders to his army of corpses. His soldiers began swinging at the bubble, trying desperately to break through.

BOOM!

BOOM!

Two more portals opened. Alec was speeding things up, desperation his motivating factor.

Only one more to go!

I sent as much fire as I could at the barrier, it was broken in so many places, but not enough to rip anyone from the circle. It was frustrating being so close but not close enough to do anything.

And with a final nail in the coffin…

BOOM!

The last portal opened.

The glee in every Titan and Olympian's face was impossible to ignore, especially Cronus who laughed loudly, drunk with what was probably the biggest power rush of his existence.

Cronus roared to all the Grigori, demons and dead attacking the protective barrier. "You are but measly creatures! We are gods! You will bow before us!"

A giant blast of fire burst from the circle like a nuclear bomb, pushing all attackers back as if they were leaves in the wind.

Ryan, Elisha and I only got the tail end of it and were knocked to our feet, but some of the closer dead and demons were incinerated instantly. A few Grigori appeared singed, but nothing could kill a Grigori, which helped my stress level at the moment considering Owen, Talan and Antel were right next to the blast radius. Jack and Penny were unscathed as well.

And since Asmodeus and Terence were airborne they were also thankfully spared from any injury.

I stood up and stared at my allies screaming in pain and anguish, burning from a fire that shouldn't exist – and I froze. The world was ending, and it had nothing to do with my mission. Standing next to Ryan, the target of my Atlas mission, I almost wanted to laugh. Checking my internal clock, we were less than an hour from the four-day countdown: thirty-six minutes to be exact. Maybe this was how the curse was supposed to end.

Me dying.

Maybe it had nothing to do with Chelsan at all.

And for a moment, I thought maybe we had been wrong about Alec. Maybe Alec was just Alec and the I.Q. Collective had truly died months ago. Maybe he wanted to end the world and he needed the gods to do it.

And where were Gaia and Chelsan? Didn't they promise to help in this fight?

I stood motionless, watching my worst nightmare come true...

SWOOSH!

Every Titan and Olympian froze, their expressions of utter joy suddenly erased, replaced with blankness. They all looked comatose.

Alec, in contrast, looked downright elated. His eyes turned to mine and they had a slight white glow to them, reflecting his insides swimming with power.

Then something happened, none of us expected, not even Alec.

The gods began to scream.

I rarely rattled easily, but hearing the Titans and Olympians shrieking with an overwhelmingly intense volume was terrifying.

But one interesting thing pulled me out of the horror.

Alec looked shocked.

Alec may have been able to place the souls of the I.Q. Collective into the deities surrounding him, but he hadn't counted on one thing –

The gods were fighting back.

Their screaming became more sporadic but some of the more powerful gods were stronger, fighting for control. They seemed to be winning.

One of them was Cronus.

His eyes desperately sought me out again. "Sister! Help us!"

Sister? Really? I wanted to let the I.Q. Collective take over every one of their bodies, just to spite them – but sociopaths were a lot harder to predict than gods who acted like infants.

The next second, Cronus and the others who had been gaining some traction were back to screaming. The I.Q. Collective were fighting hard.

But a soldier always sees an advantage.

The gods were down for the moment and we needed to shut the portals.

I spoke to Talan and Owen in my mind: *Take down those gateways, I'll try and stall the gods.*

Talan responded, *On it. We can't let the I.Q. Collective take over the gods' bodies completely. We don't know what their ultimate plan is, but I fear them more than the Titans and Olympians.*

Agreed, I answered back. *The devil you know…*

Speaking of… it looks like Asmodeus is losing control of the demons. I think Alec isn't just gaining control over the gods, but the demons and dead as well, Owen added.

As if hearing our conversation, Elisha confirmed, "I've almost lost all control of the dead!"

Alec is the key to all this. If I could get close to him… I shook my head in frustration.

Talan answered, *I'll crack open the shield, it's weak enough now. I don't know what kind of magic he can use against you, but be careful.*

Looks like I'm beating up a seven-year-old, I groaned. Even knowing Alec was at least a hundred years old, he was in a clone's body that was still a child. But I had to stall him, stop him, anything to prevent the Collective from becoming gods.

I believed in the Grigori. They *would* take the portals down.

Just in time for my Atlas mission to fail.

I could already feel the rumbling of the ground beneath my feet. The curse was ready. Ready to tear the planet apart until I killed Ryan Vaughn. Which was impossible. Only thirty minutes left.

I shook the thought from my head.

Priorities.

Gods and portals first.

I moved fast, running toward Alec, having complete faith in Talan's ability to crack open a hole for me to reach him.

As I neared the shield: CRACK! I saw the hole. It was right under Ares and Poseidon's clasped hands. I slid through like I was going to home base. The shield sealed up behind me.

Now I had nothing between me and Alec, but I also was in a shielded circle with Titans and Olympians that would gladly kill me right now if they had any wits about them. Added to the fact that, if the Collective took over, they'd want to kill me too.

So, yeah.

Not a very smart move.

But necessary.

Alec's eyes were closed in concentration.

Good.

Using my Atlas strength, I punched Alec in the center of his chest.

It was as if my hand had hit steel.

Before I could pull it away and mutter the appropriate 'Ow!' expression, Alec grabbed my wrist and his eyes popped open.

He smiled with triumph, "Exactly the juice I need."

The feeling was all too familiar. Alec was draining my strength.

I could physically see the wave of power he took from me and siphoned it to the I.Q. Collective.

I had to stop him.

Yanking my wrist free took all of my strength, but his hands were that of a seven-year-old. Magic or no, I was still stronger. Once contact was broken, I felt energy flow back into my system as I rooted my feet to the ground, pulling the Earth's power into my body. A great perk from being the daughter of Mother Earth.

Not wanting to get near Alec again, I sent a blast of white fire his way. White fire was used for control, my hope being that I could force him to stop the Collective from taking over the gods' bodies.

As the flames reached his body, they snuffed out before making contact.

The creepy smile hadn't left his face.

It didn't bother Alec for a second that I was in front of him, waiting for a fight.

Alec stayed in a defensive position, forcing me to take the offensive. It was a disadvantage: he knew there was nothing I could do but attack.

I lunged forward, grabbing his small arms and tossing him across the circle. I was shocked when it actually worked. Alec's body flew across the ground, slamming into Cronus's feet.

Before he could recover, I ran in for another attack – but before I reached Alec I slammed into an invisible barrier. Falling to my feet, I scrambled to stand back up, when I noticed…

…the screaming had stopped entirely.

It was eerie, only hearing the chants of the Grigori as they tried to seal the gateways, combined with the rumblings of the dead and demons, who continued to pour out of the portals.

I peered up at Cronus.

His eyes no longer held the anger of a petulant child.

Then, looking at each god, all eyes staring directly at me, I realized I wasn't facing my deity family anymore.

I was facing the I.Q. Collective.

Chapter Fifteen

Five Years Ago

CHELSAN

Chelsan stared at the acceptance letter for Geoffrey Turner High School, along with a partial scholarship. It arrived that morning and Chelsan was in a panic. Logically, her mom and everyone else she knew in her trailer park expected Chelsan to go to Forester High, a public school. A free school. Not the most expensive school in the state.

But Forester was five miles away and Bruce would collapse into a mush of bones and guts if Chelsan left her four-mile radius mark. And it wasn't like she could find a way to have her step dad stay at school with her all day. The amount of concentration it would take to keep Bruce lively *and* do her schoolwork would be too much. She'd probably pass out by noon.

So her only option had been applying to Geoffrey Turner High, super expensive, but well within her radius. Her mother was going to flip out when she found out that Chelsan was going there. Janet Derée had made her feelings quite clear with how she felt about Vice President of Population Control Geoffrey Turner.

She hated him.

As in, *really* hated him.

Chelsan never knew why; her mother didn't elaborate on the reasons she despised Geoffrey Turner so much. Chelsan learned not to talk about him much, which was a feat unto itself since Turner was in the news constantly. Not to mention the fact that he was the voice and face of all the world leaders. You couldn't go very far in this world without knowing every wrinkle and crevasse on the face of the Vice President.

Maybe that was the problem? Her mother was an age-ist. Chelsan had to admit it was revolting seeing the skin sag and wrinkle like that, but sometimes she found it comforting and sweet. She'd never admit it to her mother, but every once in a while, Chelsan felt a kind of connection to Geoffrey Turner.

So going to the high school named after him was weirdly serendipitous.

"What's that?" Janet's voice sounded from behind Chelsan.

Chelsan tried to cover the letter with her hand, but her mother was too quick. She snatched it up, reading it with shocked disgust.

"Answer me! What is this?"

"You know what it is. You're looking right at it." Chelsan flinched at her own attitude. She wasn't the kind of kid who talked back to her mother, but seeing the anger in Janet's face made her respond defensively.

Janet stared at her daughter with a mixture of surprise and... Was that... fear?

Chelsan didn't understand that particular emotion. What did her mother have to be afraid of? Especially when it came to what high school Chelsan went to.

"The scholarship covers almost all the tuition. I can get a part time job to pay for books and the rest. You won't have to pay for anything." Chelsan gently took the letter back from her mother.

Janet stood there for a moment, then sat down across from her daughter.

They sat at the rusty Formica-topped kitchen table resting on top of the peeling linoleum floor beneath their feet.

Chelsan kept Bruce sitting in his easy chair, watching holo-tv, occasionally she'd make him laugh. It was a trick of hers to hide the fact that Bruce was dead. She wondered if her mom ever thought that Bruce had some sort of brain damage since that day Chelsan had killed him. The amount of times Chelsan had forgotten to make Bruce appear 'alive,' were more than she could count. Drool and inactivity were the things Chelsan tried to avoid when it came to controlling her step-dad.

Janet sighed deeply, then said, "Why can't you go to Forester High like the other kids in the park?"

Chelsan couldn't answer Janet without admitting that she was a murderer and her victim was laughing at a random piece of footage on holo-tv that probably wasn't even funny. So Chelsan replied, "I want something better in my life. Geoffrey Turner High is the best school in the state and one of the best in the country. If I graduate from there, I'll be able to go to any college, probably on a free ride." Which was true. And Chelsan wanted to go to the best schools she could. She loved learning. The public middle school she had graduated from wasn't top notch. Her advanced classes had been a breeze, enough to earn her a perfect grade point average. Plus, her teachers all adored her and had sent letters of recommendation for Geoffrey Turner High, which was probably one of the main reasons she had been accepted. They saw it as a great opportunity for her.

So why couldn't her mother see it the same way?

"I just…" Janet began, trying to regain her composure. "…don't want you going to a school with that vile human being's name on it. I just can't."

Chelsan rolled her eyes like she always did when her mother spewed hatred for the Vice President. "You know Geoffrey Turner doesn't live there, right? He's probably never stepped foot inside."

"It doesn't matter. He's evil, Chelsan. I can't let you go there." Janet reached across the small table to grab the acceptance letter again, but Chelsan pulled it away.

"Mom." Fear raced through Chelsan. If she couldn't go there, she couldn't go anywhere. She knew her mother didn't like Geoffrey Turner, but never imagined that she'd forbid her to go to a high school named after him.

Something in Chelsan's eyes must have caused Janet to listen to her, because she pulled her hand back and looked at her daughter thoughtfully. "Is it because it's…closer?"

Another wave of fear coursed through Chelsan. Did her mother know about Bruce? Had she figured it out? Why would she ask about distance?

Chelsan could only imagine how she looked, her eyes wide with indecision about how to proceed.

But her mother set her at ease when she said, "I know the Hover-Shuttle is only two stops away from *that school*, and Forester is ten. You hate taking the shuttle."

Relief flooded through Chelsan. She could work with that. "Yes. It's much closer. And I need to be closer." That was as much as Chelsan was willing to share. She hoped it would be enough.

It was.

Janet looked at Chelsan for a few more moments. Finally she

said, "You know I'd do anything for you."

"I know, Mom. Same here." And Chelsan had. She'd kept Bruce animated all these years, ever since she was seven. Her entire childhood had been spent making her mother believe Bruce was alive.

Janet grabbed Chelsan's hand and held it tight, which surprised Chelsan. Her mother's eyes were intense as they stared into her own. "Promise me, that if it ever came to it, you'll leave me and Bruce behind. You'll save yourself."

"Save myself? Mom, where is this coming from? Save myself from what?" Chelsan had never seen her mother so serious before.

Janet still held Chelsan's hand tight, staring at her like she desperately wanted to confess something to her.

"It's only a high school." Chelsan broke the quiet.

Slowly, Janet nodded and pulled her hand back. "You're right. It's only a high school," she repeated. Then, as if the tense moment had never happened, Janet smiled at Chelsan. "I'm very proud of you. That school is very difficult to get into, especially for a trailer kid. We'll make sure you get the money to stay."

Chelsan didn't want to question the turn-around from her mother. At this moment in her life, she just wanted to go to school. And the only school she could go to was Geoffrey Turner High.

Besides, maybe going to this school would somehow let Janet see that the Vice President was a pretty cool guy.

Somehow, Chelsan doubted it, but at least her mother was on board with her going. Every muscle in Chelsan's body relaxed.

Chelsan would never leave her mother.

Not for anything.

Not for anyone.

Present Time

All I could see for miles and miles was gray: the trees, the dirt, the rivers, the sky and clouds... only Gaia and myself were in vivid color. People walked past us, heading for the bright light of the portal a hundred feet or so behind us. From the expressions on their faces, I could tell they thought they were headed to the Promised Land. But they might really be headed for the end of their existences.

Gaia watched the people go by and said, "It used to be that in the Underworld, one's soul was at peace, but they would have no consciousness. They were but shells housing a soul. But when Jack Norbin and Pandora took over, they wanted the people to live in happiness and peace. To truly *live* in their afterlife. A very human decision."

I wondered aloud, "If they're so happy why are they trying to leave?"

Gaia smiled gently. "They want to see the ones they left behind – just as your parents are trying to find you."

Then Gaia pointed.

And there they were.

I knew my mother instantly though it took a second longer to recognize my father. I'd only seen him in visions. But walking toward me, only twenty-feet away, were my parents. They were black and white like the rest of the souls in the Underworld, but for me they might as well have been in full color. My heart nearly burst from seeing my mother again. I almost fell to my knees. My brain couldn't function. It was an emotional overload. She had been my everything. And she had died for nothing. For a grudge. I was shocked that my being could be so filled with love for my parents and hate for my grandparents all at the same time. But seeing my mother again and trying to block out the images of her dying was nearly impossible.

Suddenly my mother's eyes met mine.

And she ran. Ran toward me, arms outstretched, ready to pull me close, tears flowing down her face as she exclaimed, "Chelsan!"

I raced the last few steps and instantly felt her arms wrap around me tightly. I couldn't seem to let go of her. I was afraid if I did, I'd lose her again. And we cried. No matter how hard I tried, I couldn't keep it together. When I felt my father's arms wrap around us both, my knees did wobble then. Everything I'd ever wanted was right here. I didn't want to leave. I wanted to die to be with them forever. Rationally, I knew that wasn't true, but my heart felt a desperation in that moment, feeling their embrace, and I couldn't help thinking like that. I'd lost them both so violently. I didn't want to lose them again. I couldn't. I didn't think I would survive it a second time.

After what felt like hours, though I knew it had been only minutes, my parents pulled back enough to see me. Their eyes sparkled with such love and pride I wanted to burst.

"I only saw you as a baby," my father said, a slight catch in his voice. "You're so beautiful."

Mom held my hand and placed it on her cheek. "I hated how I left you and I worried I'd see you here soon after. I left you so vulnerable." Her eyes flicked toward Gaia. "But Gaia brought me to your father as soon as I got here, and she has let us know everything you've accomplished. We're so proud of you."

The fact that Gaia could travel to the Underworld *and* know all that was happening with the world while imprisoned in the Metlod made me realize that the magic prison wasn't the torture Zeus had wanted for his grandmother. Gaia was Mother Earth after all, which probably meant nothing went on without her knowledge.

Dad held my other hand, clinging tight. "I know it was difficult, but I am glad you have a relationship with my parents."

I almost pulled my hand back at his mention of the Turners, but my love for my father was too strong. I tried to sound as calm as possible when I said, "They're the reason we're not together."

Dad's grip tightened on my hand, his expression one of understanding. "I didn't say it was a perfect relationship, but from everything Gaia has told us they do love you. And I know it's hard to believe, but they were good parents to me."

For some reason my defenses kept prickling up. "They kept you a child for a hundred years, how can you say that?"

But it was Mom who answered, "No one is defending their actions, Chelsan, but they are the only family you have left."

"How can you say that after what they did to you? They killed you!" I was getting angry now. This wasn't at all what I had wanted. I wanted a big hug fest for all eternity. Was that too much to ask?

Sensing my growing outrage, my mother and father exchanged concerned glances. Then Dad said quietly, "When you die, Chelsan, all that hate and anger goes away. You see things more clearly. My parents acted out of desperation and then vengeance because when they love, they love with everything they have. They knew about the prophecy. About you. And they knew if they kept me a child, I could never have a child myself. When Janet took me away on Kala's orders, I was so happy I could finally physically grow up, and I loved your mother with every fiber of my soul. I didn't think I could love anyone more – until *you* were born. When my parents cast the spell that killed the both of you, I felt my soul break in

388

half. I didn't want to live if I couldn't be with you two. So I brought you back to life, unwittingly giving you my powers and fulfilling my part of the prophecy." He squeezed my hand again, lovingly. "Don't you see, Chelsan? No one hates my parents more than they hate themselves. Everything they did to prevent the prophecy only made it happen. And they've been punishing themselves and everyone around them ever since."

"They *should* hate themselves," I shook my head, confused. "But why are we talking about them now? We are finally reunited, and we end up having a conversation about Turner and Roberta? This isn't what I imagined when Gaia said I'd see you again."

Mom and Dad exchanged glances again and I knew something was up. I may not know my dad's tells, but I knew my mom's. "What? I know you, Mom. You have that should-I-tell-Chelsan-or-shouldn't-I look on your face."

Mom nodded her head, freeing her hand from mine and touching my cheek. "The prophecy, Chelsan. You have to fulfill it."

A sense of panic welled up inside of me. "But how? I don't know how!" I finally said it. I'd been able to ignore this prophecy for four days now with everything exploding all around me, but time was running out…

I turned to Gaia. "We're running out of time, aren't we?"

Gaia nodded. "There are merely minutes until the Atlas mission must be fulfilled or the world will crumble."

"But the portals! Won't the world end because of those, too?" I didn't know why that came out of my mouth. It seemed like a distraction at this point. Like I wanted the world to end another way that I wasn't responsible for.

Gaia shook her head. "The Earth could survive the opening of the gateways." Her eyes bore into mine. "But it can't survive the curse of balance not being fulfilled."

"But Kala can't kill Ryan. He took the serum. How am I supposed to break this curse if I don't know how?" My mind couldn't take in the enormity of everything that was being placed on my shoulders. It didn't seem real. And being in the Underworld in a palette of all gray didn't help to ground me in reality, either.

Then an odd thought hit me. "Why did you bring me here?" I asked Gaia. "If time is truly running out, shouldn't I be back there? Where the action is? Give me a chance to try...something?"

It was my mother who answered, "We can't tell you why, but you'll understand soon. Trust me, Chelsan, coming here will help you break Kala's curse."

It made no sense, but I trusted my mother, and a desperate part of me wanted to hold onto any kind of hope that I'd somehow manage to make everything right and break this curse for Kala. My instincts were screaming at me that something was off, that I was being manipulated somehow, but I didn't want to care. Seeing my parents like this had been a dream come true and I'd be forever grateful even if Gaia had something up her sleeve.

The ground shook and the portal wavered from the impact.

Gaia spoke, "It's time. The I.Q. Collective has taken over the gods' bodies and Kala needs our help." Another jolt to the ground. I almost lost my footing. "The portal will close soon. The Grigori are close." Gaia turned to me with sympathy. "Say your good-byes."

I turned to my parents, but the three of us had no more words. We pulled each other in for another embrace, my hands clenching the clothes on each of their backs. I needed them. I didn't want to leave. I couldn't. It was safe here. Quiet. Peaceful. I didn't want to jump back into the mayhem that was my life. The portals were open, the I.Q. Collective now inhabited the Titans and Olympians...

and oh yeah… the world would end if I didn't figure out how to break some mythical curse! And I had zero magical ability!

The Underworld was looking pretty good right now, shades of gray and all.

Gaia's hand landed on my shoulder. "I'm sorry, but we must leave now, Chelsan. I can feel the Earth breaking apart." She looked at me with concern and patience. "I can always bring you back here to visit them."

That thought gave me a strange kind of hope I couldn't describe. "You'd do that?"

Gaia smiled, "If I'm alive, yes – but I won't be for long if we don't return."

She was Mother Earth. If the Earth died, then so did she.

I couldn't let that happen.

And neither could my parents. Mom placed her hand on my shoulder. "Go, now. You can do this."

I nodded, though I felt no confidence.

But the mere thought of being able to spend time with my parents again was enough to get my mind back in order. I was ready. I had no idea what I was going to do, but I was ready.

I clasped Gaia's hand. "Let's go."

In a blink of an eye Gaia and I were suddenly in the center of the circle of Titans and Olympians all holding hands, all staring at…

Kala.

Next to her was Alec, thrilled beyond measure. Then I realized the gods were calm, calculating and radiating power.

The I.Q. Collective.

It was strange how I could tell the difference. No more peacocking or whining, only confidence and no emotion. I never thought I'd miss temper tantrums, but I'd take Cronus's monologuing over the cold calculation of an I.Q. kid any day.

Alec held his hands out high. "My brethren! Kill the Grigori!"

I watched in horror as the Titans and Olympians let go of one another and began spewing fire of every color from their hands and into the surrounding Grigori.

That was when I noticed that three of the eleven gates were already closed. The Grigori kept their chanting going as they were engulfed in the fire from the gods. It seemed to hurt them, but they were withstanding the pain in order to close the rest of the gateways.

Kala grabbed my arm. "Where have you been?! We only have fifteen minutes left in the countdown! Can you break it?!"

She was referring to the curse and I still had no clue.

Alec sent fire into Kala's back, throwing her forward and causing her to let go of my arm.

That pissed her off.

Kala whirled around and attacked Alec with a blast of searing, pain-inducing green fire. It glanced off his arm, but grazing him caused Alec to cry out from the brief contact. It was enough to scare him, and he ran into the melee of fighting gods.

Some Grigori had broken off and were attacking the gods, while Asmodeus, in his dragon form, and a second man-dragon kept swooping down and shredding the Olympians and Titans with their black, gnarly talons. There was no circle at this point, supernatural beings were running wild within the heat of battle.

And the earth was shaking.

As in, seriously breaking apart.

Kala and I were alone in the center of the battle chaos. She motioned to the jolting ground. "Unless you figure it out, this world with crack open and humans will become extinct. Only the people who took the serum, like you and your boyfriend, will live and you guys will be floating in space, suffocating, then reviving, suffocating then reviving, *forever*. That's your future if you don't hurry up!"

"Thanks for the visual." Was I just being sarcastic? I think I was just being sarcastic. But Kala's threats kind of made me angry. It wasn't as if I knew what I needed to do and was refusing to do it. I honestly had no freaking clue what to do. So what? This was it? The gates to the Heavens and Hells pour out onto Earth as it explodes into floating asteroids?

All because of me?

"Maybe we should have been trying to figure this out a little harder over the last four days," I grumbled, knowing that with all the noise no one could hear but me.

I was knocked to my feet by a blast of green fire.

Pain instantly flooded to every part of my body. I screamed from the shock and agony of it. It only lasted seconds, though, as Talan ran into view, hands out before him, casting a magic shield over me.

Then I saw Ryan.

Running toward me.

Hearing my scream he must have realized I was back and, despite the monstrous battle going on around him, Ryan came for me anyway. I closed the distance between us, and we were in each other's arms in seconds. I felt his lips touch mine with fevered desperation. He was terrified. I could tell by the frantic way he kissed me. When he pulled away all he said was, "This is all my fault."

"What? No! Don't say that! It's my fault for not having an

answer. I'll think of something. We have – what? Ten minutes left?" I almost laughed at the absurdity of that statement.

Ryan cracked a small smile, but his eyes were full of terror and, what was worse, guilt. He was taking on the burden of my mistakes because his death was Kala's mission and, because of Fortski's immortality serum, she could never fulfill it. But what he didn't seem to understand was that, serum or no, I'd *never* let him die. It was selfish and wrong of me, but I knew it in my heart. I would have never let it happen.

Isabelle, Dean and Derek had entered the fray. I could see them with three of Derek's UVC guns, blasting at the gods/I.Q. kids, causing them to scream in pain.

Elisha joined us, along with Ashliel, Turner and Roberta. I could see a shimmering glow around the four of them as either Ashliel or Roberta protected them from the flying fire and spells darting around the battlefield.

It made me wonder: where were we? There were no hover cars above us, no humans anywhere in sight. It must have been some kind of dead zone that the gods staked out years ago, knowing where they'd break open the dimensions and create a new world. It was probably Alec who had persuaded them, guiding them to all their choices. For all the hate the gods held toward humans, they ended up giving their entire beings to one without realizing it. I'd almost feel sorry for them if they hadn't been warned a bagillion times by Kala.

Despite the massive attack, though, the Grigori still managed to shut down two more portals. Only six left. I could feel the dead bodies walking through those gates that were still open. Through my Metlod, I was able to control them if needed, but I could feel Hades's (or, more specifically, whichever I.Q. kid took over his body) grasp on more than half of the corpses. I wasn't sure if I could win a battle of wills between the Death God/I.Q. kid and myself – and, honestly, I didn't think there'd be any time to anyway.

But seeing Alec in the distance, amongst the gods that were the I.Q. Collective, his face befuddled by the Earth crumbling and shaking.

Alec hadn't expected the Atlas mission to fail.

I would have thought that more mayhem would only make the Collective happy, that destroying the planet was their ultimate goal. But no. They wanted their god puppets to rule a new world, a world of all the Heavens and Hells colliding into one. But, if the planet ended, they'd rule nothing. They'd be nothing. Floating in space like Kala had said.

Turner's words brought me out of my thoughts. "Alec is the key!"

Kala and Talan huddled with the new arrivals, Kala keeping her eyes on Alec. "Yeah, we know. Him and the Collective have completely taken over the gods' bodies."

Turner shook his head. "That's not what I mean. Alec is the key to killing the I.Q. Collective permanently."

That sounded promising. "How?" I asked.

Ashliel answered carefully, "We have to kill Alec."

My defense mechanisms kicked in immediately. "We can't. He's taken the immortality serum." The serum was the ultimate protection.

It was Ryan's protection.

Ashliel exchanged concerned glances with Talan.

Kala noticed. "What? What do you two know?"

Roberta's eyes were on me when she answered, "They know how to remove the serum."

The ground shook underneath us, knocking me to the ground. But it was Roberta's words that had truly knocked me down.

No.

"That's not possible," was all that came out of my mouth.

Talan tried to sound calm amongst the chaos around us. "It's always been possible. The Grigori have known how to do it since we learned of its existence."

Kala's eyes flashed mine. "I didn't know. I swear."

Rage.

Yes.

I felt rage.

I didn't believe Kala for one second.

She had planned this as a last resort. Of course Kala knew there was a possibility that I wouldn't be able to break the curse, so she gave Ryan the serum to convince me she was trustworthy, knowing full well she could kill him if she needed to. Jason's suspicions had been right. I kicked myself for not taking his theories more seriously.

Instinctively, I placed Ryan behind me.

To Talan I said, "Go. Remove the serum from Alec and destroy him and the Collective, but if you come one step near Ryan, I will end you." I sounded like my grandparents, but I didn't care. I meant it.

SLAM! SLAM! Two more gates closed.

Four left.

It was Ashliel that ran for Alec, though, maneuvering his way through demons and gods, but Alec was now guarded by the big guns: Cronus and Zeus. The two I.Q. kids controlling those gods knew that they would be Alec's best defense. The fact that they were guarding him also alluded to the fact that they always knew that losing the serum was a possibility. It also told me that Alec was indeed the key. Kill Alec, kill the Collective.

I didn't want to kill anyone though.

I wanted to take Ryan, find Nancy, Bill, Max and Jill, and just be. Maybe jump into one of the Heaven dimensions before the Grigori closed them up.

I needed to get Ryan and me away from Kala.

I began backing up, Ryan right behind me.

Ryan's whispers cut like knives to my heart, "Chelsan, you have to let her complete her mission. I can't be responsible for the world ending."

"You won't be responsible. I will. We're going into one of the Heaven dimensions." I said, voicing what I had fantasized out loud. It made it sound like I had a plan. Let's face it, I was running on panic alone at this point, the seconds slipping by as the noose tightened around us.

The battle raged.

The ground shook.

Giant cracks opened up around us, causing the dead and demons to fall down into the abyss of a dying world.

Kala inched closer. "Chelsan, I am so sorry. You'll never know how sorry I am."

"Get away from us!" I screamed.

Then suddenly I couldn't move.

Not an inch.

I could feel Ryan beside me. He was frozen in place as well.

I watched in horror as Talan walked calmly over to us, his eyes full of sadness as he said, "It must be done."

I wanted to scream, but my vocal chords were frozen too. Turner and Roberta made a dash toward me, Roberta's eyes telling me that

397

she'd do anything to protect me. But they were instantly frozen as soon as they began moving. I was shocked that I felt a pang of love for the two of them as I knew they were going to help save Ryan. They understood. They knew that love was all that mattered.

Talan placed his hands on Ryan's head. I could barely see from the corner of my eye as a slight yellow glow formed around Ryan. Then I heard a small splash of liquid as it hit the ground, Talan turned to Kala. "It's done."

My insides were screaming.

Tears streamed down my cheeks.

I couldn't see straight.

She couldn't look at me as she walked up to Ryan, pulling out her gun.

A gun.

Pointed at Ryan.

This wasn't happening.

I struggled with all my might to move, but nothing I did worked.

Ryan was telling me he wanted Kala to do it, that he didn't want to be responsible for killing billions of lives. I could barely hear him my panic was so heightened.

I was stuck watching the love of my life be killed by a god.

My eyes met Gaia's, pleading for help without words, but what I saw in her expression made me shudder. And suddenly I knew why she had taken me to the Underworld to see my parents. Gaia knew this was what was going to happen. She knew I'd be stuck here, forced to watch Ryan be murdered. She brought me to my parents and made them talk to me about Roberta and Turner to see how far I'd go to keep Ryan safe. Gaia wanted to provoke me into what I was about to do...

And it worked.

Gaia knew I'd never let Kala hurt Ryan.

She counted on it.

Kala turned to me and said, "I'm so sorry."

Then she aimed the gun and pulled the trigger.

BOOM!

I blasted through the Metlod inside my head, shattering it to pieces.

With powers I didn't know I had, I disintegrated the bullet before it touched Ryan's temple. Then I shattered Kala's gun.

Kala stared at me and for a second, I wondered what I must look like to her, because her eyes were full of fear.

Talan leapt to grab me while Kala reached down to snap Ryan's neck.

SLAM!

I felt something inside of me snap.

With a terrifying ease, I connected to the gods', demons', angels', and humans' lights.

My body filled with power as I took control of every single one of them.

Chapter Sixteen

101 Years Ago

KALA

Talan pulled Kala close as they lay in bed in her apartment. They had made love and Kala had felt a bit frantic before and during their love making. She was much more relaxed now and, in a rare moment, she snuggled in close to Talan.

Forehead to forehead, Kala took in the beauty that was Talan. His perfectly chiseled features were only a bonus to his sparkling, kind eyes. Kala could get lost in them for hours on end, and sometimes she would. It was better than thinking of the Atlas mission countdown, which ticked inside her head as if a stopwatch had been surgically added to her brain.

Talan couldn't seem to help himself and leaned in to kiss her. His soft lips sent a thrill through her body that immediately made her want to jump his bones again. Pulling slightly away, Kala said between kisses, "Why do you love me?"

She hadn't meant to go there, but the words fell out of her mouth before she could stop them. And she needed to know. If their roles had been reversed, Kala knew, she would despise Talan. Sleeping with Asmodeus, having a child with him, then mission after mission, one more vile than the next. How could Talan love someone who had done such terrible things? Kala could barely look at herself in the mirror anymore. She was afraid of what she'd see there if she looked too hard.

Talan stopped kissing her, his eyes full of empathy.

For her?

Why was he so good?

Maybe being an angel had something to do with it, but Kala had met plenty of Malaks and Grigori who were dicks, so that couldn't be the reason.

Talan was just good. It was who he was, built in every cell in his body.

Unlike Kala.

Kala was about to push her way out of bed from self-disgust when Talan pulled her head in again so they were back to forehead-to-forehead.

"Kala Hicks you are so full of light, I could never imagine being with anyone else. You're funny, you're brilliant, you're the most stunning being I've ever seen. How could I not love you?" Talan said this with such sincerity Kala could almost believe it for a brief second.

But self-loathing took over quickly, as it usually did.

"I'm a monster." Her voice was small.

Talan's hand cupped the side of Kala's face, his eyes boring into hers. "No one would exist on Earth without you. Every being on this planet owes you their life. That doesn't make you a monster, it makes you a savior."

Unexpected tears came to Kala's eyes. "I don't feel like a

savior, I feel… broken."

His expression was one of helplessness. Talan didn't know what to do any more than Kala did.

But his hand felt strong against her cheek and Kala took what comfort she could from it.

"You've already lived with this curse for two hundred years. If the prophecy is right, you only have a hundred years to go," Talan said, as if that would make her feel better.

"A hundred years." Kala let those three words hang in the air. "That's over nine thousand more missions." The number was staggering, and it made Kala feel lost and anguished.

Talan, seeing the error of his words, kissed Kala gently. "And I will be with you for every one of them. You don't have to do this alone."

"But I do. The very nature of being Atlas is the fact that I have do it alone. No one can complete my missions for me. I wouldn't wish that on anyone." Kala shrugged, "Except Zeus. I'd wish it on him and Cronus, although he'd probably like it."

Talan smiled, "They wouldn't complete one single mission. They don't have the stomach for it. And they want the world to burn anyway. You're the only one strong enough. *Atlas* couldn't even perform his own punishment. He'd rather watch the humans he tricked go slowly insane." Talan suddenly realized mentioning *insane* probably wasn't a good tactic.

Kala smiled back. "You know, you're not very good at the whole cheering-up thing." She kissed him. "But I appreciate the effort."

Talan stared into Kala's eyes with such a love that it always left her breathless. "Let me show you your life after the curse is broken," he said.

"Can you do that?" Kala couldn't hide the hope from her voice.

"I can try." Talan's hand firmed up where it cupped Kala's cheek.

Kala felt the familiar rush of colors and blurred scenery as Talan gave her one of his visions. The images moved so fast, Kala couldn't differentiate one from the other. This wasn't normal, not since Kala had grown used to navigating Talan's visions.

"What's happening?" she asked, bewildered.

Though she couldn't see Talan since her sight was enmeshed in what he was showing her, Kala could only hear his voice.

"I'm not sure. It's as though the future isn't set, so I can't show you." Talan, too, sounded confused.

Panic seared through Kala's veins. "Does that mean the curse doesn't break?"

"No. It's not that. It's just… there's some kind of block. Like the universe won't let me see the future."

When the images wouldn't form into anything coherent, Talan finally stopped.

His face came into sharp focus as Kala fell out of his vision.

Talan's eyes were full of regret. "I wanted to comfort you, but I feel like I made it worse."

Kala leaned in and kissed him again, then said softly, "Don't be sorry. Seeing the future can be worse sometimes. Knowing your fate. What if you showed me the curse locking in place and never going away? I don't think I could live with that."

Talan nodded, but the guilt stayed in his expression.

"I need to have a little faith. All those years ago I met the girl, Chelsan, who would save me. I hope she's as good-hearted as she seemed, because I believe that she will break the curse someday."

Kala said the words and found that she truly meant them.

Chelsan was her salvation.

Chelsan would save her.

Only a hundred more years to go.

Present Time

This was bad.

Very bad.

I couldn't move, and from what I could see, no one else could, either. Even Terence and Asmodeus were hovering motionless mid-air above us. At least Chelsan had the presence of mind to keep them from dropping like stones to the ground. I was surprised that Ryan was stuck, too. Chelsan must have pulled this off without knowing what she was doing, which meant everyone got caught in the crossfire.

The earth shook violently. It was the only sound against the silence. No more fighting, no more chanting, no more moving. Chelsan had stopped it all.

One minute left in the countdown.

It was over.

I found myself not trying to break free of Chelsan's control. I was surprisingly calm. I had been preventing this moment from happening for three hundred years now. Now that it was out of my hands, I felt a strange kind of peace. I could rest now. I was so tired. I didn't think I'd had a good night's sleep since before I became Atlas. It would be nice to sleep. It would be nice for it all to be over. I had felt like this before, years ago, and I had only admitted it to one person: Asmodeus. The fateful three days I spent with him when Terence was conceived. Terence had given me new life, new hope. He made me want to live and keep this world spinning for him.

But Chelsan was going to let it crack and burn.

For love.

I envied her. I could see Jack frozen with Penny next to him in the distance. I had chosen to kill him to save the planet. I chose billions of lives over his. I chose strangers over the man I loved.

Everything was in slow motion.

Chelsan stood there, soaking in the immense power she had tapped into. Her eyes glowed white, brimming with the essence of connecting to the souls of gods, demons, and angels. I had seen it before when she had connected to the pregnant women in Havenville and then the clones a few months back. But those had been humans. Powerful, yes, but nothing compared to supernatural beings. Chelsan had tried these last few days to connect with Hades and failed each time, his light too powerful for her to connect to. Somehow, now, she had broken through that barrier. She owned us all.

I tried to test for a weaknesses in Chelsan's hold.

Nothing.

Suddenly Terence slammed to the ground with frightening force, followed by Asmodeus. Apparently, keeping them afloat took too much concentration for Chelsan. Asmodeus groaned and transformed back to his human self, though still frozen in place, but Terence...

My heart squeezed in anguish as I stood, paralyzed, frantically watching to see if my son was alive.

His body didn't move.

I wanted to scream.

I pushed as hard as I could against Chelsan's hold, but I

might as well have been a wooden puppet. I had no control over my body.

Ten seconds left.

Giant cracks tore through the surface of the ground, causing motionless bodies to tumble into the depths that opened up underneath them. I felt guilty for feeling relief that no one I cared about had been one of the victims.

It was almost over.

I felt two things when I saw Terence transform back to himself and saw his chest move up and down in slow breath: relief that my son was alive and terror that he was about to die with this planet.

Five...

I failed.

Four...

How could Chelsan watch the world die? Without the serum, Ryan would die anyway.

Three...

I wanted to scream to the people that I loved and tell them I was sorry and that I loved them, but Terence and Derek were unconscious, and Owen was out of my view – even Asmodeus was too far away to see. But Talan... He was there in front of me, and when my eyes met his, I wanted to cry. I spoke to him telepathically, not knowing if he could hear me or not. *I love you.*

Two...

Talan's voice filled my head as I waited for oblivion to take us all, *I love you, too.*

One...

My body yanked forward as if strapped into a giant leash that was just pulled violently.

I tried to look down to watch the Earth break apart. This was it. Front row seats to the end of everything.

Another wrench forward.

Then I realized…

My body wasn't moving.

I looked up to see: Chelsan staring at me, her eyes still white glowing orbs. Then she spoke, her voice was clear and calm, somehow overriding the deafening thunder of the ground breaking apart. "I see things now, Kala. I see it all. I see the curse inside you. It's a living breathing thing."

The roar of the Earth rolling and shattering became a backdrop to Chelsan's small, angelic voice as she smiled at me, "I'm going to kill it now."

With one last yank, I felt a part of me rip out of my skin. It was as if my intestines had been pulled out of my body through my throat. But, instead of what I expected to see – guts – I saw an orange colored cloud being yanked out of my mouth. It felt like Chelsan was pulling out a rope that had no end in sight. It wasn't just the curse she was taking from me.

It was Atlas.

All his memories, his being, everything that made Atlas who he was, left my body in the form of the orange cloud. I could still feel his strength and his powers inside me, but the essence of Atlas was being pulled out of my body. All the barriers that Talan had built inside my brain to house a god without losing my mind dissipated with the smoke, no longer needed.

When the last of the orange smoke left me, it disintegrated in the air above until there was nothing left of it.

I was Kala again. Just Kala. Half-Gaia/half human.

But the Earth continued to rip apart.

The curse of balance had been placed back into the Universe's hands and it still wanted blood.

Ryan's blood.

His death was the mission.

A burst of light shot out of Chelsan's chest, directly into the sky itself and she screamed.

But in a flash, Chelsan was calm once more, her eyes back to an eerie glow.

Silence.

The ground had stopped shaking. As if I had completed my mission though Ryan was very much alive.

Chelsan still controlled us all.

Her voice, though aimed to me, carried to everyone there. "It's done. Your curse is broken."

And it was true.

I could feel it in my soul. I was whole again. No countdowns. No missions. No more access to Atlas's memories. No more Atlas. I was me again. I would have cried from happiness, but I was still frozen in place.

And Chelsan didn't look like she had plans to let any of us go.

Chapter Seventeen

Two Years Ago

CHELSAN

Chelsan sat with her two best friends, Nancy and Bill, at one of the booths in *Mel's Ice Cream and Sodas,* where she worked. The store was closed now, and Mel had given Chelsan permission to close up and have a couple of scoops of ice cream on him for her and her friends. Mel had heard about how Jill Forester had tried to humiliate Chelsan in front of the school assembly by 'accidentally' showing a holo-image of Bruce and her trailer, to show how poor Chelsan was and how 'trashy' her stepfather looked.

Internally, Chelsan didn't mind much. If Jill had known that Bruce was dead, she probably would have been impressed at how great he looked – for a corpse. But Jill's mission had been successful: the entire school laughed and threw Chelsan disgusted looks the rest of the day.

Mel didn't mind making money off rich kids, but he didn't like them very much. At least not the Jill Foresters of the world.

Bill and Nancy though?

They were his favorites because they risked social pariahdom by being Chelsan's friends.

Bill ate a bite of his chocolate-chip-mint, double-fudge scoop of ice cream and his eyes closed in delight at the taste. "Mel has the best ice cream on the planet."

"I don't know about the whole planet," Nancy took a bite of her triple-caramel, pecan, vanilla, "Okay, the planet." Her eyes rolled back in her head. "I can't even." She turned to Chelsan. "How do you not eat this all day? I'd be five hundred pounds if I worked here."

Chelsan laughed, enjoying the moment of being with two of her favorite people. "I somehow doubt Mel would let me stay if I ate all the merchandise."

"Oh, he totally would. He loves you to pieces." Nancy motioned around the 1950s-decorated restaurant. "He trusts you enough to let you close up without him. And he trusts you enough to let your hooligan friends hang out here with you." Nancy eyed the ice cream counter. "I might have to eat a scoop of every flavor. And then die of my stomach exploding."

"We can't have you dying just yet. You have to marry Jason Keroff first," Bill teased.

Nancy batted her eyelashes. "Ah, yes, Jason Keroff: the most beautiful man to ever exist. And probably the sweetest most selfless, brave person ever. Did you see the news piece he did on Virtual Reality bars? He probably saved thousands of lives."

Bill chuckled at that, "How is talking about Virtual Reality bars saving lives?"

Nancy shrugged with a laugh. "I don't know, but he made it sound like he was uncovering something underworld-y. The point is: he's perfect in every way."

Chelsan and Bill both laughed at that. The first thing that Chelsan had learned about Nancy was her raging crush on the famous reporter, Jason Keroff. At first, Chelsan had agreed wholeheartedly, mainly because it bonded them in a way. But now that Chelsan was on her fifth tutoring session with Ryan Vaughn, her fleeting crush on Jason had come to a screeching halt. Both Ryan and Jason were completely out of her league, of course, but Ryan she saw every day. The torture was real.

Chelsan ate a bite of her own double-chocolate fudge ice cream and had to agree with her friends. There was something magical about every bite of Mel's ice cream recipes. It was all homemade, with ingredients from all over the world. Mel only picked the best for his ice cream. His store was a world landmark, which basically meant people from everywhere would come to Los Angeles just to have a scoop of delicious goodness.

Bill's expression turned serious, "Sorry about what Jill did today. That was messed up."

Chelsan took another bite of ice cream. "I'm not ashamed of where I live or my step dad, so it didn't bug me as much as I'm sure she wanted it to."

Bill's face flushed with embarrassment. "I didn't mean that you should be ashamed... I just meant all the laughing... and the dirty looks... That sounded horrible. I'm such a jerk."

Nancy nodded, mock-serious, "That's exactly the word I'd used to describe Bill Merryweather: jerk."

Chelsan laughed, "I wasn't trying to make you feel bad, Bill. I knew what you meant. The things that Jill Forester would be embarrassed about in her life are not the same as mine."

Nancy guffawed. "Tell me about it. I'd be embarrassed just *being* Jill Forester. She's truly a horrible human being."

Though Chelsan wanted to agree with her enthusiasm, she knew that people were rarely mean without reason. It would have to be a big reason though because Jill was a nasty piece of work. A part of Jill's ire came from Bill being friends with Chelsan, of that she was certain.

"I need to develop a tougher skin. I somehow doubt Jill will let up for my entire high school existence." Chelsan realized with clarity that Jill Forester would be a thorn in her side until they all graduated.

"Maybe I should talk to her. She'll probably listen to me," Bill offered, though his face looked as if he'd rather eat razor blades.

"Nah," Chelsan let him off the hook. "It'd make it worse. She has the hots for you and any conversation where you say nice things about me would probably send her into a rage-filled tirade."

"That's definitely true: the hots and the tirade," Nancy agreed, taking another bite of ice cream. "Seriously, this is so freaking good. I think I'm going to have a heart attack."

"Jill doesn't like me," Bill seemed appalled by the idea.

Chelsan and Nancy both laughed at his ignorance.

Nancy answered first, "Bill, you're funny."

Chelsan added, "Jill looks at you like you're her soul mate."

"No way." Bill couldn't seem to accept what they were saying.

"I don't know, Bill. I think it's too perfect: the King and Queen of Geoffrey Turner High… Bill and Jill. It has a nice rhyming ring to it," Nancy teased.

Bill's face turned bright red and he glanced at Chelsan to see what her reaction would be. Even teasing that Bill would date Jill made Chelsan feel a pang of hurt. Not because she liked Bill in that way, but because Jill was such an integral part of what made school miserable for her.

412

"You *wouldn't* date her? Would you?" Chelsan asked and was surprised that her voice sounded frightened.

Bill's eyes were loyal and fierce as he said, "Never."

Chelsan nodded slowly, finding herself more relieved than she would have thought possible. "Good." She paused in the silence, then said, "You're too good for her."

"That's putting it mildly," Nancy broke up the tense moment. She scraped the bottom of the bowl as if more ice cream would suddenly appear on command. "Bill, your family is the richest family alive. Buy me another ice cream?"

Bill grinned and it was contagious. Both Chelsan and Nancy smiled back as Bill said, "It would be my pleasure."

Chelsan watched as her two best friends went behind the counter and scooped themselves up some more ice cream.

In that moment, Chelsan felt true happiness.

She didn't need the school to like her.

She didn't need Jill Forester to like her.

Chelsan had two friends who loved her unconditionally and that meant more to her than she could possibly dream.

"I've got a killer milkshake recipe if you guys are interested?" Chelsan smiled with her eyebrow raised in question.

"Um, yes please!" Bill answered immediately.

Nancy nodded like an eager puppy. "Yes, yes, yes, yes!"

Chelsan stood up and walked over to the shake machine and began to make the three of them milkshakes.

Nancy was the first to drink the shake. She sighed in pure joy, then said, "You're trying to make me fat so you can have Jason Keroff, aren't you?"

Chelsan and Bill laughed.

Memorizing the moment and the contentment she felt,

Chelsan knew that she'd be friends with Bill and Nancy forever.

"I love you guys," Chelsan smiled.

"We love you, too," Bill answered back.

"Love you to the moon and back," Nancy smiled as she took another sip of her shake. "These should be illegal. Are there drugs in here? I'm pretty sure there are drugs in here."

Present Time

I did it.

I destroyed the Atlas curse. The Universe had still wanted Ryan dead, but that wasn't going to happen so I stopped it. And if there were ramifications later on, I'd stop those too. I also destroyed what was left of the being Atlas as well as the curse, but that was because I didn't know how to tell the two apart at first. I had still been figuring out how to use the power I had surging through me. I was pretty sure I left Kala with all of Atlas's super powers simply because they weren't attached to the god's memories and essence.

A little voice screamed inside my head: *Chelsan! Disconnect! This is killing you!*

What a strange thing to say. I felt better than I ever have. How could staying connected to these beings *kill* me? It didn't make any sense. Not logically anyway. The power was a part of me now. It *was* me.

Energy flowed through me as if it was my own blood pumping through my veins. At first it had been overwhelming, to a point where I thought I'd lose myself forever, but then everything became clear:

I was a god.

Not like these creatures in front of me that called themselves gods. When you broke it down, they were just old supernatural beings with super powers. No. Not like me. I was truly a god. I could create something from nothing. I could bend this world any way I liked. I could destroy everyone here if I wanted. It was simple. I could see *everything*. And I knew how to do *anything*.

In fact...

I closed the rest of the portals instantly. It was so easy, like shutting doors. Why had it been so difficult for the Grigori? It was so simple. I accidentally sliced a few demons and dead people in half, since they had been frozen in the doorway, but it couldn't be helped. The gateways needed to be closed. Now they were.

Next.

Alec and the I.Q. Collective needed to go away. I thought I had destroyed them months ago. I had been forced to kill all of the Franklin clones to do it and apparently, I had failed. I didn't like that. It made me angry. And the Collective hadn't cared how difficult it had been for me to murder hundreds of versions of my father as a child. They just jumped ship and flew into Alec's head when I robbed them of their living vessels. Although, thinking about it now, it wasn't as emotional for me as it used to be. I strangely felt numb to my feelings. Everything felt more matter-of-fact.

The voice screamed at me again: *Chelsan! Come back! Where are you?! Stop before it's too late!*

Come back where? I was here already. I was everywhere. Too late for what? I was fixing things back to the way they should be. It was so obvious, why would anyone question that?

I shook the voice from my head and turned to Alec, who was frozen a few hundred feet in front of me. As I walked over to him, I saw that his eyes were full of terror. I didn't know why he thought *I* looked so scary. What was so scary about me? *He* was the creepy child clone.

I stared at the face of my father and was again reminded at how I had a complete lack of emotion about it. It was almost as if I wasn't in my own body. Or I was disconnected from my feelings somehow.

It felt wonderful.

I chastised Alec, "You should have died a few months ago."

His eyes were screaming, but it meant nothing to me.

He had been living on borrowed time anyway, really. I was just ending his short-lived ride. I added, "I hope you enjoyed the power while you had it. Think of it as a nice parting gift."

Barely moving my hand, I ripped out the serum from Alec's body and it splashed gently to the ground. Everything was so easy, felt so right, as if I was creating music that only the universe and I could hear.

I saw the white, glowing souls of the I.Q. Collective inside the gods' bodies and I pulled them out as if they were made of metal and my hands were magnets. Lastly, I pulled Alec's light from the clone it inhabited and combined it with the other souls, making them into one bright light above my head. The clone's body fell to the ground, unconscious.

Staring at the light, it looked like a mini sun. It was fascinating, knowing that the bright orb above me was the I.Q. kids' souls swarming around, trying to live. It was time to end it.

With a blink of my eye, I snuffed out the light and destroyed every last I.Q. kid for good. I thought I'd feel relief or happiness, but surprisingly I felt nothing.

I looked down at the unconscious clone and decided to let him live. Without the serum and without my grandparents giving him

Age-pro, this clone could grow up and be… my father? Maybe. I felt a tug on my emotions, but I brushed it aside. Had it been happiness? I couldn't tell anymore.

Next.

I didn't like that Roberta was tied to the King of Demons. She shouldn't have that kind of power; and now I could take it away. I snapped their connection with a mere thought.

Roberta's eyes met mine and she seemed utterly terrified.

Why was everyone was scared of me? I was just a god. It wasn't as if they hadn't seen one before. Not as powerful as me, but still.

Maybe Roberta was scared because she thought that I was going to kill her. I guess severing her ties to a demon might give her that impression. But I found that I didn't want to hurt my grandparents. My hate for them felt distant, out of reach. So did my love. Because I *did* love them. I could admit that now with no feelings of shame or guilt.

I needed Roberta to be safe, so I yanked out the soul of the clone she was inhabiting. The bright light glowed above her head and tears began to stream down Roberta's cheeks. I didn't want to destroy the clone's soul. She was an innocent.

So I opened the Underworld's gateway once again.

Then I sent the clone's soul to live there in peace. Now Roberta's soul was safe in the clone body.

In the doorway of the newly opened Underworld stood my parents. They were frozen, too, along with everyone behind them. A whole army of the dead. I was controlling them without even trying.

A pang of…something.

Mom.

As a great sadness began to bubble up inside of me, I pushed it down.

Roberta and Turner needed to apologize to my mother and father.

I controlled Roberta, Turner, and my parents like puppets. Although I was sure I could save Mom and Dad's souls if they stepped out of the Underworld, I didn't want to risk it, so I made Roberta and Turner step into the Underworld.

And I released the four of them.

Roberta fell to her knees and begged for Dad and Mom to forgive her, just like she said she would if given the opportunity. Even Turner was wracked with emotion, tears falling from his eyes at seeing his only son. I was shocked when my mother was the first one to embrace Roberta. They had killed her. Desecrated her corpse. But she hugged Roberta anyway.

As Dad embraced Turner, I felt something inside me again.

Peace?

Yes, it was peace.

I liked it.

I froze them in place again: Dad with Turner and Mom with Roberta.

It felt good.

I wanted to keep them that way forever.

Like a nice snapshot I could go back to and see anytime I wanted.

This strange sense of calm was invigorating.

I wanted to share this feeling.

Terence.

He needed peace.

And I liked him.

I controlled Kala to stand in front of her son and I opened up both of their minds. They grunted from the pain of it, but they'd thank me later. I let them both see how much they meant to each other, how much they loved each other. They were fighting me, too stubborn to share how they felt. But I was a god, so I was stronger. And within seconds I could see the sparkle between them. Pure love.

It felt nice.

I liked these feelings I was feeling.

Being a god wasn't an abuse of power. Not the way I was using it. Look how many people I was helping.

Then I remembered Elisha and her wish to die.

Turning to her, I yanked out the immortality serum, letting it splash to the ground.

"I'll let you decide your own fate," I said to Elisha, then I pulled away all of the barriers Talan had set in place to protect her from the memories of the evil deeds she had committed. "But if you choose life then you have to live with what you've done. I won't let you hide from it."

Elisha was still frozen like all the others, but her eyes were screaming. No peace for her. But she didn't really deserve it.

I was judge and jury, but I wouldn't execute her.

I wasn't a killer.

Was I?

Alec and the others.

I had just killed them all.

The voice yelled in my head again: *Chelsan, I love you! Please come back to me!*

Ryan.

A flood of emotion raced through my body. Ryan!

Devastation threatened to take me over and drown me. I had just killed hundreds of human souls. I had murdered them like it had been nothing.

"Ryan!" I screamed aloud.

But I didn't unfreeze him.

I didn't unfreeze any of them.

My brain fought with the power surging through me. The power was winning. It was stronger than me.

"Help me," I managed to croak out, but it was barely a whisper.

Desperate, I used my powers to try and help me break free.

Nancy and Bill suddenly teleported in front of me.

I had done that.

I had wanted them there, and my mind brought them here.

My anchors.

When Nancy saw me, her eyes went round. "Chelsan! Are you okay? Where are we?"

Nancy and Bill looked around at all the frozen bodies and were genuinely shocked, at a loss of what was happening.

I couldn't form the words to explain.

I had hoped that seeing them, my two best friends, the only two who had stood by me in high school, our original trio, hearing them, having them near me, would help me break free of this power, but I was still locked inside my own head.

Nancy stepped forward to embrace me—but then stopped mid-step.

They both did.

Frozen.

Like the others.

Did I do that?

Did the power?

Gaia's voice sounded in my head: *Your friends will be fine. You will be fine. But first you must complete the prophecy.*

I was able to speak back to her inside my brain: *I did! I broke the curse! Why can't I disconnect from everyone?!* I was terrified. But even that was beginning to fade, the power taking away my emotions once more.

I don't want to be a god. I tried to fight back.

But you are one. For now anyway, Gaia replied, hearing everything I was thinking. *You know what you have to do.*

No, I don't, I answered honestly.

Gaia quoted the prophecy as if hearing it would explain everything. *A beginning to the end and an end to the beginning. A new paradise shall be born. The Fated One will be the last. The Fated One is the first. The first of us all.*

And? I didn't want to feel stupid, but I felt pretty stupid. None of that made sense to me.

The more I was able to think like myself, the more I was able to distance myself from the raging power within. Maybe I could disconnect...

Gaia's voice was strong and commanding, *Cronus and the others can feel your weakness. They're fighting back for control.*

She was right. I could feel them trying to break free from my hold. I wanted to let them. I didn't want this kind of power surging through me. I didn't want to lose myself. I didn't want to become like them: obsessed with power.

Chelsan, what do you think Cronus and Zeus will do when you let them go?

I hadn't thought of that.

I didn't want to.

Gaia continued, *What were they trying to do before the I.Q. Collective took over their bodies?*

Destroy the world, I answered.

421

Do you think they'll stop now? she asked, though she knew the answer already.

And so did I.

No.

Gaia spoke to me as if she was a teacher trying to maneuver her student to figure out an equation on their own. *So we need to stop them for good, right?*

Like dead? I gulped. *I can't kill anymore. Please don't make me. And besides, I can't kill gods. No one can.*

Kala can. She did it with Atlas, Gaia said with clarity.

So why are you talking to me? Make her *do it.* I was suddenly defensive. I had killed the entire I.Q. Collective *again* and I wasn't sure how I was going to live with myself. Now Gaia wanted me to kill her children and grandchildren?

You're the only one who can save Kala if she consumes them. Gaia's voice sounded desperate. She didn't care about Cronus and the others, but she obviously still loved Kala.

Cronus's hand moved.

He was breaking free.

Chelsan, please, Gaia pleaded. *I love my children, but I am the Earth itself and I won't have them destroy it.*

I thought of the prophecy's words. If the gods were truly gone then this would be a beginning to the end of their time here on Earth, but also an end to the beginning of the time when they were created. Kala was the Fated One. She'd be the last of the gods, but the first of her kind, because if I succeeded Kala would have the power of every god I made her consume.

I knew what I had to do.

Gaia was right. I was the only one who could potentially save Kala after she consumed the Titans and Olympians.

I couldn't believe I was about to do this.

If Kala did survive, she'd probably try to kill me after.

But it was the only way to destroy the gods for good.

I turned to Kala, "My turn to be sorry."

Kala looked at me with confusion.

Then I fully tapped into the power of all the supernatural beings' souls. Flushed with energy, Cronus locked into place once again.

Focusing on Kala, I commanded: "CONSUME!"

Chapter Eighteen

50 Years Ago

KALA

Kala sat on her knees, wondering who she was anymore. It was one of her bad days, which made it hard to remember ever having a good day.

After completing her last mission only minutes before, Kala found that she couldn't move. Killing people was always the hardest for her, ironic since she had been a sniper when she was human.

But this time?

With an Olympian involved?

And almost consuming him…

The two burnt corpses still smoldered from the fire Kala had used to destroy them. They had been burned so badly they barely registered as human.

But Kala needed to stay.

She needed to see what she had done.

For what? To save the world?

On days like this, it didn't seem worth it. The two corpses would probably agree.

"You going to stay here all day, buttercup?"

Asmodeus.

And, in that moment, he was what she needed. She hated that about herself, that there was a part of her that would always be connected to Asmodeus. That he would make her feel better in her darkest moments, when Talan couldn't. Maybe it was because he was a demon and she felt like that was what she deserved. Or maybe it was because Asmodeus understood her dark side better than she did and he knew what to say – or, more accurately, what not to say.

Or maybe it was because he was the father of her son, the one person she loved above all others.

"That smell is making me hungry. You want to grab a bite?" His voice was friendly and nonchalant, but Kala knew why he was there.

"Talan sent you, didn't he?" Kala already knew the answer.

"The only good thing I can say about that Grigori is that he knows you well." On the surface that would normally be taken as a compliment towards Talan, but Kala knew Asmodeus meant it as a way to prove that he was the only one who could pull Kala out of her depressions, and that Talan knew it enough to send the demon.

Which only made Kala feel both love and guilt toward Talan. He loved her so much, he'd send the being that she had betrayed him with.

Asmodeus held his hand out for Kala to take and she let him help her up.

Before she could stop herself, Kala wrapped her arms around

Asmodeus, needing to feel his embrace. Asmodeus, hesitant at first, quickly drew Kala in, holding her tight.

Kala spoke into his chest, "Sometimes I want to let go of everything."

"Doing what you do, I'm not surprised," Asmodeus said gently. "But then what would I do? I'd be bored and it would be all your fault."

Kala let out a small chuckle and found herself melting to Asmodeus's charms. "You're such an asshole."

"No argument there. But I was kidding about the smell, it's pretty horrendous. Can we get out of here?" Asmodeus pulled slightly away within their embrace to see Kala's face.

With one last glance at the corpses, Kala teleported herself and Asmodeus to a mountainside in the Swiss Alps.

Asmodeus looked around. "Well, this is... cold."

Kala disentangled herself from Asmodeus and walked to a small ledge. Viewing the cinematic view in front of her always took her breath away. It was spring so there was still a little snow on the mountain tops. It made Kala feel like she had stepped into a painting, as if she could escape entirely from every responsibility she had in life.

Asmodeus's hand felt warm on her shoulder as he stood next to her. "What happened with those two toasties?"

After a moment, Kala finally confessed, "I had to get past Hermes to reach them. He was protecting them for some reason."

"Hermes? He's so boring. I haven't heard about that guy in years." Asmodeus seemed genuinely baffled about hearing of the Olympian's involvement.

"The only way I could get him to leave was to start to consume him. If he hadn't teleported away..." Kala looked up

426

at Asmodeus, not afraid to show the terror she felt. "I could feel him dying, becoming a part of me, taking a piece of my brain like Atlas..." Kala shook her head, terrified. "I know it's my ace-in-the-hole against supernatural beings, but I can never do it again, Asmodeus. I can't."

Asmodeus pulled her in for another hug. "You won't have to. The simple threat scares us immortals. Hermes was probably trying to see how far you'd go. I'm sure he thought you were bluffing, or that the Atlas thing wasn't real. That you were just another one of the humans that Atlas tricked into taking his place. With that pill that everyone can take now, it's hard to tell the immortals from the... human immortals."

His logic made sense. Hermes hadn't been in the picture. Maybe he didn't believe the other Olympians when they told him of what Kala was capable of and had to find out himself.

And he did.

Kala could still taste him inside of her.

It had felt like she was going to lose herself.

It was worse than death. Kala knew that for a fact, ever since she had died and gone to the Underworld.

"I can't consume anyone, Asmodeus. If I consume, I'll be dead. Lost forever." Kala looked up at him within the circumference of his arms.

"You're stronger than that." Asmodeus's expression showed that he truly believed his words.

But Kala didn't.

"I don't think so," was all Kala could say as she turned her head away from him.

Asmodeus forced eye contact with Kala. "Well, I know so. You're stronger than anyone I've ever met, and I'm pretty old and very social, so that's saying a lot. If it comes to it someday where you have to consume another god. You *will* be fine. I promise you that." Then he smiled. "When have I ever been wrong?"

Kala wanted to believe, but deep down she knew…

…if it came to consuming another god, Kala wished she would die first.

Present Time

Hearing the word 'consume' sent terror to every cell of my being.

I focused on Terence in front of me for some kind of solace. What Chelsan had done had been nothing short of a miracle. Our barriers had been broken. Terence finally knew that he was my everything, that I loved him more than I'd ever love myself. And I felt his love back. Through all his bitterness and anger, he truly loved me. It had been exhilarating.

Now, as I looked at him, his eyes screamed with agony.

We both knew: I wasn't going to survive this.

I was going to die.

But I was a soldier.

I was Atlas.

I felt a strange calm.

I would save the world one last time by eliminating the beings who wanted to destroy it.

My last mission.

All at once, Cronus's body hurtled toward me as if he was in some kind of wind tunnel and Chelsan made my mouth open wide. A force within me opened up. I had felt it before. I had been furious at the time, my emotions out of control. I swallowed Atlas whole, and I was about to do it again.

It felt like a giant worm as I breathed in Cronus, his essence, his soul, his power. He became a part of me, his body dissipating inside of me. All his memories and experiences flooded my brain. I stumbled. I was blacking out, like I had done right after I consumed Atlas. I no longer had Talan's protections in place. I didn't think they'd help anyway. Cronus was ten times more powerful than Atlas. I'd find out soon enough if he was strong enough to take over my body.

But he didn't.

Like with Atlas, even though I knew every thought Cronus had ever had in his entire existence. That was it.

He was dead.

No conscious thought trying to fight back.

No anger at being stuck inside of me.

He was gone.

Truly gone.

But his thoughts were too much for my brain to contain. Only the force of Chelsan's hold on me kept me on my feet, kept me conscious.

And just when I thought I might be able to regain some kind of semblance of sanity, Zeus was sucked inside of me.

I was gone then.

My mind floated on a cloud.

I couldn't see anything anymore, only darkness around me.

I was only slightly aware of god after god flying into my body, being devoured until they no longer existed. I would be the last of them. No more gods. Only angels and demons. Only me.

I didn't know who that was anymore.

My name was too distant to see.

It was on the tip of my tongue, but every time I tried to reach for it, it slipped further and further away.

Where was I?

Who was I?

Memories of millennia of existence whirled around me as though I was in some kind of beautiful and terrifying menagerie. No longer any sense of self. Unsure of what I was. Was I god? Was I many gods?

Yes.

All those things.

With every new entity that entered inside of me, I felt more and more power. I was swimming with it. I was drowning in it.

I couldn't differentiate between life and death. Time meant nothing. So filled with life after life, existing became everything to me.

Survive.

My base instinct was simply survival. It didn't matter who I was. It didn't matter that I had hundreds of minds inside me. Only *living* mattered.

Life.

My body had stopped consuming. No more souls left to devour. It was animalistic, but I felt a surge of disappointment. I had grown used to the stacking of power as each deity disintegrated inside me like bricks on top of each other.

Swimming, swimming with life, boiling my skin, rising to the surface.

My head began to throb.

The darkness began to brighten.

Memories started to rip themselves from my mind like someone was yanking them out with toothpicks. Faster and

430

faster: conversations, battles, arguing, loving, living, escaped out into the ether, slowly uncluttering my brain.

Kala.

I was Kala.

It gave me a sense of relief and purpose and I held onto my name for dear life. But I didn't have to for long. The more memories that left me, the stronger my sense of self grew. It was like a vacuum cleaner on reverse at this point, the essence of each god being sucked out of me at lightning speed.

Until…

I was just me.

I hadn't realized my eyes were closed. I opened them slowly.

My legs gave out and I started to fall.

Terence caught me.

We were moving again.

I looked around: everyone was moving. Chelsan had released us all.

But there were no gods.

Only Gaia.

I felt their powers inside me. Such a strange sensation… My mind and body swam with abilities I'd never experienced before. But years of being Atlas and even more years of living like a soldier, I knew I could keep these powers at bay. I could control them.

Chelsan looked at me with concern, "Are you okay? Did I break you?"

Before I could answer Chelsan collapsed to the ground, unconscious. I couldn't fathom that her human body had lasted this long. Without the serum running through her veins, she would have died the moment she tapped into us all.

Her crew was immediately huddled around her. Ryan propped her up and held her in his arms.

I knew how good that felt. I turned to Terence; I knew he was waiting for the answer to Chelsan's question as well. "I'm okay," I told him. Then I smiled. "Better than okay. I'm really, really good."

His smile sent a warmth through me. He hadn't smiled at me like that since he was a kid.

It was over.

Over.

I couldn't believe it.

Talan raced over and embraced me tightly. He could see the love between Terence and I and his face radiated happiness.

Terence shook his head, slightly embarrassed. "Don't look so shocked. I planned on forgiving her after the curse was broken anyway."

I smiled. Whether it was true or not, my son was joking with us and it felt… perfect.

Gaia nodded to me. Her expression said a million things at once. She saved me. She loved me. She was going to be in my life for good now. Her voice carried to everyone as she turned to Jack and Penny, who stood in front of the Turners and Janet. "Let's return these souls back to the Underworld."

Jack nodded and gave me and Derek a wave of good-bye. Penny waved as well, though it had never been comfortable between us.

I watched as Turner and Roberta gave Franklin and Janet one last embrace as they stepped out of the Underworld gateway. There was genuine affection for Janet in their expressions. It shocked me and it gave me hope. Maybe I'd earn their forgiveness someday. I certainly hoped so.

Within a few minutes, all the walking dead were gone along with Gaia, Jack, Penny, Franklin and Janet as Gaia closed the gateway behind her.

"Don't go hogging my girl." Derek's voice filled me with joy.

Talan gently let me go as Derek's arms pulled me into a bear hug. He whispered in my ear, "I'm glad you're okay."

Asmodeus walked up to us, accompanied by Owen.

Asmodeus waved his hand and all the roaming demons disappeared. "They'll be grateful to be home. Earth was never really their happy place." Then he looked to the field where the gods once stood and asked, "Are they really gone?"

I nodded. "I felt them die inside of me." I glanced over at Chelsan, who was slowly coming to. "Chelsan managed to pull out all of their essences, though. It's just me in here." Then I added, "Me and all their powers."

Terence whistled low. "Remind me to never piss you off."

I laughed. Laughed.

Everyone looked at me like I was another person, which made me realize how rare it was that I had shown any kind of humor. The last three hundred years hadn't been peaches and roses.

My heart filled with the kind of joy I couldn't describe when Terence looked at me with adoration, as he had when he was little. I hoped I could finally be the mom he wanted me to be. And, seeing him smile, it truly hit me:

No more missions.

No more countdowns.

No more...

Visions!

I could actually watch a screen without seeing my Atlas mission on repeat.

"Who's up for binge watching every TV show ever created for the last three hundred years?" I asked with a smile.

Though I was half-joking, all five of my guys nodded and raised their hands.

Derek laughed, "I'll bring the beer and pizza."

My whole body relaxed, and I didn't think I'd ever felt more at peace than I did at that moment.

Life was good.

Finally.

Chapter Nineteen

Seven Years Ago

CHELSAN

Chelsan woke up with a smile. She couldn't believe that she was eleven years old today. Life was getting much easier for her. She had finally worked out all the kinks with controlling her dead stepfather. It had taken four years to do it, but Chelsan was pretty proud of herself. None of the neighbors pointed out Bruce's odd behavior anymore. In fact, they all seemed rather pleased that he seemed to be over all his 'ailments.' Ailments being when Chelsan would momentarily forget to control Bruce and he'd drop suddenly in the front yard, or when she'd think she was controlling his legs, but it was his arms, so Bruce ended up hand-standing down the front steps instead of walking.

But all that was over with now. Bruce walked and talked like a totally normal human being. He didn't hit, he didn't yell, he only helped around the house and watched holo-tv (and occasionally showered when Chelsan remembered, or when Janet told Bruce to clean up).

Chelsan heard her mother cursing outside the window. From the neat rows of black swirling holes on the ground, Chelsan could see that Janet had failed in her gardening skills yet again.

It was time.

Chelsan felt confident in her control over Bruce, so now she would extend her powers to her mother's garden.

Quickly dressing in t-shirt and jeans, Chelsan passed Bruce in his easy chair, and flew outside to see her mom.

When Janet saw Chelsan, her entire face lit up. "Happy birthday, birthday girl!" Then she apologetically nodded toward the dead garden. "I thought I'd pick some of your favorite flowers for your birthday, but, yeah, they kind of died."

"Mrs. Tolstey said she had some magic cure for growing plants. She said it worked almost instantly. Some new science thing," Chelsan half-lied. Mrs. Tolstey was her fifth-grade teacher and had told the class about new and revolutionary ways of growing plants, but it was all off the market stuff. Still, Chelsan figured, if her mother talked to Mrs. Tolstey about it, at least her teacher would unknowingly back up the lie. "She let us bring some home, should we try it?"

Janet appeared thrilled and nodded in excitement. "Yes! Go get it and let's see if science can save my black thumb."

Chelsan raced back in the house and wondered what she would use as her fake 'cure.' Going into the kitchen, she grabbed a cloth bag and filled it with a mixture of sugar, flour and a heap of paprika for color. She hoped her mother wouldn't look too closely.

Running back to join Janet, Chelsan wildly threw the concoction all over the dead plants. Janet laughed at Chelsan's enthusiasm, not realizing it was her daughter's way of hiding the made-up fertilizer.

436

When Chelsan finished, she stood next to her mom. "It should only take a few minutes."

Janet took Chelsan's hand. "If it doesn't work, I'll be okay, Chelsan. You know that, right?"

Chelsan ignored her mother's attempt to prepare her daughter for the chance of failure. "It'll work."

Janet smiled and together the two of them waited.

Chelsan figured enough time had passed and connected to every single black hole in Janet's garden.

And brought it all back to life.

She may have gone a little overboard making each flower, vegetable, lettuce, beet, and fruit grow almost six feet high. It went from dried, dead corpses to a jungle of green and the brightest colors imaginable.

But Chelsan only heard silence. No gasps and ahh's like she thought she'd hear from her mother, so she looked up to see what was wrong.

Janet stood there, clasping her daughter's hand, and tears fell from her eyes.

"What's wrong, Mom? I thought you'd be happy." Chelsan felt a pang of disappointment.

Janet peered down at Chelsan with an awed expression. "It's the most beautiful thing I've ever seen."

Chelsan beamed inside. She had used her powers to make her mother truly happy, and that in turn made her feel blissful.

Kneeling down to Chelsan's eye level, Janet said with eyes that sparkled with joy, "You know I love you with every fiber of my being, right?"

Chelsan hugged her mother around the neck. "I love you back."

"Happy birthday, my beautiful girl."

Embracing Janet a little bit tighter, Chelsan smiled.

This was her best birthday so far.

Present Time

I lay awake staring at the ceiling, wishing I could fall asleep. It had been a few days since I destroyed the Titans and the Olympians, and I was having trouble sleeping at night. I had barely grown used to the idea that gods existed before being the one who forced Kala to annihilate them. I wasn't sure how I felt about that. Once I let go of everyone's lights, it took me a while to come back to myself. I still had moments where I felt lost and terrified. I didn't talk about it to the gang. I didn't want to worry them.

I knew it would take time.

I also knew that I still had the power to connect to any being on the planet. Including Kala. I never wanted to go there, though. I never wanted to be put in that kind of position again. I hoped now that the prophecy was over that my life could finally go back to normal. Graduation was in a few weeks and I shocked myself when I had invited the grandparents to attend.

Though I was initially angry with my parents for defending Turner and Roberta when I saw them in the Underworld, letting them have their reunion and a chance to say good-bye helped me beyond measure. It somehow made it easier to possibly include them in my life. They were in charge of the world again, but Jason was in control of the media now, so at least they weren't going to be able to hide anything from the public anymore. People had gone into utter panic at Cronus's surprise announcement after forcing them to witness the world's leaders rot in front of their eyes. So the familiar face of Turner telling them that it would all be fine, and that his granddaughter had removed the threat, pretty much made everyone fall in line. That was what people did when they were afraid. They held on to anything that made them feel safe, even if it was my not-such-a-good-guy grandfather.

The whole end-of-the-world-thing changed Roberta and Turner, though. I could see it. I think they always doubted that the prophecy was real. That their only son died for something they never believed in. But seeing me fulfill the prophecy… and seeing Dad one more time… It truly did give them peace. I could see it in their eyes. Also, they didn't have access to Cronus and Hades's powers anymore and I think that was a good thing too. I knew first hand that too much power corrupted your soul.

I felt like a part of me broke that day. With the love of my friends, I could feel it healing, but that kind of power wasn't meant for humans. It probably wasn't even meant for gods.

Looking over at Ryan, sleeping peacefully next to me, my heart filled with love. I felt like the luckiest girl in the world. It still scared me that I had been willing to let the world end to save him, but I couldn't help who I was or how I felt. I feared that me letting him live despite the Universe wanting him dead might haunt us someday. I just hoped I could fix it. He was my life-line and I didn't want to think about the 'what-ifs' anymore. I did what I did and I would accept the consequences.

I hadn't told anyone that I had defied the Universe and saved Ryan though I was positive Kala knew. She'd been performing Atlas missions for three hundred years after all. Once I yanked out the curse from her insides then realized the ground was still breaking apart, she had to have known that the mission hadn't been complete.

But she never said a word to me afterwards. Apparently, she wanted it a secret as much as I did. Kala wanted to rest, needed to rest. She deserved it. Blissful ignorance.

A part of me even wondered if the Universe wanted Ryan dead at all. Maybe none of our theories had been right about why killing Ryan was Kala's last mission. We had thought it was because it was the one thing that would provoke me into destroying Atlas's curse. But what did the Universe care if Atlas or Kala or some duped human completed the missions as long as they were completed?

No.

The Universe needed me to connect to the Titans and Olympians, not to save Ryan, but to gain the ability to connect to any living thing in the Universe whether it was supernatural or not. And when I broke the curse, the Universe wanted even more from me. It needed me to make Kala consume all the Titans and Olympians, making her indestructible.

We were essentially the two most powerful beings in existence.

So what did that mean?

Was something coming?

A shiver ran down my spine.

Yes. Something was definitely coming.

But not right now. Not in this perfect moment.

I snuggled in close to Ryan, resting my head on his chest, listening to his heartbeat. Fortski had given Ryan the immortality serum again and this time no one was taking it away from him.

I wondered when Kala and I would cross paths again. If my suspicions were correct, then I feared it might be sooner rather than later. It was strange to go through so much with a person, but coming out of it, our lives were so altered, I was afraid our next meeting would be awkward, to say the least.

But I'd like to talk to her as a person, not as mission-girl. Maybe I could pick her brain about my grandparents, since she knew them before they ruled the world. I found myself looking forward to that day.

As for tomorrow, I tried not to think about the fact that I had my Physics final.

And I hadn't studied at all.

Ugh.

Other Books

The Riser Saga:
Riser
Reaper
Ripper

The Atlas Series:
Atlas
Grigori Returned
The Underworld

Riser Saga/Atlas Series Finale:
Atlas Rising

Alexis Tappendorf Series:
Alexis Tappendorf and the Search for Beale's Treasure
Alexis Tappendor and the Search for Atlantis

The Dream Diaries:
The Dream Diaries
The Dream Diaries: Blood Ties

Jeraline's Alley

Love & Dark Series (co-written with Hina McCord):
Vessel
First Born
Gutian Code

Bio

Becca fell in love with storytelling at an early age. The first book she read was The Lion, The Witch and The Wardrobe and she's been looking for the door to Narnia ever since! Becca is a passionate reader, consuming anything sci-fi or fantasy. Mix it in with YA and she is a fan for life. So it's no surprise that she writes in these genres as well. When Becca isn't writing, she loves to sew. From Mortal Instruments rune pillows, to elaborate Firefly/Serenity bags, Becca loves to create!

www.ingramcontent.com/pod-product-compliance
Lightning Source LLC
Chambersburg PA
CBHW022018050726
47499CB00004BA/1059